FORGOTTEN PATHS

Forgotten Paths

A Novel

Beth Schiemer

Beth Schiemer

iUniverse, Inc.
New York Lincoln Shanghai

Forgotten Paths
A Novel

Copyright © 2007 by Beth Schiemer

iUniverse books may be ordered through booksellers or by contacting:

iUniverse
2021 Pine Lake Road, Suite 100
Lincoln, NE 68512
www.iuniverse.com
1-800-Authors (1-800-288-4677)

Because of the dynamic nature of the Internet, any Web addresses or links contained in this book may have changed since publication and may no longer be valid.

ISBN: 978-0-595-44237-9 (pbk)
ISBN: 978-0-595-68575-2 (cloth)
ISBN: 978-0-595-88567-1 (ebk)

Printed in the United States of America

This is a work of fiction. All of the characters, names, incidents, organizations, and dialogue in this novel are either the products of the author's imagination or are used fictitiously.

bschiemer@comcast.net
bschiemer1@hotmail.com

CHAPTER 1

▼

THE DREAM

"I think it's time," said Jon.

"Time for what," asked Autumn.

"It's time for you to come home. I know this all seems very strange right now. However, I know in my heart that you are the right person."

"The right person for what? What home are you talking about? You are right. This does seem strange. I don't even know who you are," stated Autumn becoming more and more anxious.

"Soon …" Jon said as he vanished.

Autumn awoke from the third dream in three nights. Each one was as real and confusing as the next. They involve short conversations with an elderly southern gentleman by the name of Jon McFarland. He gives vague yet prophetic messages about her future. The dreams are very short but memorable. Autumn began having the dreams a week after graduating. At first, she attributed her dreams to the stress of finals with the excitement of graduation. Then the dreams continued with increasing clarity. The dreams seemed to be set in a den or library of a large home. The only outstanding details of the three dreams: the man, the room, and his message. However, there were too many things to be done to give much serious thought to dreams. In the morning, Autumn was packing to return home and begin her career search.

With the last moving box down, the mail carrier arrived with a certified letter addressed to Autumn N. Hummel. Certified letters are always concerning particularly when you have never received one. In the few moments between acknowledging the mail carrier and signing for the letter, Autumn had visions of the college rescinding her degree, a large unpaid college bill, or a notice that someone had sued her. Her rational mind knew that none of those were possibilities but she was not rational at the moment. Rather than ripping the letter open, she studied the outside of the envelope as if it would reveal a clue. To her confusion, the letter had a return address of Georgetown, South Carolina. Autumn's family vacationed for twenty years or more at various beaches in South Carolina including Horry and Georgetown counties. In all of those journeys, the family had never made any long-term relations with any Carolinians. The address not providing any clues, her gaze turned to the name on the return address. Amazingly the addressee was a Master Jonathan McFarland. Suddenly her dread was replaced by an eerie sense of completion. It was almost as if she had been expecting such a letter to arrive. The letter read:

Dear Ms. Hummel,

It is my duty to inform you that upon the reading of Mr. Jonathan McFarland's Last Will and Testament that you have been named sole heir of his estate. The transference of this estate must be handled according to Mr. McFarland's request in his home town of Georgetown, South Carolina within the next fourteen days. You will be contacted by phone from someone in our offices to make arrangements. Please notify us immediately of any difficulties you may have in fulfilling these requests. If you are unable to be in Georgetown within the allotted time should you decline the estate it will be left to the South Carolina Historical Society.

Our deepest sympathies go out to you at your loss. As stated before, contact us immediately of any questions or concerns regarding this matter.

Sincerely,

Eric Dravo, Esq.

The law firm seemed to be assuming there was a relationship of some sort between the two people named in the document. Autumn went back upstairs to call the office and explain things when the phone range.

"Hello," asked Autumn.

"Hello. May I please speak to Ms. Autumn Hummel," asked the voice on the other end of the phone in a thick southern drawl.

"This is she."

"Ms. Hummel? My name is Shelia. I am calling in regards to a letter Mr. Dravo sent you. Have you received the letter?"

"I just received it five or ten minutes ago. I was about to call and tell you there has been a mistake."

"A mistake? What sort of mistake?" The once sweet and easy voice now sounded a little tense. "Are you Autumn Nicole Hummel of Barberton, Ohio born October 4th, 1970," asked Shelia.

"I am. You have all this information about me," asked Autumn. She felt violated by a stranger knowing so many things about her. "No. That is all correct. The mistake is that I do not, rather, did not ever know Mr. McFarland. That is the mistake!"

"Ms. Hummel, it is not our job to explain how or why. We were simply hired to take care of Mr. McFarland's wishes upon his passing," Shelia replied. "Since you have read the letter, you know you have fourteen days to claim your inheritance. I am calling to set up several things. First, we need to set a date of departure to hire a car to take you to the airport. Second, we need to discuss where you will stay while you are in Georgetown. There are several inns, hotels, and Bed and Breakfasts'. If you prefer, you may stay at the McFarland farm. It is up to you." Shelia finished, unfazed by the fact that Autumn did not know Mr. McFarland.

"Well," started Autumn. She had no idea what to say next. Sheila's requests sounded very inviting. "I am driving home to my mom and dad's today. Other than that, I haven't made any solid plans. That could probably wait. So, how about tomorrow? I'm all packed. Sure. Why not?" Autumn said all this as much to Shelia as to herself. Autumn and Shelia began working out the details of her trip. A car would arrive at eleven in Barberton to take her to the airport. The airport was forty-five minutes from her parents' house. Jon McFarland's private plane would take-off around half past noon. Touch-down would be expected at two in the Myrtle Beach Airport. From there, a car would take her to the Carolinian Inn in Georgetown because Autumn decided it would be weird to stay in a recently deceased stranger's home alone and hundreds of miles from family. Once Autumn checked into the hotel, the driver would take her to Mr. Dravo's office for a meeting at four. Mr. Dravo would give her a personal tour of the estate and discuss thoroughly the financial holdings she was to inherit before being asked to sign anything. Speaking to Shelia for over an hour, Autumn discovered Sheila was a truly kind-hearted and warm person. What had begun with fear and confusion was transforming into the prospect of a wonderful adventure. Autumn actually found herself excited about what mysteries lie ahead in South Carolina.

Back in Barberton, the next day dawned. Autumn awoke with an increased enthusiasm about her trip. Autumn passed her dad on the stairs. Normally a very stern man, the morning was the time he was most amicable. This morning, he passed her silently shaking his head and smiling. Autumn was not sure what to make of this but, not being a morning person, she was not about to ask him why he was smiling like the Cheshire cat.

"You are not going to South Carolina on this farce," Autumn's mom stated. Her mother's voice sounded calm but it was merely the calm before the storm unless Autumn called the trip off.

Autumn mumbled, "And good morning to you, mom."

"You know nothing about this Jonathan McFarland or about this inheritance."

"That's why I'm going, mom. How am I going to find out anything until I go and see." Autumn wearily poured herself a bowl of cereal knowing that this discussion was far from over.

"Now, we have been down there how many times in your life and never seen anything but tobacco and soybean farms. They were nothing to write home about."

Autumn sliced a banana into her cereal bowl not really feeling up to this since the car would be picking her up in just a few hours. "That's true mom but, in all those trips, we have never seen anything that wasn't on the beach or along the interstate that took us to the beach. From what I understand, South Carolina is a rather large state." She knew the moment she said it that her sarcasm would only antagonize her mother.

"Well," her mom scoffed, "you are the college graduate in the family. I should just send you off to God-knows-where to fend for yourself."

Autumn's dad came back downstairs still smiling. "I don't know why you two are arguing. Autumn is going to do whatever it is she wants. Always has. Always will."

"Aren't you worried about your daughter?"

"She knows how to dial a phone," Autumn's dad stated flatly.

"Humph! You won't be just a phone call away when she's in South Carolina."

"No but that stubbornness that you are fighting now is the same quality that will keep her from doing anything she doesn't want to do when she's a thousand miles away." He took a piece of bacon from the plate sitting on the counter and sauntered off. Autumn smiled as she watched him walk away. There had been a time when her father could huff and puff with the best of the big bad wolves. With age had come grace. Precious little ruffled his feathers anymore. It might have been his demeanor or his words. Either way, he took the wind out of his wife's sails.

"I bought you a new straw hat. Remember to wear it when you're out in the afternoon sun."

Autumn walked over to her mom, hugged her, and kissed her on the cheek.

The car arrived promptly on schedule. Driving the forty-five minutes to the airport, Autumn could not help but daydream about her trip to South Carolina. She could almost imagine standing on the beach. The thing she loves the most about going to South Carolina is when she could smell the sweet salt air. The plane was ready to go when she arrived at the airport. Autumn, however, was not. Flying was not her favorite mode of transportation. She had only flown twice in her life. Those trips had been on large commercial jets. This was a small jet. The pilot came out of the plane to reassure her. He explained that private jets are safer because they are better maintained than commercial jets. Pilots of small jets were the greatest asset. This was Mr. McFarland's personal jet and crew. The plane only logged a third of the air miles a commercial jet of the same age. The flight crew knew this plane inside and out. The pilot finally convinced Autumn that she would be perfectly safe. The lavishly decorated interior of the jet convinced her to stay.

The cabin of the plane was completely redone to not look like the cabin of a plane. Walking up the stairs, Autumn entered a living room of plush champagne colored carpet. The furniture and color scheme was an interior decorator's dream come true. Everything was done in various shades of white. The elegant furniture had a linen look with large bronze pillows finishing the look. The curtains over the plane windows gave the illusion of regular windows. Towards the rear of the plane, where you would expect to find the toilets, there was a full bath. The bath was decorated a little more masculine than the cabin. It was done in gold and deep rich blues. Autumn was very intrigued by all of this. If the airplane looked like this, what would await her in Georgetown? After all, Mr. McFarland could have been the son of a sharecropper with a shanty, a couple over worked fields, and Confederate money for all she knew. That hardly seemed a plausible situation by the looks of the private plane. Autumn's head was filled with the wondrous possibilities awaiting her at Mr. Dravo's office. Everything was very mysterious and unknown but a little more elegant.

Landing in Myrtle Beach, she hooked up easily with her driver. While driving down King's Highway, Autumn was flooded with a warm familiar feeling. It was a feeling she always got in South Carolina. When she was a teen, part of her had always wondered if she hadn't lived a past life in The Palmetto State. The feeling was always hard to put into words. It was almost a "coming home" feeling. Autumn had seen Myrtle Beach go from a beach community of one motel and a few doctors' summer cabins to being "The Grand Strand". What once faded into obscurity at Murrell's Inlet was now commercially developed down the coast to Georgetown with a short break in the development of the coast due to Huntington State Park and Debi Dew. Both are large stretches of coast that have been designated as nature preserves. Debi Due was the gated community of Debordieu with large vacation homes in only a small area of land. The rest of the land, including the coast, is protected. The land stretches on undisturbed from Debi Due until the Atlantic Intercoastal Waterways. Sea water and fresh water meet at the Intercoastal Waterways to create the cradle of the former Rice Empire. Once cars crest the enormous bridge passing over the waterway, Georgetown lies directly on the other side. Georgetown is not a tourist trap of neon lights and piercing parlors like the Grand Strand. The town is large, the second largest in the state, but full of antebellum charm.

Just after crossing the bridge, the car pulled up to the Carolinian Inn. As the elevator opened to her floor, Autumn was still awash with excitement about being in Georgetown. She rushed to her room which was decorated in the colors of magnolia blooms. The bed linens were a creamy white with a deep green embroidered pattern. The walls were a rich green like the leaves of the elegant tree. The accents in the room were the deep burnt cranberry color found deep within the blossom of the magnolia. After flinging her bags on the bed, Autumn found a home for all her clothes. She decided to take a quick shower and change clothes. The process made her feel terribly antebellum. It was almost as if she was Scarlet getting ready for a dinner engagement. Her thoughts left all the mystery and excitement of the moment and turned to Georgetown.

Georgetown is one of the three oldest cities in South Carolina. The elegant homes in the Historic District tell of Georgetown's affluent past with their pillared porches and large sprawl. The town had been one of the busiest seaports in America. The indigo grown in the region had a high demand all over the colonies and Europe. As indigo became available in other locations around the world, rice became the cash crop for the local farmers. The money and demand drove farmers to buy more land for more crops. The farmers then needed more hands to work the field. The earliest settlers tried to use captured Native Americans but to no avail. They would either run away or die. The Native American inhabitants of the South Carolina coast were not built for hard labor in the hot Carolina sun.

European diseases killed most of them. That is when the institution of slavery began.

Farmers would buy slaves or indentured servants to work their fields. Driven by the almighty dollar, the institution thrived and grew until it almost ripped the nation in two. Georgetown stands as a living reminder of that past. As a student of American history, Autumn was glad that Georgetown existed. The financial success of the South allowed the thirteen colonies financial independence from England. Many people believe that the first shots of freedom rang out in New England on Bunker Hill. That was not the case. Charleston, South Carolina was where the first shots for liberty and independence first rang. All that America had left of that prosperous time reminds us that it had been a freedom bought with the lives of crown traitors and slaves. The wounds of slavery still ring throughout the United States of America. They exist to remind us of a grand but inhumane past. Some may not see it that way. As a student of history, Autumn knew that it's simply the facts. When people forget the past, they are doomed to repeat it.

Though nervous and excited about her meeting with Mr. Dravo, Autumn found herself basking in being at the Carolinian Inn. It was late May in South Carolina. The air was warm and heavy with that familiar "ocean air". Someone told her years before that the increased ozone levels in the air along the coast are responsible for that smell. To Autumn, it just smelled like sand and salt water. The magnolia trees had just begun to bloom. They smell like heaven. It was hot but a gentle breeze brushed the Spanish Moss hanging from the trees with the coolness of spring. Autumn could come to South Carolina in the dead of night and know where she was. As soon as her feet meet dirt in South Carolina, roots she never knew would rise to embrace her. Autumn's sixth sense and nose told her where she was. The quiet was suddenly interrupted by a knock at her door.

When she opened the door, a small pale gentleman in a suit greeted her. He clearly was not a native Carolinian. "Ms. Hummel," asked the man abruptly. "I hope your plane trip went well. I would recommend selling. Are your accommodations suitable?" The little man shot all this at Autumn before even introducing himself.

"Yes, why, and yes. Who are you," Autumn shot back.

"Sorry. Eric Dravo. Shelia told you I'd meet you at four. It is now 4:03. Can we begin?"

Much to Autumn's dismay, Mr. Dravo was not a southern gentleman at all. She quietly accepted the fact that this pale individual was not the lawyer she envisioned on her plane ride down. That lawyer was tall, dark, handsome, and unassumingly charming. Mr. Dravo was a big city lawyer from somewhere up north where the lawyer to client ratio is better. Mr. Dravo, never Eric, had never met Mr. McFarland. They communicated by phone or through Shelia. Shelia clearly possessed more people skills than her employer. All Mr. Dravo could tell Autumn about Mr. McFarland was what existed in the legal documents. Legal documents do not really tell much about the person who had them drawn up. Sadly, Autumn still did not know much about Master Jonathan Calhoun McFarland. Mr. Dravo did enlighten her about what she was to inherit. Apparently, Mr. McFarland was not a poor sharecropper with small spent fields. Mr. Jon C. McFarland was the last of the McFarland's; a prominent and wealthy family in South Carolina for generations. He had no heirs. Jonathan was an only child. There were no relatives, immediate or distant, to will the estate. The inheritance came to Autumn under no penalty or obligation on her part. Essentially, it was a gift with no strings attached. Autumn was not naive enough to believe there were no strings. She thought the strings would show up later. Any taxes or transferences were to be paid from a tax free account Jon McFarland had setup to take care of any costs charged for inheriting estate. There were some very strict stipulations to be met before Autumn could claim the inheritance. The first stipulation was that, legally, the estate keeps the McFarland surname. Second, the house and land be kept as a whole. Autumn could sell it or donate it providing the future owners also promised to keep the farm whole. The third stipulation was the stickiest. It stated she must occupy the estate for five years. If Autumn left at any point before the five years were up, the land would go to the Historic Society of South Carolina to be preserved as a historic landmark.

Mr. Dravo, once having delivered the legalities, reminded her of the fourteen day period. Autumn need not reach her decision immediately. However, a decision had to be in his office thirteen days from today's meeting. It was a lot of information for Autumn to process in a very short span of time.

"Would you like to go see it," Mr. Dravo asked.

"Sure," replied Autumn who was not at all sure she did.

In a very old Volvo sedan, the two rode out to the McFarland farm. The drive lasted only around twenty minutes. Mr. Dravo was clearly not a man of conversation. That short drive felt like an eternity. Leaving the interstate, they made their way down a small country road. The forest on either side was beginning to be reborn. Had Autumn come in the throws of summer, the road would have been fully overgrown and looked even less like a road that was barely wide enough for two lanes. At the first right, they passed an old church that had a cornerstone marking its erection before the Revolutionary War. They drove on and out into the middle of nowhere.

Breaking the silence at last, Autumn asked, "So, how much farther?"

"What do you mean," scowled Mr. Dravo. "Until we get to the house?"

"Sure or the farm itself, either one."

"Well, you are here," he said flippantly. "That little church we turned at is the McFarland family chapel. The land on either side of this road is the farm. The house is four miles up from the chapel."

In disbelief, Autumn slumped down into the car seat. The church was huge and beautiful. She had visited churches in New England built around the Revolution. None of them had belonged to or had been built by or for a single family. All Autumn's studies told her that this chapel served a different purpose. Wealthy landowners of the coast would have had traveling ministers hold service for the family at the church. Children of the family would have had lessons in the church. The slave children would also have gone to church and school in that building although not at the same time. The plantation owners of this region of the country insisted that their slaves and the children of those slaves be Christian. As such, many traveling ministers commented in their writings that some of the slave children knew their Bible verses better than some of the white children in New England. The gift of Christianity gave the Underground Railroad the language to make it work. Negro spirituals used biblical themes that served two purposes. One was to praise God while the other was to give directions to freedom.

The scenery that rushed by made a strong impression in her mind. The open fields had some sort of crop growing in the fields to the right of the road. To the left of the road were sparse clumps of cows grazing in the evening sun. Apparently, it was a working farm though not large enough to be a commercial farm. Mr. Dravo explained that the crops were sold to local distributors based on quality and quantity. The more the workers produced at a low cost, the more money they were paid. Mr. McFarland only kept what he needed to tend to the herd of cows and seed for the next season. As Eric and Autumn got closer to the house, a small pecan orchard appeared. Pecans were one of the many gifts of the South. The orchard gave way to a private drive lined with very old live oak trees. Autumn had no idea how the trees came to be called "oaks" because they look nothing like the oak trees that produce acorns. The "live" moniker seemed an oxymoron since they are obviously live. Southern oaks are slow growing trees that have massive roots that stick out close to the top of the soil. Autumn saw one in a Georgetown church cemetery years ago. The roots looked as if they were cradling the grave stones in its massive roots. The leaves of live oaks are small, sparsely clumped, and deep green. Live oaks live a very long time if left alone. Spanish

Moss must prefer these grand southern hosts' because one won't see a tree of any size not draped in moss.

The live oak drive led up to a giant Georgian style home complete with a massive pillared porch. The entire house was a great alabaster beauty set against the green landscape. The windows had black shudders that coincide with both the architecture and the stately home's proximity to the coast. Mr. Dravo's car pulled up to the main house whose broad porch begged spending an afternoon enjoying finger sandwiches and mint juleps. In awe, Autumn made her way out of the car. This was something out of a dream.

"Welcome home," chirped Mr. Dravo sarcastically.

As they crossed the threshold of the home, all of Autumn's years of study kicked into gear. This home, like most mansions of the era, was not like Scarlet's Tara. The home in the movie was this impressive and elegant mansion with a grand central staircase. Most plantation homes did not start out as stately mansions. Most were the meager farmhouses of European farmers who claimed as much land as they could farm. As they were financially able, they added more land with more crops. Soon these people who would never have been landowners in Europe found they owned massive farms with all the free albeit forced labor to work the fields. With money not an issue, the modest farm home began to reap the benefits of wealth. As the farm grew, so did the family and the house. They typically built onto, up, and around the existing structure which was more practical than tearing everything down and starting over again. Occasionally, fire would level the original home but that was not the case with the McFarland home. The entryway and sitting room would be the kitchen and living area of the original farmhouse. The walls were plastered and polished to "fit" into the new house. As it became stylish to eat dinner at a formal table, a dining room would be added to the old house. The upstairs would be reached by ascending a simple set of stairs very unlike Tara's. There would be bedrooms for mother, father, and children. The husband and wife sleeping in separate rooms reflected their financial status and the social mores of the era. Sometimes a modest kitchen was at the rear of the house generally used as a winter kitchen or staging area for fancy dinner parties. The McFarland house was slightly different.

The original McFarland farmhouse had been converted into the kitchen and servants dining area. It was almost as if the builder knew he would have many "house slaves" because nothing was remodeled in the old part of the house. It did, however, reflect the humble beginnings of the first McFarland. Because of the treatment of the original house, a large staircase sat on the left wall of the entryway. The Federalist style of woodwork prevailed in the house. All the woodwork was painted in matching or accent tones to fit the rooms. Upon entering the home, the formal dining room was to the left. To the right was the living room with a beautiful marble fireplace and two twelve pain windows. Behind the living room was the most shocking room. It was the den, library, or cigar room depending on the era. The room would have been where the gentlemen would gather to discuss important topics of the time while they enjoyed an after dinner smoke and drink. The room was shocking because Autumn had been in that room before.

Mindlessly, Autumn wandered from Mr. Dravo's side. The den looked very masculine. It was dark and rich with what seemed to be oak or mahogany furniture and trim. The book shelves held a small personal library. The formal desk had stationary and lamps that must have facilitated the business of Mr. McFarland. Closing her eyes, Autumn could still smell the warm bitter sweet aroma of fine cigars rolled from the finest tobacco the South could grow. To the right of the doorway on the wall facing the desk was a portrait of Jonathan C. McFarland and his dogs. This was the room in Autumn's dreams and the man in the portrait was the one who had visited her in those strange yet vivid dreams. Autumn walked through the room stroking the walls, the books, and the furniture as if they could tell her something of the man in her dreams. Finally, Autumn came to the desk. On the desk was an envelope with her name on it. She snatched up the envelope in hopes that the contents might reveal some answers. The note inside was hand written. It read as follows:

My Dearest Autumn,

All of this must seem a mystery to you. For that, I am glad. I knew I would have to spark your interest to get you here. As a historian, you know how to research and where to look for answers. Now, you must use those skills to unwrap the mystery I have set before you. Use all of your skills and believe what you see. That is how you will solve this mystery. Answering the simplest question will catapult you onto the more important questions.

Why you? One day, I was driving along the streets of Georgetown when I saw a face from the past. It was not a ghost or the delusions of an old man. It was a real person. She had a head full of brown hair. Her hair was almost as dark as this mahogany desk. When she smiled, the world was a better place because of that smile. I knew her face from somewhere but where?

I stopped my car to go and find out who she was. Shop keepers usually do not share such information. I just happened to be friends with the owner of the store the girl had just left. She had bought a handful of Confederate money on a credit card. Once I found her name, the rest of the information was easy to find.

That young lady was you. The woman you reminded me of was my Great-great Aunt Florence. She was the last great lady of the Old South to live in this house. I figured it was fate's answer to my last earthly concern: what would I do with my family's legacy. I was the only child of only children. Therefore, there is no family to name as my heir. Then, one summer day, I found you. That is the first and only answer I will give you. A fabulous story fills every inch of this land and house. I hope you stay long enough to find out the history of this old home. All that I am is now yours. I only regret never meeting the young lady behind the smile.

Truly Yours,

Jonathan

The letter opened the door for more questions. To Autumn, what began as a wonderful mystery had become the mystery of a lifetime. After all, the land had been owned and farmed for several generations. The letter seemed a little sad to Autumn. Mr. McFarland had no children. He had no real family with which to share all that he was. In fact, he gave it all to someone who, for all he knew, could be very uninterested in this great mystery. The only thing Jon knew about Autumn was what a name could tell him. Mr. McFarland's only safety net in this venture came in the form of legal restrictions governing the sale or donation of the home and land.

Autumn carefully slipped the note into her purse as Mr. Dravo burst into the room. "Ms. Hummel, I'd appreciate your complete attention as we tour the property. You'll have plenty of time to wander around later."

Autumn decided she really did not care for Mr. Dravo and his innate ability to rain on her parade. It seemed to escape him that this was all very weird. Autumn wondered if he even cared. "My apologies, Mr. Dravo." Autumn's apology was more sarcastic than sincere. "You will have my undivided attention." Autumn's promise was simply to make her time with him as short as possible.

The house was located almost in the center of all the land. Mr. Dravo shared that it was the second largest privately owned land in Georgetown County. The largest, 125 acres, belonged to Mr. McFarland's neighbor, Mr. Boyd Masters.

The back half of the property contained a few well preserved or restored buildings. One building was the kitchen where all the cooking would have been done in the eighteenth and nineteenth centuries. The other two small outbuilding buildings currently did in the summer what they once did all year. The buildings had been and were quarters for field workers. Now, the few field workers employed on the farm followed the harvest. These modern workers would travel up and down the coast following the planting and harvesting seasons in each region of the country. These migrant workers started as far south as Florida and ended the season as far north as Maine. From the house, the property backs into a marshy wetland off the Pee Dee River. Mr. Dravo explained that it was once where the great rice crops were grown in antebellum days. Rice still grows wild in patches along the shores of old plantations. For the most part, the land had reverted back to the fox, deer, and waterfowl. Hunting had been a passion in the Old South and continued to be for Jon McFarland. The young woods toward the left of the property were where Mr. McFarland would run his dogs. There was also a derelict cemetery on the left side of the property. To the right of the main house was a radiant flower garden where the family traditionally held family weddings. Oddly, Autumn found herself drawn to the dingy cemetery amidst all this beauty.

"I'd like to go see the cemetery, please."

"But, Ms. Hummel," almost whining, "it is of no significance or beauty. Why don't we take a look at the garden? I'll introduce ..."

"I want to see the cemetery," Autumn said firmly.

"Fine. I will not go with you. The mosquitoes have just come alive. They are the reason people moved to the coast for the summer months. You will be chewed up but I will be here when you return," snorted Mr. Dravo. "There is a small path leading from the first out building on the left. Follow it into the woods. You will stumble over markers before you see a 'cemetery'. Have fun."

Autumn really could not explain why she wanted to go to the cemetery. Cemeteries had always been interesting to her. Once outside of Nashville, Autumn had stumbled across a cemetery that dated back to the early 1800's. The markers had been fascinating to read. Each stone had enough information about the deceased that one could almost imagine them. The land had appeared well maintained by the rangers but no flowers or markers had been placed by the graves in over a hundred years. The fact that the cemetery no longer had been visited made it even sadder to Autumn. Wandering from stone to stone, Autumn had felt as though someone had been following her. She had felt that it had been a young boy looking for someone to play with him. Autumn seemed to recall smiling in his direction and whispering, "It's time for you to follow the bright light. If you follow that, you won't be alone anymore." She quickly bolted for her car in terror of the realization that she was talking to a ghost.

Autumn followed the dirt path into the woods. Being late spring, the forest floor was just awakening. The undergrowth was not too troublesome. The air smelled of Carolina yellow pine. After a long walk into the undergrowth, Autumn could see the remnants of a partial fence. In the middle of the cemetery appeared a cross that was new and made of stone. Around the cross and within what remained of a fence were "things". Small slate sheets stuck in the ground. A circle or two of stones were in the outline of what must have been a grave. There were rotted pieces of wood on the ground that showed signs of being hewn. Most of the earth simply showed signs of being disturbed. Autumn knew from Mr. Dravo's description that this cemetery was a slave burial ground. She had never seen one before though many stories have been written about them. To Autumn, the place spoke volumes about that darkest part of American history. Cemeteries tell a lot about people's lives through how they are committed back to the earth. What this place said was unthinkable to Autumn. It was as if the landowners had buried family pets rather than people. "Unmarked graves in an unimportant place for people who were not people," thought Autumn.

The cross was made of a material that could survive the Carolina heat, humidity, and acidic salt air. What few markers could be found had most likely been placed there by friends, relatives, or loved ones to consecrate the land in some way. The slaves, ironically enough, were Christians. The concept stands in drastic contrast to the ideology of slavery but it is a documented fact. This did not mean that the landowners perceived them as people. So in death as in life, these people had been buried without a thought given to who they had been. Like that sad cemetery in Tennessee, this burial place had been forgotten by time. Sadder still was the fact that no one had cared enough about those interned here to record their names. Tears streamed down Autumn's face and she became overwhelmed by the brutal reality of slavery. As she turned to leave, she heard a voice in the distance. It was a lady's voice tinged with a lazy southern drawl. Autumn looked around nervously reliving the panic she felt in Nashville. The voice came from nowhere and everywhere at the same time. Suddenly, a heavy set woman appeared from the path. She was wearing a light blue cotton dress, a straw hat, and garden gloves. Her warm smile and friendly gaze put Autumn immediately at ease. It did not hurt that she was a real life flesh-and-blood person.

"I'm sorry, dear. I didn't mean to startle you," she said. "Mr. Dravo said I would find you out here. Not the prettiest place on the estate. At least the cross gives a little back to these folk and their final resting place. Come now. Let me show you the prettiest place on the property."

Autumn followed along as this truly welcoming lady slowly made her way through the undergrowth. "Where are we going, ma'am?" Autumn asked in the hope of ascertaining the destination as well as the name of her guide.

"Oh, my! Where are my manners? I am Fanny. I'm the gardener for Mr. McFarland. There is no Miss or Mrs. Just Fanny. My last name is Young just like most people around here. The garden had been Mr. McFarland's sanctuary," volunteered Fanny through her labored breaths. She appeared to be a very matronly woman. "Fleshy" as Autumn's mom would put it.

"Pleased to meet you, Fanny," shouted Autumn as she looked around to get her bearings. "I don't know anything about Mr. McFarland but he doesn't strike me as a garden buff."

"I wouldn't say he had been a garden buff. Didn't know a daisy from a rose. I planted whatever I liked. His only directive had been that there be blossoms until the frost came. I think he needed the beauty and the quiet to regroup. He had loved nothing or no one as much as he had loved this land. Here we are!" Fanny collapsed onto the concrete bench at the entrance of the garden. Surely this was what the Garden of Eden must have looked like. Two large magnolia trees stood sentry in the center of the garden. The blooms filled the air with their clean sweet smell. The trees stood on either side of a little gazebo made from Carolina pine. The gazebo was draped in a beautiful vine of wisteria covered with bundles of delicate purple grape-like blossoms. There were roses, black-eyed Suzie's, poppies, and so many other flowering specimens. The palmetto trees that gave the state its nick-name bordered the garden.

"It's beautiful, Fanny! I can't believe you take care of all of this by yourself," declared Autumn.

"Oh, it is a labor of love." Fanny seemed to swell with pride.

"And it shows," continued Autumn. "How long have you taken care of this garden?"

"All of my life, I suppose. My mother had been the gardener before me. I used to come and help her during breaks from school. Her father had been gardener like his mother before him." Before Autumn could form the question, Fanny asked and answered it. "Am I related to the folks buried out there? I sure am. That's why all my family pitched in to put the cross in the cemetery. We may never know who was buried out there but the cross gives them some dignity. It says that someone cares. Someone remembers them. I hope they can look down and see what has become of their home and children. I hope they're proud. That is what keeps my children on the right path. They gotta live the life those folks only could dream about."

Autumn's heart swelled, tears filled her eyes, and a shameful blush flushed her cheeks. "How can you stay here knowing that? Why wouldn't you leave and never look back?"

"First, wipe those tears from your eyes and the shame off your face," Fanny said firmly. "Were you here a century ago? Have you ever in your life owned another human being?"

"No," whispered Autumn the way a shy second grader answers her teacher.

"Then, dry those tears from your eyes and wipe the sin off your face."

"But everyone at the time had known about slavery and had done nothing about it for so many years. I don't know who had been worse. Those that had owned the slaves or those that had known about it but let it continue."

"Now listen. That was a long time before you and me. There isn't anything you or I can do to right the wrongs of the past. All we can do is be better for their mistakes. The slaves' hardship resulted in my opportunities. I owe it to them to make the most of what this world has to offer. You owe it to them to not stand in my way. Now, that's all. I don't want to hear anymore about this. It is what it is but we've got to live here and now," Fanny said resolutely.

The two shared a long talk as they strolled back to the house. The day was growing long and Mr. Dravo's patience was running thin. Fanny enlightened Autumn somewhat to who Jon McFarland had been. Jon, as Fanny called him, had been a serious fellow who had felt passionately about the things he had loved. The farm had been one of those passions. The land had been claimed as farm land. He had promised himself that the land would always be farm land. The main house had been another passion. Jon had believed a home looses its soul when no one lives in the building. The building affects the owner and the owner affects the building. He had once told Fanny that no matter what became of his estate, the house would have to be lived in even if it became a museum. As far as Jon's fortune, some of it was inherited from generations past. The McFarlands had followed their brethren in the Civil War. The McFarlands' had not believed in the separation issue but they could not have lived in the state they had loved and sided with the Union. As a result, the family fortune had remained in Boston investments and banks. The currency in the house and pockets at the time may have been Confederate but that was all. The rest of the fortune Jon amassed with his business savvy in the stock market and investments. Jon had been gifted in the business of finances yet it had not been a passion. To him, finances had been something he did and not what he loved.

Autumn's day concluded in an amazing frenzy of sights and stories. As Mr. Dravo dropped Autumn back at the Carolinian Inn, she could finally pause and reflect on the day's events. Rather than returning to her room, Autumn decided to go out for the night. Much had happened. Unwinding would require some effort. Mr. Dravo rented her a car for the next two weeks. Autumn pulled out onto King's Highway to see the old familiar sights of South Carolina. Turning north, she drove until she reached Pawley's Island. The sun was just beginning to set. It was going to be a beautiful sunset. The sky was a deep topaz. The clouds looked like pink balls of cotton candy with a heavenly halo around them. As the sun neared the horizon, the sky was turning a pinkish orange shade. Autumn recalled an old seafarers saying, "Red sky at night, sailors delight. Red sky at morning, sailors take warning." It really had nothing to do with what she was feeling and thinking. It was just one of those things that jumped in her brain.

She parked the car near one of the walkways along the beach in Pawley's and dumped her shoes on the front seat of the car. Autumn needed to see the ocean her first day in South Carolina. Her heart ached for something real, familiar, and constant. As she crossed the dunes, her feet sank into the warm white sand. A gust of wind blew through her hair as the thunder of the surf roared a familiar greeting. As she reached the surf's edge, the water swirled around her ankles. She sank into the shore more and more with each passing wave. Looking down, Autumn remembered standing on the edge of the shore as a child and loosing her balance. The waves washing one way and her body sinking into the sand confused her sense of balance. As a child, she easily tumbled into the surf. Tonight, she turned her gaze to the horizon just before she tumbled into the water. Her gaze wandered down the coast line. On a clear day, beach goers could see all the way to Debordieu. This evening's storm clouds were rolling in from the northeast. It was bringing cool breezes and lightening. Autumn looked around the beach to try and catch a glimpse of the Gray Man; a ghostly figure that wandered the beaches of Pawley's Island before hurricanes and other big storm events. Autumn chuckled to herself at the thought of seeing a ghost tonight. That would have been just a little too much after what had proven to be an overwhelming day. The shore was growing dark. Pawley's Island, a nesting beach for Atlantic Sea Turtles, had no lights on or pointing towards the beach after sundown. Even though Autumn and her family love the ocean and swimming in it, they possessed an even greater respect of it. The beauty and serenity that could be found in the ocean was balanced by the power and force that it could also hold. Nothing was more daunting than the ocean at night. It stood as a world full of unknown treasures and mysteries. The beach represented her day perfectly.

Autumn drove down to her family's favorite restaurant on the island, Shabby's. The parking lot was fairly empty due to the hour and the season. In mid-summer, there could be a forty-five minute wait even at 9:00p.m. The building was unassuming and shack like. That could describe almost everything on the island. Seafood was the specialty of the house: crab cakes, creek shrimp, and the catch-of-the-day. Their hushpuppies were the best anywhere on the planet. Shabby's served them with honey butter. The hushpuppies melt in your mouth. Autumn could never tell if it was the honey butter or hushpuppy that was the best part. Together they were quite the pair. The servers at Shabby's were so generous with these golden delights that people could eat themselves sick before their meal ever arrived. In her experience, the best seafood to order in South Carolina was either the catch of the day or the shrimp. Autumn, being a fan of all seafood, could not pass up shrimp. Shrimp boats out on the horizon were a common sight. It would insult the people who harvest the little gems from the sea to batter and fry them. Shrimp was prepared two ways in Autumn's opinion: boil-and-eat option or sautéed in butter and garlic. Autumn went for the sauté because the peel-and-eat just seemed like too much work. The food nourished her body and soothed her soul. Like a baby's security blanket, Autumn found comfort in being in a familiar place. Once her pecan pie and coffee arrived, she could begin to process all that had happened. She marveled at it all and made a plan for the coming day. Back at the hotel, she planned to call her best friend Kendra to seek some legal advice. Autumn's parents needed to know what was happening. If Autumn had trouble falling asleep, the legal documents Mr. Dravo gave her to read should be boring enough to lull her to sleep. Tomorrow, Autumn would head back to the farm.

A soft breeze drifted through the sheers of her room as the sun ushered in the day. The world was clean and fresh after the night's thunderstorm. The storm was far more entertaining than all the legal forms she forced herself to read. Autumn had drifted to sleep during Mother Nature's light show only to wake to a beautiful sunrise. Showering and dressing quickly, Autumn scurried down the hotel's staircase and burst through the doors. In the small lobby, there was a continental breakfast laid out for guests of the hotel. Autumn grabbed a donut and a cup of coffee for the drive out to the McFarland farm where the day had already begun. Workers were working in the fields as she sped past. The purple coupe pulled around to the garage on the right side of the drive. She bounded up the seven steps of the porch when she heard a voice say, "Well, someone sure lit a fire under your butt this morning!"

Autumn looked around but didn't see anyone.

"I'm down here," said the voice. A thumping sound came from underneath Autumn's feet. "Down here, under the porch. The old root cellar wall fell in with all of last night's rain. Don't worry. We just pack the fallen dirt back up then mortar the old bricks back in place. Don't tell the building inspectors about it. We told 'em years ago that we filled the old root cellar in with concrete. I assume you are the new lady of the house. I'm the caretaker of this old beauty. Ian McClusky is my name and jack-of-all-trades is my claim to fame. I'll be up in a southern second. If you don't know what that is, I suggest you grab a seat on that chair."

Autumn sat down for around five minutes before a man in his late twenties or early thirties emerged from a little door underneath the porch. Clad in a canvas jump suit, the balding blonde man emerged wearing a toothy gaped-tooth smile. "See. A southern second has nothing to do with the functioning of that small third hand on the face of a watch. I learned that early. Otherwise, I would have pulled out what little hair I have left," he said. He tussled the wispy blonde hair on the top of his head.

Autumn recognized a fellow Yankee by the rhythm of his speech. Ian was indeed from the north. Surprisingly, he had gone to school in Ohio. He had received his degree in Computer Sciences. Ian had worked with one of the first companies to bring the Internet to PC users everywhere. After five years at computers, he walked away from financial success and failing health to make a new life in South Carolina. Ian met Jon McFarland during his computer days. When Ian began sharing his story, Jon had told Ian that his sanctuary was his home in South Carolina. The more Jon and Ian talked about the farm, the more Ian knew that South Carolina was the place for him. Ian had asked Mr. McFarland if he needed any help at the house. Ian had come to the McFarland farm to create an intranet for Jon. As time passed, Ian offered to fix little repairs around the house. Now, Ian was the official handy-man at the McFarland farm. There was very little Ian could not manage at the house. He was fairly versed at simple repairs. Anything major just took a little research and ingenuity. Even Ian admitted the repairs might not be done the right way but the outcome was generally the same.

Autumn spent the day exploring every inch of the main house and out buildings with Ian as guide. He explained that there was no basement to the house. The house predated furnaces and indoor plumbing. Therefore, the structure had no need of a basement. There was a root cellar under the front porch that had been crumbling since it was created. It leaked like a sieve and did not stay too cool. The house was plumbed and heated in the mid-1930s. The furnace and hot water tank were hidden inside the pantry of the original farm house. The wiring came later. There was a natural gas deposit on the property that supplied the lighting in the house until the 1960's when houses were inspected and building codes enforced. There were fireplaces in virtually every room. There were panels on either side of the fireplace in the dining room. These giant panels concealed two hidden doorways. The door to the right appeared to go upstairs but actually dead ended. The panel to the left opened to what appeared to be a large closet. Both doorways had other purposes. The stairs hidden to the right lifted up to conceal people or valuables in a large area underneath. The stairs had once led to the master bedroom but had been sealed off after the Civil War. The closet to the left had a false floor that dropped down into the corner of the house. It was a brick and mortar space that had no apparent function. Despite the condition of the root cellar, this room was rather cool, dry, and in very good shape. Very little of the architecture of the house had been changed since the two additions had been made back in the 1800's. Each owner may have had color preferences and given in to the interior decorating styles of their generation but the architecture remained unchanged from one generation to the next. There were more interest-ing decorative touches such as panoramic paintings in the upstairs hall and hand printed wallpaper in the master bedroom. The house stood as an example of the best and brightest styles in interior decorating from the past century. The most interesting discovery in the house was found in the attic.

The attic was in the third floor. What had once been the nanny's living space now served as storage space. However, glimpses of its former self could be seen. Autumn decided to clear out the room. She figured all those boxes needed to be looked through. Some boxes could even give her a window into the enigma known as Jon McFarland. As she was clearing out boxes, Autumn opened the bedroom closet. Inside, on the back wall, was what looked like a family tree. There were no last names. Letters were printed backwards. Some names were spelled incorrectly or phonetically. The only logical explanation was that one of the slaves lived in the big house to care for the family's children and wanted to preserve what little of her family history she could. How such a piece of history remained untouched all this time was purely a matter of luck. The information contained on that wall could be precious and valuable. The author and date were, however, a mystery. Autumn might never know the family the tree recorded. She decided to seek Fanny's input on the discovery. Fanny told Autumn that she owned a family Bible that goes back generations. It might contain a link or a clue. Unfortunately, the family tree in the closet was mostly indiscernible. Fanny's

Bible would have been more helpful if they could decipher the writing on the wall. Hopefully, time would provide them with the key to this mysterious puzzle.

Autumn's thirteen days were spent walking the grounds, talking to all the people who worked for Mr. McFarland, cleaning up the neglected chapel, and sorting through boxes in the attic. The chapel had apparently been shut up for years and years. Whoever took the time to close off the building had done it so lovingly and well that all Autumn had to do was clean away the cob webs and dust. There were beautiful sacred pieces gathered up, covered, and locked in the minister's room near the altar area. A person skilled or familiar with early American religious artifacts and art would have thought they had entered heaven. The items were simple but elegant. As for the attic, the vast majority of the boxes contained old curtains, antique lamps, and all the other things one could find in an attic. The holiday decorations ranged from modern artificial trees to Pre-WW II glass ornaments. A genealogy chart could be made from all the other things in the attic: family birth certificates, marriage licenses, photos, and personal letters. Autumn found it all very interesting though it brought her no closer to knowing why she was here. The McFarlands had married well. That had been how they had acquired most of their land. The land had been given as dowries for the brides of the McFarland men. With little under two weeks to spend in the attic, Autumn could only separate the mess into titled boxes. Photos went into a box of their own because all of the faces were strangers to Autumn. Autumn figured she could put a history of the McFarland family together. It seemed the least she could do for her generous benefactor.

Other parts of her days on the McFarland farm were spent combing over legal documents with Kendra. Everything contained in the documents legally was on the up and up. There were no loop holes or sucker punches at the end of the deal. Still, Autumn had not made a decision. Maybe it should have been easy but it was an awesome prospect for someone just out of college. There was so much history here. The inheritance was a dream-come-true for someone with Autumn's education. She would be saving the McFarland legacy from whatever fate awaited it in the hands of the Historic Society. Autumn had nothing against historic societies. Maintaining a house that was over two hundred years old was a lot of work that required a great deal of money. Rarely, privately funded societies have the resources to take on such a project. The farm was a historic jewel that could eventually go the way of other houses from the era. On the other hand, how could Autumn possibly run a farm, manage an investment firm, and live hundreds of miles away from everything familiar to her. All of that hardly mattered because Mr. Dravo was expecting her at his office at the end of two weeks.

"Today's the day, huh," smiled Shelia. "You'll do okay no matter what you decide. I'd love to see you a Carolinian, hon. Just follow your heart."

"Thanks, Shelia," whispered Autumn as she reached for the door. Autumn felt like an errant child entering the principles office after being caught in the act.

"Okay. Your decision does not matter to me and I am not here to hold your hand while you make your decision. I've got three hours to file these papers. So, what is your decision?" Mr. Dravo was as charming as ever. Whatever her decision, Autumn would be glad to get rid of this snotty little man.

"I accept. I'll be Mr. McFarland's legal heir." The words came out of her mouth but she was shocked to hear them. Her heart had spoken and now her mind had to catch up. It was too late to retrieve them. She signed the papers with trembling hands.

As Autumn walked out, she barely heard Shelia say, "So, what is it?"

"Carolinian." Her mind was still trying to come to terms with what had just happened. Autumn went back to The Carolinian Inn to pack and move to the house. The rental car would be picked up at the McFarland house at four. Mr. Dravo presented her with all the keys for the farm and Mr. McFarland's black convertible. The act of packing was the only mindless activity Autumn could manage.

Driving out to the farm, she sat in the driveway wondering how she got to the farm safely. Autumn's thoughts were still racing. "How could I have done that? What did I just do?" The reality came rushing in as she sat her suitcases in the entryway of the McFarland mansion. She was home. This was her house.

Autumn's thoughts were interrupted by what had become a familiar voice. "I just made a bed. Would you like me to get Ian to help carry your bags?" Fanny's gentle manner slipped Autumn out of her daze.

"How did you know I would be back?"

"I saw the look in your eyes every time you looked at this grand old house. You could never leave. You most certainly couldn't let the State or Society care for this old southern belle. Now, let's get you settled. Do you want me to get Ian?"

"Thanks, Fanny. I'll get my stuff. You probably have something more important to do than help me move in tonight." Autumn almost burst into tears.

"I think you could use a little company. Besides, what are friends for?"

With that, Autumn could not hold back the tears any longer. All her emotions came streaming down her face in the form of tears. The pressure of making the big decision and then bearing the weight of that decision had become too much of a strain. Fanny's presence and company was a blessing. Autumn could take strength from Fanny's easygoing nature. In no time, the two had most of Autumn's luggage put away. Fanny suggested that Autumn go grocery shopping. Autumn thought that was a great idea. Surrounding herself with as many comforts of home could make the sprawling mansion seem a bit more like home. Before she left for the store, Autumn quickly called her parents. They should be the first to know she was leaving Ohio.

"Mom," Autumn said in a quivering voice.

"Hi, my girl. What's wrong?"

"Oh, I'm fine. Just a little tired. I wanted to call and ..."

"You made a decision," her mom interrupted. "Well, what did you decide?"

"I," Autumn hesitated because she did not know if she was emotionally ready to have a big fight with her mom. "I decided to be the inheritor. I know you probably don't think it's a good idea. You don't think any woman should live alone in a strange place. I feel it must be fate that brought me here. I owe it to Mr. McFarland to stay a little while." Autumn braced herself for her mother's comments.

"I'm very proud of you. I can't think of anyone else who would be better at such a challenge. As for living in a strange place, well that's simply not true. You've been going to South Carolina every year since you were five. I think you are right about fate. Good for you. Are you okay with this decision? You sound a little shaky."

Autumn was pleasantly surprised at her mother's reaction. Autumn received the love and support she needed so desperately at the moment. Suddenly, all her anxiety and uncertainty faded away. This was her decision and it was a good one. Autumn and Mrs. Hummel made plans for her family to come down in a week for vacation. Her mom said the family decided to add a week in order to stay with Autumn at the big house. In just a week, everyone would be down for a two week visit in South Carolina. That news gave Autumn something to look forward to as she thought, "That's how I'll manage this. I'll just take it one week at a time."

Autumn set out to Litchfield for groceries. Fanny said there was a store closer but Autumn was familiar with the grocery store in Litchfield. The drive would help calm her nerves and emotions. It was odd to go grocery shopping and not worry about how much they cost. Autumn had bought groceries while in college. That had been an experience in buying as much as possible for $25 or less. Now, Autumn could shop like she was on vacation every week. She returned to the house and carried the bulging bags in through the back door right into the kitchen. Everyone who cared for the mansion had done an excellent job maintaining the home since Mr. McFarland's death. The cupboards had been emptied, scrubbed, and relined. Autumn never thought putting groceries away could be such fun. The kitchen was enormous. Finding even the simplest thing was an adventure. Once everything was put away, she got a glass of milk and took the potato chips and dip into the sitting room to watch TV. The TV made her feel less alone. Before she sat down and turned the TV on, Autumn glanced out the window. The house was so far from anything. Whoever said, "Silence is golden" either did not live alone or was the bravest person alive. It was so quiet. The nearest streetlight was four miles away on the highway. The absolute lack of ambient light was foreign to Autumn. It seemed so strange after living in the center of a college town where there was always something or someone out making noise. Autumn checked the doors one last time and set the alarm. The TV was only on for half an hour when Autumn decided she was too tired. Turning off the last light in the house, Autumn collapsed into a randomly chosen bedroom.

CHAPTER 2

▼

THE GRAND LADY

With each beautiful spring dawn, the days flew by and Autumn slowly grew use to her new surroundings. She still felt like a stranger living in someone else's house. Her belongings arrived four days after agreeing to take ownership of the estate. Once she had gone through her boxes, Autumn had found very few things she needed to keep and even fewer that fit the décor of the home. That, of course, meant a shopping spree. The McFarland mansion had a beautiful interior décor and furnishings. While sifting through the photos of people taken in and around the house, Autumn thought the McFarland home had much in common with the White House. The White House changed residents while the house changed little. It was the same at the McFarland house. The furniture was rearranged and a few things were added with each new lady of the house. Otherwise, the interior of the house had changed very little over the centuries. Autumn's goal was to continue that tradition.

The antique markets had always been Autumn's favorite place to window shop. Now, she could finally buy some of the goodies that caught her eye. She found a circ. late 1700 spinning wheel for the sitting room. She had always wanted one since watching Sleeping Beauty. The spinning wheel was the vehicle for all the wicked workings in the story but Autumn had been enchanted ever since. As the owner of an old home, a spinning wheel would have been a common feature in any home before the Civil War. So, the spinning wheel would be her contribution to the McFarland house. Other items Autumn wanted to bring down from the attic to join the spinning wheel were the beautiful antique crystal set from Germany and the china that certainly belonged to one of the very early Mrs. McFarland's. There was also a large Gothic hall mirror with a genuine marble foot in the attic that could sit at the top of the staircase.

Once Autumn settled into the house, her next priority would be to meet all the people who had worked for Mr. McFarland. It took weeks before Autumn knew-everyone's names, what they did, and how long they had been employed for the McFarland's. She tried to do this over the phone or through e-mails with little or no success. Autumn needed faces and places to put with the names. So, she went to the office. They also needed to get to know her and know what kind of "boss" she would prove to be. When Fanny said the strawberries were ready at a near by farm, Autumn planned the first of what she hoped would be many employee lawn parties. Mr. McFarland's caterer could not wait. It had been a long time since they had prepared a party menu for the mansion. Autumn said they could plan the menu without approval from her. They were far more experienced in this area than Autumn ever could be. Autumn sent printed invitations to each employee and their families. Autumn traveled with Fanny to pick-up the strawberries. Autumn wanted to prepare enough homemade strawberry pies for the party.

The day of the party was set for Sunday June 1st at one. The attire would match the atmosphere of the day: casual and informal. The last little bit of planning came once the replies were confirmed. Autumn wanted it to be a family affair but very few parents could enjoy a party if their children just wanted to know when they could go home. To remedy that, Autumn hired a local carnival company for the day. Children five to twenty-five could ride rides or play games and win prizes. For the younger crowd, there would be baby-sitters to watch the little ones. All Autumn needed for a perfect afternoon would be a gorgeous South Carolina day. The carnival would set-up Saturday and the sitters would arrive early Sunday. The final step was to fill all the pie shells with fresh strawberries and homemade strawberry glaze.

When June 1st arrived, it could not have been a more perfect summer day. As the people pulled up to the house, a bright beautiful day greeted them. The day was going to be warm but the air wasn't stagnant. Autumn made sure to greet each and every person as they arrived. The sheer glee of the small children when they saw the carnival was a wonderful sight. When the teen-agers saw the set-up, they lost their "Just so you know, I don't want to be here" faces and began being truly gracious young adults. There were tables with red and white checked tablecloths to add to the picnic atmosphere. The food, according to the caterer, could only have been better if his momma had done it. About two hours into the party, when families with babies would have had to call it a day, they quietly slipped off to put their little ones down for a nap. The complete warmth and friendliness of every employee was a welcomed relief. Each could not express how much the Lawn Party meant to them. Autumn could not thank them enough for coming and accepting her in her new position. She had explained that there was no aspect of the business that she was familiar with but she was eager to learn with their help.

While standing with a small group of people, one of them remarked, "Look! You even got people to come in antebellum attire. I guess it truly is a lawn party."

As the group turned to see what the guest was talking about, Autumn laughingly brushed it off by replying, "I didn't." To her amazement, there were three ladies standing under one of the massive oaks with parasols, hats, gloves, and beautiful nineteenth century gowns. The group looked to Autumn. When they all looked again, the ladies were gone.

One of the older gentleman in their company said, "You must have thrown a wonderful party. The ladies only gossip at the best parties. Of course, they were figuring out how to throw a better party!" They all had a good laugh and went back to enjoying the party.

As Autumn made her way to the backyard, some children were running to see their parents. Autumn made it over to where the families were in time to hear what the children were saying. The children were telling their parents about the living history display Autumn arranged in one of the out buildings. The parents wanted to hear all about what they had seen and done. The group of children was made up of early elementary aged children who excitedly recanted what they had seen.

"There were five people in kind of old fashioned clothes," said one little one. "Yeah. Like they'd been worn a lot. Like worn everyday," an older boy said. "There were two ladies cooking in the fireplace. One lady was taking care of a baby."

"The two guys were working on making something or fixing their house or something," another boy chimed in. "They said they finished working out in the fields for the day. That gave them time to work around the house."

"Yeah, we asked them, 'Why do you work here?' and they said they had to earn their keep and work hard or Master McFarland would put them in his pocket," said a savvy ten-year-old with freckles bridging her nose.

While the children shared their stories, one of the fathers walked with Autumn to the out building where the children said they had seen the people. He followed her because Autumn looked confused and scared. As they came around to the front of the building, Autumn explained that she had not arranged for anything like that. The gentleman asked why anyone would come on the property.

Autumn could not imagine why someone would do this or what she would do when she confronted these five people. Autumn was told that the buildings were locked and shutters were latched closed to protect the buildings from weather or vandals when there were no workers. Nervously, Autumn reached for the door with a trembling hand. The door was locked.

Ian saw Autumn running toward the out building. He came brandishing the keys. "What's wrong? Has something happened," he asked in a hushed tone. "I saw you coming over. You look as scared as anyone I've ever seen."

"Did you have this door open earlier this afternoon? The kids said they were in here with five people 'acting' as slaves. I'm just confused."

"I told you these buildings stay locked tight until the harvesters begin arriving in August."

Ian unlocked the door and the three of them walked into the building with the curious kids tagging close behind them. There it sat. The building was empty: no furniture, no fire, and no other people but those who just walked in. The dust in the air of the boarded up building and the stale smell reassured Autumn that it had been closed since the planting season ended. There was no fire in the fireplace. Not even a warm ember.

"You're sure this is the building," Autumn asked.

All the kids nodded. They even took the adults around to the places they saw furniture in the small room and where each person was.

"Well, you learned a lot today. How about some ice cream," Ian said.

The kids did not give the bizarre story one more thought after the mention of ice cream. One of the moms leaned over to Autumn and said, "I guess its part of the wonder and mystery of the South. Good thing southerners are so laid back. Don't worry. Just smile and go about your day." Autumn assumed this was one of the many lessons on being southern that she needed to learn. The situation did not seem to upset anyone like it upset her. The woman said not to worry and that was what Autumn did. What else could she do?

The party was a tremendous success. Everyone seemed to sincerely have a good time. The last guest left around six thirty. By eight, no one would ever have known there had been over three hundred people and a carnival on the property. The infants and toddlers were cared for by wonderful dear grandma-type ladies. Parents could not have been happier. Autumn should have been more exhausted but there were too many new friends made and weird experiences had today to just crawl in bed for the evening. It was time for her to try and wrap her mind around the unusual guests at the party. The sun was not going to set for another hour. Autumn thought a horse ride would relax her. After changing into long pants, she headed out to the stables.

Joe was just finishing up when Autumn got down to the stables. He reluctantly saddled up "the finest horse in the state". Autumn thought the black horse looked like one of the prettiest horses she had ever seen. Admittedly, Autumn had only seen three horses up close. This horse had a southern temperament. Ebony never got too excited, rarely spooked, and was never ever in a hurry. All those qualities were desirable to Autumn who had never ridden a horse until she moved to the McFarland farm. The first horse anyone would ride should be a horse that knows how to be ridden. Ebony fit that description to a tee.

They headed out of the stables at a slow gallop. After rounding the far northwest border of the property, Autumn stopped to watch the sun set over the field of her neighbor. The sky was pink and slowly glided into a dazzling red glow. "Red sky at night, sailor's delight. Red sky at morning, sailors take warning. Well, Ebony, it looks like a good night wrapping up a good day. Let's get going before the sun is completely gone." Autumn turned Ebony toward home, but Ebony bristled. After some coaxing, Ebony turned. However, she refused to go forward. Out of inexperience in horse riding and worried about the fading day, Autumn spurred Ebony too hard. Ebony jumped and kicked. Before Autumn even knew what happened, she was on the ground gasping for air. A quick self-examination and Autumn knew no serious damage was done but the wind was knocked out of her. Autumn had only herself to blame. "If someone had kicked me squarely in the ribs, I'd have tossed them off, too," Autumn whispered to Ebony once she caught her breath.

Before she could get to her feet, Autumn realized the throw from the horse was not her problem. Just feet away from her, a large copperhead lay coiled up and ready to strike. This had clearly been Ebony's reason for not wanting to go when Autumn prodded. Now, Autumn was alone in the middle of nowhere. It would be dark shortly and there was a large deadly snake at her feet. The first thing she told herself was as long as she remained perfectly still, the little hisser would slither off to find some place nice and warm to sleep. Next, she wondered if she would be that nice warm place he decided to slither off to once the sun set. Then she thought, "God knows what else could be out here in the dark wooded areas of South Carolina: alligators, other snakes, poisonous spiders."

"I could go on but that might scare me," she said sarcastically to herself.

BANG!

The once menacing snake was laying in tiny snake pieces around the giant crater where the snake had been sitting.

"Great," a little voice in Autumn's head said. "The snake is gone but you are out here in no man's land with a gun wielding psycho. Could I please have the snake back?" She rolled to her feet to face whoever it was.

"You need to listen to your horse. They won't put themselves in harm's way," a deep smooth southern male voice said. The voice sounded like the rich, warm, sweetness of Southern Comfort on a cold night. The sun was long gone leaving Autumn with the stars as her only source of light. She held her hand out in front of her but could not see it. The voice was followed by the scent of burning wood, soap, and men's cologne. Regardless of how irresistible he smelled, this was a stranger brandishing a gun. "It's one of the first things you come to know about horses. They'll save your life when you are too stupid to do it yourself."

"I should say thank you to you and my horse. Except," Autumn gazed up to where the voice was coming, "I know my horse's name but I don't know yours." She swallowed hard after mustering all the composure she could under the circumstances.

"Ebony's one of the finest horses in the state. She'll always take care of you. Especially if you thank her for throwing you. My name is Boyd. Boyd Masters. You're welcome."

"I really do appreciate you blowing up the snake. I prefer my deadly snakes headless. It was going to be a lonely cold night out here. I'm Autumn Hummel. I ..."

"You're the mysterious girl Jon couldn't get out of his mind. I know," Boyd said. "I'm pleased to finally meet you. Since you're new around here, would you mind if I walked you and Ebony back to the stables. I can only imagine what could happen if I let you go alone."

"I could manage by myself, thank you very much. If you would like to keep us company, I'd be happy to let you walk us back. Although, I can barely find my way from the house to the stables in broad daylight." Autumn chuckled at the joke she made at her own expense. It was funny and it was true.

"Let's head back. There won't be any moonlight tonight because of the new moon."

"So, you knew Mr. McFarland. How," asked Autumn who never was at a loss for words.

"Jon and I were neighbors. I own the farm next to his or, rather, yours. It is a horse farm that has been in my family for generations just like this one." He laughed and Autumn saw a sly grin crawl over his face in the light of the approaching stables. "The horses from South Carolina have been the backbone of those famous Kentucky race horses." Boyd reached down and patted his mount. "Cheyenne is the best of six generations of horses from South Carolina."

"He's beautiful."

"But," he leaned toward her.

"But what," asked Autumn.

"You were going to ask me something. Go ahead and ask."

"I'm not very up on horse racing but why is he here and not running for the Triple Crown or whatever they call it." Autumn knew that she once again let her inquiring mind come before her finesse. Here she was in the presence of a gentleman and she insults his job, his family, and his horse all in one sentence.

"Cheyenne is a breeding horse not a racer. When he was two, he blew out his knee. That ended his racing days but his sons and daughters have gone on to be champions. Pretty bold question. Most women wouldn't ask because they'd be too afraid of what I'd think. I like straightforward people. No hidden agendas. Jon would like that too."

"Thanks," Autumn said softly thinking, "You really dodged the bullet on that one. Try and keep your mouth shut, please."

The lights were still on in the stable when they arrived so Autumn could get Ebony settled in for the night. The light afforded Autumn her first real look at Mr. Masters. Now, in the light of the stables, she had a face to put with the deep rich voice. As he slid off Cheyenne, Autumn could see he was a man with a very athletic build. His muscles shifted and flexed underneath his shirt as he took Cheyenne over to a stall. He was perfectly proportioned in build, not as bulky as a football player but no featherweight. The grin fell on a handsome face with flowing chiseled features. He had a strong lean jaw-line with long high cheekbones. Despite his blonde hair, he had very dark brown eyes that were mesmerizing. Boyd could have been carved out of an artist's granite. The Master Himself beautifully, proportionately, and lovingly crafted each and every aspect of him. Autumn did notice that when he was not smiling, his expression seemed intense and almost fierce.

Suddenly, Autumn turned her thoughts from his appearance to hers. She ran her fingers through her hair and dusted herself off. Being thrown from a horse, held captive by a snake, and saved by what could have been a madman generally took a toll on appearances. Boyd noticed her attempt to pull herself together.

"You look great. There must be some southern blood in you. Only a belle could go through what you did tonight and still look beautiful." He took water and oats over to Ebony and Cheyenne.

Autumn met Boyd at the stalls with sugar cubes. "I know they are not good for them," Autumn smiled. "Joe would storm around muttering under his breathe if he ever knew. I figure they deserve a reward for tonight."

"You're going to reward the horse who threw you?"

"Cheyenne for bringing aid and Ebony for putting me in need of that aid." Autumn could feel herself blush. "Would you like a ride home? Four wheels not four legs."

"Thanks."

The drive was a little awkward at first because of the silence. The ice was broken by questions. Boyd knew Jon but had never seen Jon's place. So, as they passed the house, fields, and finally the church, Autumn and Boyd had something to talk about as they left. Taking the few short turns to Boyd's house, it was he who had the story to tell. They were now on his land. The little she could see in the dark of the Masters' place was a wide-open field. Boyd explained that his family had almost always bred horses. Before horses, the family had raised indigo in the first crop dynasty of the South. When indigo was followed by rice, his family did not follow suit. Autumn's property was between his and the river. She had the water for rice. He had the land for horses. Generations of crops depleting the soil made the land barren. Now the land could barely grow enough grass to sustain the horses. As they approached Boyd's house, Autumn was a little surprised. Unlike her home, Boyd's house was a log home. Hand-hewn logs met at the back of the grounds near a dense forest. The home was every bit as sprawling as her own. The electric candles in each window made it seem particularly welcoming.

"You're surprised by my house," Boyd said as he turned his gaze down to the floor mats. He suddenly seemed vulnerable and timid.

"It's wonderful. The lights and the woods make it nestled in like a warm memory. It feels like a place from the past; warm and familiar. If I seemed surprised, it was not by its appearance but how it made me feel when I saw it." Autumn responded almost in a whisper. It was partly in response to the shyness she saw in him.

When she stopped the car, she met his gaze. He was smiling at her and said, "Well then, you gotta come in. I feel the same way every time I come home."

The inside of the log home was just as charmingly rustic as the outside. The home was decorated to fit the style of the house. The house Boyd grew up in had been built after the War of 1812 but caught fire. When the builders were gutting the home, they discovered the original farmhouse. It was a small log house with a loft made of black cypress dovetailed logs. There was no way to know how old the dwelling was but the singed logs were in excellent condition. So when Boyd decided to build his house, they used the logs to build the new log home. The original builders would have used the logs over again as well. Boyd decided to stay with the style for two reasons. His ancestors chose the design when they were building their first house. The log home fit both the land and Boyd. There was a large fireplace that served as the focal point for the great room as well as an oven for the kitchen on the opposite side. The stones for the foundation were taken from the fields and the original log cabin foundation. The symbolism of which he expressed best when he said, "A strong future is built from the past's good foundation."

The two of them said their goodnights not long after coming to the house. It had been a long night. Besides, southern society would frown upon her staying beyond a polite tour at such a late hour. As she slid behind the wheel of her car, Autumn kicked into autopilot. Without much more thought, the day passed into another night at the McFarland farm.

With dawn, the promise of romance filled her head when her mind turned to Boyd Masters. Those thoughts gave way to the strange events at yesterday's party. Autumn wondered who those people were and why had they appeared. No harm had come from their actions but it was unnerving. Autumn decided to talk to Fanny about the events of the party. Before she could, Autumn wanted to stop by the stables and check on Cheyenne. Joe would be a little more than surprised to see Mr. Masters' champion stud in his stables. When she approached the stables, she could hear two voices. Autumn felt a flutter in her chest and her step quickened. Even if she had not thought about it before, Autumn was glad to see Boyd again.

Joe greeted her. "I told you it was too late to be out riding. You're so bull-headed. You are just."

Autumn interjected, "Lucky someone was there to save me. Good morning Mr. Masters. You are here bright and early this morning."

"He didn't want Cheyenne getting spoiled over here. He might decide to jump ship and let someone who knows how to take care of horses tend to him," growled Joe.

"You had the choice, Joe. You chose Jon. Good morning, Ms. Hummel. How is the fall feeling this morning?" Boyd was choking back a chuckle.

"Southern ladies may have hard heads but northern girls can take a hard fall now and again. Thank you for asking. I was just coming down to check on Cheyenne and fill Joe in on what and why." Autumn had a good night rest under her belt and was ready for whatever today brought. Nevertheless, she had to lock her knees so she would not shake at the sight of Boyd. Obviously, a night's rest found its way to him as well. Autumn wondered if the newly shaved face and pressed shirt were for her. "I see that everything is okay here. So, I'll say thank you to the both of you. I've got some mysteries to uncover today. I hope to see you again Mr. Masters."

"The pleasure would be mine, miss," Boyd said with a smile and a nod of his head.

Autumn could hardly keep from skipping out of the stables. For as handsome and mysterious as he seemed last night, Boyd was ten times all that today. Boyd was wearing intoxicating cologne that lingered. She planned to ask him to join her for dinner when she went to visit his stables to return Cheyenne. It would have been out of character for her. To this day, Autumn had never even walked up to a man she found attractive let alone ask them out on a date. It would not be proper for a woman to do that. Southern etiquette still ruled in parts of the South; the rules of the society Boyd knew from birth. She did the right thing by playing it the way she did. Her interest in Boyd was acceptably casual yet definitely noticeable. There could always be a neighborly reason to see him. Though meeting Boyd was the highlight of yesterday, there were more pressing events to be explained.

Autumn met up with Fanny in the garden. "Fanny, can I talk to you. I have a couple things to ask you if you don't mind."

"Okay. You know I don't mind. Besides, I could use the company. There's nothing to be done till the end of summer except water and weed." Fanny sat on a small stool yanking mercilessly at the garden weeds.

"First, can you cut magnolia blooms for the house? They are so beautiful and smell wonderful. I thought they would be perfect for vases around the house. With the days getting longer and warmer, the flowers seem to be dying." Autumn thought a slow start would be better than, "So, were those ghost's at the party yesterday or what?"

"You're right. Summer steals the life from magnolia blossoms. You go right ahead and cut some. In the air-conditioned house, they'll last weeks in a vase. Make sure you cut some with leaves. The heavy waxy leaves set off the white flowers nicely."

"Great. I'm still working on the writing in the attic closet. Have you had any luck?"

"Ian told me about the uninvited guests at the party yesterday."

"Oh … So, who do you suppose they were? I can't imagine how they got here without anyone noticing."

"Girl, you really think the folks you saw yesterday were real. I mean flesh and blood?"

"What else could they have been," Autumn asked. She did not want to lead Fanny in any way. In the back of Autumn's mind, she also did not want to think that her new home was haunted.

"Honey, these lands have been in the McFarland family for generations. People were born, raised, died, and buried here. God only knows what else went on here. You are in the South now and there are two things to be said for southerners. One is that we don't hide our crazy relatives in institutions. We sit them on the front porch with everybody else. The other one is that northern folk wonder if there are such things as ghosts while southerners just wonder which ones they'll see on any given day. Yes. They were ghosts." Fanny patted Autumn's lap and shook her head. "My guess is that your Lawn Party struck a chord with this old house. The McFarland ladies were renown in their days for the fabulous parties. The ladies were known to get the best the world had to offer to make a splash in society circles. One party even had blue glacier ice brought in from Canada for drinks. The ladies were probably jawin' about your party, deciding if it were up to snuff. The family those children met were probably from the same time. You may have just ripped a hole in the veil. That's what caused all of that. Just a small tear." Fanny turned back to her attack on the unwelcome vegetation.

"A tear ... the veil ... what," stammered Autumn.

"Okay, okay. Take a deep breath," said Fanny in her motherly tone. "Some folks, especially Christians, see the world in three layers. There's heaven on top, hell on the bottom and our world sandwiched between the two; three separate and distinct layers. Then you start thinking that people belong in one of those layers. We never occupy more than one. The concept of ghosts is scary because the three layer view makes them either an angel from heaven or monsters from hell. Scary, right?"

"Right." Autumn replied as she attempted to wrap her mind around the concept.

"There is another view of the universe, however. That view of the universe believes that we go on to the other side of life. Choosing the time, the place, and person we want to be. Wherever we were our happiest, we stay there on the other side. They are living life but in that happy place. So, we are in sort of a parallel world to this one but every once in awhile the veil is lifted. We see that other world. That is what probably happened yesterday. The veil brushed aside for a few moments."

"Okay. So the young ladies in their party dresses make sense. Beautiful girls in beautiful dresses enjoying the life of southern belles but the slave family?"

"Happiness is relative to the rest of your life. Being another man's property is not a happy situation. That moment, place, or experience may have been the happiest time in that life. They were home and surrounded by the ones they loved. That is what made them happy in a life wrought with such unhappiness. Remember, they are not here. They are in their world. The veil lifts every once in a while and we get a glimpse. It's like turning on a TV. You see a picture but cannot interact with what you are seeing. You may learn something from what you see but that is all. On this old farm, you'll probably see more of the other world than you care to see. Have you had any luck with the writings in the attic?"

Autumn had no idea who could have made them or why. Autumn told Fanny about the family research made available by the Mormons. Autumn thought she would transcribe what was on the closet wall and take some photos. The historical society may know what to do with her discovery. A web page could also allow African-Americans researching their family tree an entry point. Any branch or twig would take them one step closer to their roots. With all this on her mind, Autumn thought she should take some photographs and visit the Georgetown Historical Society. After running upstairs to snap some quick pictures, Autumn dropped the film at a one-hour photo lab and headed downtown to the historical society which was housed in an office inside The Rice Museum. The groups worked together in preserving the history of the area. Some people have been offended by the society's efforts to preserve the history of the Antebellum Era with its plantations, aristocracy, wealth, oppression, and slavery. The supporters would say that the only way not to repeat the mistakes of our past was to remember them. Autumn stood firmly on the side of history. A lovely older lady greeted Autumn when she entered the office. Her name was Lillian. She was born and raised in Georgetown. Lillian said she knew everyone in town but had not yet met Autumn. Autumn explained that she had only been in town a few weeks. That's when Autumn told Lillian about the writings she found. Lillian thought they were a priceless treasure. Lillian told Autumn she would file them after she cross-references the names with some of the old slave record books the society owned. The information would be valuable to many families out there. She asked Autumn which house was hers because the location would also be helpful in cross-referencing the names. When Lillian found out it was the McFarland Farm, her eyes lit up and she raced off to show Autumn "something of interest."

When Lillian returned from the small back room, she had an old leather bound book in her hands. The gold leafing on the spine and cover showed wear but still bore the name McFarland Family Bible. Jonathan had donated the book thirty years before his passing. With no children, he had thought the society would be the best place for it. Lillian said it contained family stories and information about lineage back to 1809 when Liam and Miriam McFarland were married at the farm. Every lady of the house had kept a record of the life and times of the family McFarland. Since the book now belonged to the society, it had to stay in the office. Lillian assured Autumn that she was more than welcome to read it whenever she could stop into the office. Though it was tempting to stay and see what wonders could be found in the beautiful old book, Autumn took her leave for the day. There were many mysteries to be uncovered at the McFarland farm but each one would be found in its own sweet time. The writings upstairs would be first. The writings could open the door to more mysteries.

Autumn went in to pick-up her photos at the drug store. The hot humid day gave way to a torrential down pour in the afternoon. The young lady behind the counter told Autumn her prints were done but the lab technician was reviewing the pictures. When the young lady returned, she seemed a little sheepish as she handed over the prints. Autumn smiled and thanked the girl. While Autumn perused the pictures, the girl kept glancing up. One would have thought that Autumn had some risqué photos. So far, the photos of the house, land, and party were wonderful. Everything seemed just fine. Then she saw the photo of the third floor. At first, Autumn could not really figure out what was in the pictures. Once she had a moment to compute what she was seeing, the shock covered her face. The once glancing girl now fixed a stare and asked, "Is there something wrong with your prints?"

"Well, I think so. I'm not sure what I'm looking at but it is not what I took a picture of. I was just," Autumn paused, realizing she was rambling. "Could I talk to the lab technician? Maybe he could explain what happened to my pictures."

The shy girl scurried to the back office and returned with a man in a white lab coat and glasses. "We wondered about those. I checked the negatives after the prints came up. The image on the prints is in the negative but it isn't a double exposure or a flaw in the film. What is in those photos was there when you snapped the picture. That is the only thing I can tell you. Do you have any ideas?"

The photo of the room with the closet in profile showed a woman clutching what appeared to be a small boy about five or six years old. The second photo was of the closet straight on with the same woman trying to hold on to this young boy who was being pulled by unseen hands from her grasp. The next three were photos of the wall inside the closet. There was no image of the woman or the boy in these photos. Instead, it was just the names painted on the wall in black writing. That was what was in the closet of Autumn's third floor. The unusual part of the poorly written names, dates, and family lineage were the red letters in excellent penmanship that appeared as last names over each family group. There were just a few surnames for each group, not hundreds. The photos with the names could be keys given to unlock the mysterious family tree that appear on the inside rear of the closet. Autumn was energized. Not only did she have an important piece of local and national history but she had the key to get this information to the people who would treasure it the most. Someone or a great many people on the other side of the veil would like to be found by their descendants. Suddenly, what started as confusion, disbelief, and fear turned into a mission. Autumn was going to place these names with their families no matter what she had to do. That gave her an idea.

Autumn made it to the McFarland Office just before four o'clock. There was an hour before the office would close. Autumn called everyone to drop whatever he or she was doing to help her with this project. She told everyone about the names in the closet, her hopes to find their full story, and dispense all of the information anyone in the office would find. Autumn gave them surnames to put with each group but did not tell them how she knew the surnames. Peggy, Jon McFarland's secretary for more than twenty years, was promoted to office manger on Autumn's first day as director of the estate. Peg offered an old slave ledger that could match names of when they were sold and to whom. The ledger also contained the surnames of some of these individuals once they were freed. Todd was the office computer guru who said he would post a web page if Autumn would spring for the costs. He could have it up and running in two to three days. Cheryl ran the 401K for all of Mr. McFarland's employees. She offered to get the information to the local Family History Libraries where people go when they are looking for their families. Autumn spent the last hour of the office day profusely thanking her office staff. She sent everyone home while she finished cross-referencing the names on the ledger with names from the closet wall. By six fifteen, Autumn found all but two names in the ledger. They were two men who appear on early dates on the wall. Autumn resolved that they lived and died on the farm and may have died before being sold or freed.

It was around seven when she arrived home. The old farm was really starting to feel like home. She could feel herself unwind at the sight of the stately mansion. Fanny left the lights on. As Autumn came closer to the house, she saw someone sitting on the porch in one of the Pawley's Island rockers. Her heart leaped when she recognized the person

"Welcome home, Ms. Hummel," he said in his smooth, warm, and easy southern drawl. "You have yet to master the hours of a southern lifestyle."

Autumn chuckled, "Why Mr. Masters, to what do I owe the pleasure? Has your horse jumped ship to come live at my stables?"

"You do know that no one in South Carolina says 'to what do I owe the pleasure' anymore, right?"

"Okay. You caught me in a 'Scarlet' moment. I think that's going to happen until I can walk up to this house without 'Tara's Theme' playing in my head. Would you like to come in? I haven't had dinner yet and I'm starving."

"Well, that's why I'm here. I wondered if you would like to go out to dinner. There's this little restaurant that sits on Winyah Bay."

"Seafood?"

"Seafood? Seafood what?"

"Does this little restaurant by the bay serve seafood?"

"Whatever you would like. Is that a yes?"

"Yes and thank you. Can I take a minute to change?"

"Sure."

Within minutes, Autumn returned with a new do, dress, and sprits of lilac perfume. Boyd had driven over in a beautifully decked-out classic blue 1969 Mustang convertible. It was a gorgeous early summer night. The rain drained the humidity from the air and the intoxicating sea air was reaching inland for miles. Out on the farm, with the nearest street lamp being four miles away, the beautiful blues, purples, pinks, and oranges of dusk were vivid. Just before crossing the bridges over the Intercoastal Waterways, the restaurant sat on the bay at the edge of Georgetown. The restaurant was set so all the tables faced the bay or the Sampit River. There were recreational boaters heading out to enjoy a lovely and relaxing evening on the water. Sun burnt fathers, sons, buddies, and brothers were returning from a day of sun bathing, and fishing. Some were a little green from "the motion of the ocean". Boyd and Autumn started the evening with wine and ended with Plantation Pecan Pie. The moments in between were the best part of the evening, day, or week. The two shared stories of growing up. They found out they had a great deal in common with each other though they were from completely different worlds. Boyd's dad traveled all over the world showing, buying, and breeding horses. His mom was the stay-at-home type but home involved more than just running the house and raising the kids. Mrs. Masters ran the family business while his dad was out of town. Boyd and his three brothers were very close even though they live far apart. Growing-up, everything was a contest: dirt bikes, horse riding, breaking horses, cars, and girls. No matter who won which contest, victory was not sweet. To the victor went a serious beating at the hands of the losers. When Boyd was older, he traveled with his dad when it did not conflict with school and other activities. His family traveled a lot. Two weeks every year, the Masters traveled as a family all over the country. His mom felt there was too much in this world to do and see to just sit at home. Boyd was the only son to go into the family business. It was completely of his choosing. His parents encouraged all their children to do what they loved.

As the sun set over Winyah Bay, they took a walk along the newly built Georgetown harbor walk. Boyd told her about the rise, fall, and recent resurrection of Georgetown. The town never really recovered from being a great farming and shipping port. The town had benefited from tourism in South Carolina and the reawakening interest in American downtowns. As they made their way past beautiful Greek revival homes, Boyd had a story for each home: people, events, and ghost stories.

Autumn started noticing a prevailing trend among these houses. "Why are so many of the porch ceilings painted light blue?"

"Oh, you noticed that. Well, there are guidelines for homeowners in the Historic District. It dictates what changes the homeowner can make to the structure and the property. There is a specific list of colors to paint your house. Porch ceilings fall under those guidelines. It was, however, based on a belief from the Gullah people." Boyd seemed to swell with pride when talking about his hometown.

"Wow! I just thought I was asking a simple question. Now, it's starting to sound scary."

"As long as you are not scared of ghosts, you'll be fine," warned Boyd.

Autumn chuckled, "Tell me your ghost story and I'll tell you mine. Then, we'll see whose ghost stories are scarier."

Boyd lifted his one eyebrow and grinned curiously, "Okay. The ceilings were painted light blue because it was supposed to keep evil spirits from following you home and across the threshold. Now, what's your ghost story, missy?" He playfully nudged her as they continued their stroll.

"No. Not here. You got to tell me your ghost stories where they happened. Take me home and I'll tell you my ghost story."

They made their way back to the car. With the top down, they tried to convince each other of who had the more embarrassing moments in high school. Once at home, Autumn and Boyd went into the kitchen to make coffee. Boyd hopped up on the center island while Autumn threw the coffee together. Autumn laughed as she shut the cupboard door with a bang. "Do you ever wonder why we have such huge kitchens? Heck, I amaze myself at how stupid I feel slapping' together a PB and J sandwich in a kitchen right out of a home interior magazine. The amazing thing was that no matter how hard I try I only ever use the two feet of counter space on either side of the sink. My mom's whole kitchen would fit where the refrigerator and stove are. The thing that is weird to me is how much noise one person in a huge kitchen can make!"

"So, are you going to tell me your story or what?" Boyd tried to sound impatient but it did not come off that way.

Autumn shared the whole thing from the writing in the closet to the pictures she got earlier that day.

He hopped off the island with boyish excitement. "You've got to show me those pictures."

They took their coffee into the den. Autumn's computer sat with the photos and her transcription of the writings. The photographs intrigued Boyd. He was staring so intensely at the pictures that everything else in the world faded out of his sight. His brow was furrowed and his jaw was set in deep thought. With a sudden shift in expression, Boyd's gaze turned to Autumn. "Who do you think she could be," Boyd said with a sadness and sincerity that caught her by surprise. "What do you think was happening in those pictures? I mean, God only knows the sins committed against these people. It's so damn sad." His hand brushed the transcription. "You've found some of the people written on the wall? Is that what all this is?"

Autumn explained the search she and her staff were putting out. The timer on Boyd's watch suddenly went off. It was midnight.

"It's been a most interesting and adventurous evening, but I should say goodnight before we give people something to talk about."

"I'll see you out, then." Autumn felt it was the polite thing to do and say. Still, she was not tired nor did she want the evening to end. She told herself there would be more times with Boyd. The two made their way to the foyer. As she opened the door, Boyd took her hand in his. The joining of their hands was like an electric shock, not painful but rather like a circuit completed. Autumn could feel the warmth of his hand and the gentle strength it possessed.

He turned and said softly, "You know, I think I could become very fond of you, Miss Hummel. Thank you for a great evening."

With that, he brushed the hair back from her face and gently placed a kiss on her cheek. By the time Autumn had regained her senses, Boyd's headlights were streaming down her drive.

The cornfields were ready for picking in early June. The fields of tobacco would follow at the end of June into July with the cotton in very late summer or early fall. Autumn was raised in the city. Outside of a small garden plot out by the local reservoir, Autumn had never really "taken in a crop" before she moved to South Carolina. The field foreman, Tom, explained the procedure and the time frame for harvesting each crop. Tom already sold the crops to the best buyers. Anything harvested above the estimated yield was sold right in Georgetown at the Farmer's Market. Much to the surprise of the farm hands, Autumn went out every morning to join them in the fields. She loved being out there working and getting a great tan at the same time. She realized there was a time when it was not becoming for the lady of the house to look like someone who worked in the fields all day but times have changed. In the beginning of this farm, everyone would have worked to bring in the harvest. As time passed and farmers became the aristocracy of South Carolina, the ladies would never have thought about stepping foot in the fields. The woman's role had been to bare children but not too many, care for the slaves, and be the hostess of the farm. Those times had long passed and Autumn figured the only way to truly get to know the land she inherited was to see how it worked. More than that, she loved the look on the workers faces as she stood out there keeping pace with the most experienced of them. The harvesting would take about two months. During that time, Autumn lost her appetite, lost weight, and lost her iridescent northern skin. It was the best tan of her life. At least that was what she told her sister. Autumn had one complaint about the experience and it was tobacco beetles. They do not bite, sting, or even eat the crops themselves. The beetles only passed through her fields on their way from one tobacco farm to the next one. Her complaint was that they were creepy looking and scary. More than one field worker laughed himself or herself to sleep thinking about Autumn's screaming and swearing at the innocuous bugs.

Throughout the summer months, Autumn's evenings were spent in the company of Boyd Masters. Summer was a very slow time in the business of thoroughbreds. All the horse owners were focused on racing their beautiful horse. Boyd made his way, by day, to a few of the big races. By evening, he was back either at his home or Autumn's. It was a record-breaking summer for heat. Neither Boyd nor Autumn minded the heat wave. They spent the hot nights of mid-summer riding horses, boating on the PeeDee and Black Rivers, or just sipping lemonade on the front porch. As for the names in the closet, people claimed ancestry to more than a dozen of the names. The relatives made their way through the internet, Family History Libraries, or Fanny's word-of-mouth chain. It seemed that there were not many people in Georgetown or Horry County who did not know Fanny. The relatives of those people lived all across the United States. They also came from every walk of life. Many people contacted Autumn to thank her. Most asked if they could come visit her house someday. They simply wanted to see the farm to feel connected to somewhere. Autumn invited every single person who contacted her. That's when she decided to go one step further. Autumn sent out invitations to each and every person who contacted her about visiting the McFarland farm. She invited them to a McFarland Plantation Reunion. Autumn guessed that a lot of these people would be distant relatives to each other. In addition, all the folks who wanted to visit could now do it in one day rather than randomly throughout the year. The response Autumn received was tremendous. Autumn said she would provide all the necessities and the lost relatives could provide the food and beverages. Boyd was out of town for two weeks at the end of August which seemed the perfect time for the reunion. In less than two weeks, there would be over five hundred people at the McFarland farm for the second party of the summer.

People from as far away as the state of Washington came to the reunion. The very old to the very young made the trip to be united with their history. Some of them described this homecoming as being the closest they could come to a "homeland". Tears were shed, families torn apart were reunited, and old wounds were addressed. Each family brought picture albums, scrapbooks, family trees, and heirlooms to share and trace. The most special moment of the day came when the family of the young boy in Autumn's ghostly picture approached her. The boy in the ghostly picture had apparently been sold to a plantation owner in Virginia along with one of his cousins. Emancipation moved south slowly. This boy became literate and wrote many letters to the mother he would never see again. The letters had all been returned because his mother was still a slave. As this boy became a man, he told his children and grandchildren the story of the day he said good-bye to his Mama. He told them how she wailed and cried as if someone was tearing the heart from her chest. That day his mother had vowed to love him always and he would be in her heart no matter where he found himself. The family and Autumn quietly made their way to the third floor. By the closet door, the family sat a dozen red roses in her honor. One by one, family members introduced themselves to the matriarch they had never known. There were a doctor, a college professor, and the list went on. Their closing words were, "Out of your pain, suffering, and hardship we were born. Thank you for being strong enough and brave enough to see us become a reality. May we, everyday and with every action, make you proud."

Autumn joined them in their tears and celebration of their past.

CHAPTER 3

▼

THE HANGMAN

As the temperatures began to rise, the days melted into each other. A two-week trip for Boyd in late August stretched out longer than planned. The farm had become quiet with the passing of summer. The fields were harvested and let to run their growing season. All of the outside house repairs and maintenance were completed before the reunion. Ian left to visit his family up north. The once beautiful lush gardens and lawns were now struggling to stay alive. The plants of spring and early summer were replaced by tropical flowering plants and ground cover. The sprinklers watered the lawns every night but it was just enough to keep the grass alive. The only really bountiful plant was the Spanish Moss. The humidity intensified ten-fold in August and September. Locals said that a long moist spring coupled with a dry hot summer was just the thing the moss needed. The moss made the South look mysterious. It draped down from every tree. A live oak would not look the same without it. Autumn found piles of it in her front lawn after a particularly nasty tropical depression brushed the coast. When she raked it all up in a wheel barrel, she took it down to the stables for Joe to burn with his other rubbish.

"Why'd you rake all this up," Joe groused.

"The storm knocked it off the trees. I thought you could just burn it," Autumn stated. She was accustomed to Joe's naturally grumpy disposition. "Besides, I'm cleaning up to plant a garden next to the big live oak."

"Didn't anybody tell you? You can't burn this stuff. Thanks to blight in the 1970's, Spanish Moss was almost wiped out. You can't burn it. Plus, it's not dead. Just leave it near the woods. It will do fine till a wind or a bird picks it up and sets it in a tree or a bush."

"But, it's been out of the tree for several days."

"Don't care. It's an air plant. Draws all it needs as far as food and water from the air. Has it been closed in a plastic bag this whole time?"

"Well, no?"

"Then?"

Autumn strolled away without a word. She was not going to give him the satisfaction. So, she made her way to the far side of the woods near the river. Autumn picked up armfuls of the moss and tossed it up and out over the foliage. Autumn thought she would give it help back up in the world. As she was winging moss into the air, Fanny came by and asked, "What are you doing?"

Autumn turned around to answer Fanny but she had to wait. Fanny completely lost it. Tears were welling up in her eyes. Suddenly, Fanny let out a laugh that could make old Iron Sides smile. Fanny's laugh was an all over laugh. Once Fanny could catch her breath, she reached in her pocket to withdraw a compact and handed it to Autumn. Without saying a thing, Autumn opened it and looked at herself in the tiny mirror. Just as Autumn looked, she burst into laughter. It seemed that some of the Spanish Moss found Autumn's head a perfectly high enough point to rest. While they continued to laugh, the two pulled clumps from Autumn's head and set them loose on a near by bush. When Autumn could control herself, she put her hand on Fanny's shoulder. "I'm glad to see you. For more than one reason," snickered Autumn.

Autumn knew that Fanny had probably the greenest thumb in the county. Fanny would be the person to ask about planting a new garden. Autumn explained that one of the ladies of the house, Elaine MacBruce, had a garden "beneath the large old oak". Elaine had been only the third Mrs. McFarland. Autumn thought it would be nice to have a flower garden she could cut flowers from and it would also recapture a little more of the past of the stately home. Fanny gave her a fine list of annuals that would make for beautiful cut flowers: hydrangeas, lilies, orchids, zinnias, Australian daisies, and lavender. These were all beautiful fragrant flowers that enjoy full sun in most climates. Fanny said they would do wonderfully in the shade of the live oak. The little shade they would get from the tiny leaves on the tree would protect them from the scorching heat of the day but not steal too much of their sunlight. Fanny said she would be happy to help with the new garden. So, they started to work right away. By dusk, the two had measured and marked where the garden would lie. The partners agreed that was good enough for now. Fanny would be back at ten in the morning with the flowers, fertilizers, and topsoil. Autumn volunteered to ask Tom for the rotor tiller, shovels, rake, and hoe.

As night settled in, Autumn's thoughts turned to Boyd. It was almost three weeks since he left. She had not heard from him since. Joe would meet up with some of the farm hands that work for Boyd and get the latest news. Joe passed any information on to Autumn be it begrudgingly just to get Autumn from moping around the stables. She knew Boyd was safe and that he would be gone longer than originally anticipated. Autumn could not be upset that he had not called her. They were dating but did not warrant a phone call from abroad. Their romantic encounters had not gone beyond holding hands and goodnight kisses. Autumn decided to stop fussing about it and get ready for bed. As she turned off the lights and crawled into bed, she suddenly heard what sounded like a crowd of people outside. Autumn shrugged it off and pulled the covers up around her neck. She giggled and thought to herself, "I never thought I'd be sleeping with covers when it was seventy-three degrees at night. I must be becoming a Carolinian."

Just then, the crowd she had heard earlier became frighteningly loud. The voices seemed angry. She heard horses neighing and stomping their hooves. When Autumn rolled over, light was coming up from the yard. It almost looked like light from a fire the way it was flickering on the walls. Autumn dashed to the window fearing a fire had broken out somewhere on the farm. When she reached the window, she could not believe what she was seeing. There were at least thirty people gathered in her lawn carrying torches and yelling. Most of the people were men but there were a few women. Four or five men were on horseback. The men had the reigns pulled tight because the horses seemed spooked by the fire and loud crowd. Autumn grabbed the phone and dialed nine-one-one.

The officer asked, "What is your emergency?"

Autumn searched for words. Stammering, she blurted out, "Men yelling on my lawn!"

The operator asked, "Could you repeat that, ma'am."

Autumn finally found words to describe what she was seeing. The dispatcher told Autumn to stay upstairs and to leave the lights off. The dispatcher kept her on the line until the officer radioed that he was coming down the main road. The officer confirmed that he saw flickering lights and a crowd in the distance. The police then turned their lights and siren on as they sped down the drive.

Autumn headed downstairs to see what was happening. As she reached the midpoint of the stairs, Autumn sped up in astonishment. She ran to the dining room window and moved the sheers aside. In the front lawn, the police officers were there and the lights from the squad car. Those were the only things in the front yard. The officers walked around the front and back of the big house. The two patrolmen then made their way up the front porch. Autumn met them at the door. "I'm so sorry. They were here. I know they were." Autumn looked around incredulously. "Right there. Right out front here."

"Well, ma'am, there is no one here now. We'll drive the grounds just to be sure. That should give you some peace of mind," the middle-aged officer said.

"Where were they on the lawn," asked the other officer almost as if he really did not want to know the answer.

Autumn pointed out toward the large live oak. "Right under that tree."

The middle-aged officer asked her to come out and look at something. The men accompanied her to where she told them the angry mob had been. There was a cold spot where the mob had been as they reached the foot of the tree. The spot was cold enough to make the threesome shiver out loud. The officers were carrying flashlights and turned them to the ground. There in the dry dusty ground were many sets of footprints. The last party was at least a week and a half ago. The tropical depression that had rained buckets and blew the Spanish Moss from the trees had come through since then. The prints were definitely not from the reunion guests. Even more amazing were the hoof prints around the perimeter. They were not prints from one or two horses but several.

"We don't know what to tell you other than that there is no one here now," said the middle-aged officer.

"Then, what did I see," queried Autumn. "I mean, I wasn't dreaming. I was on the phone with the dispatcher for over ten minutes while I watched the crowd from my window!"

The younger officer agreed with Autumn. "We saw flickering lights and shadows from a group of people. Just as we got close enough to distinguish something for sure, we saw nothing."

"Well ma'am, call us if you have anymore trouble. We will be on the grounds for another hour just to be sure. We'll swing by the house once more before we head back out to the main road," stated the older officer completely unfazed by what had or had not happened.

Autumn was scared, nervous, and unsettled by the events of the evening. "Excuse me, sir," Autumn said in voice that hopefully hid her annoyance. Something real or perceived had happened. The officer was acting as if he had rescued a cat from a tree. "Why are you so calm about all of this?" The strain of the events erupted in her voice.

"Ma'am, I protect the citizens to the best of my ability. You do not appear to be in any danger. We are going to search the area to make sure you and your property stay that way. There is no one here to arrest or I would. It is not, however, my job to figure out the 'whys' of a situation. I stopped trying years ago." He finished his statement just as he slid into the police cruiser. "Goodnight. We'll wait here until you are back inside."

Autumn closed the door and flashed the porch light to let them know she was okay. The patrol car headed down towards the stables and fields. Autumn gave the whole incident one more replay in her mind. To her surprise, she was no longer shaking or worried about what had happened. Fanny's veil theory fit the situation and that gave Autumn comfort. Once her body felt the soft cool sheets, the fear of seeing a torch carrying mob paled next to the physical exhaustion of working in the Carolina heat all day. Like so many bizarre days at the McFarland farm, this day would soon be a memory.

The next morning, Autumn met Fanny under the tree where so much had happened. "Looks like someone had a party out here last night. Are you sure you want to plant a garden here?" Fanny asked completely oblivious of last evening's events.

Not ready to have a great philosophical or metaphysical discussion so early in the morning on another picturesque summer day, Autumn responded, "Yes, I'm sure." Autumn chuckled half-heartedly because she still had not wrapped her mind around what happened last night. The footprints and hoof prints suggested something real. It was at least real enough to leave physical impressions on the earth. If the people on the other side of the veil could do that in the physical world, Autumn wondered what else they might be able to do.

Fanny and Autumn made short work of the small garden. The grass was not very deep here. Once they got down an inch or so, it could just be pulled off. Fanny cut the circle and Autumn pulled up the sod. Between them, they carried nine wheel barrels of dirt to the garage so they could replace the sandy soil with topsoil. Autumn shoveled the topsoil while Fanny raked until the garden was level. Fanny had the brains and experience. Autumn had youth and physical stamina. The pair each took a trowel and watering can. Fanny told Autumn to dig a hole, fill it with water, plant the flower, and water the newly planted flower until the water began to pool around the hole. That technique would ease the plant's transition into its new home. They both knew they would need to end the work for the day by three o'clock. The heat would shock newly transplanted flowers. Working in the soil felt good to Autumn. "It's nice to have something normal to focus my attention on," thought Autumn. She and Fanny would pause occasionally to admire their handy work. There was a cool refreshing breeze coming from the east. The scene, to Autumn, was awe-inspiring. She looked around her and felt as if she were living a dream. The classic design of the McFarland home, buildings and lawns were picture perfect. The cliché of being Scarlet on Tara came to Autumn's mind again. Ashley and Rhett were nowhere to be found. Autumn knew this was not a movie. She did have a leading man for her movie. Autumn's leading man was the best of Ashley and Rhett. Boyd was classically handsome and rough around the edges like Rhett but every bit the southern gentleman of Ashley. Autumn found herself wishing he were home from his trip.

Shortly after showering from the garden experience, Autumn heard a ring at the door. She rushed down the steps in her robe and bare feet. "Not exactly how a lady of such a grand manor should greet someone at the door," thought Autumn as she raced for the door. When she opened the door, there was a large arrangement of beautiful roses with babies breathe. Autumn laughed when she saw them. They were perfect in every way with each bud just slightly opened to reveal the classic rose shape. The roses were a deep maroon and throughout each petal were veins of a deep gold. They are a new breed Autumn read about a while back called "Hocus Pocus". The name is what made Autumn laugh.

A voice came out from behind the arrangement, "Ms. Hummel?"

"Yes," replied Autumn as she relieved the man of the bouquet. "Thank you so much! I'll be right back." She sat the beautiful arrangement on the foyer table and grabbed a tip for the dear elderly man who delivered them.

"Someone must be in love," the delivery man said with a broad grin.

"Oh," Autumn said in surprise, "I hadn't thought of that."

"You don't send roses if you don't have a very special lady in mind. Enjoy, miss."

In a dumb stupor, Autumn rushed to the flowers to retrieve the note. The note said:

Thinking of you. See you before Labor Day.

Boyd

Autumn felt herself blush like the day she saw Boyd at the stables. She clutched the card to her chest. When the doorbell rang, Autumn danced over to answer the door. Before she reached for the door, she ran back to replace the card in its holder. Still a little light headed, Autumn announce, "Just a moment." She raced upstairs to throw some clothes on and then opened the door.

"Hello," announced Ian. "Well, I'm back." He thought she might have forgotten he was gone because she did not respond. "I just got back last night from my parents'." Ian leaned in a bit. "Are you okay? I heard you had a project you wanted my help with. Just tell me what it is and I'll get on it."

Autumn apologized for her mind being somewhere else. She snapped out of her romantic daze enough to welcome Ian back. Autumn explained that she wanted to paint the ceiling of the porch.

Ian laughed a little and asked, "Are you superstitious?"

Autumn explained it was purely for historical aesthetics. She saw all the homes in downtown Georgetown and made a decision to follow their lead. Ian told her he would get the paint, drop clothes, ladders, and paint brushes if she wanted him to start today. "Oh no, I don't want you to do it. I want us to do it together. I have nothing against a little of my own elbow grease going into this place. Plus, the porch is almost forty feet by ten feet. We could have it done by sunset today if we do it together. So, how about it?"

"Sure and you will sleep a little better knowing no one can get in the house."

"Yeah," agreed Autumn.

"Not that you are superstitious, right?"

"Right," said Autumn unwittingly. "Okay, smarty. I'll go get the paint."

By the time the catty-dids started singing that evening; Ian and Autumn were sitting on rolled-up drop clothes drinking rum coolers. They were amazed at how different the porch and front of the house looked with the blue. That of course led to a discussion of how different they looked with blue paint in their hair. Eventually they got to more serious topics. When Ian commented on the new garden, it led to a long discussion about the history of the house. Autumn really did want to paint the porch because of history. Due to the weird and unexplainable events, being superstitious could not hurt. Ian agreed that the events were strange. Mostly, the two of them agreed that this sort of thing either did not happen or was not spoken of in Ohio. They decided ghosts and spirits were a southern phenomena.

Autumn laughed. "Maybe southerners see them because they move through life so slowly."

"Maybe southern ghosts are just friendlier than our northern specters," Ian joked.

Laughing, the two finished cleaning up. By the time Ian left, it was beginning to get dark. Autumn slipped into her favorite pajamas and came back downstairs. She curled up on the family room chair facing the foyer and the roses. Autumn suddenly realized how much she was missing Boyd. Before he left, she saw him everyday. He was always dropping by for lunch or to take Autumn out some place she had never been in all her other visits to South Carolina. Having him next door, even though it was a couple miles away, made her feel safe and not so alone out in the sticks of Georgetown County. Before heading to bed, Autumn realized Labor Day was eleven days away. Labor Day suddenly would be a greatly anticipated holiday in Autumn's life. Again, she had no trouble settling in for the night. "Several hours of painting above your head will do that," thought Autumn. "The rum coolers didn't hurt either."

Autumn woke to agonizing screams outside. She rolled over to see what time it was. The clock said three in the morning but was blinking. The power must have gone out about three hours ago. The shrieks were deep and gut wrenching. A little more composed than she had been the previous evening, Autumn apprehensively approached the window. She braced herself for the worst before looking outside. Autumn peered down at the oak tree to see what was happening tonight. She let out a shriek as she collapsed on the floor. Shaking, she reached for the phone to call the police. The dispatcher recognized the number from night before and sent a cruiser with two officers out immediately. Autumn could not even speak to explain what her emergency was. She hung up the phone and crawled to the window. Below the oak, a woman and three children appeared. The woman was in a heap on the ground wailing. Up on the lowest branch of the tree, a man hung by his neck. Hanging was a horrible way to die and a particularly gruesome sight.

Autumn was paralyzed with fear and felt sick to her stomach. When the police arrived on the scene, an officer ran to the tree with his gun drawn while screaming for the other officer to radio for an ambulance. The officer steadied his hand and shot the rope from the tree. The man, woman, and children all vanished when the shot rang out in the night air. The police suddenly turned their attention to the woman who was inside the house. The police had to break in the door. When they found Autumn unresponsive upstairs, they radioed the dispatcher that there was another victim at the scene. The paramedics arrived but could find no one in the front yard but rushed Autumn to the local hospital. When she awoke the next morning, Autumn had no recollection of where she was or how she got there. The nurse was happy to fill in the blanks for Autumn. Apparently, Autumn went into shock from what she had witnessed. When she arrived at the hospital, her vitals were stable but she was unconscious. They made sure all of her vitals were monitored but figured she would sleep the shock off. The police needed to finish their report from last night and came in shortly after the nurse reported that she was awake.

The officers explained that they had radioed in a man hanging from the tree. They also reported the discharge of their weapon. Autumn asked who the person hanging from the tree was and if he was dead. The police could not answer any of those questions. Upon firing, the man simply vanished. After they retrieved her from the up-stairs bedroom, the paramedics could not find anyone on the property. If her memory of last night coincided with their report, they just needed her signature on their report. Autumn quickly read through the report and agreed with what the report contained.

Shortly after the police left the room, the doctor came in and explained that stress could sometimes cause an anxiety attack. If those attacks go undetected and untreated, the victim could loose consciousness as the body attempts to protect itself. That was what happened to Autumn. The doctor recommended that she take it very slow for the next couple days and needed to get some extra rest. He felt it was okay for Autumn to go home but she should see a doctor about any further attacks. Other than a little embarrassed, Autumn left the hospital feeling worse than she had in months. The garden and painting had clearly been too much to do in one day.

When she arrived home, Lillian was waiting for her on the front porch with Fanny. Fanny ran down the steps to hustle Autumn into bed for the day. Autumn assured Fanny that was not necessary. She would join the ladies on the porch for a visit. "Lillian was at the grocery store and asked what happen last night. She heard something happened out at the McFarland place but didn't know what." Fanny grabbed Autumn a glass of her special homemade lemonade. "I feel just awful that none of us told you about the hangman."

"What? How did you know?" Autumn almost dropped the glass from her hands in shock.

"Oh, honey. The hangman. We don't know anything other than he appears around the 21st of August. Someone sees him swinging in the tree and then he disappears for another year. I'm so sorry I didn't tell you. The story of the hangman is as old as this farm I think. It's something you just forget about because you assume everyone knows the story. I'm so sorry." Fanny could not have been more sincere in her apology.

"When Fanny told me what happened, I left the store to go get the McFarland Bible out and see if it had any such stories. When I began flipping through the entries, I realized that there was a lot of material. Fanny told me about the August 21st date, so I started searching through just those entries. I started sticking paper tabs to mark entries that contained something about the hangman." Lillian lifted the book up for Autumn to inspect and there were over twenty colorful tabs.

"What did you find out about the hangman," asked Autumn. She was delighted that there was such a big clue to this mystery. Autumn sat back and sipped the lemonade with jasmine. The jasmine was Fanny's secret ingredient for her lemonade but everyone knew she used it.

"The entries start as far back as the War of 1812. The entries are all very similar. Someone on the plantation, whether slave or master, catches a glimpse of the man hanging by his neck in the front lawn. The man seems to disappear as soon as someone sees him. Several journal entries say that when they got someone else to look, the man would be gone." This was clearly the most fun Lillian had ever had as the director of The Georgetown Historical Society.

"What about the other people I saw?"

"What other people," Lillian asked leaning in a bit. This was a fish Lillian was not ready to reel in just yet. "There is nothing in the journals about *other* people."

Autumn told Fanny and Lillian about the woman and three children she saw. In fact, had Autumn not heard the woman's screams, she never would have seen the hangman. Lillian flipped through the journal one more time to see if anyone referred to other people during the sightings. Other witnesses described it as a most horrific sight of a man "hung by the neck" until dead. Lillian and Autumn decided that the woman and children were probably there with the man but he sort of monopolized the scene. Fanny did not think that was true. The police saw the man but did not report seeing anyone else. Fanny speculated that this may not have been the usual visit by the hangman but something unique to Autumn.

"Gee, thanks. That's a comforting thought."

"Well, I certainly don't mean to frighten you anymore than you already are. I'm just saying that it was a *woman* and child that appeared to you in the attic through the photos. I just think that a woman and children in another scene is more than coincidental. Besides, you said if you had not heard the woman's screams, you probably would not have seen the man hanging in the tree. That's all I'm saying."

"So, what's the connection," asked Autumn who began to look at the situation analytically rather than emotionally. "Why are they appearing to me and why women?"

"I think that's obvious," Lillian interjected with excitement. "There are mysteries that have been unrecognized and unresolved for generations because they weren't mysteries to the McFarland's. Fanny even forgot because her family is as much a part of this farm as the McFarlands. Not one of them would pay attention any more. You didn't grow up on the farm. They must know that you can and will help them because you haven't grown up knowing there were skeletons in the closet."

"Oh, girl. You have learned something over the past couple of years," squealed Fanny. Lillian was a lovely white lady who learned much about the Gullah culture from Fanny.

Just as the two of them quit laughing, Autumn could here the faint strains of "Carolina in the Morning". Lillian suddenly looked very uncomfortable. "Please tell me that you are hearing the song, too." Lillian was far more interested in reading and hearing about ghosts than seeing one.

"Don't get your nylons in a bunch. I hear it. Who do you suppose it could be?" Fanny stood up and shaded her eyes as she looked down the drive.

Autumn had been giggling the whole time. "I know exactly who it is." Just as she said that, a heavyset lady with a rosy complexion and a large brimmed straw hat came into view. One could hardly say the lady was strolling down the drive. Her gate was not graceful or easy but rather like someone who had a sore back and hips. The song she was singing went this way:

> "Nothing could be finer than to be in Carolina in the morning.
> Butterflies all pucker up and kiss each little buttercup at dawning.
> If I had the chance to be a hundred and three, I'd make a wish
> And here's what it'd be:
> That nothing could be finer than to be in Carolina in the morning."

The song itself made Autumn's shoulders finally come down from around her ears. The discussion between Lillian and Fanny had been very interesting but was doing nothing to inspire her confidence in spending another night alone in the house. The lady coming down the road was just what Autumn needed. Autumn was not surprised at all that the woman singing was here. Autumn rather expected and hoped that this would happen today.

"You obviously know the lady coming down the drive. Are you going to share?"

"It's my mom!" Autumn leapt off the porch and ran down the drive.

Autumn's mom dropped her bags just in time to catch Autumn's embrace. Her mom gave her a big kiss and then took Autumn's face in her hands. It was a tradition of her mom to closely inspect her children's faces to make sure they were really all right when they *said* they were all right. There was no lying to mom. Mrs. Hummel could tell just by looking at her children if they were not okay. Autumn picked up the small carry-on bag and took her mom's arm as they made their way down the rest of the drive to the porch. The two of them were knee deep in conversation about everything from fried bologna to things that go bump in the night. Autumn felt as though she could finally breathe again.

"I hate to interrupt, but could you tell us who this wonderful lady is," laughed Fanny.

"You must be Fanny. Autumn has told me so much about you. I would love to sit down and have a long talk with you someday while I'm here. There are so many things that we could really chew the fat about. Thank you for making my Autumn feel so at home. She said you have been such a help."

"Thank you so much. Anytime you want to have that talk, you let me know." Fanny and Autumn's mom acted as if they had known each other all their life. It really was not that surprising to Autumn. Fanny had always reminded Autumn of her mom.

Autumn introduced her mom to Lillian. The four of them shared another glass of lemonade while finding out why Mrs. Hummel came to Georgetown so unexpectedly. Autumn's mom had a weird feeling last night. Mrs. Hummel woke her husband and said she couldn't find Autumn. After trying to convince his wife that she was nuts, Mr. Hummel told her to call Autumn. When Mrs. Hummel couldn't get an answer in the middle of the night, she hung up and called the local airport. By 4:00 in the morning, Mrs. Hummel had booked the 6:30A.M. flight and was packing.

Autumn explained the events of last night that resulted in her being hospitalized. Fanny and Lillian shared what had been discovered before Mrs. Hummel walked up the drive. At the conclusion of the replay, Lillian apologized for having to head back to the office and took her leave.

"Fanny, I have to agree with you. Autumn is obviously the key to these weird events. We just have to figure out what she is the key to. I think I'll stay and take care of her. Autumn can focus on what all this means."

"You don't seem to be very concerned about what Autumn saw last night," Fanny said.

"I've seen lots of things in my twenty-six years as a surgical technician. Some of the things I saw in an operating room were far scarier than a ghost. Plus, I believe that they are spirits who need something answered before they go to the other side. I would think spirits would ask those questions once on the other side. Either that or the questions would loose their importance when they die. These must be some serious issues."

Autumn and Mrs. Hummel passed the day with much talk about everything particularly the beautiful roses in the entryway. Autumn missed her family. They are all very close. The distance had not changed that. It was good to talk about every little stupid thing Autumn could think of with her mom. The two headed up-stairs at around midnight. Fanny had made up the bedroom next to Autumn's but Autumn wanted her mom closer than an entire room away. So, Autumn set up the rollaway bed at the foot of her bed. Mrs. Hummel wanted to make sure her baby would be okay. Autumn took the rollaway bed and gave her mom the big bed. It took over half an hour for Autumn to fall asleep. She had forgotten how much her mom gnashed her teeth at night. Before Autumn fell asleep, she thought to herself, "Watch. Now that someone is here, nothing is going to happen."

It was a nice thought but at four in the morning, the two Hummel ladies awoke to shrieks of terror coming from outside. In the darkness, Autumn could hear her mom say, "It's all right, honey. I'm right here." The two clasped hands as they made their way to the window. The night was stormy. It was raining fairly steady. The dark was illuminated sporadically by lightening flashes. Outside, no figures could be seen. The screams were the same as the night before but there was no woman to go with them. The two made their way downstairs and turned on the exterior lights. When the lights came on, they could see a noose hanging from the old tree. It was exactly where the police had shot the rope down. Autumn's mom suggested they call the police. As quick as news travels in small towns, this just might be someone playing on Autumn's fears. "After all," her mom said, "How hard would it be to sneak out here with a couple of friends, tie up a rope, and have someone screaming in the distance?"

Autumn thought her mom was making a lot of sense. Rather than dialing 911, Autumn dialed the police station and asked to speak to one of the officers she talked to at the hospital. Within twenty minutes, the cruiser was there. They checked the grounds and the property. Everything checked out just fine. The officers were going to patrol the farm until dawn because they felt that it probably was a prank. Autumn and Mrs. Hummel could not go back to sleep after all the commotion. They sat in the kitchen and made plans for the day. The two headed to bed early that night. They thought they should get a few hours in before another restless night. Autumn shared a little request with Mr. McFarland in her mind. She told him that she was very appreciative of everything but the specter thing could go away. Much to her surprise, Autumn awoke late the next morning. The clock beside her bed said seven in the morning. She tip-toed over to the window to look outside. Her mom began stirring in the bed. "Is it really morning? I missed it, didn't I," said her mom in a mix of sleepiness and disappointment.

"No, I don't believe we have," Autumn paused as she pulled back the curtains. "I don't think we missed it. I think he has been waiting for us to wake-up." Autumn could feel her stomach sink and her knees tremble.

"What's wrong? What are you talking about?"

Autumn motioned for her mom to the window. After Mrs. Hummel threw on her housecoat, she looked out the window. There in the cool light of dawn stood a man in old-fashioned clothes motioning for someone to follow.

"Let's go find out what he wants, Autumn. You need to put this to rest if you are going to stay in this house."

"Are you nuts," exclaimed Autumn. "Hello, he's a dead man. I am not following a dead man anywhere thank you very much."

"I think you have to or this haunting is just going to keep happening. It's morning and I'll be right with you. Come on."

Autumn reluctantly walked with her mom out to the front lawn. The man kept moving away but motioning for them to follow. They kept a good distance from the man. Autumn had wished the distance was greater but her mom was intent. The man led them to the family cemetery out on the right edge of the property. Once there, he motioned for them to follow him into the cemetery. Autumn was not about to do that. She thought it might be inviting trouble. Following a ghost into a cemetery typically is. The man walked slowly over to one of the stones and laid his hand affectionately on it. Then, like a mist, he just vanished.

A loud voice caused both ladies to scream. "I'm sorry you two but what are you doing out here so early and in your PJ's?"

"Okay, you just scared the pee right out of me! What are you doing here so darn early," Autumn snapped.

"You know I can't handle the heat. It's supposed to be ninety-six today. I figured I'd get in early and work. Gees. Someone sure woke up on the wrong side of the bed this morning."

"Mom, this is Ian. Ian, this is my mom. You know what I've been through the past couple of nights?"

"Actually, no I don't."

"Well, let's just start off with what just happened this morning. There was a man standing in my front lawn motioning for someone to come with him. Like fools, we did. We kept following him until he led us here. Then, he vanished. Now do you see why we screamed?"

"I'm trying to figure out why you followed him?"

"Very funny. If you are not going to help us, please go somewhere else to work."

"No. I'd like to help. Sorry, Mrs. Hummel."

"It's all right dear. You didn't know." Autumn's mom joined the conversation to ease the atmosphere a bit.

"I am sorry Ian. I think all this is really starting to wear on my nerves. I always appreciate you being here and helping out." Autumn smiled a weary yet sincere smile and the three set off to look for clues. The man wandered into the cemetery and then disappeared just as his hand fell on a particular gravestone. There did not seem to be anything unusual about the stone. It was worn and weathered like all the other stones. It laid flat on top of the burial site like the ones in New Orleans where they buried their dead above ground because of the water. In South Carolina, the bodies were all buried under ground. These large markers led down steps to a burial chamber where several family members were buried. The stone told who was buried in the chamber and how they were related. This one contained Alyson McFarland, beloved wife of Charles McFarland and her children Michael, Thomas, Sarah, and a stillborn infant. The three kept reading the stone to see if they were missing something. Alyson died at the old age of seventy-two. The story this marker told was grievously sad but no sadder than the other stories that could be told during the time period. People died giving birth, being born, fighting wars, catching plagues, and simply living before the modern age of medicine. The time frame for this family would put them pre-Revolutionary War through post-Revolutionary War. The three amateur detectives were just about ready to give up when Ian realized something. They had been looking too hard for a hidden secret. The one thing they missed was that the beloved husband and devoted father were not buried here with the rest of his family. He must be the man who Autumn and Mrs. Hummel saw this morning. That was just the beginning. If Charles was the hangman and the woman with the three children were Alyson, Michael, Thomas, and Sarah then where was he buried? If it was Charles, the master of this house, why was he hung in front of his own house and in front of his own family?

Autumn and Mrs. Hummel thanked Ian for his help and headed back into the house to get dressed. They figured their next step was to visit Lillian and take a look at the Bible. Lillian could not believe her good fortune. She thought that yesterday was the highlight of her whole month. Now, not only did she get to find out who the hangman" was but she would get to research the mystery around his life and tragic death. Lillian flipped carefully through the old brittle pages to where Alyson had written her last entry before her death which passed the McFarland Farm onto her son Michael. The entry was ordinary. She had listed her progeny through great-grandchildren. The gift she was leaving each of her children was spelled out for posterity's sake. Autumn did not believe they would find the answer to their question in Alyson's last journal entry. So, Lillian flipped back in the book to where Alyson was a young woman and mother to small children. Each entry depicted life in her day. The farm had just become fifty acres. There were a few slaves, she called them "taskers", on the farm. The entries told of how hot the summers were and the brutal nature of winter in those days. She had been a fortunate woman to have survived childbirth three times. Her children were lucky to have survived being born.

The ladies reading the entries remarked from what healthy stock these people must have been because Alyson lived to be a very old woman. Her entries were quite extensive. Mrs. Hummel, Autumn, and Lillian slowly covered the entries until they came upon the ones that spoke of the Revolution. As a wealthy land-owner for his time, Charles had been rather reticent about severing ties with England. He had much to loose and revolting against the crown would have meant disaster for him. As time went by, he had begun to think King George took much from the colonist and had given less and less back.

After returning from many weeks in Philadelphia, Mr. Rutledge had called all the men of South Carolina for a meeting. Charles and his eldest son, Michael, rode the short distance down the coast to Charleston. Mr. Rutledge explained what had happened in Boston. The British had been planning an embargo on all ships that sailed from the colonies. That would have effected the South both in terms of selling their goods and receiving goods. After careful consideration, the men of South Carolina had voted to go along with the call for independence but only if a southern colony had suggested it. Where South Carolina went, the rest of the deep South had followed. Charles McFarland had not been happy but he stood by his brothers when independence had been declared.

As the war made its way north from Charleston, Mr. McFarland had opened his land and his home to the rebel troops. He had instructed his sons and wife to stay clear of the men. That way, if the war had gone sour, his family could have honestly said they had remained loyalists despite Charles' stand. Without warning, Lillian, Autumn, and Mrs. Hummel found the entry they were looking for at last. The date was December 17th, 1776. Independence had been declared earlier in the summer. There had been much success in holding the British at bay. However, in late November, the British had taken Charleston. By taking Charleston, the British had controlled all the ports including Georgetown. Because the McFarland home had served as refuge, hospital, and camp for the Freedom Fighters, the British had sought revenge on all they had found in between Charleston and the McFarland farm. Any rebels found on the farm had been killed or imprisoned. The family had been spared because the commander could not kill children or take their mother from them. Charles' fate had been sealed. It had been war and his crime had been the highest crime you could commit in war: treason. His sentence had been death by hanging. The sentence had been carried out immediately in the large live oak tree on the front lawn of the house. Troops had to restrain Mrs. McFarland and her children until the deed had been finished. Once Charles had been pronounced dead, the troops had left with some of the family's food stores and several slaves. After weeping for several hours at the foot of the tree that took her husband's life, Alyson had looked up at her children and "picked up and carried on for they were all that was left of him now."

Two of the male "taskers" had come to cut Mr. McFarland down. The male slaves and their wives had readied the family cemetery for his burial until Mrs. McFarland's brother had come to the farm. He had suggested that Charles not be buried in a marked family plot. The Red Coats had a reputation of returning to farms and displaying corpses as a warning to others who might join the Revolution. So, the slaves had taken Charles and buried him in a location only known to them and Mrs. McFarland. That was the last journal entry about the ill-fated Charles McFarland. The journal was very little help. Now Autumn and Mrs. Hummel were left with more information about their mystery but were no closer to solving it.

Mrs. Hummel said, "Did you read that sweet little poem Alyson wrote about Charles?"

Lillian and Autumn both replied, "What poem?" Apparently, they had been so focused on the front of each page that they missed the backs of the pages. The poem was on the back of the last page in the book. Autumn had no idea what her mom thought was sweet about the poem. The poem read:

> Into the ground he loved so much
> They interned his body thus.
> Unknown to strangers; friend or foe
> He's safe inside the ground below.

To find him, you must use their key
For they buried him for me.
My love, your truth will be told
When youth has passed and I am old

As they finished reading the poem, they realized it was a clue. The slaves had buried Charles in an unmarked grave in the *slave* burial ground. No one would have thought to look for the master of the house there. The key to finding him was to figure out what symbol the slaves would have used as "their key". Obviously, Mrs. McFarland had forgotten to tell the secret burial spot of her husband. The reason the hangman came was because he wanted to be buried with the rest of his family. Now the three ladies were just one step away from granting Charles' eternal request.

Autumn asked Lillian, "Do you think Fanny would know what the key in the poem is?"

"If Fanny doesn't know, she'd surely know someone who would." Lillian squealed with excitement. "Isn't this exciting? You must let me know what you find out."

"Well of course we will. The two of us wouldn't have gotten this far without you finding reference in the Bible about the hangman', rather Charles."

Mrs. Hummel was bursting with excitement. She suggested they stop by the local health department to find out the details of exhuming and moving a body for burial.

"How about we wait until we find the body," Autumn suggested. After a light lunch at Land's End, they returned to the farm to find Fanny. She was in the garden, of course, planning next year's beds.

"Well, you girls look like you have had quite a day. What happened?"

Autumn and her mom took turns telling all the information they had gathered.

"So, there is a key that marks the unmarked grave of Charles McFarland?"

"I think that is why he keeps appearing to the residents of this house," Autumn said, proud of her reasoning in such a mystical matter. "The weeping lady and children was the key to finding the identity of the man in the tree. I think they came to me to help him end his eternal quest."

"This girl of yours has come a long way in the short time she has been here," Fanny whispered to Mrs. Hummel.

"Okay, now what could be 'their key'? Just give me a minute and I'm sure I'll remember." Fanny sat down on the bench near the garden. Had the bench not been concrete, it would have collapsed under Fanny.

"You mean you actually know what the key might be," Autumn asked.

"I would be forsaking my heritage as a Gullah if I didn't know. Now, it is more than just a simple symbol. These slaves had to keep everything a secret from their white owners. It would be a combination of symbols. It would be," Fanny started. "The first symbol would have come with them from Africa. The most powerful symbol was a circle. It represented life: no beginning or end. The second most powerful symbol was that given to them by their white slave owners. It represented the beginning and the end in the white man's beliefs. It was the cross on which Jesus died. He is the alpha and the omega. The cross being the end of one life and the beginning of another. They would have been superimposed on each other. That way neither one would dominate the other."

"Great, we just need to look for a circle with a cross inside of it." Autumn hopped up to search the slave cemetery.

"Whoa, child," Fanny grabbed her arm. "I told you that these were very complex people with a very complex code to hide their real meaning. A circle with a cross is no great code. The last piece you need is the river."

"You mean there would be a symbol for the river in the key. What would they have used to symbolize the river?"

Fanny laughed, "You white people still don't get it. I guess my ancestors were a little cleverer than generations of white people would give them credit!!!"

"Okay. Ignorant white girl puts her foot in her mouth. AGAIN! Not really a news flash. So, enlighten me," Autumn said as a she blushed.

"The top of the cross, you know how the cross stick is not in the middle of the upright stick but higher, would be pointing toward the river on the key. You find the circle with the cross that points to the river and you will find Charles' grave. How 'bout that for a memory? Can I come with y'all?" Fanny slowly pulled herself up off the bench.

"A pair of eyes that actually knows what they are looking for would be great! I don't want to tear you away from something more important."

"Don't fool with me girl. Finding the answer to one of your ghost stories is a thrill. Now, come help the fat lady up."

"After that, she can come over here and help this fat lady up," joked Mrs. Hummel.

Ian always took great care in mowing the tall grasses around the slave cemetery. Fanny showed him early on what were weeds and what were the flowers the families had planted to decorate the graves. The flowering plants and foliage were over one hundred and fifty years old. Autumn recalled reading about the people who originally settled in Pawley's Island. At one point there were one hundred and fifty white people and over six hundred African-American people living on the island. Even though it was a small parcel, picking through each grave was a slow and tedious process because much of the graves were lost over time. They found several graves with the circle-cross sign but they did not face the river. Luckily, Autumn possessed an uncanny sense of direction because the river could not be seen from the cemetery.

Mrs. Hummel was not used to the intense August heat. She decided to take a break while the other two wandered through the cemetery. The eternal gardener, Fanny had a fist full of weeds she was pulling as she made her way through the cemetery. Autumn was getting tired of going from row to row to row. She broke off from Fanny and headed to the extreme northeast corner of the cemetery. As Autumn made her way over, she noticed an uncharacteristic mound in the earth. Because it stood out, she thought that would be a good landmark to make home base for her new search. As she turned to look at the earthen mound a little more closely, the rock formation on the mound started to take shape. There after one trip to the hospital, two scary nights, and over a hundred years of sightings, was Mr. Charles McFarland's grave.

"Mom, Fanny, he's here! He's right here! I can't believe he's here!"

Autumn raced over to collect Fanny and take her mom's arm.

Fanny verified the "key". Mrs. Hummel said a little prayer as they bowed their heads. Autumn made a pledge to *this* Mr. McFarland that she would see him home as soon as possible. It turned out that would be easier said than done.

The Health Department was very helpful in processing all the special permits necessary. Ian contacted the local funeral home to aid in the exhumation and reburial of Charles. Everything seemed to be going well. The date was set for August 5th for the exhumation and reburial. The politicians caught wind of this story and wanted to be a part of this momentous occasion. Autumn did an interview with a local reporter that was a tell-all about the appearances of "The Hangman", the reported sightings over the years, the search to find him, and to put him to rest with his family. The plan took several weeks to choreograph. Autumn wanted the media to be there when the presentation was made. The whole affair stirred up issues for everyone.

The federal government got involved because of the role this individual played in the course of America's history. The Federal Government was satisfied with two things. Autumn gave them an authenticated copy of Mrs. McFarland's journal entries related to her husband's final clash with the British. The other promise came from the local Veteran's Association. They promised to include his name in their records and decorate his grave every Memorial Day. The farm was made a historical landmark by the state of South Carolina. It assured that the land, house, and cemeteries could never be sold or disturbed under state law. Lillian wanted to get a formal marker for Charles since he died as one of the first martyrs in the fight for independence. Autumn told Lillian she would pay for a marker that would sit at the opening of the family burial chamber to include Charles and the role he played as a South Carolina freedom fighter.

An African-American group from up north was appalled that such a fuss was being made over a slave owner. The group was challenging. They would require a soft and delicate touch. Autumn thought of a solution to their outcry but it would take a lot of research on her part and Fanny's help. Fanny knew everyone from Charleston to North Myrtle Beach. She was not partial to the color of a person's skin. Fanny was also the most charismatic person Autumn had ever met outside of her mom. Fanny talked to everyone she knew about the issues and got their thoughts on the matter. The leaders of the African-American group who raised a fuss came to town on September 2nd. They planned a rally for that day. There would be a formal protest in Charleston on the 3rd. The 4th would be the day the protest would begin outside of the McFarland farm. Autumn made sure that every media outlet in the country would be at the rally on the 2nd. Anyone who wanted to come to the rally was welcome and encouraged to speak their minds.

Autumn sat quiet as the protesters presented their points. They listed the horrors of slavery, the greed that had motivated the sin, and the fact that the institution had been tolerated so long in a nation that declared "all men are created equal" from its inception. There was no arguing their points. They were valid and sound points. The only thing Autumn could do was present the other side of this story. Autumn was not going to argue the sins or virtues of the man. She was going to present the other facets of this man's life outside of being a slave owner. He had been a patriot who had been murdered for standing with his countrymen against the English monarchy. Charles McFarland had done no more than follow the lead of other famous slave owners of the Revolution who had been named "The Founding Fathers": George Washington, Thomas Jefferson, Richard Henry Lee, and Edward Rutledge. Autumn's intent was not to honor the man so much as it was to honor the cause and the sacrifice Charles had made for the nation's independence.

Just as Autumn was concluding her presentation, over fifty women and men of African-American descent entered the hall arm-in-arm doing a Gullah "shout". The sight was awe inspiring. The sound of their voices united to sing this very powerful and significant piece of living history stopped everyone, including Autumn, in their tracks. Fanny stepped forward from the crowd holding the hand of a very aged woman. The two made their way to the podium. Autumn embraced Fanny as she passed. Fanny introduced Safrina. Safrina spoke in a voice that was coarse from its long service. The entire crowd, black or white, was perfectly still and silent.

"Yo heyr wad we cuma singn? Cus yo dun no. Oni Geechee sing da song." The dialect of Safrina was Gullah or Geechee. Geechee is a cross between Elizabethan English spoken by the slave traders and the native African language of Angola. It is a Creole language was only spoken on the coastal plantations. The culture and language, like Safrina, were very much alive in South Carolina where the descendants of over 40,000 Mende, Kisi, Malinke, and Bantu brought the soul of Africa to America's shores. Safrina explained that the song she and her friends entered singing was the oldest of plantation melodies. Her ancestors made rhythmic translations of forbidden drum cadences to communicate storms and other events in the lives of the slaves as well as a code for freedom. She asked the African-Americans "rasin da fuz" why they were ashamed of their slave ancestors.

The crowd was stunned into silence but one man in his early forties answered Safrina's question. He told Safrina slavery implied that black people were a weak people who could be dominated by another race. Safrina scolded him as a mother scolds her child. She told him he was not old enough to answer her question and directed him to sit down. Safrina did not know where his people came from but *her* people were a proud strong race. They were dominated by the warring between tribes. They were dominated by tribes capturing enemy Africans and selling them to the white slave traders. They were dominated by the technology and communication of the white man. Slavery had little to do with race. Had Europe been black and Africa white under the same conditions, it would have been the white man serving the black man back then. Safrina's ancestors had lacked the unity of language and culture that the white man possessed. Her people were intelligent, resourceful, and deeply religious with a strong sense of culture.

One of the ladies passed a beautiful handmade basket around the crowd. Safrina pointed out that the only two places in the world where you could find baskets made like this was coastal South Carolina and the west coast of Africa. The Smithsonian has a sweet grass basket on display that is five hundred years old. She admonished the people gathered here to protest the burial of Charles McFarland. He had been a man doing what people had done in the late 1700's in the American Colonies. Safrina did not know if he had been a good man or a bad man but everybody has a right to be buried with their family.

One lady spoke-up irreverently, "Well, I suppose you see no harm in flying the Confederate flag either?"

The ladies that had come in with Safrina shook their heads and gasped. One lady said, "Oh you did *not* just say that?"

Safrina told the lady that her mamma should have done a better job raising her. In her younger days, Safrina would have knocked that tone right out of her mouth. She would not answer that belligerent and disrespectful question.

Tyler, a kind faced gentleman of about sixty, stepped up to help Safrina down and into a chair. He returned to answer the lady's question. "Y'all from the South," Tyler asked in a soft even voice. "Raise your hand if you're from any part of the South." Tyler waited but no hands went up. "Y'all don't know. Most of us here, we were born and raised here like our fathers and mothers. It goes back to when our ancestors had come over from Africa. We are the pride of our slave ancestors. You don't get it. If we bury the past by ignoring it or deciding it is not politically correct enough to talk about, we are bound to repeat it. I am the dream of my slave forefather. I own land. I vote. I live a free man all because of their sacrifices. My life honors the horror that was slavery. My people were a great people who in a very short time have overcome much in this world. I think people in the South should not be allowed to fly the Confederate flag. Not because it stands as a symbol of slavery but because it is the symbol of a rebellion that almost destroyed this great nation.

"So, you all need to look hard and deep at *your* slave history and hush-up about this poor man who gave his life for our country. Now, any of you want to know more about us and how we feel, stay around. We'd be all too happy to pull up a chair and chew your ears about the slaves you are trying to honor." Tyler left the stage quietly with his hands inside his pockets.

The tone among the group shifted dramatically from race to culture. Ladies answered questions about sweet grass baskets and "long strip" quilts. Both are popular folk crafts indigenous to Africa and the coastal Carolina region. Sweet grass is the soft reeds that grow in all the marshes and swamps in the South. The baskets are made with sweet grass, the long pine needle of the yellow pine, and palms from Palmetto trees. The art is very time and labor intensive. A basket that is four to five inches in diameter could cost the buyer ninety-five dollars depending on the weaver's proficiency. Much of the Low Country food comes from the

Gullah people. The slaves had eaten whatever they had been given and the rest would have been whatever they could catch, find, or hunt. Hush Puppies, which are a staple in the South's restaurants, come from a practice called "The Whistling Walk". Like Autumn's house, kitchens had not been part of the main house until much later. Slaves would have had to prepare the meals in the separate kitchen and would carry them to the dining room in the main house. Some slave owners had noticed that their food had been sampled along the way. To eliminate the slave's practice of eating while they had carried the food, they had been told to whistle from the kitchen to the dining room. No one can whistle and eat at the same time. Most of the slave owners had been great hunters and had many hunting dogs. When the slaves would whistle, the dogs would run and topple the trays of food. To prevent this from happening during "The Whistling Walk", slaves would have deep-fried little bits of cornbread tucked into their apron pocket. When the dogs came running, the slaves would throw the bread to the dogs with a firm, "Hush, puppies!" The night air continued to be filled with such stories and information as Autumn quietly thanked Fanny and slipped out.

September 5th arrived early with a knock at the door. A courier was sent with notice that the Governor of South Carolina, Congressmen from South Carolina, and the State Representative from Georgetown County would attend the ceremony. The letter told her that special arrangements were made to accommodate the honored guests. Autumn was almost too afraid to find out what the special accommodations were. The nights were non-stop with the appearance of Charles, Alyson, Michael, Thomas, and Sarah. The lack of sleep was taking its toll on Autumn. Fortunately, Mrs. Hummel was still in the house. The two learned to sleep through the nightly visitations. The special accommodations were the local high school band, a giant American flag with a flag poll erected at the cemetery, and an army full of media persona. Not only did Autumn have to witness the disturbance of a very old grave, now she would have to look her best and put on her best smile for a bunch of photo opportunistic politicians. Autumn drug herself into the kitchen to have breakfast and make some coffee just before there was a knock at the door. She opened it to find the governor's personal assistant standing there with two very large garment bags.

"Hello," Autumn sneered at the unsuspecting man.

"I hope it's not too early." He did not stop to hear Autumn's reply. "Did you get the letter we sent? Everything is already set-up. The buses just pulled in. The limos should be arriving in about an hour or so. I called to confirm the arrangements you made for the whole affair. They said everything was in order. The last thing I needed to do was drop one of these off. I've been told you are the history whiz. You can decide which one is more appropriate."

"Which one of what is more appropriate?"

Autumn slowly sipped her coffee as the hyper man rambled on. "The dresses of course," he sighed as he whipped the two dresses from their bags. One dress was a daffodil yellow chiffon mess pretending to be an antebellum gown. The other was a simple cotton dress with pantaloons, undergarments, and corset pretending to be from Colonial times.

"What are these for," asked Autumn as the headache she predicted manifested itself.

"They are for you or, at least, one of them is for you."

"Why would I be wearing one of these?"

"Well, the Governor thought it would be a marvelous photograph with the lady of the house dressed in period attire. The gentlemen will be in suits representing the Revolutionary War era."

"And did any of these gentlemen bother to ask the lady of the house her opinion? I'm afraid the lady of the house will appear as a woman from her own century. Thank you."

Autumn opened the front door to show the gentleman out when Mrs. Hummel appeared at the foot of the staircase. "It's not like you to pass up a chance to wear a historic costume or be so sour?"

"M-o-o-m," Autumn whined.

"Oh that's right. You are not a morning person. I don't know where she gets it from," Mrs. Hummel turned to the man in the doorway who could not tell if he was coming or going.

"Good morning, ma'am. I'm sorry to have disturbed you so early this morning."

"Leave the cotton dress and paraphernalia. She'll be there with her best smile. Thank you so much for bringing it by this morning."

Autumn's mom was so delightful to everyone all the time that it regularly got on Autumn's nerves. Unfortunately Autumn's last nerve was spent three or four days ago.

"Mom, I am not going to participate in the three ring circus they have planned. It's insulting to everyone involved but especially Charles."

"Who are you kidding? It's wonderful that this is going to get so much attention. You just drink your coffee and wake up a little more. You'll have fun. I, however, will be standing by in my comfortable summer dress." Mrs. Hummel cheerfully made her way into the kitchen. Autumn grabbed the gown as she grumbled all the way up the stairs to take a shower and change.

The high school band was spit polished and all ready to play their patriotic hearts out. The politicians were there in their period outfits. None of them considered that it was September in South Carolina. Period suits were made of the finest cotton, all four layers of it. Autumn smiled at the fact that the pompous posers were as miserable in their get-ups as she was in hers. As she looked out into the audience, she saw many familiar faces. Some of the faces were locals and a few were among the protestors she saw at the rally.

They exhumed the original gravesite earlier in the morning because it required brushes and small shovels rather than a backhoe. The Health Department was certain the coffin would have been wood and most likely gone. That would have left the remains unprotected from such heavy machinery. As it turned out, the coffin had been made of some sort of hard wood. There was speculation that it was made out of the large crates that brought rum from the islands. The remains were respectfully transferred to a new coffin before the crowds arrived. The family burial chamber was also opened in preparation for the burial. All they had to do was carry the new casket into the burial chamber as a local minister said a few respectful words. Politicians have a way of making everything simple terribly complex.

Autumn gazed at the program that announced that each of them would be addressing the crowd. To her surprise, she would also address the crowd before the minister ended the ceremony. Suddenly, the nightmare that had been happening every night since August 21st was preferable to this horror. Autumn was looking up from the program as she felt a warm hand slip around her waist. She looked down at a man's hand. Turning, she met Boyd's eyes. He was smiling at her like he knew her thoughts about this side show. His familiar cologne blew past as he leaned in to say, "You look beautiful, Ms. Scarlet."

"Why, Rhett, you devil."

They both giggled quietly to each other. Mrs. Hummel was standing in the front row. She winked at Autumn and gave the "thumbs up" sign discreetly to her daughter. Autumn felt more confident just having Boyd there. As Autumn made her way to the podium, she was formulating an appropriate yet brief speech. When she got there, she said, "I want to thank you all for being here. It is fitting that we honor a patriot with such a ceremony. I pray that we all appreciate the sacrifice Charles and his family made for our freedom. May he find peace with his wife and children."

The three politicians and Boyd volunteered to carry Charles down into his final resting place as the minister read from the Bible and said a short prayer. With that, they replaced the large stone that sealed the burial chamber. The politicians answered questions from the media. The band finished with "God Bless America". The crowd wandered around the farm for a while but everyone was gone by three o'clock. Boyd slipped into the house with the Hummel ladies. He had tucked a change of clothes in the car with him. Autumn could not tell who got out of their ridiculous formal wear faster, Boyd or herself. Fortunately, Mrs. Hummel snapped a quick photograph before the two were in their casual clothes. Autumn found Boyd and her mom in a heavy discussion about what had happened since he left. Autumn did not want to interrupt. She slipped into the kitchen to make some lunch for everyone. Autumn came in to call the two to the table when Boyd ran over to Autumn and swept her into his arms in an embrace that took her breath away. She could feel his breath on her neck and his heart beating hard and fast. Surprised at first, she gradually melted into his arms. No matter the motivation behind the hug, Autumn was happy it happened. Trying to lighten the moment she said, "What? Its just lunch."

"I can't believe that you have gone through all of this by yourself. I should have been here. I should have called." He held Autumn's face in his hands and stared into her eyes. She knew he had intense eyes but the eyes she was looking at today led deep into the very soul of the man. Autumn had to look away because it was too intense for her.

"I'm just fine. Please."

"I'm here now and I'm not going to leave you again for a long time. I should have called. I should have been here to help you. I'm sorry."

"Okay you two. I'm starving. You won't leave my girl alone again on this big old farm. You, young lady, be quiet and let him take care of you. That's what you do when you are in love. Now, let's eat."

As Autumn turned toward the kitchen, Boyd grabbed her arm and pulled her back to him. Autumn could feel his warm soft kiss upon her lips. He had a hand on the small of her neck and the other in the middle of her back. As he pulled her closer, Autumn lost all sense of time. The nonsense of the last week faded like a bad dream. This hot blooded passionate man was letting her know in no uncertain terms what his feelings were for her. With all of her being, she was happy he was home and happy to have found a place in his heart. His time away seemed to have allowed him time and space to find out what his feelings about her were.

Boyd stayed until late in the evening but told the ladies he would be right over if they needed anything. He had even volunteered to stay in the guest room if they would feel safer. The thought was very kind but Autumn and her mom felt that the burial today would end the visits from Charles and his family. Autumn walked Boyd to his car where he offered one more time to stay with them. Autumn assured him that they would be fine. She promised to call if anything, no matter how small, happened.

Autumn shut the door and turned off all the lights in the downstairs. As she made her way up the steps, her mom yelled down, "Are you alone?"

"Of course I am."

"I don't know if I would have done the same thing in your position. Talk about a sweetie and that body." Mrs. Hummel feigned light-headedness as she joked with Autumn.

"Thank you, Mom. Good night. I hope I don't see you until morning."

"I hope so. I'm going to call your dad before turning in, okay?"

"Sure. Tell dad I miss him."

"I will." Her mom leaned over the bed to tuck her in and kiss her goodnight.

"I'm going to miss you when you're gone. It's been so nice having you here. All of you guys being so far away is the only really bad thing about this place. We'll just have to have lots of long visits."

"We miss you too but you are only far away in miles not in our hearts."

As her mom settled in to call home, Autumn rolled over in her bed and could over hear one half of the phone conversation. Mr. Hummel was not a man of many words. He thought all the ghost talk was a bit of nonsense. Logic prevailed in his world and ghosts just did not fit into a logical world. He thought that there was someone staging all of these nightly events. Autumn's mom and dad clearly had different ideas about the subject. The conversation eventually turned to Boyd. Autumn could infer from her mom's side of the conversation that Mr. Hummel thought that maybe Mr. Master's had something to do with these mysterious events. Mrs. Hummel argued in Boyd's defense. Mr. Hummel thought it was suspicious that the "haunting" started when he supposedly left town on business. Mr. Hummel seemed to have suggested that they could probably count on one more "haunting" this evening. Mrs. Hummel yelled that she did not think that Boyd would play such an adolescent prank. Mostly, there was no way that Boyd could have faked the visitation by the hangman in broad day light that led them to the cemetery.

Abruptly, Mrs. Hummel seemed to have turned the subject to her travel plans. They discussed the airport gate, times, and airlines so that he would let the whole Boyd thing go. Nothing had been happening at home except the high school football team had started their two-a-day practices. Mr. Hummel had gone to football practice since he was a freshman in high school thirty-five years ago. He must have mention that he would be glad to have her home because he missed her cooking because she replied, "We've been married for almost forty years and you have done nothing but complain about my cooking!" The laughter was followed by whispers. Autumn's parents were not openly affectionate but they had their moments behind closed doors and in whispers.

Tears rolled down Autumn's cheek as she thought of home. Moving to Georgetown gave her so much: wealth, a house, two different businesses, and Boyd. It had been a trade. In that trade, she lost the security of being in the bosom of her family and hometown. Autumn cried herself to sleep with memories of home.

Autumn shot straight up in her bed. The sun was up and it was a beautiful day. She threw the covers off and ran down the hall. Before she reached her mom's room, the smell of bacon and eggs cooking caught her attention. Mrs. Hummel was up and had started breakfast. Autumn ran down the stairs. She was both elated and sad. Autumn was elated that nothing happened last night. The sadness came because the smell of bacon and eggs. It reminded her of home. Mr. Hummel had eggs and bacon every morning of his life. The fact that her mom was cooking meant that she was leaving. Autumn burst into the kitchen and said, "You're leaving?"

"Good morning, honey. How would you like your eggs?"

"Are you leaving?"

"Well honey, it's been almost two weeks. You haven't had any more panic attacks. The hangman has found peace in the family cemetery. Besides, Boyd is here for you."

Autumn had not even noticed that Boyd was sitting at the small kitchen table. "Hi, I just wanted see how your evening was. Your mom asked if I wanted scrambled or over easy eggs. I hope that's okay?"

Autumn's attention turned to Boyd. "I am thrilled that you are here. Our night was great! There were no bumps or boogiemen in the night. Thank you for coming over to see, though. I'm also glad mom asked you to stay. I'm going to need you with her leaving today. I hope you are okay with that?"

"I'm okay with that. Why do you think she is leaving today?"

Mrs. Hummel slid a plate of bacon onto the table. "Because I'm cooking. If her dad's not around, I never cook breakfast." That was a true statement but Autumn could not blame her for taking a vacation from the usual breakfast routine. "Honey, your life is here now. My life is over a thousand miles away and it's time that I get back to it. Besides, your dad actually misses my cooking. You know that means I've been gone too long. I have spent over forty years killing his taste buds. If I stay here any longer, some of those taste buds may grow back."

"I guess you're right. It's just that I'll miss you so much. I could not even think about you leaving." Autumn pulled up a chair next to Boyd as she poured the orange juice. "You just sort of caught me off guard. That's all. So, you didn't see or hear anything last night?"

"You didn't tell me what kind of eggs?"

"Dippy eggs."

"No. I did not see anything or hear anything unusual last night and I was up late packing. I decided to go home after I got off the phone with your dad."

"I know that this is a very touchy moment but could one of you tell me what a 'dippy egg' is?" Boyd was hunched over his plate trying not to laugh.

"Are you making fun of me, Mr. Masters?"

"No." He could not contain himself any longer and burst out laughing. The laughter was contagious. Soon, no one was eating because they were laughing so hard.

The three finished breakfast. Autumn and her mom got showered and dressed while Boyd carried Mrs. Hummel's luggage down to his car. The only way to get back to Ohio on this particular day was to fly from Charlotte to Akron. The drive to Charlotte, which was about three hours away, was filled with laughter and tears. Autumn had made plans to come home to Barberton in the fall. Boyd promised to come with Autumn. Autumn made her mom promise to call the minute she got home. They worked out a regular schedule of phone calls so no event would pass without sharing it with each other. Boyd thought the two of them seemed more like best friends than mother and daughter. The two ladies considered that a great compliment. They were still very much mother and daughter but had become best friends along the way.

The Charlotte airport was considerably larger than the one in Myrtle Beach. The three made their way to the gate. There were big hugs and kisses. Autumn tried to keep the tears at bay for as long as possible. Mrs. Hummel did not do as well. Her face was flushed and wet. She could not even say anything as they parted. Mrs. Hummel made her way down the gangway heaving and sobbing. Autumn yelled down the gangway, "I'll see you in a few weeks. Call me when you get home."

As the plane taxied out to the runway, Autumn broke down. Boyd quickly ran over to Autumn. He did not say a word but held her until she was ready to move away from the gate. The first half hour from the airport was spent in total silence except for Autumn's occasional crying jags. "The wonderful thing about Boyd," thought Autumn "is that he did not say anything. Boyd isn't uncomfortable with the silence between us."

The heat of summer, relentless and never-ending, passed into fall. Autumn decided that fall must be the reason people move south. The forests of South Carolina were mainly cypress, live oaks, and yellow pines. All were evergreens. The land just goes to sleep. Back in Ohio, fall paints a beautiful farewell picture before it drifts into the sleep of winter. This was a slow time for Autumn's farm. Autumn and Boyd were able to spend the days becoming more familiar with each other. Boyd took pride in showing Autumn all the sights of South Carolina no tourist ever sees when visiting the Grand Strand. Autumn had never been deep-sea fishing and was sorry she had not kept it that way. It was hard work fishing at sea and also quite smelly. Boyd took her on an all day cruise of the intercoastal waterways where the remains of old rice fields still stood. The river still grew rice. It was almost unable to give up the crop that brought it fame and fortune. Autumn's favorite hobby during this time was cruising all the plantations that were now museums or preserved homes.

The homes were all beautiful and well maintained though none of them had been as well maintained as the McFarland home. Most of these beautiful plantations were inherited by family members who, at one point or another, could not afford the expenses of such large old homes. As a result, they sold off what they could to keep the house from being lost in debt. The items sold ranged from furniture and art work to moldings and mantelpieces. The only things original to some of these houses were the shells. Even some of the out buildings were "rebuilt" from pictures of houses in the area. Seeing the old mansions made Autumn very proud to be the owner of the McFarland farm.

One evening, Autumn decided to hang out on her front porch. Just as she curled up in the hammock, she could see a cloud of dust ahead in the drive. In minutes, the sporty blue car revealed that it was Boyd coming over for a visit. As he strolled up the piazza steps, Autumn could smell the faint hint of his cologne on the breeze. Each time she smelled it, she felt warm and safe all over. She noticed he had a masculine gate as he strolled over to the hammock. He had a cock-eyed smile. It was just the way he smiled. He rolled into the hammock beside Autumn and snuggled into her shoulder to place a kiss on her neck.

"Why, Mr. Masters, I was wondering when you were going to get here," Autumn said with a laugh.

"Close your eyes and hold out your hands," Boyd whispered.

"Why?"

"Just do it."

Autumn held out her hands as Boyd poured seeds into them. Autumn opened her eyes in bewilderment. "Why'd you dump seeds in my hands?"

"The one thing that is missing from this farm is rice."

Boyd reached in his pocket and handed her a small piece of paper with a name, address, and phone number written on it. "So, I looked into rice cultivation. Trust me; it was not easy to find someone who still grew rice along the rivers. This guy even uses the old equipment and techniques."

"What guy?" Autumn had taken the paper but had not looked at it.

"Oh, Albert. His family still farms the river with rice. He sells his rice to different places that market it as a souvenir in Charleston and other historic sights. The rice he grows is antique red rice from the days of plantations. Well, what do you think?"

"I don't know what I'm supposed to think?"

"He said he would farm his crops here for you. His crew would do the necessary planing of the river swamps and build the trunks. You would be responsible for buying the wood to build the trunks, renting the equipment to plane the swamps, and the seed rice. They would do the rest and run their business from your farm instead of the land they now use. Other than the initial investment and expenses of creating rice beds, there would be no financial out put on your part. Does that help you think?"

Autumn was so enthusiastic about Boyd's idea that she called Albert the very next day. The workers for Albert arranged for the equipment and supplies they needed to prepare the river for the rice fields. Autumn was astonished at the willingness of these people to do this hard physical labor. The creation of rice fields from swampy riverbeds was a laborious process even with diesel-powered land moving machines. The trunks had not changed in design since the 1850's. The new ones Albert and his crew built and set in place looked identical to the ones that could be seen all along the Waccama and Black Rivers. The earth underneath all that river muck was black and rich from years of sediment washing up from the rivers and the bay. It smelled horrible but was fertile. Autumn always thought that smell was from the paper mill in Georgetown. It actually came from dredging the river's shores. By the time all the work was done, they had planed enough land to grow a crop that would yield about three thousand pounds of rice. That sounded like a lot of rice but Georgetown County once had a maximum yield in 1860 of five hundred thousand pounds of rice.

Autumn had no idea if they could sell three thousand pounds of rice as a novelty food. Albert assured her that he could sell that and more. It seemed that Albert was not the backwoods farmer he appeared to be. He was marketing his particular brand of rice to gourmet chefs in New York who were always looking for something unusual and trendy to cook. Albert cooked up some homemade gumbo with his rice and had chefs in New Orleans try it. The chefs were convinced that his rice was originally meant for gumbo because it cooked up firm while thickening the gumbo and held its flavor. Restaurants bought river rice by the pound for their authentic Low Country cooking.

Once the fields were created, Albert and his workers left the farm. He explained to Autumn that nothing more could be done until spring but was grateful she let them start the work in the fall. The days could still be pretty hot in the spring and could also launch the first hungry round of mosquitoes. The fall was cooler and drier. That let them work longer. Spring would see the land harrowed and plowed for planting. By April, Albert's crews would return to hand-sew the rice seeds that would then be flooded until the rice sprouted. The water would be drained and the sprout would be allowed to grow for three weeks until the first of May. That would be the point flood that would cover the rice almost to the top of the plant. The long flow would drain the water slowly until water only covered half of the plant. The water would stay at that level until the plant was strong enough to stand on its own. The water would then be completely drained off. The lay-by-flow happened in mid-June or the first of July where water would be added gradually until the plants were completely submerged. By the first week of September, the rice would be ready to harvest.

All the farm workers were gone now until spring. Albert and his crew were through planing the rice fields by the third week of October. Fanny was done with the gardens after the first hard frost. After the frost, she prepared the beds for next year and said her farewell. Ian would be around in case of an emergency. Otherwise he would be doing freelance computer consulting during the winter months. Joe would be in everyday because the animals would have to be taken care of even in the winter. For the most part, Autumn would be alone on her very large farm. She did not mind. She had gone to the local library and checked out a few books on the history of the places in and around Georgetown. Lillian was still at the Historical Society everyday. Autumn popped in every now and again to see what fascinating things she could find in their collection of information. The ocean was so near that Autumn would occasionally pack-up for the day and spend the daylight hours on the beach. The ocean had a life cycle she had never seen before visiting. During the cooler weather, dolphins could be seen in droves fishing off the coast.

Boyd was always there to fill her days and nights. Autumn spent more time at his place because there were so many business phone calls for him to take this time of year. The time passed quickly because of the short days. Boyd always marveled at her arriving on brisk fall days with just a sweater or a sweatshirt. He would have a heavy fall jacket over his sweater or sweatshirt.

"This is like back-to-school and football weather back home. Winter coats don't come out until the first snow or early November," Autumn explained with a laugh. "This is my kind of weather. If it stayed like this or a little cooler, I'd be happy all winter."

"Well, then you are in luck. This is winter in South Carolina. It rarely gets snowy or as cold as it does in Ohio."

"You are kidding me," Autumn gasped in astonishment. "Then we are going to have to pack your winter coat, hat, and gloves for our Halloween visit. You might freeze to death."

"You mean it might be colder there?" Boyd could not believe his ears.

CHAPTER 4

▼

HALLOWEEN HOMECOMING

Born and raised in the South, Boyd never visited places north in the fall or winter. Autumn knew he liked the warm weather from his antagonistic remarks about winter sports. He just could not understand how people could have fun while being out in the cold and the snow. Autumn tried to explain that some people could think he was crazy horse riding or dirt biking during South Carolina's summer heat. Autumn called home to ask her dad what the forecast was going to be like for the week. Lucky for Boyd, it was going to be a mild low sixties kind of week.

"I thought you loved this weather?" Boyd could not figure out why Autumn was disappointed.

"I do. It's just that when it is that mild around Halloween, it usually means it is going to be rainy. The leaves and punkins look so beautiful when they are set against a bright blue sky. That's all."

"Hey, it's my first Halloween with multicolored leaves, Indian corn, hay rides, and *pumpkins*."

"Are you trying to point something out?"

"You don't say that word right."

"What word?" Autumn smiled because she knew what word.

"Pumpkins."

"How do I say it?"

"Punkins."

"That's what they are. Punkins."

"It is not, unless you are referring to a different orange squash frequently carved into jack-o-lanterns. They are pumpkins."

"You are right. They are pumpkins but when you decorate your house with them, have signs with them all over the place, and stick a candle in them, they become punkins for Halloween."

"You're goofy."

"Thank you. I come from a long line of goofy people who would be proud to hear you say that. Now let's get packing."

The trip was about twelve to fifteen hours long. Autumn and Boyd decided to drive it in a day. Autumn had never seen the Great Smokey Mountains in the fall. The misty mountains were even more beautiful painted in shades of red, gold, and orange than summer's deep greens and blues. It was the first colors of fall Boyd had seen in such abundance. As they got closer to Autumn's parents and northeastern Ohio, fall had begun to fade slightly into winter gray. As they approached the expressway exit for Barberton, Autumn gently reminded Boyd that her family home was nothing like their houses in South Carolina. Her parents' home had been a three bedroom and one bath house Mrs. Hummel changed into a two-bedroom and one bath house. There was a living room that was a living room, family room, den, and study all wrapped into one. The third bedroom had been turned into a TV room for the sanctity of her dad. He liked to sit alone and watch TV when the family gathered. The basement would be where the annual Halloween party would be held. Even though Mr. And Mrs. Hummel had it finished, it was still a basement.

Boyd leaned over, "I'm southern, remember?"

Autumn elbowed him in the ribs and blushed. It was not that she was ashamed of her parents' house. She had never brought someone who grew up in a mansion home. Then she thought, "Maybe no one else's opinion really mattered as much as Boyd's?"

When they pulled to the curb, the small saltbox house was decked to the gills with Halloween decorations. There were corn stalks and pumpkins in the front yard. Black cats, silly ghosts, and paper jack-o-lanterns filled each window. As they stepped out of the car, Autumn's heart filled with all the warmth and memories of home. Halloween was her mom's favorite time of year. She went all out with the decorating. Autumn got her name from her mom's love of autumn. When they opened the back door, the house smelled like Sloppy Joes, apple pie, and homemade sugar fudge. Autumn did not know if she really smelled those things until Boyd asked, "What smells so good?"

"Mom's been cooking. I told you that's what she does, right."

"You told me but she didn't do it when she was visiting you?"

"When she's not home, she doesn't cook. She's an old fashioned girl with old-fashioned tools. She knows how hot her burners and oven get. Most of the things she cooks, she has a special pot or pan that she makes them in. She goes outside of those rules and her cooking is not always a success."

"Well, whatever it is, it smells awesome. Let's get in there."

Just as Autumn and Boyd entered, Autumn's mom sent a flaming dishtowel from the stove to the sink. "Hello you two. How was your trip? I hope you didn't stop somewhere for dinner. I have Sloppy Joes and homemade apple pie ready."

Boyd leaned over and whispered, "Isn't she concerned about the fire in the sink?"

"Who her? She's been trying to burn down the house for years." Mr. Hummel appeared from the living room in his purple polo shirt, purple windbreaker, and purple South Carolina hat. He casually reached over and turned on the water in the sink. "Ever since I became Fire Chief, she's been trying to set the house on fire. How's my girl?"

"Just fine. Where are you off to?" Autumn asked even though she could tell from his attire where he was going.

"There's a play-off game down at the stadium tonight. Barberton's playing some Catholic team from Cleveland tonight and probably going to get the snot beat out of them." Autumn's dad had a grouchy way about him that frightened most people. Boyd was not afraid but Autumn could tell he did not know what to think of Mr. Hummel.

"Dad, this is Boyd Masters. Boyd, this is Mr. Hummel." The introduction had happened, now they just had to wait for the fireworks to ensue.

"Nice to meet you. You look like an athletic young man. Did you play football?"

Autumn had prepped Boyd on almost everything but not football. She thought the season would be over already. "Yes sir, I did. I was the quarterback for three years when we won the state championship." Autumn had not prepped him but he could not have given a better answer.

"Well then, maybe you wouldn't mind joining me down at the stadium tonight. It should be a complete slobber knocker. There should be some highlights despite the poor match-up. What do you say?"

"I'll leave that decision up to your daughter, sir."

Autumn was impressed with Boyd's ability to dodge the loaded gun pointed right at him. Now, she had to answer her dad. "We'll be down after we eat but I can't promise how long we will stay. That drive always wears me out."

"So, you'll be down. Okay. There are two tickets on the TV. I better go." Mr. Hummel sauntered out the door and strolled casually to the car. After sitting in the car for two or three minutes, the minivan pulled out cautiously from the curb.

"I thought you said your dad is a fireman," Boyd asked.

"He is. Why?"

"I just wondered because he just said he was in a *hurry* to get to the game?"

Mrs. Hummel raced to the table with food. "Would you two come eat? If you're not there by the last few minutes of the first quarter, you won't be allowed to leave before the end of the game. Besides, my cooking has a certain peak period and you are about to miss it." Autumn's mom had been ignoring the football conversation and busily putting dinner on the table. "Boyd, you did not think that was fast?"

"Well, I didn't mean anything but," Boyd was embarrassed that Mrs. Hummel heard his comment.

"I know. You might as well kiss goodbye whatever was on fire rather than count on him to save it. I've been married to him most of my life and have never seen him run. He clearly must have at work but otherwise his pace is that of a snail. Doesn't matter what's going on. That's all the faster he moves."

"Plus, you can't just hop in a car and go," Autumn chuckled. "It takes two minutes for the oil to leave the pan. You have to give a car at least two minutes to warm-up. Five in the winter." Autumn was clearly imitating a speech her dad had given her. Autumn and her mom burst out laughing.

The long weekend started out with the football game. The hometown team prevailed despite a serious size deficit. It was a clear and crisp fall night. Everything gave Autumn memory flashbacks. Her dad took his traditional post up at the top of the stadium. The fight song and alma mater she still knew by heart despite her long absence. Even the smell of the hot dogs cooking in the band booster's concession stand under the home bleachers reminded Autumn of her "glory days". Autumn had been going to football games since she was nine months old. Her dad had not missed a home game since he graduated. Boyd enjoyed listening to "Coach" Hummel discuss the ups and downs of the game. Autumn could only smile at the two of them. Mr. Hummel clearly liked this young man because he was speaking to him. Boyd was the first beau that Autumn let her dad meet that did not act terrified in his presence. Autumn and Boyd enjoyed the game and the beautiful evening so much that they stayed until the game ended.

When they returned to the house, they all sat around and had homemade fudge. Boyd was grilled about the details of the trip. Mr. Hummel had driven that route over twenty times and could tell you when he got gas, how much gas each car he ever owned needed to drive the trip, and how many hours. Boyd had not paid much attention to those things but, as Autumn pointed out, normal people rarely do. Autumn saved Boyd several times by saying, "We got here. That's all that matters, right?" That usually changed the line of questioning for a few moments. Mrs. Hummel finally put an end to the questions by telling "the children" they had a long day and needed to go to bed. At that, Mr. and Mrs. Hummel retired upstairs. Autumn made sure that Boyd was all settled in for the night and headed up stairs to the small bed in the hallway. Autumn could not help but lie there and think of all the years she had spent in the house.

The following morning, she heard Boyd and her Dad sharing football stories. Autumn grabbed her robe and scurried down the twelve steps to hopefully inter-cept any fireballs her dad could soon lob at Boyd. When she got there, they were having a really good discussion. Her dad seemed to be behaving himself. Autumn slipped off into the kitchen to visit with her mom who was already cooking a large breakfast. Autumn was sent to call everyone to the table for breakfast. When she emerged from the nook, she heard her dad say, "You're looking at the best football player Barberton High School never saw."

Boyd beamed at the comment. He could tell that her dad was referring to her tenacity and drive. He could not ignore, however, what an odd thing it was to say about a daughter. Without saying anything, the three made their way to the table for yet another one of mom's feasts. Autumn quickly changed the topic of con-versation to what was planned for the day. Mrs. Hummel said, "Well, the hay-ride is planned for one. Then, everyone's coming here for the party. Beggar's Night starts at six and runs until seven or eight. You can do all, part, or none of it. It is completely up to you two." Autumn knew that last part was not true. Everyone had to do everything. It was not spoken just expected. Plus, Autumn looked over at Boyd and could tell that he was not about to miss any of the fall fun.

The hayride was out at a small farm. The tractor towed a flatbed loaded with hay and people through the pumpkin and corn fields. The ride was a relaxing way to enjoy the fall air. At the end of the ride, they could choose their own pumpkin from the thousands harvested at the farm. The rule in Autumn's family was that the pumpkin could be as big as you could carry. Boyd took this rule literally.

Being a healthy and fit young man, he chose a pumpkin that weighed thirty or forty pounds. He could carry it therefore he could have it. Later while Autumn's nieces and nephew bobbed for apples, Boyd wanted to carve his pumpkin. When Boyd cut the top off, he seemed stunned when he peered inside the enormous gourd. Either he had never carved a pumpkin before or someone had always cleaned the pumpkin out for him.

Autumn walked over and looked in with him, "I think we better take this one outside to clean it." Boyd and Autumn scooped out seeds until it was time for dinner. Boyd admitted to Autumn that he just did not think about how much more insides would be in a large pumpkin. After the traditional meal of hot-dogs, chips, salad, and popcorn balls, Boyd carved a ferocious jack-o-lantern and placed it on the front steps with the other pumpkins. Boyd was giddy about handing out treats for the trick-or-treaters. Having been raised on a remote farm, he had never participated in such a neighborhood phenomena. He had comments for every little one who came. Boyd would shriek with horror at the scary ones, chuckle at the silly ones, and playfully tease the comics in the crowd. They saw over two hundred kids in the two hours Beggars Night lasted. The "Great Pumpkin", as Boyd's pumpkin eventually became named, glowed well into the bewitching hours of All Hallows Eve. Linus himself would have been impressed with the tales that were being told by children of "The Great Pumpkin" that lived at the Hummel's house. The night ended with the grown-ups sitting around telling tales of their various Halloween adventures.

Boyd and Autumn turned to the road very early Monday. Despite her best efforts, Autumn cried for the first forty-five minutes of the trip. All she could think was, "Boyd is going to think I am crazy. I cried when we took mom to Charlotte. Now, I'm crying because I'm leaving home." Autumn finally calmed down enough to say, "Do you think I'm crazy?"

"Why would I think you were crazy? First, it wouldn't bode very well for me. After all, if you are crazy, what does it say about me? No, I don't think you are crazy. You are a young woman living a thousand miles away from your family and friends. I grew up traveling the world. Your world was your hometown until you heard the name Jonathan McFarland."

"Don't you think that makes me shallow? My whole world was my hometown? How could that be good?"

"I am a little jealous of you for what you have. Your mom and dad live minutes away from their children and grandchildren. You all love your hometown with all of its idiosyncrasies. I don't have that. It doesn't make me a bad person or a better person. It is just the way things are. You are who you are because of where you grew up. I love you and I love who you are."

Autumn was taken back by his casual pronouncement. She leaned over and kissed his cheek and tearfully whispered, "I love you, too."

"Now I think you're crazy. Why are you crying? I thought hearing someone tell you they love you is a good thing. Especially if they mean it." Boyd nudged her off his shoulder playfully.

"Just shut-up and drive."

"Yes, ma'am."

CHAPTER 5

▼

CHARLES TOWN

Summer returned to South Carolina. Since Autumn's arrival just over a year ago, Autumn was plunged head long into a history quest. Fortunately, South Carolina was jammed with historic places. Boyd cleared his calendar to accompany Autumn to Charleston. His goal was to make what could be an overwhelmingly boring trip an adventure. Though they both lived only a little over an hour away from Charleston, it would be the first time Autumn had been there. Boyd booked a suite for two nights and three days. He knew that a day trip to this very old town would only tease Autumn's thirst for knowledge. Boyd also knew there was the very distinct possibility that Autumn needed a little break from all the fun and festivities of the McFarland farm. Staying at an inn in Charleston would really give her a sense of "being away".

Autumn looked forward to getting away with Boyd. The fact that he was taking her to Charleston was mere icing on the cake. Autumn had been collecting pamphlets and brochures about the pre-Revolutionary War town since moving to South Carolina. There were so many places to go and things to do that Autumn had no idea how she would do them all in one day. As she packed her things, Autumn was a little concerned that Boyd might actually discover what a huge history nerd she really was. Then, in true form, she chuckled and thought, "I've never cared what anybody has ever thought of me before. Why start now? I'll be me. He'll be him. That way the two of us can really decide if we want to be together."

The sound of his horn honking in the drive roused her from her thoughts. She dashed down the steps and pulled the door behind her. The smell of his cologne greeted her as she slid into the little blue sports car. When the car turned out of the McFarland property, Autumn could only see what lay before them. All that was life on the farm was laid in the dust of the old drive. The day was clear and warm. Boyd filled Autumn in on all the things that he thought they could do on this trip. The road from Georgetown to Charleston was lined for miles with forests. The few red lights along the way were in small little towns no bigger than an intersection. The only other thing that could be seen on the road was the vast expanse of Francis Marion National Forest. It wrapped around on either side of the road during different moments in the drive. As the park wore away, the road soon became dotted with small stands selling baskets. After seeing more and more of these stands, Autumn could no longer contain her curiosity. "What are the baskets?"

"Aren't they beautiful?"

"They are really extraordinary. I've never seen anything like them. I mean I've seen the woven baskets of Nantucket. So, is there a story behind them?"

Rather than answering Autumn's question, Boyd glided to a stop at what seemed to be the smallest of the stands. The baskets were in any array of sizes. The lady who was minding the booth sat weaving a basket. The baskets were beautiful and unique. They were unique because of their hand made characteristics. Autumn picked up one the perfect size for handling sewing scraps or yarn. As she admired it, she heard Boyd shout, "Hey, Gali."

"Boyd Masters. You old swamp rat. Ain't seen you-," Gali said in a thick southern drawl.

Boyd interjected, "Yeah, it's been awhile. How y'all doing, lady?"

"Whoa, girl, you'd better watch yourself with this one. He can sweet talk a sour egg sweet." She laughed.

Autumn was starting to sense that the two knew each other. "Okay, does somebody want to let me in on the secret?"

"Gali's mother was my nanny. Gali and I sort of grew up together."

"Shaw. That'd be assuming I lived in the big house. I didn't. That much is for sure. Boyd here got to learn that not everyone in South Carolina lived like him and his."

"She's right. We'd spend some afternoons over at Gali's house. The playground was only across the street. I learned a lot in the games of tag and baseball. Gali's mom gave me a real spiritual sense of what it is to be southern. Fanny reminds me a lot of Gali's mom. Proud to be black, southern, and descended of slaves."

"What you doing down this away?"

"Autumn is the new owner of the McFarland place. She's from Ohio. Thought she'd like a personal tour of Charleston."

"Come here, child." Gali's tone suddenly changed. The sing-song tambour left her voice and the smile that lit her whole face vanished. Autumn walked over to her. "May I see your hands?"

Autumn offered them to Gali without a word. When she took Autumn's hands, the smile returned. "You a strong girl. Knows what you want and does what you want. That's good with that scallywag you traveling with. You also powerful. You gonna need that in the near future. People at that old farm gonna be testing that power. You believe in it and listen to it. It ain't never gonna let you down. Now, you listen to Gali, you have to tell them what they need to hear. Don't you go nowhere without a big bag of sea salt. They say we come from ash and ash we will return but it's wrong. All life comes from the sea and we go back to the sea. Sea salt helps. You'll see."

Boyd admonished Gali, "We didn't come here for you to scare the girl, Gali. We are here on vacation. I brought Autumn to see your baskets and so you could answer her questions about the baskets. Do you always have to be so oogy-boogy about everything?"

"Don't let him fool you. He knows about these things and will stand strong beside you." She patted Autumn's hands. "Don't need some uppity white boy from the country givin' me a hard time."

Autumn bought four baskets but Boyd insisted that they stay with Gali until the return trip. It was either the baskets or their luggage. With that, the two continued on to Charleston. Gali slid a large bag of sea salt into Autumn's hand as they made their good-byes. Boyd explained that voo-doo was practiced in South Carolina more than anywhere else. Autumn knew voo-doo was alive and well in New Orleans but had no idea that it reached all the way over to South Carolina. Boyd explained that voo-doo was in South Carolina before the Creole ever arrived in New Orleans.

"So, the Gullah believe in voo-doo," Autumn asked.

Boyd laughed. "Only some. Gullah or Geechee is its own faith system but some have added voo-doo. Not many, though. Do you have any idea what the sea salt is for," queried Boyd.

"I think so. I'll let you know later if I'm right." Autumn grasped the bag tightly in her hand and then slid it into her purse for safekeeping.

Charleston was unlike any city Autumn had ever seen. The pictures she had in her mind were not even close to what she found. Autumn and Boyd crossed a great body of water to get to Charleston. That must have been why it was such an ideal location for both an early settlement and later a powerful shipping port. The city was surrounded on three sides by water: two mighty rivers and the Atlantic. As they crossed the bridge, Autumn could see both Charlestons. There was the historic downtown that had been faithfully preserved on the coast. Further inland on the other side of historic Charleston was the modern metropolis that reflected the historic side of town. Needless to say, Boyd and Autumn's sights would be set on the historic downtown of Charleston.

The scale of the city sincerely surprised Autumn. The buildings were much smaller than modern buildings. There were buildings that were painted cool pastels to reflect Charleston's link to the islands of the Bahamas. The inn Autumn and Boyd were staying at could have been lifted right out of the French Quarters of New Orleans with their stucco exterior and iron railings. The architectural similarities were easy to justify. New Orleans had once belonged to France before Thomas Jefferson's famous Louisiana Purchase. The French Huguenots were the first large European settlers in South Carolina. The streets were so narrow that two cars could barely get down them. Some were so narrow that the only thing in the twenty-first century to get down them would be pedestrians or bicyclists. There were a few streets still made of cobblestone. Off of King Street, every street looked down to a church. Boyd told Autumn it was by design. The city planners wanted people to see God wherever they turned as a constant reminder of His presence. Other streets went right to the ocean. Apparently, Charleston has been slowly moving over the centuries. What were now roads were once landings and docks. The city "goes with the flow" when nature decides to move the cities boundaries.

The whole area of historic Charleston was probably only six blocks by ten blocks but there was an enormous amount of history packed into that area. After all, Charleston had been the city to fire the first official shots of both the Revolutionary War and the Civil War. It was rarely remembered for the first but always that later. Charlestonians say the ghosts of her patriots protected the city from pirates and other criminals before the War of Northern Aggression. During the Civil War, however, those ghosts left the city with broken hearts. Boyd showed Autumn all the wonderful sights of Charleston. Nothing in the city was without a story. Admittedly, some of the stories were legend more than fact. It did not really matter to Autumn because it gave the town even more charm and character.

The food in Charleston was without comparison. Whether it was traditional Low Country food or gourmets with innovative twists on tradition, the food was without rival in Autumn's opinion. The seafood was all brought in on Charleston's docks. There was everything one could imagine and some things one could not imagine but needed to try. Because of Boyd's familiarity with the town and its people, every occasion was a special occasion. Dinners that should have lasted one or two hours would frequently tarry on well into the latest hours of the night. Autumn enjoyed every moment. Being with Boyd had felt as if she were on the arm of a famous celebrity. Everywhere they went they were treated like royalty. The down side was that Autumn and Boyd typically left each establishment a full one to two pounds heavier.

The days were mild and warm. The nights were just cool enough to send a chill when the wind blew. There was not an inch of the historical downtown that the pair did not comb. Without using much imagination at all, Autumn could envision herself back in time since the city was so layered with the past. Autumn had always been sensitive to the presence of ghosts or lapses in the time-space relation before she moved to South Carolina. In many ways, she expected to find a spirit around every corner and in every doorway. The spirits and their events in Charleston were so bountiful that it was like sleep walking through the past. Cemeteries in Charleston were dignified and quiet. The folks buried in those places had enough living relatives to remember the past that the deceased in Charleston were content. If the stories were not the truth, the specters seemed even happier at that. It appealed to their southern preference to hear a good rumor rather than a boring truth. Many of the buildings in Charleston had been so damaged by the two great fires that the buildings seemed to have been exorcised of their tragedies or malicious specters. The provost and dungeon was being renovated for future generations. It had a long and varied history as one of the first buildings in the original Charleston settlement.

At night, Boyd and Autumn walked the cobblestone streets along King Street. If they paused for moment, Autumn could almost hear the sound of a horse drawn carriage and beating hooves making their way to a fancy dinner engagement. Battery Park sat on the bay looking out at Fort Sumter. Autumn chuckled every time they made their way to that end of town. Battery Park had played a very critical role in the Revolutionary War and even more so in the Civil War. It had been dedicated after the Civil War when the Union Troops left their occupation of Charleston. As a sign of good faith, Union troops had left Charleston cannons and cannon balls. That would allow the citizens of Charleston to defend them from attack. However, the cannon balls were too large for the barrels of the cannons. Autumn thought it must have been another one of those wonderful oxymoronic things of post war. Another one had to have been Charleston green. In the historic district, there are only certain colors the exterior of a home may be painted. It was the same principal as in Georgetown's historic district. In Charleston's case, one of the colors was Charleston green. To Autumn's perception, Charleston green was just a shade of black with a green hue. Black paint had been left after the Civil War by the Union. No self respecting Charlestonian would ever have used black to paint there home. Black was the color of death and grieving. Some clever fellow discovered that adding just a touch of an equally unpalatable yellow would give the black a green cast. Hence the birth of Charleston green. Autumn thought it amusing because Charleston green looked black to her.

Boyd and Autumn discovered something during their stay in Charleston. All the things that Autumn thought Boyd would find quirky and unusual about her were the very things that he delighted in. He appreciated the fact that she could and would slow down to peek at a hidden garden between two rather unassuming houses. He marveled at her memory. There was not one story or fact told to her during their stay that she forgot. Boyd rarely remembered the names of people he had known all of his life but had not seen in years. Autumn remembered every restaurant owner, waitress, or acquaintance they had encountered over the several evenings of dining out. The other thing he loved was her chattiness. In fact, one evening while dining at the most famous seafood restaurant in town, an elderly lady made her way over to their table and said, "It is wonderful to see two young people in love. I hope you appreciate each other as long as you live. You never know when it is your last day with your best friend." Then, she laid her wrinkled frail feminine hand on his broad youthful shoulder and whispered, "With her, you'll never be lonely." Boyd and Autumn just sat there and watched her make her way out the front door until she disappeared into the night.

All of the observations Autumn made the first night she met Boyd were now some of the qualities she loved the most. His know-it-all way of speaking was just his way. The physical presence he exuded from the moment she met him was from the very core of his being. Boyd was a defender and provider. It gave Autumn a sense of well being she had never known with anyone else. His perspective of "life is just a series of one adventure to the next" kept Autumn from dwelling unnecessarily long on the moment. Most of all, Boyd was full of passion; passion for life, people, horses, adventure, and Autumn. Boyd and Autumn discovered that they were a perfect fit for each other. The qualities each possessed complimented the other.

They stopped on the way out of town and loaded the car with baskets. By the time they left Charleston, Autumn thought of several places where she could use the beautiful baskets and what wonderfully unique gifts they would make for the family back home. The baskets were costly but Autumn did not mind. Autumn had not come from a wealthy family. That family never placed much importance on money being the key to happiness. After inheriting the McFarland legacy, Autumn knew that money was not the key to happiness but it did not hurt!

Somewhere between the ghosts and the holidays, the farm had become home to Autumn. At the end of a particularly hectic day, she looked forward to driving up the lane of what she now thought of as home. The noises that the old house made at night were comforting and familiar. It was home and Autumn was happy to call it home. Someone once told her that everything was relative. That certainly would be true about human beings. There was a time not long ago that Autumn never thought she would be able to live through the Carolina summers. Now, they seem no longer or more oppressive than other summers.

Over the past year, Autumn managed a nice assortment of odds and ends that made the house hers including the baskets from Gali. This summer Autumn renovated her bedroom, added a copper kettle to the house, and a paint job on the front porch. Ian was the muscle behind all of these endeavors. Autumn made her bedroom an upscale recreation of her grandmother's which was lilac and lace. The copper kettle was a happy accident. Autumn saw it at a traveling antique market but the seller had no idea it was an apple butter copper kettle. The cost of the copper alone would have made the item twice what she paid for it. However, it needed some serious cleaning in order to even find the copper. Ian's knowledge and elbow grease cleaned the copper pot back into shape. Autumn promised him he could have as much apple butter as he wanted this fall. The front porch had only gotten the ceiling painted the summer she moved in due to all the weird happenings. When it did get done, Autumn made sure the roof of the piazza remained sky blue. A little superstition went a long way when you live in a haunted house.

CHAPTER 6

▼

OLD FRIENDS

"Are you going to buy something or just eat your way through everything," Autumn scolded as Boyd helped himself to his third free sample. "The new library won't build itself."

"Don't be so hard on him, dear. I think the reason he is lingering has less to do with what we are selling than who is selling it," Elizabeth said giving Autumn a gentle nudge. "Why don't you take him to get a bite to eat? Maybe he won't be so hungry for baked goods with a little food in his belly."

"Are you sure? I hate to leave you out here in the sun by yourself? The town fair is going on all day, we could step out later."

Autumn was interrupted by Elizabeth. "I am just fine. I can sit if I need to. Get a cool drink if I need to. Worst case, I can leave the booth and slip inside for a few minutes to cool off. Now, I wouldn't have said it if I didn't mean it. Besides, your friend just helped himself to another taste!"

"You are completely impossible, you know that don't you." Autumn rolled her eyes at Boyd as he helped himself to another brownie. "Stay here. I'll be right back. Try not to eat anything!"

Autumn slipped inside the library for a moment to get Lillian to sit with Elizabeth. When Autumn returned, she saw a small group of teenage boys run over to the table. "Miss Hummel, are you still hosting the Halloween party out at your farm next weekend?"

"Yeah."

"Can we still buy tickets for the party? We'd like to do something fun on Halloween with our girls that won't get their parents all worked up."

Autumn laughed. "How many tickets do you need?"

"Eight, please."

"Okay, it'll just take me a minute." Autumn snapped around to Boyd, "I will break your hand if you eat one more thing!"

"Oooh," teased Boyd as he dropped a fifty dollar bill into the collection cup.

Elizabeth joined in the fun, "I think she means it this time."

Autumn ran into the library office to grab eight tickets for the Halloween party. Boyd was talking to the boys. She couldn't hear exactly what they were talking about but by the hushed "cools" and "sweets" her guess was they were talking about the house.

"Miss Hummel, is it true your house is haunted," one of the more awkward looking boys asked.

The boys flanking him slapped him across the top of his head. "You don't ask that?"

"It's alright. Yes, my house is haunted."

"Have you ever seen any ghosts there," the shortest of the four asked.

Boyd couldn't resist. "Has she? Not only has she seen them, ask her how many she has seen?"

"You're incorrigible, Boyd Masters. Y'all have to come out on Halloween and find out for yourselves. Now let's get going before Elizabeth changes her mind and Lillian melts like a hothouse flower. See y'all on Halloween!"

Boyd and Autumn strolled off in the direction of Nancy's Café. Boyd leaned over and whispered, "So, when did it happen?"

"When did what happen, you pastry-thief?"

"When did Miss Ohio Valley become Miss Southern Belle?"

"I truly have no idea what you are talking about," Autumn playfully teased Boyd.

"You'ns and you guys but never y'all."

"Well," Autumn shrugged, "it happens to the best of us."

During lunch Autumn grilled Boyd about the haunted house stories that he was planting in everyone's head. People knew the house she came to inherit under unusual circumstances. The fact that she spent the better part of the first year in the house dealing with ghostly visitors was a well guarded secret. Autumn wanted people to come to the Halloween party to have fun. She wanted people to eat popcorn balls and apple pie, bob for apples, and carve pumpkins. Boyd argued that on Halloween everybody wants to go to a haunted ... something. He was just trying to insure a good turn out. "Plus, you said I could do the whole haunted side of the old plantation."

"Yeah, I thought you would tell ghost stories out by the bonfire. I thought you could use local legends and lore. I never expected that you would want to turn my haunted house into a real haunted house." Autumn's tone was half-serious and half-joking. She knew deep down that Boyd was right. The only way any girl or young lady would get their beau to go to a Halloween party was if there was something scary. "Okay. You do what ever you like but you've got to censor yourself soon. Kendra will be here in a few hours and I told you."

"I know. I'll be good. When is her plane arriving today?"

"She gets in just after four today. I'll have enough time to finish working the bake sale to drive into the airport."

"How did you ever get her to fly down here? You've told me several times that she is terrified of flying. I can't imagine how thrilled she was to be getting on your little puddle jumper."

Autumn couldn't help but laugh. Kendra and she had been best friends since the seventh grade. Unlike Autumn, Kendra was afraid of many things including highway overpasses, roller coasters, and airplanes. "I used the 'I can't believe my best friend will never see my new life just because she has this irrational fear of flying. Essentially, I guilt her into it by reminding her that she was flying in my own personal jet. If she had any reservations, I'm sure Jerry will give her the same reassuring speech he gave me before I got on the plane for the first time."

"You say it's an irrational fear but it's not," Boyd who jets all over the world several times a year argued. "Planes can crash. That's a pretty rational fear."

"Kendra is not afraid of them crashing, taking off, or landing. She is afraid of the actual piloting of the plane. She is a control freak. When we were in high school talking about going on the Blue Streak at Cedar Point, she very calmly explained to me that she would ride the roller coaster if they would let her drive it. She feels the same way about planes. Kendra would be happy as a clam if she were allowed to pilot the thing."

"Okay. *That* is irrational!"

After a very delicious and filling lunch, Boyd walked Autumn back to the library.

"So, did you sell everything yet," Boyd hollered when they got back.

"No, we still have food for you to mooch." Elizabeth was sitting having a mint julep.

"Oh, please. You know that stuff goes straight to my hips and, after all, a boy does have to watch his figure," Boyd said as he did his best to imitate a feminine posture. The truly comical part was that, being so masculine, the feminine just came off as awkward and silly. "When should I be over tonight to pick you ladies up?"

"If you could be there by six, we'll leave for dinner at six thirty."

"Sounds like a plan. Well, ladies, have a good afternoon. I hope you sell out before you close down."

"We'll do a lot better now that you're leaving," Elizabeth teased Boyd.

Boyd's wish did come true. The library raised at least two hundred dollars with the bake sale. There was not one sweet morsel to be found by two thirty. Elizabeth headed for home at around one. The heat started taking its toll on her after three hours. Autumn cleaned up the tables and put everything up against the large tree on the curb for the firemen to collect at the end of the fair. Despite the unusually high heat on this late October day, the firemen's fair had a nice turn out. People from all over Georgetown and Horry County came for the quaint event.

Autumn easily made her way to her car and the Myrtle Beach airport by four to pick up Kendra. To her surprise, however, there was no Kendra. Autumn had thought she missed her getting off the plane but the airport is so small there was no way Kendra could have gotten by her. Autumn waited until she saw Jerry and the crew coming off. As they came through the doors, Autumn asked if they knew where Kendra had gone. The flight attendant said that Kendra was the first person to bolt out the door when the plane taxied to a stop. Autumn thought that was odd since she couldn't find her either at the gate or the lobby.

"She may be in the restroom," suggested the flight attendant.

"I don't mean to seem ungrateful but I've been here for a half hour. I don't think that she could have been in there that long."

"Your friend seemed to be, well," Jerry hesitantly said.

"Oh, no!"

Autumn raced to the restrooms. Autumn could tell by the hesitation in the Jerry's voice that Kendra had obviously done something to allow herself to get through the hour and forty-five minute flight. As Autumn turned into the bathroom, she saw Kendra in front of one of the mirrors.

"Good grief girl, you scared me to death. What's wrong? Was the flight that bad?"

"Hi, hon. I'm sorry I scared you. No, the flight was great. I'm fine. There is nothing wrong." Kendra looked peaked but otherwise well.

"I've just been here for a half hour and you've been in here the whole time. Something must be wrong."

"Oh, stupid me. You know how I am about flying," Kendra said as she put the finishing touches on her hair. Autumn would think it funny if it were anyone but Kendra. How many people do their hair before they see their best friend? That was just Kendra.

"Yeah, you are terrified of it. Hence the reason it took you fourteen months to come see me."

"Right. Well, I didn't know how I was going to get on the plane when my mom suggested that I take one of her little pills. She takes them when life gets just too-"

"Oh. Knocked you on your butt, didn't it?"

"Autumn, I slept the whole way down. They had to pretty much shout to wake me up before we landed."

"The flight attendant said that you were the first to jump off the plane when it landed."

"I did," Kendra added as she sprayed a little perfume on before zipping up her purse. "I couldn't meet your new boyfriend looking like a drooling pillow head. So, I made a break for the bathroom to fix myself up before I met you. However, the mad dash to the bathroom made me a little lightheaded."

Autumn laughed, "Are you okay?"

"Yeah. I'm fine. Why are you laughing?"

"I swear. You are like a breath of fresh air. Home can be so far away sometimes. It's good to see you."

"So, where's this new cutie in your life," Kendra asked as she scanned the airport for Boyd.

"I just left him at the bake sale. He'll be over tonight to go to dinner and, oh my, he is *so* cute!"

"Wait, you're not cooking a big homemade supper for me tonight?"

They both broke into hysterical laughter. There were many things these two young women could do. Autumn could quote the chronological history of our country. Kendra could trace the history behind any piece of modern law. Cooking a homemade meal was a little beyond the grasp of either of them. The only time they had decided to make a home cooked meal to impress their boyfriends at the time, they discovered that there truly is an art to cooking. It seemed preposterous to either of them that they could be so worldly in so many ways and yet not cook a simple meal. Mrs. Hummel was a wonderful cook who felt that her children had their whole life to cook and clean for themselves. Needless to say, Autumn learned very little except maybe the basics. Kendra's mother was a busy professional with very little time to spend in the kitchen. "I've gotten much better since living away from home for a year. I still think you would prefer a nice meal cooked by a true professional."

"Boyd doesn't know you can't cook, does he," Kendra asked as she lifted her luggage off the belt.

"Sadly, he does. Luckily, he's no better at cooking than I am. So, how was your flight?"

Kendra could tell by her tone that she was mocking her. "I have no idea how my flight was. I was looped by the time we took off. How embarrassing? So, let's get out of here and see that house of yours."

The trip from the airport to the farm was forty-five minutes worth of quality girl talk. They kept up their weekly phone calls they started in college. Autumn had attended a small private college just thirty minutes from the large infamous state college Kendra chose. Despite the short distance in miles from their schools, their lack of wheels and time during their undergraduate days meant that the phone was the best way to keep in touch with their ever changing lives. The phone calls had always let them keep in touch but it was nothing like being in the same place with each other. In person, they could just talk about whatever came into their brains. When the meter is running on the phone, people have a tendency to plan their call. When in person, they could discuss all the newest idiosyncrasies that were driving them nuts about their moms. With Kendra and Autumn, the "Mom List" filled up most of the trip to the farm.

When they reached the main drive of the McFarland Farm, all Kendra could say was, "Shut-up!"

"Did you think I was lying, ya big brat," Autumn screeched with a chuckle.

"No. You know me. You've told me about all of this. You know I have no imagination. I couldn't picture something in my head unless you give me a picture of it, make me stare at it, and then I just *barely* get it."

"Well, now you're here."

"So, where does your property start?"

"That chapel we saw at the corner is where it starts."

"You mean all of this ... Wow! Now, where is Mr. Masters' home?"

"The farms are so big that you can't see our houses from each other. He is next door but there are several acres separating the actual homes."

"This is unreal. You and I grew up reading about farms but never being on one. Now you own a huge farm. What is that like?"

"Ken, this has been the most amazing year of my life and I like to think that I have had many. It took months for me to wrap my brain around Mr. McFarland leaving me, a stranger, this wonderful home, huge farm, and everything else.

So …" Before Autumn could finish her thought, Kendra gasped. Autumn slowed down a little bit when she reached the beginning of the old live oaks that line the drive heading to the house. Autumn knew the feeling of disbelief upon seeing the McFarland home. It was just over a year ago that she was in the same shock and awe. For the first time since the two had laid eyes on each other today, Kendra was silent. As Autumn turned to the right of the house and the garage, Kendra lifted herself out of the seat to turn and stare at the house.

"Home again, home again, jiggedy jig."

"Your mom has always said that. What the heck does it mean," asked Kendra who was slowly pulling herself back together.

"It means grab your stuff and let's get going. Boyd's gonna be here in an hour to pick us up for dinner."

"Well, he is just going to have to wait because I am not running through your house just to go have dinner. Sister, he can wait till we are good and ready to leave."

Autumn laughed, "Okay, this is one of those things I told you about living in South Carolina. If we were home, that would mean that he would be here and then we would leave. In South Carolina, that means he will be here, we'll chat, have a drink or two, and then we'll leave for dinner. Relax. You'll get the full price tour for free. Are you ready?"

"You bet."

The two walked the small distance from the garage to the front steps. Kendra slowly climbed the seven broad steps to the house, gazing in awe at the stately porch and pillars. Upon entering, Autumn suggested that she sit her bags in the foyer while they looked around. The staircase to the second floor was large but with a simple elegance. Autumn took Kendra through the left arch and into the dining room first. All of the pieces were antiques from the McFarland family. Autumn added a sideboard in order to display the beautiful German crystal and china that she discovered in one of the many boxes in the attic. Next, they passed through a swinging door into the huge kitchen. Autumn offered Kendra an adult beverage. Kendra decided she'd be better off with a soda until the medicine was completely out of her system. Kendra joked that she would prefer Boyd's first impression of her not be that of someone who needs a good rehab clinic.

They worked their way back to the front door and proceeded into the living room. In the short time Autumn had been in the house, this was the room that reflected her personality the least. Autumn let it stay much the way she saw it in all the family photos but there were a few pieces added to make it homey. One of her favorite items was a fabulous afghan of many colors that her aunt made her after graduating from high school. "You live alone for a year and see what weird security items you hold dear," Autumn said pointing to the blanket. The next room they entered was to the rear of the living room. This room was probably Mr. McFarland's office or den. Kendra asked if it was original to the house. Autumn explained that in antebellum times, the men would retreat to this room to discuss, smoke, and do whatever gentlemen of that time did when they were together. The room she calls the living room would have been where the ladies would have gathered to chat, knit, sew, and whatever women of that time would do.

"Wouldn't they have done that in the kitchen or maybe the dining room?"

"Never! You have to remember that these are people who had slaves. These ladies probably had no real idea what their kitchen looked like let alone shared the space where the 'taskers' were. The dining room for women was a microscope. Men judged a woman on two things: the fairness of their skin and the size of their waistline. Women used to eat before attending socials so they wouldn't feel the urge to eat a full meal at the party. Plus, imagine trying to eat anything with a contraption squeezing your middle so that you were only eighteen inches around at the tummy. I don't even know how they breathed!"

"I don't know how they got eighteen inches," Kendra laughed as she grabbed her belly.

"Yeah, really," joined Autumn until she realized that midriffs were still something women obsessed about and men cared about.

"It still smells like cigar smoke," Kendra said crinkling up her nose in disgust.

"It has ever since I first came to the house but I kind of like it," Autumn shrugged off Kendra's disdainful look.

"Have you ever tried to do anything about it—cleaners, sprays, candles?"

"Yeah, but look," Autumn stepped out of the room.

"What just happened?" Kendra looked around.

"I don't know? What happened?"

"It smells clean in here. There isn't any more old cigar smell," Kendra turned and took several stiff breathes through her nose just to be sure.

"I know but watch." Autumn stepped back into the room.

"Eew, it's back again," Kendra leaned over to smell Autumn. "Is it you?"

"Yes, it's me. I smoke big giant stogies when no one's looking. That and I have hair on my back. Of course, it's not me."

"Then what the heck is it?"

"I don't know. Before the first party at the house, I had the house professionally cleaned. When they were done, the crew leader walked me through every room in the house to make sure I was pleased. I walked into this room and asked if there was nothing they could do to get rid of the cigar smell. The crew leader looked appalled at the smell. At that particular moment the phone rang and I ran to answer it while he searched over his map to find out who cleaned that room. That's how I found out that the room only smells like cigars when I'm in it."

Kendra just shook her head, "And you don't think that's weird?"

"Yeah, but what about my life the past year hasn't been weird."

"Well," Kendra said clapping a hand on Autumn's shoulder, "That's true."

"It reminds me of the meetings the gentlemen of this house would have had in here. The first talks of secession could have happened here. Who knows, the first delegates to the Continental Congress from South Carolina could have come here to persuade their fellow Carolinians to leave Britain."

"I don't know about that, but it does stink when you are here. Is this where you found the letter?"

"Yep. I come in here when things get crazy with the farm and the business. I feel the closest to Mr. McFarland in this room. Sometimes I almost feel like I can hear him talking to me. That might sound creepy, but it is really helpful when I am faced with a big business decision. You know me and my serious lack of business knowledge."

"Sure and your dad's serious 'who gives a shit' attitude when pressured. No, I know what you mean. He was a good businessman, John McFarland?"

"From what people have told me, he was the best. My bank account says they are right. It apparently ran in the family. Though the McFarlands came here as poor farmers, it was only one generation before they were running the farm and not working the farm. That was pretty much unheard of at that time. Let me show you your room and we'll get your bags upstairs." Autumn helped Kendra get her bags upstairs. They headed first to Kendra's room which was at the far end of the hallway. This room was the largest of the four bedrooms in the house. The room sat across the hall from the stairs that led to the third floor. The best explanation for this arrangement was that the third floor had been where the mammy of the house would have lived. The room at the bottom of the stairs would have been the nursery.

"Who the heck is mammy? What are you talking about?"

"Okay. We are in the South," Autumn said leading her.

"Duh. Okay," Kendra said.

"Well, when this house was built, there were slaves and masters," Autumn said.

"Would you just spill it? You, history major. Me, not." Kendra was rarely up for the hoops that Autumn liked to make her jump through. It was fair in the end. Kendra would do the same to Autumn when Autumn had a legal question.

"Okay, mammy was more of a title than a name. She would have been the one who took care of the family's children. She would have changed diapers and gotten up in the middle of the night. The mammy would have chaperoned the girls to socials and parties. The children would have been her only assignment until the children were grown and married. That's why this room is so large. The babies were usually born close together and would have shared this room until they were adolescents."

"That is so incredibly sad," Kendra said.

"It is as an institution but so many of these children and mammies had a true love for each other. The children were like those mammy's surrogate children. Come on let's get you settled."

"How can you live with all this horrible history around you," Kendra said as she shook her head in disdain.

"Wow. How can I explain this to you? The history was written well before my day. I can't change it and I wasn't responsible for it. That is part of how I can live with the history of this home. I also know that there are wonderful people who may not have been here without the practice of slavery."

"Okay. Who have you been talking to? That is just not like you. How did you get to this place in your life?"

Autumn laughed. It was good to be around someone who knew her so well. "You really do know me. On the first day I came to the farm, I met this wonderful woman. She is the ancestor of the people who were once slaves of the McFarland family. For generations, her family has taken care of the grounds and gardens. I gave her all my tears and guilt. She set me straight."

Kendra was chuckling. "That's Fanny, right?"

"Right. Now, get unpacked. Boyd will be here." The words didn't leave her lips before the doorbell rang. "Okay, go. I'll get the door."

"You're ready?" Kendra always had to get ready. Autumn usually was ready.

"Thanks and yes. Go."

Autumn bounded down the hall and ran down the steps.

Boyd Masters was at the door. He was all spit and polished for the introduction. The cologne which he insists he never wears, from the first moment they met, melted her heart. He was wearing a crisp dusty blue dress shirt with three buttons undone at the top and well fitting blue jeans. Autumn still swooned whenever he was around. His devilish looking grin was Boyd. There was always more than meets the eye with Boyd but what meets the eye was great. Over the year, the two had become best friends and much more. There was a boyish charm to this brooding and sullen man that intrigued Autumn. He reached through the door and pulled Autumn close.

"Miss me," he asked after a long kiss.

"You know I did. Come on in."

"So," Boyd said leaning in the doorway, "where's Kendra?"

"Upstairs. We may as well go get a drink. She'll be up there for awhile."

Boyd strolled in as if relieved.

"Are you nervous," Autumn asked jokingly.

"No. I had struck a pose in the doorway and wondered ..."

"If you wasted it on just me? Thanks. So, was the kiss just to impress also?"

"I don't know. Did it?"

"You are hopeless."

"I try." Boyd hopped up on the counter like he always did in her kitchen. Autumn suspected that it was one of those things he just wasn't allowed to do growing up. "Was her flight okay," Boyd asked as he popped the lid off his bottle.

"Yeah but she got hammered before it took off. I found her in the bathroom of the airport after the flight crew told me she had a little trouble."

"I'm surprised," laughed Boyd. "Being your best friend, I would have assumed she walked the straight and narrow like you. I might like this girl yet."

"The straight and narrow," a voice boomed from the dining room followed by a sarcastic, "Yeah, right."

Boyd managed to hop off the counter and strike another pose just as Kendra swung open the dining room door.

"Her? Straight and narrow. That's laughable. Hi, I'm Kendra." Kendra reached out to shake hands with Boyd while catching Autumn's eye. Kendra mouthed, "Nice!"

"Nice to meet you Kendra. Autumn's told me so much about you."

"And yet, left out all the good parts I see." Kendra grinned. She knew this would get her off on the right foot with the new boy and make Autumn squirm at the same time.

"Don't start. I'm hungry. Let's go." Autumn grabbed her purse and Kendra. "I'm sure you need to eat something after the day you have had." Autumn hoped that would keep Kendra quiet for a few minutes. It would have but Kendra's luring comments about Autumn's deep dark secrets were too much for Boyd to ignore. It would be like handing a five-year-old a brand new exciting toy and saying, "You can hold it but don't play with it." The child would explode before obeying.

"So, what do you know about Ms. Hummel that I do not?"

Kendra realized the bait worked. "Well, because she is my best friend, there are things that you only share with each other. I will tell you that she is not as innocent as she likes to appear. Like the night you became a Little Sister at SAE."

"You really are a brat. You know that, right? I always thought your mom was exaggerating but it's true." Autumn scolded her in fun. This was all just part of being best friends.

"I do not know what happened the night she became a Little Sister to a Fraternity House. That alone is a new revelation to me," Boyd said sounding ever more intrigued.

"Well …" Kendra started.

"You are really going to tell him that story," Autumn interrupted.

"I am not going to let him continue a relationship with you under the guise that you are pure as the driven snow. He deserves to know the true you."

"I do, don't I," quipped Boyd with a wicked gleam in his eyes. "Please, go on."

"I want to be perfectly clear that at this moment I hate you both. Please, go on." Autumn settled in the car seat for a long stare at the scenery between her place and Land's End.

"Miss Autumn became friends with some of the Tri Deltas who traditionally were the Little Sisters of the Sigma Alpha Epsilon fraternity at her school. Through those friends, she came to know several of the brothers and attended a good number of their parties."

"Okay, now you are just lying. I had gone to two parties over at the house. One of those parties really wasn't even a party. They were just having a pizza bash at the house because one of the other big frats on campus was having their casino night. Now, go on."

"Needless to say, she had become friends with some of the brothers. Teresa knew this senior who didn't have a little sister and asked Autumn if she would be his Little Sister. Autumn agreed. Long story short, Autumn became a Little Sister. The ceremony took place in the ballroom of the frat house which is up on the third floor. When it was all said and done, people were going out to one of the two local bars the college kids frequented. Her 'brother' wasn't much for the party scene, bar scene, or drinking scene. As she was about to leave and say goodnight to her 'brother', a group came by and asked if they were going. His answer was no."

"And, I was not going to go if my 'brother' didn't go. I thought that would be rude. Continue."

"The group of guys insisted that she go and promised her 'brother' that they would take care of her. Now, I said that she had gone to parties at the house but she never drank."

Boyd gasped, "You went to frat parties and never drank?" He almost sounded incredulous, as if the two could not go together. "Isn't that the point of going to a frat party? That was always the reason we had parties."

"Shut-up. No, I never drank. What do they usually have at frat parties?"

"Beer."

"What can most college students afford to drink when they go to bars?"

"Beer."

"Right, have you ever seen me drink a beer?"

"There is something desperately wrong with you. You don't like beer. That is impossible. Everybody likes beer. Even if they don't at first, they acquire a taste for it." The stunned tone in his voice made Autumn laugh.

"Would you two be quiet and let me finish the story?"

"Yes, let's not make me suffer any longer than I have to, please." Autumn turned back to the window.

"So, she goes with the firm resolution to NOT drink at the bar. She would have a coke and sip it all night. After about a half an hour of being at the bar, one of the 'brothers' she came with was appalled to see that she did not have a beer."

"My response to him was that I did not want a beer."

"And I suppose, having been a 'brother' myself, he would not hear of it."

"Exactly, he said that I could just have one."

"Well, over the course of two hours, she never made it to the bottom of the glass. No problem. Beer just doesn't seem to bother her. So, she's hanging around socializing when she sees one of the guys by the nickname of Fish trying to get one of the girls to do a shot. Autumn came to the rescue of this girl. Fish still wanted someone to do a shot with him. Her friend was a little tiny thing who was slight of build. Plus, Autumn thought she had not even had one whole beer. What would be the harm, right?"

Boyd reached over, grabbed her leg, and smiled at Autumn. The loving expression in his eyes told her that all this was being done in fun. "Right."

"So, she's never done shots before but, after understanding the challenge before her, jumped in with both feet. She slung the shot and did the beer chaser." Kendra paused because she was laughing so hard.

"And I almost got sick right there. I asked Fish what was in the shot because it burned all the way down and was killing my stomach. His answer was 'Prairie Fire'. This meant nothing to me but I wanted to know exactly what was in it because there was no way I would ever drink it again." The mere thought of the experience caused Autumn's stomach to turn.

Boyd laughed out loud and shook his head in disbelief. "Your first shot was 'Prairie Fire': tequila and Tabasco. Not a timid person's drink. How did you feel?" His eyes twinkled when he asked her that question.

"Kendra started this debacle. As soon as she can pull herself back together, she can finish this."

Wiping the tears from her eyes, Kendra started again. "Okay, okay. I'm back. As you clearly know already, shots have sort of a boomerang affect on the shooter. Not so bad in the beginning but they come back to bite you in the butt once you metabolize them. Feeling pretty proud for saving an 'innocent' and tossing one back with a pro; she excuses herself to the ladies room. Upon returning, she was gloating about how many Little Sisters were celebrating their new family by hurling in the bathroom. No sooner did the words escape her mouth when the room started to spin ... violently. She excused herself from the company at the bar to collapse in the bathroom."

"Y'all didn't? You got sick?"

"No. No. That would have been preferable to what I was experiencing at that moment in time. I could not keep the world from spinning. I had no idea which way was up and slumped against the bathroom wall in a stupor. After what seemed an eternity, my head felt as if someone had beaten it in with a baseball bat. When I hadn't returned, Fish got another Little Sister who was a roommate of a friend of mine to come in and check on me. I could not stand. The guys stood at the bathroom door and pleaded with me to come out and I just cried because I could not. Before long, Fish, who was a big football player, came in and carried me out. I passed out before we even left the bar."

"I'm proud of you. At least you didn't get sick," Boyd said with his hand over his mouth to hide the smirk.

"Very funny, getting sick would have been better. At least I would have gotten rid of some of the alcohol in my system. I can see you grinning so quit it!"

"Well, they couldn't take her back to the dorm. If anyone had found out she had gotten drunk, especially at a frat event, her conservative religious school would have had their heads. So, they did the only thing they could do which was to take her back to the frat house."

"Why Miss Hummel, I would never have guessed you would have spent the night inebriated in a house full of college men." Boyd was laughing out loud at this point.

"Get off it. To hear her tell it, I met with a horrible fate. It can be a fate that can cause colleges' scandal and young women psychological torture. Michelle, Fish's Little Sister, took me to the guest room in the frat house. Apparently, back in the day when the house mother lived in the fraternity house, it was her suite. The guys just kept it for visitors or whatever. Fish brought me some of his clothes to change into and I slept it off. The end"

"Now what do you think of Little Miss Innocent." Kendra stated in righteous indignation.

"Love her."

"But," Kendra said with a little fake sadness.

"No buts. Now I know a little bit more about her. Everyone has a wild oat or two to sew. I sowed enough in my day for four or five hundred people. I now know why she rarely ever drinks and, if so, always in moderation."

"You people are no fun," Kendra snorted as if to be disgusted by the lame affect her story had on Boyd. "So, let's hear about some of your sordid past Mr. Masters?"

"Look, we're here," Autumn announced.

"Okay, you're safe for now. Let's eat."

The next day, Autumn and Kendra spent the afternoon at the beach. The weather was too cool in October to sun bath or swim. With the mild air, they could sit and enjoy the beauty and awe of the ocean. The summer months make doing that almost unbearable. They were lucky enough to have gotten a glimpse of a school of dolphins making their way down the warm southern currents from Florida and the Bahamas. They combed the beach for a few hours and then drove down into Murrells Inlet for lunch. Murrells Inlet was once a quiet out of the way place where there was one good seafood restaurant owned by locals. There had been a time when the only reason people would come to Murrells Inlet was to go fishing. People would either go fishing in the inlet or take chartered deep sea fishing boats out for the day. Because of the inlet, there was no beach front property or even land enough for a golf course. Back in the day, the marshy land and inlet served as the perfect hide-out for the famous pirates of the Caribbean. Over the years, however, developers figured out they could expand upon the restaurant business in Murrells Inlet. Now, where dense Carolina pine forests and wetlands once stood is home to every sort of restaurant imaginable. Kendra and

Autumn opted for one of the big steak and seafood chains since they were in the area.

To finish the day, they went shopping in Conway's Outlet Mall until dark when they drove down to the Grand Strand in Myrtle Beach. Both Autumn and Kendra spent many fun nights during their adolescence in the sultry neon glow of the Grand Strand. Kendra didn't believe Autumn when she said that the Grand Strand was a completely different place during the off season. Many of the shops closed down until summer. Other places on the Grand Strand ran limited or weekend only hours. The biggest difference was the lack of people. In the summer, a teenager could live a whole week on the energy that surrounded the boardwalk. The warm summer wind gently blowing off the ocean and the lights strung everywhere to grab attention. Just the sound of life that emanated from the dance clubs, souvenir shops, and carnivals created the feeling so many people came to associate with summer: carefree days and all night parties. Who could forget the sweet but fleeting romances of summer? During the fall, the Grand Strand was a sleepy little place with an occasional winter vacationer. Kendra seemed a little sad to see Myrtle Beach that way. Autumn and Kendra agreed that they liked the picture they kept in their head of Myrtle Beach in the summer. For them, Myrtle Beach was a place where summer never ended.

Kendra's second day, Autumn gave her the full tour of the farm which included a walk down to the old slave cemetery. Just as the emotion overwhelmed Autumn at seeing these final resting places, Kendra was also moved. Autumn took Kendra to meet Fanny and her family. The weather was cool and all the gardens were prepared for winter's sleep. Fanny would be back in the spring to bring color to the canvas of the McFarland farm. From the first day Autumn came to the McFarland Farm, Fanny had been a guide, pillar of strength, and a solid motherly shoulder to cry on when necessary. Kendra could not hide her emotions about Fanny's family history. She just welled up with tears.

"What's with you white girls? Cry for no good reason? Now, is that how you meet new people? Get over here and give me a hug. I have to listen to this one talk about you all year." Fanny sounded gruff but it was all with a broad smile across her face. Kendra walked over to Fanny and the two hugged like old friends. "Now, let's dry up the waterworks so I can get a good look at you." Fanny started mopping up Kendra's eyes but the tears still came. "What did you do to this poor girl?"

"You know. I told her all the stuff and showed her and now ..."

"This is all because I'm black and my family was slaves?" With the words spoken, Kendra began to cry out loud. "Girl, didn't you tell her what I told you?"

"I told her but I don't think she really thinks you believe what you said." Autumn added. The statement could have been taken wrong.

"You better be watching your mouth, girl."

"I didn't say that *I* didn't believe what you said. I don't think *she* believes you said it," Autumn said defensively.

"Hush now child," Fanny said in her motherly voice. "First of all, I do not say anything that I do not mean. Second of all, Autumn knows better than to make up stories 'bout folk around her. It takes two seconds for the truth to get back and half a second for a lie. You don't lie 'bout anyone 'round here without them knowin' it." Fanny chuckled. Her body chuckled when she did. "First, it's true. They were my relatives. They were slaves. There ain't nothin' you or I can change about that. It was what it was. Second, I'm sure, like Autumn here, that you never owned a slave. Well, have you?"

Kendra was beginning to regain her composure. "No," she muttered through the sobs.

"Well then, no reason to feel bad about it. All any of us can do now is live our lives learning from their mistakes and hardships. After all, if they hadn't been slaves and brought to this country, I would not be here. I work hard everyday and take advantage of all that life has to offer me to honor them and the inhumanity they endured. I make sure that each generation remembers that they are the dream of their slave ancestors. Okay. That's done. I don't want to talk about that no more. Come on inside and I'll whip up some of my special lemonade."

When they went inside, Kendra was again astounded by the home she was in. For all the elegance and grandeur of the McFarland home, Fanny's home was the complete opposite. The house was barely two floors. The building resembled many rural homes in coastal South Carolina. They almost look like homes on the islands of the Bahamas. The front door opened into the living room with all its furnishings, quilts, and photos. As Kendra looked around, Autumn pointed out people in the pictures. There was a picture of Fanny as a young girl with her siblings and parents. Then, there was a picture of Fanny and her children. One picture was taken at the McFarland farm with Fanny and Jon McFarland. All the other pictures were of Fanny's two children. Her son was the oldest. He was off at Stanford University beginning his second year of medical school. Fanny's daughter was almost five years younger than her brother. Her daughter decided to study architecture at Rutgers. She took the year off, however, to do mission work in Africa. Before she returned to Rutgers for her senior year, she was also taking a three month tour of Europe. Her daughter thought it would be a wonderful opportunity. Fanny's whole being had glowed with pride when she talked about her children.

In the back of Kendra's mind, she was thinking, "How wonderful for her children but how was Fanny affording it?" Kendra was polite enough not to ask, but Fanny must have read her mind.

"Their daddy and I have been setting aside money since before they were born. I'm not saying its much, but it was something. That would have gotten one of them through the first year of a state school. When Mr. McFarland passed away, Autumn was not the only beneficiary to his generosity. Jon had created a living will five years before his death which allowed him to give a portion of the designated person's inheritance to them while he was still alive. Two of those beneficiaries are my children. Each year, he gave them $50,000 until his death last year. With his help and financial acumen, each of my children left for college with over $1,000,000 in their possession. A generous person he was, God rests his soul. That's how my kids are getting to do anything and everything their heart's desire. No mother could want more for her children. Plus, they keep in touch with their mama. That's the only other thing a mother can ask of her children. Oh," Fanny interjected emphatically, "Autumn, Safrina wants to see you before you leave today."

Autumn looked at her very puzzled. "All right, I wanted to take Kendra over anyway. Wonder what that's all about?"

"Let's finish our tea and head over."

"Is anybody going to tell me what that was all about," asked Kendra feeling a little bit out of the loop.

"Oh, I never told you about Safrina. It's a long story but I'll give you the basics. Remember when I arranged for the reburial of the McFarland that was buried in the slave cemetery?" Kendra nodded that she remembered that story. "There was a big fuss being raised over the state wanting to recognize him as a national hero, a patriot killed during America's fight for freedom?"

"Who was fighting, again?"

"There were lots of people for it. There were a small number of very vocal outsiders who thought that it was a horrible idea to celebrate a man who owned slaves and perpetuated the institution of slavery."

"You white people are a pain when you get your buns in a twist but it only takes a few black folk with big mouths to complicate things." Fanny shook her head with an air of disgust in her voice. "Some people don't know anything about the folk who live here today. I could tell them plenty."

"It's all right, Fanny." Autumn patted Fanny and turned back to Kendra. "Safrina took care of that. We had a big town meeting before the actual ceremony to smooth over the hurt and insult that it would have caused. I was there and presented the side of historic fact. Yes, he was a slave owner but he was also a patriot who died for what he believed in—freedom from England. That, first and foremost, made him a patriot. Second, he was a slave owner. It also placed him in the majority of the people occupying the Southern colonies of the day.

"The others argued that his owning of other human beings negated the patriotic act of dying for the cause of freedom. I could not argue their point because it was just as true as him being a patriot. Before either side could do anything, Safrina led a group from this neighborhood into the meeting. She enlightened everybody in the room with her perspective of the situation which was that this man had done a great thing for all Americans. She is three thousand years old and will tell you that. However, she is one of the strongest and wisest souls I've ever met."

"Y'all better be gettin' over there. You know she's sittin' there thinking 'I three thousand years old and gettin' older by the minute'," Fanny joked lovingly.

When the three ladies made it over to the small house Safrina lived in, there was a crowd outside the house. Fanny grabbed Autumn's hand, "Something's happened." The two ran to the door. One of the ladies inside the small screened porch saw Fanny and Autumn. She ran out to Autumn and said, "She keeps saying she needs to see you. Come on."

Autumn was led into the small room off the kitchen that was Safrina's bedroom. The tiny room was no bigger than a walk-in-closet in some homes. There was an old Pawley's rocker with a patchwork quilt thrown over facing the window that looked outside. Safrina was the unofficial guardian angel of the neighborhood kids. She'd sit and watch all that went on out there. Next to the rocking chair was a small bed with a very frail frame inside. It appeared that Safrina was soon going to be a real angel. Autumn went to her bedside and held her frail hand. Safrina had dainty hands that would have been very lady-like except for the calluses from years of hard work. Safrina was as dark as a cocoa bean. Years in the Carolina sun made her darker still. Autumn was suddenly struck by the contrast of her own hand to Safrina's. Autumn's hands were soft, youthful, and full of life. Safrina's were rugged, wrinkled, and leaving life. Autumn looked up to Safrina and met her gaze. Her eyes were hazel at one time she said. Now, they were an eerie pale green as a result of age. All Autumn could manage was, "I'm here Mammy."

Safrina's frail form managed to laugh at the running joke the two of them had. With that, Safrina motioned Autumn closer to her. Autumn leaned over. "I'm done. Don't let them be sad. I've had a wonderful life. I dun more than I could have dreamed or dared. I'll always watch them. Always."

"I know Safrina. It's time for you to leave us. Don't worry. I'll tell them." Autumn choked back tears and put on a convincing smile.

"They are always gonna be safe. You need to be careful. Dark times are coming. Powerful. You ain't ready yet but there'll be help. You listen. Believe it. Trust it. It's the only way. You'll know when and how. Remember, we came from it. We go back to it." With that, Safrina slipped out of this world and across the veil. It was her release and her reward for a lifetime of hardships and struggling. Autumn wept only for a moment out of selfishness. She was crying for herself. Safrina had been a wise and beautiful soul Autumn was blessed to meet. Safrina had taught everyone that the place where we were all going made the burdens and struggles of this life meaningful. Autumn stopped crying. She could not imagine her life without this beautiful soul. Now, she would have to try.

When Autumn left the room, the women who gathered to take care of Safrina rushed Autumn outside so they could bathe her and pray for her. It was a custom that could be found in many ancient traditions. They washed Autumn to cleanse her from the "stench of death" and prayed so death would leave her. As Autumn sat on the porch, the other people asked if Safrina told her anything. They wanted to know what Autumn heard when she was with Safrina. Autumn told everyone gathered there what Safrina's final message to the people she loved was.

"You get back to that handsome devil Boyd. See that this day isn't ruined for your friend." Fanny's tone suddenly brightened as she turned to Kendra. "It was a joy to finally meet you. I'm sorry it had to end this way. You have a good visit and come back when all my flowers are blooming." With that, Fanny planted a kiss on Kendra's cheek and ran off to go help the others.

"What the hell just happened back there?"

"I am *so* sorry. I would not have gone over there if I had known that she was so bad. I just saw her two day's ago but I guess when you are somewhere between ninety and three thousand, your health can turn on a dime. I hope this has not ruined your day?"

"You are *so* completely missing the point," Kendra shouted. "How many times in my life have I had someone near and dear to me die? I feel bad but I am certainly not going to have some sort of life crisis because of what just happened. I am freaking out by what you said to those people back there."

"I have no idea what you are talking about?" Autumn was leading the way back out of the housing complex.

"Hello? Safrina didn't *say* anything. She was completely unconscious the whole time. That didn't seemed weird to you?"

Autumn began to laugh because she had become completely accustomed to these sorts of things. "What do you want to know? Where should I start?"

"You are being so calm about this. Okay. What you did represents *what* to those people?"

"Well," Autumn began hesitantly because she did not know exactly how to explain to Kendra what she had just done. "There is energy in the universe. We happen to call it God. We belong to that energy. The only thing that separates us from the energy is our body and this world. I can call on it when I need it and when I don't necessarily want it. In other words, Safrina was crossing over to 'the other side'. The veil between the two worlds is particularly thin when someone is dying. So, I could hear every word Safrina was telling me."

The look of astonishment was all over Kendra's face. It took her a moment to come up with her next question. "We know this because of faith but we can't actually see it, right?" Kendra had stumbled upon a logical line of questioning and was getting less astonished.

"Well, most people can't. I can." The wind was blowing through Autumn's long deep brown hair as they sped along the road back to the McFarland farm.

"Uh, huh and how long have you been able to do such things?" The astonishment was replaced with cold hard cynicism.

"Stop acting like I'm a person from outer space! I have been able to do those things probably all of my life. It wasn't until I came here and the weird haunting started happening that I couldn't ignore it anymore. Before, I just thought I had a really over active imagination. The Gullah people, like Fanny, have guided me. What was happening to me was real and my faith would always comfort me no matter what happens. Safrina had the same 'gift'. It was seen as a blessing in her community and she was greatly respected for it. For me, being from white middle-class suburbia, people would have not have seen it as a blessing but an oddity. That's why I was so open with Fanny's friends back there. Are you gonna be okay with it?"

Kendra sat back in the car seat and was silent for several moments. She took a long breath and asked, "What other things have you seen before coming down here?"

"I can give you several for instances but I don't know if I remember all of them. Is that enough?"

"Sure."

"When I was a little girl, I was always afraid to go upstairs at my Grandmother's house. I especially did not like going to the bathroom alone. I would always make someone sit at the bottom of the stairs. Everyone in my family dismissed it as just one of those quirky little kid things until I was old enough to tell them what I was afraid of. My grandmother's house had three bedrooms and the bathroom upstairs. The bedroom right across from the bathroom had been turned into a study. In that room, my grandmother had a curio cabinet with all her precious possessions: an old fashioned floor lamp, and a big stuffed chair facing the window looking out on the backyard. Why I was frightened to go use the bathroom was because there was a man that always sat in that chair who wasn't really there. I didn't know who he was or why no one else could see him. That frightened me. Having someone at the bottom of the steps made me think about the real people in the house rather than him."

Kendra smiled. "I think all children have something like that in their lives and we just don't know what it is. For me, it was my Grandma's house and the bedroom I slept in or, rather, didn't sleep in. I never knew why but the room always made my skin crawl."

"Yeah." Autumn agreed that children were all psychic. Most normal children grow out of it. Autumn continued. "There have been other things, too. When I was going to look at houses with my sister, we pulled up to this cute colonial brick home in a quiet neighborhood. As the car came to a stop, I looked up at the house and there was a short grey haired lady in a light blue dress standing at the door. I turned to the real estate agent and said 'I thought this house was vacant?' She turned back to me and said that it is vacant. When I looked back at the door, it was closed and no one was there. There was even a realtor's lock box on the door. I went in but I could not have my sister moving in there. It would have been too creepy."

"Wow that just sent goose bumps down my back. Don't those sorts of things frighten you?"

Autumn laughed, "Not all of my experiences have frightened me. Some have been really good experiences."

"Oh," Kendra's mood lifted a bit, "there's a story I'm gonna want to hear. Please, give me something that won't give me nightmares tonight."

"The summer after we graduated from high school, I had hooked up with an old friend. We started hanging out at some of the bars around Akron University. He was working with a guy who had a house near AU and wanted me to meet his friends from work. I wasn't really feeling up to it after working all day but his friend, Andy, got on the phone and convinced me to come over. I was driving over figuring that I'd go, meet everyone, play a hand of cards, and come home. When I got to the house, Andy swung open the door and announced with a big broad smile, 'You must be Autumn!' Before I knew what had happened, he had scoped me up in his arms in one gigantic bear-hug. The astonishing thing about Andy was the light that surrounded him when he opened the door. There was a blue green aura around him that had gold sparks jumping out from it. I knew that spending time with him was going to be fun and fleeting. I was right on all accounts. Andy was one of the best looking, creative, talented, passionate, and romantic men I have ever known in my life. When we kissed, it was like sticking your finger in an outlet but in a good way."

"Was he your first," Kendra leaned in, intrigued by what the answer might be.

"No, because of all the things I told you. He wanted. I wanted. However, I knew that nothing but pain and disappointment would come from it. It was great fun while it lasted. I do not regret any moment of it."

"That's cool. So, what do you see around Boyd Masters?" Kendra winked at Autumn. "I mean, are there any sparks coming from him?"

"You are incredibly nosey. Good thing you are my best friend or I'd be insulted." Autumn scolded.

"You had to know that I was eventually gonna ask. That's what best friends are for."

Autumn became contemplative when she started thinking about the question. "Did I hit a nerve?"

"No. No sparks for Boyd. I've seen red, blue, green, yellow, and yes, gold. Boyd's aura is very much like him. It is very close to his body and changes by day and by moment."

Now, Kendra seemed worried. "Is that a bad thing?"

"I guess I see how you could think that. Auras are weird. Andy's aura was almost like a neon sign. You would think that meant that it was stronger than Boyd's. The opposite is true. Andy's reflected him. He was reckless and out of control. Boyd is very much cautious and always in control. Part of what I love about Boyd is that he is such a hard person to read. I am constantly trying to tell what is going on with him. Most of the time, I have no idea. The rest of the time I am just plain wrong."

"Let's get back to your place. I have got a lot more to ask you but a glass of wine would go a long way in helping me understand all of this."

CHAPTER 7

▼

AN UNWELCOME GUEST

The days of fall in South Carolina are gentle and pleasant with gentle breezes and frequent but brief showers. Kendra and Autumn were on their way to get pumpkins and bales of hay for the big Halloween party until they had to post pone their journey out to Sampit because of the rain showers. The two raced from the house to the stables with rain ponchos on. Autumn borrowed the pickup truck and drove from the stables down to the abandoned cornfields to collect more essentials for a good Halloween party. Joe was in his usual cranky mood and grumbled something about Halloween being just an excuse for kids to get in trouble and eat too much candy. Kendra told Autumn that he was the only genuinely unpleasant Carolinian she had ever met. Autumn assured her that Joe was all bark and no bite. Autumn compared Joe to her dad. Mr. Hummel always assumed the worst in any situation. "Dad won no matter how things turned out. If everything was fine, no one remembered him being pessimistic. If it wasn't fine, dad could always claim he knew all along. The best way to get back at Joe is to kill him with kindness."

This was exactly how Autumn got Joe to surrender the keys to the pickup truck. When Kendra and Autumn had gotten to the barn near the cornfields, Kendra got a true sense of how massive the McFarland farm really was. Taking the main drive to the house from the interstate, all you could see were fields to either side of you. Not having spent much time on a farm in her life, Kendra had no idea what was growing in the fields. They drove for about a quarter of a mile from the house back out the main road and made a quick left onto a virtually invisible dirt road. The road ended at the corn and feed barn. It was a huge barn that stored the machinery necessary to farm large fields. In the loft, the farm manager stored all the little things necessary including the seed corn for the next year, fertilizers, and ladybugs. Two extremely large metal silos stood beside the barn. They held all the feed corn Autumn's herd would need until next year's crop was harvested.

Tom O'Sullivan was the manager of her farm division. He was in the barn with a few other workers getting the vehicles ready for storage and the next planting season. By Thanksgiving, all the farm hands but Joe and her ranchers would be done until March. Tom met the truck as it pulled up to the barn. He greeted Autumn with a smile, a big hug, and an almost unintelligible southern drawl.

"Do you always greet your employees that way," Kendra yelled as Autumn ran ahead of her. "And does Boyd know that you do?"

"Now, who is this beautiful Yankee?"

"This is …"

Kendra jumped in before Autumn could finish the introduction. "Hi, I'm Kendra and you are?" Kendra extended her hand with cute tilt of her head and a shy smile on her face.

"Tom. Tom O'Sullivan, miss. I believe you have just about the most beautiful green eyes I have ever seen."

"Why, thank you Mr. O'Sullivan," Kendra replied, trying to blush.

"Keep trying. Some day you might be able to get a little pink, you faker," Autumn whispered to Kendra knowing Kendra was far too worldly to blush at such a comment. "I'm going to go get the stuff. I'll be right back."

"I'll go help you, hon." Tom went to follow Autumn to the barn. Kendra shot a look in Autumn's direction that said she better not even accept Tom's offer.

"No, no. I'm sure Rob or one of the other guys would be more than happy to help me." Autumn made sure to shoot an evil glance in Kendra's direction while she said that.

As Autumn made her way upstairs, she heard Ian and Rob talking. "Hey, mister, what are you doing here?"

"Rob and I are planning on creating a souped up tiller over the winter. We want to see how fast and cool we can make one of those babies without killing anyone or completely wrecking the tiller."

"Sounds dangerous, I'd like to talk you out of it but …"

"You know it wouldn't do you any good. I'll be up at the house in about an hour. What do you need me to do?"

"Well, you remember the pit out by the out buildings?"

"Yeah, the one they found the old plantation bell buried in. What are you doing with that?"

"I figured that would be the perfect place to build the bonfire. Would you mind building it while we go out to pick up the last few supplies for the party?"

"Not a problem. Hey, maybe Boyd could help me out. He's probably built a few bonfires in his day." Ian turned to Rob and punched him in that you-know-what-I-mean guy way. "After I help Boyd set up his Haunted Trail. The kids should get a real kick out of it."

Autumn sighed, "I told him that I didn't want him to make it *too* scary. I can see that really meant a lot. Promise me that it won't be too scary."

"Come on, how are the boys gonna get any action with their girls at this party if we don't have a haunted something?" The look on Autumn's face made Ian hastily add, "I promise nothing *too* scary."

Autumn spied the boxes of dried corn and bundles of cornstalks. "Thank you. For your information, there will be a DJ there all night. Any action can happen on the dance floor. I have to go get the hay and pumpkins but I'll be back to make sure you keep your promise."

Rob chuckled, "I guess Boyd will probably be the first one to get any action on the trail."

"Very funny, Rob. Want to help me with these things," asked Autumn.

"Sorry, Autumn, you know I didn't mean anything by it." Rob was a shy man who was generally not very outspoken. Rob and Ian had become friends in the last few months. They found each other in the same monster truck chat room. It has been motor head heaven ever since for the two of them.

"I know you were just playing, Rob. No harm. Hey, you and Katie still are coming to the party."

"We wouldn't miss it. Folks 'round here are not that big on Halloween. It'll be our first Halloween party since we were little kids." Rob sauntered over and lifted two of the very heavy boxes of corn easily. Autumn struggled mightily with just one.

By the time Autumn made it back down to the truck, Kendra was in full flirt. She was twirling her hair and flashing Tom her you-are-the-most-interesting-person-on-the-face-of-the-earth smile. Once Autumn arrived with the last of the corn supplies, Tom had Kendra over his head. No doubt he was showing her that he was not lying when he said he was strong. "I hate to break this up but we've got a lot to do today. Fred's been nice enough to give us all the big pumpkins and unused hay he has. We have to get to Sampit and back with all the stuff today. So, I'll see you at the party, right Tom?"

"You sure will. He's coming as my date," Kendra announced.

"Well, okay then. Thanks again for all the supplies."

As the two made their way back up to the main house, they discussed Tom O'Sullivan. Autumn thought Tom was not Kendra's type. Kendra disagreed. Tom being a redhead with stunning green eyes was exactly her type. What was probably freckled skin in his youth was now one big freckle all over his face from living and working outside in South Carolina. Kendra pointed out the fact that he was very muscular from that type of work. That was rarely, if ever, bad in her book. Autumn again thought he was not her type because he worked on a farm and wore jeans to work every day. Eventually, Kendra got the impression that Autumn thought she was a snob.

"I don't think you are a snob. I'm just saying that you have never been on a farm until I inherited one and probably had not thought much about farms before that. Plus, you live in a world where everyone looks forward to the day they'll be wearing suits and carrying leather attaché bags to work. It is just hard for me to imagine you being attracted to someone like Tom. He is one of the nicest people I have ever met and very ruggedly good looking. I just pictured your type to be more shirt and tie than dirt and sty."

"You're probably right," Kendra agreed. "We probably won't be able to click on an intellectual level but it's only for one night. Plus, I don't want to be the only adult at the party without a date."

"Now, that is where you are wrong. Tom is no country bumpkin. He was born and raised on a farm in South Carolina but he has his master's degree in business management. It just so happens that the business he loves to manage is my agricultural division. He is very good with a buck."

"You have divisions here?" Kendra said without realizing the implied insult.

"Hello. I am president, CEO, and owner of McFarland Enterprises. Of course, like any other corporation, I have divisions: agriculture, tourism, financing, and investment. That's how all this keeps going."

"Sorry, I thought you were the one who got all the money without actually being responsible or aware of the ins and outs of the business." Kendra's apology was sincere. "A brain and good looks? Saturday night could turn out to be a real treat."

After unloading the corn supplies back at the house, they set out for Sampit. The journey out took Autumn and Kendra into the middle of the agricultural area of Georgetown County. The interstate was awash in empty fields dotted by the occasional church here and there. Autumn explained to Kendra that if this were June or July, the empty fields they were passing would be filled with tobacco or soy beans. Fred was the gentleman who ran the rice farming on the McFarland Farm. Fred had a small garden that he worked on his own land simply for the love of farming. The last crop to be harvested was the gourds. Fred also grew straw because it will grow on his depleted fields. He uses it to cover the rice patties in early winter through spring. He heard about the Halloween party and offered the pumpkins he grew to fertilize his depleted fields. The vines took very little from the dirt but the gourds returned many necessary nutrients back to the soil when properly composted.

Fred managed a bumper crop in both pumpkins and hay thanks to the wet summer. Autumn was welcome to as many bales of hay and pumpkins as she could get in the flatbed of the old truck. The only catch was that she comes to pick the pumpkins herself. The hay was already sitting at the edge of the field when she and Kendra got there. They hopped out of the truck and into a field awash with beautiful and enormous orange pumpkins. Autumn thought the best course of action was to each take a side of the field, picks only the most beautiful ones, and work their way toward each other. Before too long, the bed of the pick-up truck was full of hay and pumpkins. They made their way back to Autumn's place to unload all the pumpkins then themselves onto the nearest soft piece of furniture they could find.

Later that day as Kendra and Autumn were recovering in the living room, they heard Boyd and Ian laughing and joking all the way up the front steps. By the time the boys had reached the front door, Kendra and Autumn were standing there. The girls had decided that Boyd and Ian had not worked hard enough setting up their part of the party. Before Ian and Boyd could come in and rest, they helped the girls hang the lights and set up the displays of pumpkins, cornstalks, and hay.

"What is the point of all this again," asked Boyd, still gassed about the haunted walk.

"Haven't you been paying attention? She's doing the best she can to make it seem like fall but without the chill and colorful leaves." Just as Ian finished replying to Boyd's question, Fanny pulled up with several full garbage bags in the back of her car.

"What are these?" Autumn wondered out loud.

Fanny hopped out of the car and tossed one of the bags over towards the pumpkins, hay, and cornstalks. When the bag finally hit the ground, it spilled open to reveal a colorful burst of orange, yellow, and red. Somehow, Fanny had managed to bring the last little touch of fall to the autumnal displays on this Carolina farm.

"Where in the world did you get these?"

"You both look stunned. It's not a good look for either of you." She gently reached over to close Boyd's mouth. "Close that, dear. People will think you're slow," she said with a little chuckle.

"Fanny, you always come through!"

"Doesn't South Carolina have fall leaves," Kendra asked.

"There are deciduous trees in South Carolina but there are not standing forests of them. Here, you'd almost have to pick them up by hand to get them from all the fallen pine needles and palmetto husks. People definitely don't have to rake leaves like back home," Autumn explained as she hoisted out the five other bags that Fanny brought.

"My cousin up in North Carolina lives far enough north that he has a whole yard full of these. The city officials made getting rid of them harder. He was more than happy to bring them down when he came to see my aunt last weekend. Now, you all have fun. Hopefully, my son will make it home for the party. See you all then. Oh, and Mr. Masters, I don't want to hear of any of my Sunday school kids having nightmares after taking your haunted walk. You hear me?"

"Nothing too scary, I promise."

After setting up the decorations and ensuring that the lights were going to stay up and work, Autumn drove over to a place on Route 17 to pick up some traditional Carolina BBQ. Carolina BBQ was not the kind covered in sticky sauce. It was more the way it was prepared and cooked that made it so delicious. Kendra made Autumn drive thru a fast food joint to get her food. Kendra insisted that there was no way she would eat the food from that place. Autumn argued it would be the best chicken and ribs Kendra could eat. Kendra argued there was no way she would eat food that came out of a cinder block garage with no sign or windows. The place only had a name so that it could be listed in the phone book. Boyd didn't understand what Kendra's problem was. Ian chuckled because he remembered a time when he felt the same way. He explained it to Boyd as best he could. Roughly, the same thing that allows southerners to wait forty-five minutes at a restaurant from the time they order their food until it arrives at their table without losing their mind. Northerners actually feel themselves go insane as their life was slipping by every minute they were forced to wait. It was just the difference in culture and lifestyle. Autumn said you either adapt, as Ian and Autumn had, or you lose your mind.

"What does that have to do with the food," Boyd insisted.

"Let's just say that unless I saw the Health Department's seal of approval hanging on the wall, a state license to operate a restaurant, and a building code inspection, I'm not eating anything they could serve up," Kendra said curling her nose up in disgust.

"Okay, but BBQ was invented here in the South. Where else are you gonna get food like this?" Boyd folded open the foil packages to reveal the tender chicken and meaty ribs held inside.

"BBQ was probably invented around the same time man found fire but you still have a point," Ian said as a little pork grease slid down the corner of his mouth.

"You are both right," Autumn added as she dished out the corn-on-the-cob and coleslaw. "The concept of the BBQ was invented in the South. It was the easiest way to feed a large gathering of people. When plantation owners threw a party, there was always something wonderful cooking on the spit. Most plantation owners were such avid hunters that it was usually whatever they had tagged on a recent hunting trip: pheasant, deer, elk, turkey, wild boar, or duck. However, it was the African-Americans who perfected the art of BBQ. Not a white face in that place. That's why this stuff is so good. No one there to ruin the experience. That's what makes it so darn good. Kendra, my dad would eat this stuff every night if mom let him. He would disappear. I swear he was there feeding his face."

"That comment does not inspire my appetite. You know how your dad is," Kendra added.

"What's wrong with Mr. Hummel," Boyd asked looking over at Autumn with a knowing grin.

"Haven't you met Mr. Hummel," Kendra asked.

"I have but what does that have to do with food?"

"Oh, so you know what I mean. Did you go out to eat with them when you were in Barberton?"

"Yes."

"Did you happen to go to one of the chicken houses in town?"

"Of course, I was told you really hadn't been to Barberton unless you had a chicken dinner."

"Did you happen to notice how her father ate chicken?"

"No, I was too busy being confused by the hot sauce phenomena. How does he eat his chicken?"

"The man puts an entire piece in his mouth and pulls out bare bones: no meat, no fat, and no gristle. That is why his endorsement of this BBQ place doesn't inspire me. He doesn't seem the picky type when it comes to food."

"What are you people talking about," Ian interrupted between gulps.

"My dad or chicken houses?" Autumn laughed trying to hold on to her greasy fork.

"I've met your dad. What the heck is a chicken house?"

"A chicken house is a restaurant that serves chicken dinners," Autumn stated.

"But, they only serve chicken dinners," Kendra interjected.

"What is so special about chicken dinners," Ian asked seeming more confused than before.

"They serve chicken that is battered then fried in lard and served traditionally with French fries fried in lard, hot sauce, and coleslaw. Apparently, it was a thing started in Barberton by Russian and eastern European immigrants. Barberton, at one time, had more chickens living there than people because of cockfighting. It was apparently a huge sport at one time that people bet on. Now, Barberton is unofficially known as the chicken dinner capital of the world because of these chicken houses."

"Why chicken houses and not chicken restaurants?"

"The only explanation I can give you is that the first two were not restaurants but houses that served chicken dinners to larger and larger numbers of Barberton citizens. They are restaurants but the house moniker stayed."

"Okay. So, this chicken and fries are fried in lard. Why aren't the citizens of Barberton dying at exceptionally high rates from arterial sclerosis? That has got to be bad for you?" Ian finished his second serving of pork ribs.

Kendra fielded this question. "There are little old women in Barberton who eat chicken dinners once a week and have all of their lives. Yet, they live to be older than Moses. The only thing I can think is that they are genetically immune to cholesterol."

Kendra sounded so confident, Autumn hated to burst her bubble of knowledge. "Or the gallons of homemade wine they consume every day. These old ladies are old world. They have a glass of wine every night for dinner and one before they go to bed."

"You answered all his questions," Boyd laughed, "Now, answer mine. What the heck is hot sauce?"

"Yummy and it would go great with this BBQ," Autumn shouted. With that, they all laughed and finished eating.

"You know you still have quite a few pumpkins in the back of the truck, right," Boyd asked as he finished the last of his beer.

"Yeah, what are all those pumpkins for, Autumn?" Kendra asked as she took a little bite of the chicken. Her eyes lit up. Boyd knew they'd be having BBQ again before Kendra left.

"The local elementary school is having a pumpkin carving in the afternoon immediately after school. The kids and their parents are going to the cafeteria to carve pumpkins that cost a dollar, but I'm donating all the money to the PTO. There will be snacks, punch, and a judged contest of all the pumpkins. However, several of them are coming back here to be jack-o-lanterns for the party."

"Awesome, we get to carve pumpkins. I haven't done that since I was a little kid," Ian exclaimed.

"Then, you clearly don't remember how disgusting they are to clean out," Kendra scowled at the thought of it.

"That's part of the fun," Ian continued, his spirits not dampened by her comment. "Can we have scary ones?"

"Yes. As many as you want to carve."

Saturday night was gorgeous. The night was so clear that you could see every star in the sky. Since the farm was out so far, there was very little ambient light to block the view of the sky. The moon was not quite full but no one would have known from looking at it. It was what astronomers called a harvest moon. That was what they called it in the fall. The same moon in June is called a strawberry moon and in September is called a hunter's moon. The moon just appears a little more pinkish/orange than white. It added to the ambiance of the night. The trick-or-treaters turned out by the truckload. In fact, an hour into the trick-or-treating someone had to make a candy run to the local superstore to purchase more goodies. None of the kids finished with less than a pound of candy in their bags. The older kids were checking out the house, the DJ, and each other. The adults were all keeping their eyes open for any of the unexpected guests rumored to show up when there was a party at the McFarland farm. None of the corporeal guests were disappointed.

Shortly after beggars night ended, the tables were full of people enjoying the roasted hot dogs, hamburgers, marshmallows, popcorn balls, and candied or caramel apples. There was a dessert table set with pumpkin, apple, and pecan pie that no one missed. The DJ started the crowd dancing right after dinner. Before long, the little kids moved on to bobbing for apples and dropping clothespins in a mason jar while the teens had rediscovered the innocent novelty of spin-the-bottle. Just as Boyd was getting ready to start his guided haunted walks, the ghost-watchers in the crowd were pleasantly surprised to see a gathering of ladies in antebellum attire chatting under the live oak tree. There was also a group of gentlemen gathered on the piazza smiling and relaxing. Neither of these groups stayed very long. Some said they disappeared before their eyes. After that, Boyd had over thirty or forty people anxiously waiting in line for his haunted walk. Just before he set off with his first group, he changed into an old fashioned suit he thought embraced the history of the farm. It was only the second suit of any kind Autumn had ever seen Boyd in. He assured Autumn that it could be the only suit she'd ever see him in again.

Just before he left with his first group of tourists, Autumn called Kendra over secretly.

"Want to see something neat," she whispered to Kendra.

"Sure."

Autumn held out her hand in front of her and whispered, "Lumina incarnate." As she spoke the words, a ball of light formed slightly above her hand like a large firefly. It seemed as if the light was hovering above her hand. "Guide his way little light. Stay with him till I call you back." With that, the hovering ball of light flew over to where Boyd was and hovered just a few inches above his head. No one in the tour group seemed to notice because they had focused their attention on the sights they might see. The guide himself was too engrossed in scaring everyone.

"What *is* that," Kendra gasped.

"Isn't it cool? I found how to do it when I was with Fanny and the power went out. As old as she is, Fanny is still terrified of the dark. I was sitting with her one night this summer when we had one of those tropical depressions move in and just blow like crazy. I still can't imagine how a hurricane could be worse than those. They are so frightening."

"Anyway, I asked her where some candles were. She told me to hold out my hand, so I did. Then she said, 'Say Lumina incarnate'. I did. As I did, a little ball of light appeared to float just above my hand. She told me to tell the light to be my guide until the lights came back. It followed me everywhere I went in search of candles. When the lights came on, I thanked the little light, made a motion like I was popping a bubble, and the light went away. I thought it would be funny to scare Boyd on his own scare tour. I also thought it would be helpful if the battery went out in his flashlight. What's wrong now?" Autumn had suddenly noticed all the color had drained from Kendra's face.

"You," Kendra stuttered and stopped. "You made a ball of light just by saying a few words."

"See, that's what I thought too. Fanny said there is nothing magic about the words. It's just Latin for make light. The magic lies in the universe. I am not creating light. I am just calling on existing energy in this world to come together and make light for me. I don't even know how I do it."

"Don't you think that's weird," Kendra asked hesitantly.

Autumn laughed, "Are you asking if I am weird. I guess I am. I do think it's weird but very, very cool. Have you ever heard of the phenomena called swamp lights or marsh lights? Fanny explained that early colonist didn't know what they were seeing but they were Indians using these lights to move in secret. The slaves used them to light their way to freedom."

The night continued on with music, dancing, and food. The kids had to be pried away from all the games and food. Most of the adults were sure that the little Trick-Or-Treaters had more than their fill of all that the party offered. Even though it was around sixty degrees, parents everywhere must universally agree that there was something harmful in "the night air." It was probably just a tried and true expression parents used when it's time to get kids inside and to bed. The dance floor was packed with teens that seemed to be happy that it was cool this evening. They were either eating or dancing. Some had enlisted for Boyd's haunted walk. The groups for the walk had been steady since he started nearly three hours ago. No one came back in tears but there were lots of shrieks and hollers coming from the woods. When the groups made it back to the party, they were laughing at those who screamed, questioning the nerves of those who hadn't screamed, and thoroughly enjoying the spirit of All Hallows Eve.

Before Boyd set off with his last group, Autumn ran over to remind him that the ghost stories would be starting in half an hour. Boyd turned to a small group of teens waiting for another turn to go on the walk and announced that this would be the last crowd. The group was disappointed but Ian showed up with another plate of hot dogs and hamburgers. The teens were more than happy to relieve him of his tray of food. Boyd headed into the shadows of the woods. Ian went to make more food for the group Boyd would bring back scared and hungry. Autumn and Kendra went to set up the graham crackers, chocolate bars, and marshmallows for s'mores around the bonfire and ghost stories. Everyone would be invited to share a scary story but Autumn, Kendra, Boyd, and Ian would be the safety net in case no one wanted to tell stories.

Before the stories started, Kendra seemed a little nervous. Almost afraid to ask, Autumn said "What's up with you? All this Halloween stuff getting to you? You seem a little antsy."

Kendra looked up at the big farm house, "I was just thinking. I saw the ladies in the garden and caught a fading glimpse of the gentlemen on the piazza. I just wondered if …"

"If what?"

"If we will have any other unexpected guests visit us tonight?"

"I'm sorry. I always forget that I have had time to get used to this house. Please don't worry. What you saw tonight is just a glitch in time. Something happens reminiscent of an event in the past and time sort of blurs. What you are seeing is not actually ghosts but like a movie rerun. The people aren't really here anymore. Well, those people aren't and most of the real ghosts have moved on. I made sure of that after I was hospitalized last year for acute anxiety attacks. The ghost thing wears on your nerves if you live here. Are you okay with that?"

"Don't understand and don't care as long as there are no haunting presences in the house. I'm fine but that had to be a nightmare for you."

"It was and, remember, it caused my mom to move in until we got everything settled. I don't remember what was worse: the haunting or the nagging."

"Is she still a neat freak?"

"You mean does she still clean even imaginary dirt? Yes. Is your mom?"

"Probably till the day she dies and then some. She'll haunt me every night I go to bed without vacuuming the carpet so the pile all goes in one direction."

"And they wonder why we can't live with them! Oh, here comes Boyd."

"S'more time children," Boyd announced in a rather condescending tone. He had apparently out done himself on the haunted walk.

The DJ was tearing down for the night and, once again, there was food to be had. It didn't take long for people to congregate by the bonfire. Boyd slipped off to change out of his costume. He apparently had been in a suit as long as he could take. Before changing, he wrapped his arm around Autumn's waist and whispered, "Don't start without me." Once the lights on the dance floor were off, all that was left was the eerie glow from the bonfire, the almost-full moon, and jack-o-lanterns. The atmosphere was perfect for ghost stories. The guests happily shared their ghost stories. So, the hostess and her cronies sat back and enjoyed the stories. The younger kids told all the cliché ghost stories preadolescents tell: the man who lost his arm and replaced it with a sickle, hook, or claw. Take your pick. One girl told the story of two guys driving stag to a dance. They picked up a girl along the way who was heading to the dance. The next day, they discovered the girl had died many years ago walking to school for a dance. The more stories told the more people wanted to tell stories. Just into Katie's story of a white ghost dog that wanders the highway with hell fire in its eyes, Autumn stood up abruptly. She turned quickly away from the group and walked towards the dance floor. As she reached the table where the DJ had been, she could see someone walking towards her from the drive. Before she could see who it was, something inside told her who it was.

Trying to avoid a scene, Autumn casually walked to meet the shadowy figure before he got too close or entered the party area. The person in the shadows slowed his pace when he saw her approaching. Autumn kept her voice low but the disdain was evident. "What are *you* doing here?"

"You are certainly going to have to work on your 'southern charm'."

"Seriously, what are you doing here?" Autumn was not backing down.

The man brushed past her and into the light of the dance floor. "This is where the Halloween Party is, right? I purchased a ticket to a Halloween Party being held at this address."

"The party is just about over and you are not welcome. I will reimburse you the cost of your ticket." Autumn stepped in front of the man with her hand extended to collect the ticket.

Gently, he took her hand and pressed it to his lips. The only reason Autumn did not jerk it away or slap him was to maintain a low key. "What's going on over there," the man asked, focusing his gaze on the ball of light sitting just over Boyd's head.

Autumn quickly made a motion with her hand. She had hoped it was subtle. The man noticed her motion. "You have become very talented. Do *they* know how talented you are?"

"I have no idea what you are talking about? The party is over for this year and you are not welcome here. Please let me reimburse you the cost of the ticket."

"No thank you, I think I would like to join the fun over at the fire." With that, he strolled over towards the group still wildly sharing their stories.

When Autumn reached the fire side, Ian slid next to her after setting out the last of the food. "Who's the party crasher?"

"No one."

"You want me to get rid of him," Ian asked. The platter he was carrying had hardly touched the table before every scrap of food was gone.

"No. He's fine. The party's almost over. Just ignore him."

"Okay but if you change your mind ..."

"I won't."

No one was aware of Ian and Autumn's conversation. No one even seemed to have noticed another person joining the ring. They were all too focused on listening and enjoying themselves. Ian did move over to sit next to the man who had arrived at the witching hour. Autumn set her gaze on anyone and anything except the stranger. She knew he was staring intently at her with a wicked smile on his face.

When the stories were over, Autumn stood and graciously thanked everyone for coming. She hoped they all had a wonderful Halloween. At the witching hour, she sent everyone home with a warning to keep an eye to the sky for any last minute spells that might be cast. Finally, she told them how their donations to the library would be a gift that kept on giving once the new building opened. The fire slowly ebbed out. Ian and Boyd wanted to put out the candles in the jack-o-lanterns but Autumn stopped them. Each one had a votive candle inside that would burn out. It seemed appropriate that they burn out as would "All Hallows Eve". Everything could wait until morning. The guys were too high on all the fun they had to just sit still and talk so they went into the house to get a round of drinks. Kendra went on a walk with Tom. It was the first time Kendra and Tom had been really alone all night.

Autumn found herself alone in the company of the few remaining guests including the last guest. Jim was his name. Autumn met him years ago as a freshman in college. Jim had been a senior and member of the SAE fraternity. Their encounters had been memorable but fleeting. Autumn never gave Jim another thought after he graduated. Now he was sitting at a table watching her every move with a smile. He seemed to want her attention but did not seek it out directly. After what seemed to be an eternity, Boyd and Ian returned with a small cooler full of adult beverages. Kendra strolled back dreamy eyed and smiling. Autumn's attention needed a change. She ran over to meet Kendra. "Well, is it love?"

"Don't be obvious," Kendra said. "You know me. I don't fall in love. I examine the facts on both sides and make an educated ruling."

"Oh, so that's a yes."

Kendra's step staggered as they both giggled like twelve year olds. "It's something in the air down here or maybe it's the accent. You and I have always been suckers for men with accents. Did you see his green eyes?"

"And the red hair. I'd love to have you closer than Ohio. I do know what you mean about the air down here. You don't expect it but you're really happy you found it. Are you going to see him tomorrow?"

"Are we talking about Tom and me or you and Boyd? Yeah. He said there was some work to be done at the barn tomorrow but he'd be done by lunch. We are going to go out for lunch. Is that okay with you?"

"I told you, I'd love for you to be my new neighbor."

"You keep saying that but Boyd's the only other person out here in the sticks."

"You're right; Tom is the closest thing I have to a neighbor outside of Boyd. Tom bought one of those stately homes in downtown except it's a real fixer-upper."

"Really, I would have thought …"

"He'd live out in the sticks on his own piece of land. Nope. He grew up on a farm. The house he bought had once been a single family home, then a doctor's office, an apartment building, and a badly done bed and breakfast. The owners who aspired to running a bed and breakfast were hard working but had no idea financially what it was going to take to restore the home. Fortunately for Tom, they had done almost 90% of the destruction. That meant he got to do the fun stuff. He is an excellent carpenter."

Boyd walked over and handed them each a cold beverage, "You talking about Tom?"

"Yeah, Kendra's in lo-o-o-ove," Autumn cooed.

"If you tell him that, I will hunt you down," Kendra said firmly to Boyd.

Boyd laughed while walking back to the tables, "I believe you. I won't tell him anything but I'll tell you something. Tom is an avowed bachelor. Loves the ladies but doesn't have much faith in relationships."

"Isn't that pretty much every man," Autumn said looking straight at Boyd.

"Hey, that hurts."

"Where's Ian," Autumn asked.

"He was just making sure all the outbuildings were secured and that the fire had enough sand on it. Here he comes."

"You drink them all," Ian asked looking for a beer. "What's everyone talking about?"

"Tom," they replied in chorus.

"Nice guy. Speaking of guys, what's up with that guy," Ian asked looking at Autumn.

"What guy," Kendra and Boyd asked.

"Don't know," Autumn replied suddenly becoming more somber.

Boyd put his hand on her shoulder, "You know him?"

"Sort of."

"What do you mean," Boyd asked. "An old boyfriend maybe?" He reached over and elbowed Ian.

"Ha, ha," Autumn said dryly.

"Hey, I was just kidding around but you're not. What's up?" The concern was obvious in Boyd's voice.

"Nothing. I'm just too tired. I think everything went well tonight and everyone had a really good time. I just want to leave it at that."

"Then, I think it is time to say goodbye to this guy, wouldn't you say Ian?"

"Sure but in a friendly *southern* way. Mind if we take him a beer?"

Autumn was so grateful that the boys were there. She really wanted to end this night on a positive note. "Go right ahead."

As Boyd and Ian went over to the table, Jim stood to shake hands with the men bearing beer. Just as Boyd introduced himself, Jim leaned around Boyd to look over at Autumn. The three sat down to enjoy their beers and talk. Before long, they were laughing and joking like long lost friends. Boyd was very protective of Autumn but was also southern. As with all things, southerners take their time. Boyd was going to get to know Jim before he decided how he would kick him out. Ian was also very protective of Autumn in a big brother sort of way. He, however, was not southern and knew the ultimate goal was to make it clear that Jim should leave. Their approach would be to buddy up to the guy and let him know as the beer went down. Both men would achieve their goal, but it would not happen quickly.

"This is going to be awhile," Autumn moaned as she tossed Kendra another drink. Autumn sank into one of the chairs while she flung her feet up on another chair. "Did you have a good time?"

"I had the best time. Tom was wonderful and the party was wonderful. You remember Halloween parties when we were teens?"

"We'd spend weeks thinking of the perfect sexy costume, go to the parties, dance, and …"

"Nothing," they exclaimed in chorus.

"This really was a great party. Your mom would be proud of you."

"That reminds me, I need to call her tomorrow. She'll want to know how everything turned out."

Kendra walked back to the house while Boyd and Autumn paid the DJ and said goodbye to Ian.

Autumn nestled into Boyd's shoulder. Boyd gently placed a kiss on her lips. "I guess I didn't heed your Halloween advice."

"My Halloween advice?"

With a smirk on his face, Boyd said, "Didn't you warn about spells cast during the witching hour?"

Autumn slid her hand into Boyd's and led him back to the house. Upstairs, a cool breeze blew through the window. Autumn went over to close the window. Boyd followed. Autumn felt his strong warm hands gently move from her waist down the contours of her hips and thighs. She took a slow deep breathe to drink in this moment as Boyd's hands caressed her abdomen. Boyd leaned down and began kissing the nape of Autumn's neck. The heat from Boyd's body seemed almost as intense as the touch of his hands. Clearly, he had been waiting for this moment as long as she had. There was no hesitation or second thought as Autumn turned to face Boyd. He kissed her fiercely as she pressed her body to his. Tonight, only the two of them existed. Autumn melted into Boyd willingly. Passion and love became one.

Autumn felt warmed by the love of the handsome man sleeping peacefully next to her. She could not help but smile when she looked at him. Boyd Masters was a powerful man both in personality and physique. That was what made him irresistible. Mrs. Hummel described him perfectly: a real *bad* boy who was a *real* good man. That was Boyd. His mood set the tone for everyone around him. Occasionally, he was easy going and could laugh. Most of the time, his mood made him cast a weary eye on the rest of the world. He was not a pessimist. He learned that he was his own best friend and his own worst enemy. Other times, Boyd could be so intense about whatever he was feeling that energy just emitted from him. Those times, people simply left him alone except Autumn. She was drawn to him in those moments for better or for worse because that was when she was seeing the real Boyd Masters. He could be dangerous but he could also be amazing. Those moments were when Autumn would hear him put into words what his heart was feeling and the words took her breathe away every time.

She gazed into the clear night sky at the large beautiful moon that bathed the ground below in an eerie light. It was Halloween night, the most magical night of the year. The party had been absolutely perfect. Boyd hadn't over done the "haunting". The guests appeared to have a wonderful night. She thought nostalgically back to being a kid at Halloween. This party would have been the best Halloween party she could have ever imagined. As she gazed sleepily out at the night sky, something floated past the moon. She saw a shadow streak across the ground. Autumn chuckled to herself as she thought, "Well, if I was one, tonight would be a perfect night for a midnight ride."

"Who are you," Autumn insisted. Rather than respond to her, Jim simply sat across the table smiling at her. "I don't know why you have come here," Autumn's temper was heating up. All the while, Jim just sat across from her smiling. Autumn was jolted awake by the phone ringing. Before she even found her voice, she answered the phone. In a half voice she croaked, "Hello?"

"You keep asking me and I'm not going to tell you yet. It was nice to be in your dreams, again. Get some rest."

Autumn was dazed and confused. She could not tell if she was dreaming or if she was awake. The clock on the night stand said 2:30A.M. Autumn figured she must have only been asleep for an hour or an hour and a half. Suddenly, she was overcome with anger and threw the phone across the room. From pure exhaustion, she slid back under the covers and fell back to sleep. Boyd rolled over and wrapped his arms around her. Fortunately, Boyd appeared to sleep through the phone call and the phone being thrown across the room.

When morning came, Autumn decided to cook. It was one of the things she did when she was upset. Kendra came down to an absolute feast of waffles, sweet rolls, bacon, and fruit salad. Autumn said half-heartedly, "Good morning, how would you like your eggs?"

"Back in the refrigerator, what happened?"

"Nothing, you don't want eggs?"

"Autumn, you can't cook and there is enough food here for several days. So?"

"So, I just thought it would be nice to have a big home cooked breakfast once while you were here. Now that I live over a thousand miles from my mother, I had to learn to cook. I don't *like* to but I can. Sit down and have something!"

"Oh," Kendra said. Being the daughter of a lawyer, Kendra was not rattled just because Autumn was shouting for no reason. "Does this have something to do with the phone call in the middle of the night? Who was it? I mean, calling at one or two in the morning?"

Autumn slumped down into a chair at the table with a great sigh. "You won't believe it. It was the guy Boyd and Ian chased off last night."

"Who? Oh! I remember the guy who came at the last minute to the party."

Autumn hesitated. She wasn't really sure how to start or if it really happened the way she remembered it. "Everyone had just gotten to sleep after a really busy day."

"Everyone," Kendra asked.

"Yes, *everyone*. Anyway," Autumn continued, "I'm not really sure if it was a dream or what. Here is what I remember. I had been dreaming and he was in the dream. I kept asking him all these questions. He wasn't answering any of the questions I asked. That's when the phone rang. I was very much in a fog having been asleep. He said to me that he wasn't going to answer my questions yet. Then he said that it was nice to be in my dreams again." Just thinking about it made Autumn angry all over again. Not only was she angry but she felt violated. These feelings were not new. Back in college, Jim would appear clearly in her dreams. The next day, he would stop her and finish the conversation they had been having in her dream. Other times when Autumn would be at the house, Jim would just sit starring at her with his wicked grin. He had even spread a rumor around the house that Autumn was a white witch. Autumn wrapped her hands around her cup of tea and pulled her legs up onto the chair.

"Wow. I think no matter what, it's weird and creepy. What the heck is with him saying 'Nice to be in your dreams again.' What is that all about? Who is this guy? There has got to be more to him." Kendra filled a plate full of all the wonderful food as she suddenly became very concerned about this fellow.

Boyd bounded down the stairs just as the phone rang. Once Boyd saw the table sagging under the weight of food, he would not have heard a nuclear explosion let alone the phone ringing. Autumn took the phone out into the dining room before answering it.

"Hello."

"Were you able to sleep last night," Jim asked.

Autumn walked briskly out into the entrance hall before answering. "I don't believe that is any of your business. What do you want?"

"Is that anyway to speak to a friend?" Autumn shuddered a little. Consciously or unconsciously, Autumn possessed a talent for knowing a lot about a person simply by meeting them. This man frightened her because she got nothing from him. Autumn got no negative emotions from him that could trigger her fear. The complete absence of anything good or bad concerned her.

"I wanted to see an old friend. Is that so wrong?"

"We were never friends and yes. Everything you do is always wrong." Autumn felt like a mouse being toyed with by a cat. The mouse meets its doom only when the cat has tired of playing with it. Nothing about this was pleasant.

"What did I ever do to you to deserve such hostile treatment?" The man paused and laughed a little. "You are a very talented lady. Most people don't understand your talent and even fewer properly appreciate your talent but I always have. Join me for lunch this afternoon so we can discuss this in more detail."

Autumn was taken back by Jim. In one breath, he asked her to lunch and mentioned her "talent" that she knew little about and even fewer knew she had. "If it will get you out of my life, I will meet you at twelve-thirty at Litchfield Beach and Golf Resort. Do you know where that is?"

"I'm sure I can manage."

"Okay. Then I will see you there, Mr. Renault."

Jim chuckled again. "Thank you for your time Ms. Hummel."

Autumn walked into the kitchen where Boyd sat gulping down a glass of milk. He kissed her quickly and shouted as he bounded out the door, "I need to get home. Call you later. Love ya."

Wiping the milk off her cheek, Autumn smiled and yelled after him, "Love you too!"

Autumn sat down and told Kendra about the phone conversation she just had.

"I do wonder which one of us is more bullheaded. If you are not back by three, should I call the police?"

Autumn laughed, "No, just give 'Bo and Luke' a ring. Boyd and Ian are all the protection I need. When are you going on your lunch date?"

"Oh, shoot!" Kendra jumped up and looked at all the empty plates. It was almost as if she forgot about her lunch date. "I have got to get ready. You, be careful. How hungry do you think I am going to be in three hours after this big fat feast you laid out! That was just so wrong of you on so many different levels."

"Look at it this way; you can eat like a bird. Won't he just think you are the perfect lady?" Autumn turned away trying not to laugh.

Kendra threw a dish towel at her and pretended to storm off, laughing the whole way up the steps.

The Litchfield Beach and Golf Resort was a landmark she passed many times traveling to and from Georgetown but had never been there. Golf happens to be a sport that no one in her family played. She never had any reason to visit "The Oldest Resort in America". Autumn turned into the gatehouse and asked where the restaurant, Webster's Low Country Grill and Tavern, was on the resort. She looked at her wrist watch. It was already twenty-five minutes after twelve. Autumn pulled in front of the restaurant and gathered herself casually out of the car. As she approached, Autumn kept an eye out for Jim. There was no sign of Jim. Autumn checked with the hostess to see if he left word for her. Autumn informed the hostess that she would be in the bar if Jim happened to show. Their cat-and-mouse game continued. Autumn wanted the upper hand by being late. Jim had won this round by being later. She giggled as she thought, "I can't remember when I have wanted a meal to be over as badly as today!" Half way through her drink, Autumn turned to see Jim standing and talking to the hostess. As if he knew she was there, he turned to her and waved. Autumn gathered her drink and tipped the bar tender before joining Jim.

"So sorry," he smirked. "Have you been waiting long?"

"Oh, no, I was running incredibly late. I thought I had missed you but decided to have drink before making the drive back home. How are you?"

"Starving, let's go eat."

Autumn was surprised. Jim's mood was far less intimidating than she remembered. So far, Jim had not given her any reason to suspect anything. The hostess sat them at a table that looked out across some of the golf course and out to the sand dunes. The scene outside the window could have been the picture on a post-card from South Carolina. When they had been seated, Jim asked Autumn if she had ever been to this restaurant. She explained that with all the fantastic restaurants closer to home, she had not been to this one.

"That's too bad. I was hoping you could recommend something. By the way, what is 'low country' anyway? I've seen it advertised in many of the restaurants around here."

Autumn chuckled because his sincerity completely caught her off guard. "You've never been to South Carolina?"

Jim shook his head.

"Well, it is many things," Autumn started. "This area of South Carolina is traditionally called the low country because it sits at or slightly below sea level. Low Country cooking is the food that is associated with this region. See," she reached over and pointed to the menu. In italics at the bottom of the menu, it announced that all meals were served with a basket of hushpuppies. She then reached over to the side dishes which lists almost any and every kind of grits as a side. "Really, it's old fashioned comfort food. They just have added a gourmet flare to it."

"Okay. That's fair but what the heck is a grit."

Autumn looked at him quizzically because she had no idea if he was serious or not. "You don't know what grits are?"

"This is the first time in my life that I have ever been in the South let alone in South Carolina. No, I have no idea what a grit is."

"The grit is the hard pit in a kernel of corn. I have no idea how they make it but they get rid of the shell and the meal of the corn. All that is left is the starchy little gritty thing. They boil a bunch of those in water or sometimes milk and, there, you have grits. I love them."

"Well, I guess I will truly not have experienced Low Country cooking without them. Since everything on the menu is served with them as a side, how can I not."

The afternoon passed pleasantly as they enjoyed their lunch. Autumn found out that Jim was now a successful business man with a large finance firm in Boston. He was living in Plymouth. There was currently no one in his life but he was very busy trying to find someone. Jim and Autumn were finishing their sweet tea when Jim asked if she would like to take a walk along the resort's boardwalk. So far, the meeting was more enjoyable than Autumn thought possible. Autumn still had enough northern blood in her to be comfortable on mid-sixty October days. The two split the bill and the tip. Jim led the way out to the small boardwalk between the golf course and the beach.

Things quickly changed when Jim said, "So, you have a gift."

Autumn turned to Jim and asked what he was talking about.

"You know, your 'abilities'." His smile did not waver or change.

Pretending not to feel the old awkwardness, she asked what he meant but her voice sounded a little less sure.

"I could not come to you in your dreams if you didn't have it. Plus, it looks like you have progressed. Nice ball of light." Jim sounded the same but when Autumn looked at him, chills ran up and down her spine. There was something wicked behind those pale ice-blue eyes.

"You know what," Autumn said indignantly, "I didn't appreciate you doing that." Autumn surprised herself. She had no idea she could sound so stern while trembling inside.

"Doing what," Jim smirked innocently.

"You know exactly what you did. I don't appreciate it."

"You don't appreciate it, huh?"

"What is that supposed to mean?" Without intending it, Autumn had fallen into his game. "What are you doing here, anyway?"

Jim's tone did not change through the entire exchange. If anything, he became more serene. Someone listening to this conversation would question the reason for Autumn's severe tone. "Let's grab a seat over there and I'll tell you." The bench faced the sand dunes and the ocean. Autumn was grateful for the view. This was her sanctuary. The ocean had a powerful calming effect on her. The wind gently blew the sea oats on the dune as the sun began its early descent toward the horizon. "You don't like me, do you?"

"It's not that I don't like you. It's just that," Autumn paused because she didn't know quite how to explain the way Jim made her feel. "Every time I look at you, I get an icy chill that runs over me. You look like the cat that swallowed the canary only you have a couple yellow feathers sticking out of your mouth."

Just as Autumn said that, Jim looked over at her. She had expected him to laugh or be hurt but that was not what happened. When he looked at her, he was no longer grinning. He had a very angry look on his face and his eyes had completely gone sallow. If she hadn't known any better, Autumn would have sworn that Jim's blue eyes suddenly became jet black. "You think this is a game. This is not a game. A silly girl playing with forces she doesn't even understand. How is it that you came to be one?"

Before he could say more, Autumn could no longer resist her overwhelming urge to flee. She made a dash back towards the restaurant when she heard a boom of thunder. It was Jim shouting her name. In a flash, he caught up with her. Just as he was about to reach out and grab hold of her, she turned around. Autumn reached into her pocket and threw a handful of gritty sea salt in Jim's path. Gali said Autumn would know when to use it.

"See. This is what you are. This is why I came to you. You are what I have waited for all my life. Jon McFarland knew it. Silly naive little girl, you don't even know the people whose land you now own. He knew what you were. I know what you are!"

Before Jim could say one more word, Autumn made it to her car and raced out of the resort's front gate. Autumn didn't even know what happened nor did she care to know. She did know that would be the last time she would willingly see Jim or talk to him. The man she saw on the boardwalk scared her to the foundation of her being. Autumn set off for Fanny's because she did not want Jim coming to the farm where her friends may be. She called Tom's cell phone to ask him not to let Kendra go back to the house alone. Fanny was the only one who could possibly believe her, understand her, or help her in this frightening situation. After calling Tom, Autumn looked down to see her hands shaking violently. Tears had been pouring down her face, leaving the front of her jacket streaked.

Fanny stood in her front yard pacing when Autumn quickly pulled into her drive-way. "I knew you were coming. Come on in." Fanny ran up to her and wrapped her arms around Autumn. She could feel her shoulders relax. If her mom could not be in South Carolina, Fanny was an amazing surrogate. Once inside Fanny's, Autumn sat down at the small table Fanny had in her kitchen.

"I put a kettle on," Fanny said while bustling over by the stove. "Tell me what happened?"

"How do you know something happened?"

Fanny suddenly stopped all her banging and clanging to look at her. They both laughed. "So, are you going to tell me now?"

Autumn gathered herself. She wanted to tell Fanny every detail of what happened during her encounter without emotion. Autumn did not want her emotions to prejudice Fanny's perception of the situation. When Autumn finished, Fanny sat down with hot cups of tea for both of them.

Fanny looked pensive. "Hmmm."

Autumn took a sip of tea and smiled at Fanny. Any other person in the world says that when they don't know what else to say. Fanny said that when she had so much to say that she did not know where to start. Autumn sipped her tea and said a silent prayer of gratitude that Fanny was in her life.

"I'm afraid that boy is going to be trouble," Fanny finally said. "Men like him are like you only," Fanny paused. "Only their hearts are dark. They don't like people like you. Especially when people like you are women. See, only women with your gift have true power."

Autumn was not following Fanny. "Power? I don't even know what is wrong with me."

"Ain't nothing wrong with you. Look," Fanny continued. "Safrina was like you. Did great things for people. People came to her for everything. They sick, she'd tell 'em what was wrong and send 'em to the right kind of doctor. Great lady. As are all healers. Then, there be people like Dr. Dunja out in the swamp. He's like your boy, Jim. He got the gift but sells it to people wishing ill on others and cursing them. Waste when Safrina could just smile and Dr. Dunja's magic be undone!"

"So, what do I do?"

"Good lord, girl, I have no idea!" Fanny shook her head and settled back in the little wooden chair she sat in. "But you will. You will."

CHAPTER 8

▼

THE UNENDING KNOT

Three days passed since her violent meeting with Jim. Autumn was getting ready to drive Kendra back to the airport. Feelings swirled inside Autumn that made her feel heavy, tired, and sick all at the same time. Most of her emotions were caused by Kendra's leaving. When the two of them planned this trip long ago, ten days sounded like a wonderfully long visit. Now that the ten days were over, Autumn could not help but wonder how ten days could go by so quickly. Any time people from back home left the farm, Autumn felt as she did a year ago when she decided to stay in South Carolina. The tired feeling came as the realization that life would go on after Kendra left. How? She wasn't sure. The sick feeling is a new twist to a familiar situation. Autumn had said good-bye to many people from her childhood home. She hadn't felt like this when the others left. The only time she could remember feeling this way was shortly after the hangman appeared. That feeling put her in the hospital. It was a fear of being in the big old house, far from everything, and far from everyone while there was a threat to her. The Hangman had not actually been a threat in the end. Jim was a flesh and blood threat. After seeing the man, she was not sure he would not harm her. Autumn drove those thoughts to the back of her mind. Now it was time to say good-bye to her best, oldest, and dearest friend in this world.

"Well, did you have a good time," Autumn asked.

"Of course I did, I just wish …"

"I know. Ten days just wasn't long enough." Autumn smiled weakly hoping to hide her emotions.

"That's not what I meant," Kendra sounded serious. "I just wish you were coming with me. I don't feel right leaving you with that maniac around."

"Ken," Autumn put on a fake but convincing voice, "I chose this. It isn't easy. It hasn't been easy but I love my life here in Georgetown. No, it's not what I would have planned for myself but that's life. You just have to roll with it."

"Jim is *not* part of this life. Who the hell is he to come and terrorize you like that? I still think you should go to the police and get a restraining order. He is clearly unstable. When I think of what could have happened to you if you had met him anywhere else." Kendra shuddered at the thought. "You have got to call me every day for awhile, okay?"

"Okay, mom. Oh, speaking of mom …"

"I won't tell her. Good grief, she'll be moving in if I breathe a word about this. You take care and don't make me sorry that I didn't tell her."

"You can believe me. He will not get as much as a word with me on the phone. You remember my fine young man? If Boyd sees him or ever hears of him bothering me, he will hunt Jim down and … let's just say, it won't be good. So," Autumn added brightly to change the subject, "what's going to happen when you get back?"

"Dad will probably give me the third degree about when he was my age he couldn't take off for ten days. Then, he'll let me know how many things got screwed up by my not being there. I'll have to listen to mother explain how I abandoned her to satisfy my own personal needs. Yep, that's pretty much what I'm looking forward to when I get home."

Autumn and Kendra made their way to the tiny airport. They parked and Autumn helped Kendra get her bags to the gate. "And what about Tom," Autumn asked as the small jet pulled on the tarmac.

"Don't know? I guess only time will tell. He said he might come up for a weekend before the spring planting starts. Well," Kendra cast an eye to the plane, "I guess this is it?"

"I'll call you tonight. Have a really good trip. Tell everyone I said hello." Autumn hugged Kendra. There were some muffled crying noises coming from each of them. They parted and collected themselves to say in unison, "I'll see you later." Kendra and Autumn broke into a laugh mixed with tears.

Autumn stood at the window until she couldn't see the tiny plane in the sky. She reached up and placed her hand on the glass as if reaching out to hold onto something that was slipping away. After a few minutes, Autumn let the world slip back in around her. When she got back to the house, the loneliness inside swallowed her entirely. There were lots of things she could be doing. There were even more things that she *should* be doing. None of that seemed to matter. Here she was again, alone and so painfully far away from home. Autumn went into the house that seemed the size of a small hotel. After locking the door and setting the alarm, Autumn made her way over to the den and shut the pocket doors. Autumn slid behind the large mahogany desk and put her head on it. She closed her eyes and could smell the cigars smoked in the room. The wood felt cold against her cheek. In a quietness that was almost unbearable, Autumn asked aloud, "What is the big deal with your family? Everyone has secrets. Why me? Why you?" With a thud, she dropped her head back down onto the desk.

Surprisingly, no one answered. She let out a huge frustrated sigh and kicked her heels up on the desk. Hoping that the walls would talk or someone would appear to deliver the answer to her question, Autumn scanned the shelves of the room. As she searched the shelves of elegantly bound books, one book suddenly caught her eye. It was not an elegant book with a gold title on the spine. This book appeared ordinary and plain. There was something familiar about the black book sitting on the shelf right in front of the desk. The book, she thought, looked remarkably like the McFarland Family Bible Lillian had at the Rice Museum. Lillian guarded it as if it were cast of pure gold. The only time Autumn had been able to see the book was while Lillian stood guard. Autumn could rarely absorb or find anything useful in the book under those circumstances.

Autumn took the book off the shelf. As she did, a small slip of paper dropped to the floor. Bending over, she recognized the handwriting almost immediately. The note was from Mr. McFarland and addressed to her. It read:

Dear Autumn,

This is the book that will tell you what you need to know about my family. Don't be confused if you have met Lillian George. She thinks she has the McFarland Family Bible. If I know her, she guards it as if it were her child. You won't ever be able to get it from her.

I hope this is valuable to you. There are bound to be more questions than answers in this book. Please don't get discouraged. Remember, more than two centuries of people have lived in this house. Start here and then dig

... the attic, the basement, the closets ... every inch of this house has a story to tell. I hope you are well.

Yours truly,

Jon

"Great," thought Autumn in the silence of the vast house, "just what I need! I am alone and a little scared. Now, I can add completely freaked out. I can't imagine how he could have thought that this would be good!"

Autumn slipped the piece of paper back inside the front cover of the book and tossed it irreverently onto the desk. "Jon, where ever you are, I can't deal with this right now. Just let me alone, okay." Autumn slid open the heavy oak doors and made her way up to her bedroom. She pulled the shades and fell onto the bed. Autumn brought the old afghan her aunt had given her. She felt like a child for doing it but the blanket still smelled like her house in Barberton. Even though the afternoon was sunny and warm, Autumn retreated under the blankets of her bed and pulled the afghan over her head. "I don't want to be here anymore. I am sorry ... I ever ... agreed to ... stay. I ... want ... to ... go ... home!"

Giving in to the despair and loneliness of the moment and with the drain of saying good-bye to a friend, Autumn cried herself to sleep in the middle of the afternoon.

"I wish I hadn't fallen asleep," Autumn thought angrily as she woke to find the daylight had disappeared. She gave up naps when she was two. Not to mention the fact that she typically functioned on very little sleep. The day was lost because she was behaving like a child. She would probably be up all night from sleeping most of the day. Autumn hoisted herself up off the bed and grabbed the phone. Kendra promised to call when she got back to Ohio. There were no messages on the answering machine and no missed calls on the phone. Before she called Kendra's cell phone and home phone, she decided to flip on the TV. To her relief, there were no accidents involving a small plane. By the time she dialed Kendra's cell phone, she felt a little angry. Kendra left all distraught about leaving Autumn with Jim but didn't bother to call when she arrived safely at home. The cell phone rang twice before a rather incoherent voice answered.

"Where have you been," Autumn shouted. "I told you to call when you got home!"

"Oh, I'm so sorry," Kendra trailed off in a fog.

"What's wrong with you? Did you take another one of those pills your mom gave you?"

"Yeah, can you tell?"

"Well, where are you? Are you okay?"

"I'm … apparently … still at the airport. Wow, my head is really swimming. I thought I'd be okay as long as I didn't drink anything. That is the last time I listen to my mother! 'Here, take these. They'll make you feel better about being on an airplane.' Yeah, right! She forgot to mention that they would make me feel like crap afterwards. OUCH! Okay, no more yelling. It hurts too badly."

"I'm glad you are okay. I'm gonna hang up and call my brother to come get you."

"No! OUCH! Shhh. Don't do that. I'm okay. I'll call a cab."

"I want to be sure you get home in one piece and I don't think you'll feel like calling me once you get home. Just get your luggage and sit there. He can be there in twenty minutes."

"I'll never live this down if he comes and gets me, you know."

"You're not going to be able to live it down anyway. I have the perfect story to tell when you go spouting off about my one night drinking binge in college."

"It's good to have such a dear friend, vicious but dear. Shut up and call your brother."

"Love ya."

"Yeah, right."

Autumn stayed in bed for a few more moments wondering what she could do with the night. Just as she reached to put the phone back on its base, it rang. She flipped the phone over to check out who the caller might be. To her delight, it was Boyd.

"What are you doing tonight," Autumn asked.

"Well, up until twenty minutes ago, nothing," Boyd said flatly.

"What happened twenty-minutes ago," Autumn asked with a slight hint of alarm in her voice.

"Well, my mom just called," Boyd's voice was soft and low. Autumn was worried because of his tone. Boyd was usually energetic about everything. She was thrown by his tone tonight. "She called to tell me that dad is …"

"Oh, gosh, what is it," Autumn interrupted. She couldn't bear to hear Boyd so torn apart on the other end of the phone.

"He's going to try and buy the mare that won the Triple Crown this year and wants me to come along. You know, to make sure she's all she's been made out to be."

Breathing an enormous sigh of relief, Autumn gasped, "Oh, is that all."

"Is that all," he asked in the same hushed tone. "That is huge. First of all, it's not everyday that my dad buys a champion mare let alone one that has won the most prestigious title in all of horse racing. Second, he is asking for *my* advice. Do you have any idea how *huge* this is?"

"I'm sorry. You are right, it is huge. What enormous compliments to have him ask your advice? It would be amazing to own a horse of that breeding, if I had any idea what that meant. I just assumed from your voice that it was bad news. Sorry. So, where are you going and when are you leaving?"

"Well," Boyd hedged, "The thing is ..."

"Okay, if you are fine and your parents are fine, just spit it out." Autumn was still depressed but trying to put on a brave face.

"I know what you have just been through with Kendra leaving. On top of that, you seemed really thrown by that guy who showed up at the Halloween Party.

Autumn had not told Boyd she met Jim for lunch. The other events of that afternoon were too odd for even Autumn to understand. She hoped that her encounter at the restaurant would be the end of the story with Jim. "So, where do you have to go and when are you going?"

"The horse is owned by a businessman in Toronto. The horse is kept and trained at a farm just outside of Washington D.C. It's Manassas, Virginia. Dad has to meet him when he is going to be in Virginia. He'll be there tomorrow night into Sunday. I'm gonna meet dad there."

"Are you driving or flying?"

Boyd flew whenever possible but the small size of the local airport occasionally made driving faster.

"You know the airport. I would have to fly to Raleigh-Durham or Charlotte first. Each layover would be around an hour. I'm just going to drive. If I leave tomorrow morning, I should be there by three when dad gets in. Are you okay with this?"

"Of course I am," Autumn said cheerily even though she could feel the darkness coming over her again. "You want me to come over to help you pack? I could at least keep you company while you did your laundry."

Boyd laughed out loud. "How did you know I needed to do laundry?"

"Can I come over or not?"

"Okay. You might have to iron."

"I'll be over in ten minutes and I'll think about ironing." Autumn hung up the phone, leapt out of bed, and ran a brush through her hair. As she turned to leave the room, she grabbed her overnight bag out of the closet that was always packed for just such occasions. Her plan was not to come back tonight alone, if at all. The house seemed too big and lonely. Tonight she would be in the warm coziness of Boyd's log mansion and his safe arms. When she saw the lights of the Masters' farm, the sadness was beaten back by the love in her heart.

Twice in a span of twenty-four hours, Autumn said good-bye to important people in her life. The day was very damp. There was a chill in the air that went straight through. The sky never looked like the sun really showed up to do its job. Kendra wouldn't be back for several months, maybe even a year. Boyd, however, would only be gone for the weekend. That left her with three days and two long nights alone. Autumn puttered around the house a little bit. She was dusting in the living room when she glanced over to the den. Autumn decided to go take a peak at the book she found yesterday. Still sitting where she tossed it, Autumn dusted the pieces in the den and finally around the desk. As she did, she wondered why on earth Jon McFarland would have written her a letter when he never met her. Then her thoughts turned to the information she might be able to find in the book.

"Whoever heard of a family keeping two identical Family Bibles," she wondered to herself. After carefully looking at the leather cover and binding of this book, Autumn realized that there were not two copies of the book but one. Lillian's book was glue and machine bound with a manufactured cover. The book Autumn held in her hand was bound by hand stitching with a tanned leather cover. Lillian had a replica of this book. That aroused Autumn's curiosity further. There could be information in this book that the other book did not contain. After all, if one were copying the family history for possible public inspection, one might want to edit some of the information. Autumn tossed the dust rag aside and pulled up a chair. She started at the end of the book to find out more about her benefactor.

Several hours passed along with many generations of the McFarlands. The entries did not tell her anything more about Jonathan McFarland than she already knew. Several of the modern entries were written by Dorothy McFarland, the late wife of Jonathan. Her entries gave Autumn a sense of the woman she must have been. Everyone that had known her called her Aunt Dot. Autumn heard that she was a kind and generous person who would have done anything for anyone. There was an entry about the first day she came to the McFarland mansion. She was completely taken aback by the splendor and beauty of the house. Dorothy had been the daughter of two rural South Carolina teachers. As

she put it, "My upbringing was overflowing with love but humble in worldly possessions." Autumn imagined that she and Dorothy may have felt much the same
when they had stepped onto the farm.

Another entry was on the day Jon and Dorothy were married. The most
touching and memorable entries were written about her and Jon's attempts at
having a family. Dorothy had been pregnant several times over the course of five
years. None of the pregnancies had ever gone beyond the first trimester. They
had consulted every specialist in the country at the time. Eventually, Jon and
Dorothy had accepted the fact that they would not have a child of their own.
There were no entries as to why they did not adopt or if they had even considered
it. Dorothy had blamed herself for being incapable of bearing a child. She had felt
unworthy of Jon because of it. Obstetrical science had known little. Dorothy's
body had just probably 'forgotten' it was pregnant by the end of the first trimester. The ups and downs of that part of their life would have been enough to have
driven many couples apart. Jon and Dorothy stayed together through the bitter
end. The last entries regarding Dorothy had been written by Jon. At the age of
59, Dot had been diagnosed with breast cancer. She had surgery, radiation, che-
motherapy, and more surgeries. Finally, he wrote that she had known she was
dying and begged him to take her home. Jon had reluctantly signed her out of the
hospital and had brought her home. Dorothy had died fourteen hours later.

The book had several of the usual family entries. The matriarch of one generation wrote of the day she married, her children's names and birth dates, who their
children married and when. It went on into the grandchildren and great grandchildren. Every once in awhile, there would be an interesting note or event that
was jotted down but mostly it stood as a family record. During the generation
before the Civil War, the men of this house had turned ugly and sinister towards
the slaves. The entries had been written by the women. They had spent their days
cleaning up whatever mess their husbands had caused to the slaves. Autumn
shuddered to think of what had happened here in those days. She found familiar
passages written by several McFarlands about the hangman. There were also
many affectionate entries made about the slaves. In the early days, the masters
and mistresses of this farm worked side by side with the slaves they owned. The
mistresses had made sure the slaves had been taught their Bible lessons, married,
and baptized. Those had been in stark contrast to the entries near the end of the
age of plantations.

Just as pangs of hunger were getting hard to ignore, Autumn found the genea-
logical thread that contained Mrs. Florence McFarland. Autumn carefully
marked the page before she grabbed something to eat. Before long, she came back

with a tuna sandwich and cold glass of milk. Autumn propped the book open with her right hand as she munched with the left; careful not to get anything on the old book. Florence McFarland had been one of the only McFarland women that Autumn heard of since moving here. Jon had told Autumn in the note that she looked a great deal like his Great Aunt Florence. Other than that, Autumn knew nothing about her.

The book entry Autumn found was written by Florence's mother-in-law, Jessie McFarland, on the day Florence married Jessie's eldest son Glen. The entries then go on to name the birthdates and children of Glen and Florence McFarland. As Autumn read down the list of names, they started to sound oddly familiar. Autumn read them over and over again. There was Pearl, Charles, Thomas, and Albert. She continued to read the entries as Glen inherited the farm and Florence became the matriarch responsible for journal entries. It hit Autumn like a ton of bricks why the names seemed familiar as she read the list of Florence's grandchildren from Pearl: Russell, Warren, Jeffrey, Lucille, Dolores, Shirley, and Charles … Hummel. Autumn almost choked on her tuna.

She hurriedly dialed her mom and dad in Ohio. They did the usual pleasantries. Autumn told her mom she didn't want to keep her because she knew that Friday was the day they went to the movies and dinner with old friends. "I just found the Family Bible in the den and I was looking through it. It made me think of Grandma Hummel's old family Bible. What was dad's grandmother's name?"

"Pearl."

"Do you or dad happen to know what her maiden name was," Autumn asked breathless with excitement.

"I don't but I'll ask your dad." Autumn could hear her mom yelling to Mr. Hummel in the other room. "He doesn't remember, why?"

"Well, does he remember any of her siblings' names?"

"Hold on." Again, her mom shouted to the other room. The next voice Autumn heard on the phone was her dad's.

"What's with the forty questions?"

"Hi dad. I was just thumbing through the McFarland Family Bible and started thinking about Grandma Hummel's Family Bible. So, do you remember any of your grandma's siblings or their names?"

"I don't think I ever met any of them. My grandma was from the South and her whole family lived there."

Autumn got a shiver up her spine when her dad said that. "Hey dad," she tried to sound cool, "What were the names of your great aunts and great uncles on your dad's side?"

"Well, there were seven of them. My dad, Russell, was the oldest. Then there was Warren, Jeffrey, Lucille, Dolores, Shirley, and Charles. Why?"

"You guys will not believe this. Your grandmother, Pearl, was the daughter of Glen and Florence McFarland. They owned this house. They lived here. I am home. Jon was right when he said I was coming home. I always thought he meant it metaphorically but he meant it. This is my family's house and farm and … *everything!*"

The conversation was a frenzy of excitement and wonder. Before they had realized it, an hour passed and her mom and dad had to go. However, Mrs. Hummel promised she would contact all of dad's relatives to see if she could find out any information about Pearl and her family. One would have thought that Mr. Hummel would volunteer for that job but on the few occasions where the Hummel clan got together, an outsider would guess Mrs. Hummel to be Hummel by birth. Autumn's mom knew everyone's names and how they were related. Mr. Hummel always acted like he was in a room full of strangers whom he didn't really want to get to know. The deep depression Autumn slipped into since Kendra left was swept away by a renewed excitement. There was now a whole house and grounds to explore.

Even though Autumn had lived in the house for well over a year, she felt like a stranger rummaging through someone else's personal effects. Suddenly the table had turned. She could now search shamelessly through anything she could find in order to fill in the leaves on this branch of her family tree. Mrs. Hummel must have been swimming with excitement as well. Autumn's family always managed to take care of her brothers and sister but it hadn't always been easy. Autumn knew very few members of her father's family. Autumn's aunts and uncles were much better off financially than her parents. Suddenly, that changed. The Hummels were the wealthy family with a heritage that dated back to the original colonization of this country. The only thing that would have made this discovery sweeter was if she found proof that her descendants came over on the Mayflower.

Autumn read and reread passages she only ever caught glimpses of when Lillian let her look at the book. Without realizing it, she read through dinner and into the evening. Autumn decided to turn in early since there would be a lot of ground to cover over the weekend. She would make the most of Boyd being away. As she slipped under the cool pile of blankets on the bed, Autumn began to wonder what kind of person Florence had been. There were so many different personalities who had owned the home. Some of them had been kind and compassionate. Others had been frighteningly callous and inhumane. The first day Autumn came to the McFarland house; Jon had left her a letter on his desk. It had told Autumn little about why he had chosen her. She could remember reading, "That young lady was you. The woman you reminded me of was my Great Aunt Florence. She was the last great lady of the Old South to live in this house." That meant that Florence had been the last lady to own the house before the Civil War.

Autumn thought wistfully of the opening of Margaret Mitchell's **Gone With The Wind**. The opening quote had always wrenched mysteriously at Autumn's heart strings. As she drifted off to sleep, she tried to remember the opening phrases. "... There was a land of Cavaliers and Cotton Fields called the Old South. Here in this pretty world, Gallantry took its last bow. Here was the last ever to be seen of Knights and their Ladies Fair, of Masters and of Slave. Look for it only in books, for it is no more than a dream remembered, a Civilization gone with the wind ..."

The sun had not quite risen in the sky when Autumn rolled out of bed. She ran downstairs and gobbled a quick piece of toast and some juice. After she changed into an old and worn purple sweat suit with the Barberton Magic's logo all over it, she headed to the third floor. Autumn rarely went into the attic of the home except for retrieving stored items and decorations. The first time Autumn had been in the attic was on a hot and humid summer day. She was grateful that today was much cooler and less humid. When she reached the top of the stairs, what used to be the mammy's apartment was directly in front of her. Autumn attempted to sort through the many boxes when she first moved here but there were so many of them. She had other things to deal with in the house before she could even think of the dusty boxes in the attic. Autumn walked over to one of the large boxes containing photographs. As she did, she passed the closet that started her first mystery in the McFarland home.

"I need to get up here and paint," Autumn thought as she saw the mended closet wall. Autumn had the wall with the writing removed and placed in the Rice Museum to safely preserve it for future generations.

Autumn sat down to go through all the photos in the box. When she originally attempted to clear out some boxes from the attic, she realized it was a daunting task that could not be done carelessly. A hasty decision could have meant losing valuable information or priceless antiquities. She had chosen to sort everything into boxes: photos, books, clothing, and miscellaneous items. Autumn felt that if she did bear such a striking resemblance to Florence McFarland, it would be easy to identify her in photos. One would have thought she would have found Florence before while going through the photos but there were so many. Autumn merely saw they were pictures and tossed them into the box.

Hours went by and Autumn had not found any photos of Florence. There were many people and many different photo styles. There were wedding photos, baby pictures, family portraits, party pictures, and death pictures. Apparently, it was a thing to take pictures of people when they had died. Autumn did not look too carefully at these. She thought they were very distasteful and morbid. Most of the people in the other pictures looked very harsh and not very happy at all before the turn of the century. Autumn felt discouraged. Florence definitely should have had pictures taken of her on at least two occasions in her life: her wedding and a family portrait with husband and children. With a dull headache from the stuffy air of the attic and the musty smell of the old photos, Autumn almost gave up when she found it. There, as plain as could be, was a photo of a young woman with thick dark hair on her wedding day. Autumn knew the lady in the photo had to be Florence but Autumn was shocked when she saw her. Florence and she did not *resemble* each other. They were identical to each other right up to the beauty mark each of them had near the dimple on their left cheek. The dress she wore had been beautiful and elegant but simple. The man next to her was several inches taller than her and dressed in a three piece suit. Unlike the other photos Autumn had seen, Florence and Glen looked extremely happy. Before she quit looking at photos for the day, Autumn found a family portrait with Glen, Florence, Pearl, Thomas, Charles, and baby Albert. The picture confirmed that this Pearl was indeed her great grandmother. Autumn remembered seeing photos of Pearl on her wedding day and knew that they were indeed one in the same.

Satisfied with her find and bursting to call her mom, Autumn was about to descend the two flights of stairs when something in the miscellaneous box caught her eye. Autumn pushed several boxes, piled high with stuff, out of her way to reach the item she saw. The box was beautiful but rather heavy. Because of its size and the lock on the front, Autumn wondered why she had not put it in the box with the jewelry assuming it to be a jewelry box. Autumn realized that the wood did not look familiar and the lock was just for appearances not security. Tired and thirsty, Autumn tucked the little box under one arm and made her way down to the living room with the pictures of Florence in the other hand.

She sat down on the living room sofa with her treasures and the cordless phone. Autumn quickly dialed Mr. And Mrs. Hummel. The phone rang and rang but there was no answer. Slightly disappointed that she couldn't share her findings, Autumn turned her attention to the odd little box. "I wonder why it caught my eye," Autumn pondered. Autumn turned the box every which way to have a good look at the outside and savoring the anticipation of opening it. The top had a beautiful carved pattern in the wood that looked like a complicated knot of some kind. The sides of the box seemed to have little stars etched all over it. When Autumn turned it upside down, she could see two things written on the bottom of the box. One was London, England. The other was an inscription: To my dear daughter, Alyson McFarland. When she turned the box over, she felt something inside shift. The suspense seemed too great to postpone opening the box.

Inside the box was a small deck of well used cards and a black velvet bag. For a moment, Autumn thought she had been wrong about the box not being a jewelry box. Autumn undid the string around the deck of cards to see what they were. They were not playing cards. The cards she found had pictures of all sorts of things on them with the name of the card written under the pictures. She thought that the cards were Tarot Cards. Autumn knew nothing about Tarot Cards other than what she had seen in bad movies involving gypsies and crystal balls. She carefully tied the little string back around the ancient cards and focused now on the little velvet bag. Before she dumped the contents out on the coffee table, she tried to guess what was inside by feeling the bag. After all, if these *were* Tarot Cards, one could only guess what could be in the bag. Autumn couldn't tell what was inside by feeling, so she got up the nerve and dumped them out on the table. To her relief and surprise, she found several small stones, gems, and crystals. There were two very small, flat, and round black stones that looked like mercury. There was a brownish-orange colored stone that had a line through the middle that made the stone look like an eye. There was a cluster of deep purple crystals. The largest stone in the bag looked like a quartz crystal. The quartz was clear and flawless. There were no streaks, cracks, or imperfections of any kind. Autumn carefully tipped the stones back into the little black bag. She wondered what Tarot Cards were and what the significance of the stones were. With clues to yet another McFarland mystery, Autumn set off to the only place she thought she could get answers—the library.

The library in Georgetown was a small building in the business district. It was an intimate library snuggled up against the Rice Museum. The two buildings had started seeping into each other as the curator of the museum and the head librarian became close friends. Autumn was glad to get out of the attic and stroll downtown. The quiet found in the library was a welcome change to the quiet in her house. Autumn had always loved libraries. She was a voracious reader who loved books—the information they contained, the feel of holding a book, and even the covers. Books were a whole bunch of words put together to express someone's thoughts or imaginings. Whenever Autumn stopped to look at what a book actually was, the magnitude of what she was holding left her awestruck.

Autumn parked on the far end of town so she could enjoy a stroll before settling in for some reading. The sky was a deep translucent shade of blue and there was not a cloud in the sky. Autumn thought nostalgically of her school days and could hear her father saying, "This is a perfect day for football." Everything about the day looked like a fall day but it did not feel like a fall day to Autumn. The temperature was around sixty-two or sixty-three. It was perfect weather for a long sleeve shirt to Autumn. Everyone else on the street that day was wearing a light jacket and looking quite chilly. Autumn passed the coffee shop and decided to pick up a drink before continuing down the road.

When she walked in, Allan, the owner, greeted her. "Aren't you freezing out there? Nothing on but a blouse."

"You keep forgetting this is my time of year. All you thin blooded Carolinians thrive in the hot house. My blood is still a little too thick."

"So, what can I get you today, hon," Allan asked as he laughed at her comment.

"The usual, please."

"You have to be the only person in the world that comes into a coffee shop and doesn't order coffee."

"Well, that either says a lot for you or very little about your coffee," Autumn replied as she looked at the unusual assortment of mugs for sale.

"Look, why don't I get you a little taste of my newest flavor. We got it just for the holidays." Allan handed her a small cup that smelled like heaven. It sort of smelled like her mom and dad's house when her mom baked Christmas cookies and made coffee.

Autumn took a little sip and was sorely disappointed. The smell was rich and wonderful. The drink was bitter and spicy. She finished the small cup and forced an "mmmm".

"So, are you changing your order," Allan asked eagerly.

"I'm sorry, Allan. It is really good and I'm sure your coffee drinkers will love it. I just don't care for coffee. Never have. There have been two drinks in my life that everyone said I would acquire a taste for. One was beer and the other one was coffee. To this day, I don't enjoy either of them."

"One cocoa cascade coming up." Allan turned to start making the drink which was mostly hot chocolate with just a shot of vanilla syrup. Before Autumn could make her way to the display of different coffees, Allan handed her a frothy chocolate drink with whipped cream and shaved chocolate on the top. She said goodbye and made her way down the street.

Autumn still could not get over how odd it was to see beach souvenirs and nick-knacks when she wasn't on vacation. There were shops that sold art prints featuring display windows full of tranquil ocean scenes in almost every color palette imaginable. The country store always had sweet grass baskets, sand dollars painted with religious verses, and salt water taffy. There was a large nation-wide book store taking up the area of at least three small downtown buildings. By the time Autumn reached the end of the business district, all that was left of her frothy drink was her sugar buzz and a little whipped cream on the end of her nose.

At the library, Autumn dove right into the card catalog anticipating the titles she would find. To her dismay, she found no books in the library on tarot cards. After fifteen minutes with no success, she started looking under divination. Next, she moved to fortune telling. Her last attempt was to look up books of the occult. The only reference she could find in the library was for a magazine article by a cardinal of the Catholic Church in the United States. The article read that the cards were believed to have been created in Italy around the fourteenth century. It was a game that Italian aristocrats played with the cards. The cardinal mentioned the fact that no one knew where or when the association with divination took place. The article then went on to explain why, when used as a tool for divination, the Catholic Church opposed them. Beyond this brief article, there was no information about tarot cards. Autumn was a little disappointed and frustrated but then thought that libraries, though public institutions, reflect the public they serve. Autumn was doubtful that anyone in Georgetown had ever found a need, let alone a want, for such books on tarot cards. Since her search for information on the cards became a bust, she turned her attention to the stones in the little black bag. There was not much more information to be found on them either. Autumn found a book that helped her identify the stones but gave her no insight as to why the stones were with the cards. As Autumn sat in the long shadows cast from a fall sun, she remembered a shop in Pawley's Island that might have information about the rocks that was perhaps more mystical in nature.

The Pawley's Island Shops were a group of stores that were both exotic and eclectic. The buildings gave the shopper a sense of the area before it had become a popular vacation destination. The small group of shops reflected the "Elegantly Shabby" style for which Pawley's Island was known. The shops were built literally amid a marsh. Wooden boardwalks took shoppers over the water and around to the little buildings nestled on the small dry patches in the marsh. The marsh had old live oak and cypress trees reaching into the watery ground. Everything was covered in moss of one kind or another. Autumn parked the car and made her way to "Earthen Treasures" on the back side of the complex. The shop sold stones of all shapes, colors, and sizes. They were playing music out over the boardwalks by indigenous people from all over the earth. In the window of the store were stained glass pieces and wind chimes. The proprietors seemed like two Love-Children who hung-up their anti-war slogans and settled down somewhere where life was a little simpler. Autumn made her way through the shop to the songs of whales.

After about five or ten minutes, the gentleman made his way out of the back room. Autumn walked over to the counter and asked, "I was wondering if you could help me with something?"

"Well, I would be happy to. What can I do," he replied in a gentle voice that was without an accent. He was clearly not a native Carolinian.

Autumn pulled the little bag from her pocket and emptied the stones onto the counter. "I was going through some of my-uh-," Autumn paused "-my grand-mother's things. I found these in this little velvet bag. I was wondering if you could tell me what they are."

"Cute little bag. Your grandmother's you said. Hmmm?" He reached under the counter and pulled out a small magnifying glass. He started with the purple stones. After inspecting the small cluster of purple crystals, he moved onto the orange striped one. He picked up the two smooth black ones and said. "Very odd assortment of stones you have here. You said that you found them in your grand-mother's things. Did you find anything else with them?

Autumn was hedging a little. She wasn't sure what he would think of tarot cards. Then, she thought that if she really wanted to know, he needed to know everything. "I found them with these." She set the little box on the counter and opened it to reveal the cards. "I have no idea what any of it is or what it means."

"Well, that makes a little more sense. Why don't you come around and have a seat." He turned and hollered to the back, "Pam! I think you might want to see this."

From out of the back room came a thin lady with crazy curly red hair. She was wearing a scarf shirt and sarong with sandals. There were many bobbles and beads decorating her ensemble. "This is my life partner, Pam." He turned to talk to her, "She brought me this and asked me what I thought it was. What do you think?"

A bright smile spread over her face and she said, "I think we'll need some tea. I'll be right back."

Within minutes, she returned with a small tea set Autumn knew was a Japanese set with green tea. When Pam had poured everyone tea, she said, "Where did you get this?"

"She found them in her *grandmother's* belongings. Do you want to tell her what she has here?"

Pam gently reached over to the small wooden box and affectionately cradled it in her hands. "Well, I have no idea *who* you got this from but," she paused to collect the stones in her hand, "whoever she was, she was very knowledgeable and possibly very powerful."

Autumn's head began spinning. She had come to the shop hoping to hear what the stones were and what they meant. She had no idea what Pam meant. Pam could see that.

"What do you know about this box?" Pam asked softly.

Autumn was relieved that Pam was not going to gloss over the fact that she had no idea what the box, the cards, or the stones meant. "To tell you the truth, I have no idea what any of it is. I was going through the attic looking for family photos when this little box caught my eye. I don't know anything more about this stuff than what I just told you. Why, what is it all?"

Pam slowly poured everyone another cup of tea. "The box is a wooden fold piece. It is something that people stored their personal treasures in, like a strongbox. The marks on the outside could be regional or family. They subtly tie the box to the owner." She spread the beautiful cards out on the small table in front of her. "These *are* tarot cards but they are terribly old. I am not the person to tell you where they came from. I would guess that they have been handed down from generation to generation. That could mean that they came from almost anywhere. Like I said, they are very old. So, the person who used them was not an amateur or a novice. They clearly knew divination."

Her husband spoke in his quiet smooth voice, "I can tell you about the stones. It has long been believed by several different cultures and religions that certain stones have powers. For instance, Native Americans see the power of the Creator in almost everything created. The different stones in this bag have been designated as having certain properties. Hold out your hand, please."

As Autumn held out her hand, he began dropping stones into her hands. The first one to fall into her hand was the stripped orange-brown stone. "This is tiger's eye. It is said to protect the carrier from harm. The purple stones are amethyst. They are a stone that purifies the aura or spirit." As he dropped the two black stones into her hand, the stones were initially ice cold quickly warmed. "These stones are hematite. They are actually not a rare stone. In history, they were called Alaskan diamonds. Explorers to Alaska took them back as gifts for the Tsars. In metaphysics, they are said to be a sort of grounding stone. If you are worried, suffering emotionally, or overwhelmed with something, they are said to be able to pull that negative energy out of the person holding them or wearing them and send those feelings into the ground. People even claim that the stones actually get heavier the more energy they are handling. Last, but certainly not least, is the quartz." He held the large clear crystal and gazed at it admiringly. "This is one of the largest and clearest single pieces of quartz I have ever seen." Slowly, he rolled the crystal around in his hand before placing it in hers. "This is a power crystal."

For the first time since he began telling her about the stones, Autumn found her voice and asked, "It gives off power?"

The couple turned to each other and laughed good naturedly at her question. "Not exactly. The power belongs to the person holding it. What this stone is said to do is channel that energy and purify it. It makes the person wearing it function at the best of their abilities. It centers them. The size of the stone is irrelevant. It is the clarity of the stone that is important. Any flaw within the crystal takes away from its ability to focus the person's energy. This one must have tremendous power."

Autumn sat there for a moment with all the stones in her hand. She paused to think about all that she had been told. These lovely people gave her so much information about the items. Yet, she was more confused than ever. "That is all wonderful. I could have spent half the day in the library and not found out any of the things you have told me."

Pam wrapped her ringed fingers around the small teacup that has no handle and said, "But, you still don't know what all this is?"

Autumn felt as if she had been holding her breath. The tightness in her chest released as she said, "No."

"I don't know if it was in your *grandmother's* possessions or where you got this. It really doesn't matter. The items you have belonged to someone very knowledgeable and very powerful. This person came from a long line of people who would have learned their skills by passing them on generation to generation." Pam paused to take another sip of tea. As she did, her eyes stared at Autumn like someone about to reveal a who-done-it. "That person was a seer, shaman, psychic," she paused yet another moment with a grin that spread over her face, "a witch."

Autumn had been struggling up to that point to keep up with the conversation. However, when Pam said "a witch", Autumn fell back in her chair as if she was hit in the head. "When you say witch you mean ..."

"This is your area, love. I'm gonna go back to sorting through the new tapes we got in today." Her husband stood up to leave. "Thank you for coming in today. It was very nice meeting you and seeing the items you brought. I have a really beautiful hematite necklace over in the case you might be interested in. See you soon." With that, he disappeared through a door behind the sales desk. Autumn could hear him humming in the back room. To her surprise, it seemed to be the eerie melody of one of the whale songs playing in the store.

Autumn collected herself to ask, "By witch, you mean?"

As if Pam was reading Autumn's mind, she chuckled wholeheartedly, which made all the beads and bangles do a strange little dance. She reached over and patted Autumn's knee. "No. Not like the witches you see at Halloween. There are no black gowns or pointy hats. I have no idea where that idea came from except for maybe the repressed psyche of the Puritan/Quaker/Anabaptist Americans of the day. Fear of the unknown gave witches that horrible image. People could take comfort in knowing that there were no witches amongst them because there was no one who looked like that. I guess that image took the guess work out of knowing who was a witch and who wasn't. No, these women and men, witches and wizards, were members of a society as ancient as the earth itself. I wouldn't really call it a religion for it lacks the basic fundamentals of a religion. It is more of a practicing knowledge. It was a way they lived their life and how they looked at the world around them."

Sheepishly Autumn broke in to wonder out loud, "Are you ..."

Pam laughed again and tossed her head back. Her wild curly red hair looked that much wilder for the tossing. "No. I just know a lot about the practice. Most of the people who practice the lifestyle do so because people in their family have always lived that way. They see nothing unusual or different about the way they see the world. Many of them belong to main stream religions because, like I said, it is not a religion as much as a way of life. Many main stream religions do not clash with the lifestyle. Anyway, the tea is almost gone and I'm sure you want to get back to the mansion. Like I told you before, the person that owned this box was very good at his or her craft."

"Well, thank you so much," Autumn paused for a minute. "How did you know that I live in a mansion?"

"I have ways. I know that you are the girl that moved into the McFarland place a while back. Thanks for coming by. Take care of yourself."

Autumn collected her box and belongings. Before she left the shop, she purchased the beautiful nine inch strand of hematite. As she crossed the little foot bridge over the swampy marsh to the parking lot, Autumn couldn't help but think, "Lovely people. They'd be perfect spokespersons for 'This is your brain. This is your brain on drugs' commercial. The sixties were very, very hard on them," she chuckled to herself, "or else very, very good to them!"

Most of the day had slipped by once Autumn left Earthen Treasures. As she made her way down deserted Highway 17, Autumn decided to stop at Shabby's for dinner. Ever since Kendra left, Autumn found it hard to once again cook for one. Shabby's was her home away from home. Autumn wasn't really hungry but she got a warm happy feeling every time she sank her teeth into their homemade hush-puppies spread with honey butter. Sure, it wasn't as good as Barberton fried chicken but it would do in a pinch. She was feeling pinched. The day started full of excitement for what might be in the attic. Leaving the attic, Autumn was excited about her find but felt a little foggy from the stuffy attic. Her head cleared and her excitement renewed as she made her way to the Island Shops. Now, the excitement was gone and her head seemed all foggy again because of the information about the little box. Autumn didn't really want to order real food. Drinking herself slushy in sweetened tea and stuffing her face with fried dough could have been enough for her. Unfortunately, the manager had become used to having Autumn dine there. He would not let her leave without a proper meal. The manager brought her something wonderful. Autumn didn't know. She ate it to be polite. As she thanked the manager and paid her bill, Autumn headed out into the night air. As the cool November night air hit her when she stepped outside, Autumn paused to reflect how ironic the air felt. The night was chilly with a gusty wind coming from the ocean. Yet, the air still smelled like summer. It was almost like she really did live where summer never ended. "Maybe," she thought, "Summer needs to take a break from being summer so it let's the other seasons slip in. It just lingers around in the wind to remind the other seasons 'Hey, you're just passing through, pal.'" With that, she hopped in the car, rolled down the windows, and took in all the summer November would let her have.

The next morning, Autumn awoke to the first real hard frost of the season. The world outside looked as if it had been sprinkled overnight with glitter. For the first time in a while, Autumn could feel a damp chill in the house. "It's going to be nice to have the furnace on again," she thought as she rolled over in her bed. Autumn truly wasn't a morning person. The only reason she ever bounded (and she rarely ever bounded) out of bed was if she were heading into the office or if she needed to clear out after a particularly haunted evening. Just as the dawn was being reluctant to fold into the day, Autumn rolled over in her bed and stared at the ceiling. Many things had happened yesterday that she would never have imagined but she was curious to find out where these pieces fit in the puzzle called the McFarlands. Not only did she have pieces to the puzzle set out by the mysterious stranger Jon McFarland, it seemed there were pieces of this puzzle that also fit into her family puzzle. This was *her* history. As if Autumn wasn't curious enough, this new development took her excitement to a fever pitch. Before long however, her head started fogging up as it did the day before; too much information and no clue as to what it all meant.

The sun refused to break through the clouds. It looked as if it might be one of those days where it looked like morning all day. Autumn always disliked this type of day. They made her sad and lethargic. Since moving to the sunny south, gloomy days affected her more severely. It was almost as if a year in South Carolina made her addicted to the sun. Most days, the sun was an addiction that was easy to feed. Maybe that was what made gray cloudy days worse. She threw off the covers and headed to the shower. She stood letting the water wash over her in an attempt to smooth out the wrinkles in her head. As Autumn dressed for the day, she saw the bag from Earthen Treasures on her dressing table. Inside was the beautiful hematite necklace. That was when she suddenly remembered what properties hematite was supposed to possess. She took the long strand of shimmering black stones out and put them on. The stones were extremely cold against her neck but warmed quickly.

Making her way downstairs, Autumn noticed that she had taken so long to get up that she completely missed breakfast. Autumn rounded the bottom of the stairs to head through the dining room into the kitchen. She stopped suddenly and picked up the telephone. Within a few moments, Fanny was on the other end of the phone.

"Hi, Fanny, what are you doing on this gray day?" Autumn asked trying to sound cheerful.

"Why," asked Fanny in a suspicious tone.

"Well, I thought if you hadn't made any plans, I could bring lunch over."

Fanny chuckled, "Sure. I have nothing planned for today. You come on over and I'll whip us up something for lunch. I suppose you been starving yourself since your friend left and Boyd went out of town."

"Well," Autumn paused and thought about making something up but Fanny knew her too well. "You're right but I invited myself over. I'll bring lunch. You just better have a fresh batch of your special lemonade ready when I get there, okay?"

"I will do that. You are in luck; I made your momma's recipe for pumpkin log this morning. You know it's best the day you make it so come hungry! You be careful comin' over, ya hear."

"Yes m'am, and thank you." Autumn decided to run her thoughts about Florence McFarland, her dad, and the little box past Fanny to see if she could make sense of it. Before long, she was on the road out to Fanny's place with a basket stuffed full of croissants and a large salad. Autumn decided to eat light so she could enjoy a large helping of the pumpkin log. As Autumn made her way out of Georgetown, the stretch of road beyond was deserted. The road wound through large farm fields that stood dead and somber in the gray November sky. As she made her way into Sumter, it stood in direct contrast with Georgetown. Sumter was a very small rural downtown that had seen better days. The streets were empty as were the few operating store fronts. During the summer, one could spot a few people hanging around the barber shop or maybe even the local bar. Against the dismal sky, the town looked much more run down. The place made Autumn's mood even darker.

As a child, she remembered passing through Sumter on their way to vacation in Myrtle Beach. It should have been a marker she looked forward to because it meant, after twelve hours in the car, they were almost there. That was never how she felt when she got here. The place sucked all the happiness and hope out of her body. She could remember as a teenager shuddering when she got through town. It felt as if someone had just thrown cold water over her head. Autumn felt the feeling was amplified today by her cloudy brain and stormy mood. Turning at the last red light in town, Autumn's mood brightened a bit when she saw the park where Fanny's children played. Across the park, Autumn could make out the matronly figure of Fanny on her porch steps waiting for Autumn. The neighborhood around Fanny's house reminded Autumn of her home. It was truly a neighborhood of days-gone-by. Everyone knew each other. They looked out for each other and helped each other whenever life got hard. That happened a lot in this small neighborhood. Fanny ran around to the driver's side to hug Autumn as soon as she got out of the car.

"Come on in. I have everything ready. Here, let me get that for you."

Autumn turned around to see what Fanny was going to get. Behind the basket of food sat the small wooden box from the attic. How it had gotten into the car when she had carried it into the study the night before, Autumn could not explain. It was another one of those weird things that Autumn had become immune to over the past year. The two made their way to the front door and into Fanny's kitchen.

"I haven't seen you since," Fanny dropped her thought while serving herself some food.

"Yeah, since that day of my lunch date, I know. I'm sorry about that Fanny." Autumn felt a hollow knock in her stomach. She did not even think about calling to tell Fanny that she had not heard or seen Jim since their meeting at the Litchfield Inn. "I should have called to let you know everything was okay. I really am sorry."

"Oh, fiddle-faddle child. Nothing was gonna happen to you so long as you stayed at the farm. That was a pretty rough experience. Then, your friend left for home. I knew that would be hard on you. You seem to love living here but someone coming for a visit tears at your heart strings a bit, don' it?"

"It does. It feels like leaving home all over again. No one ever stays long enough for me." Before Autumn could even stop herself, she asked, "What did you mean that you knew nothing would happen to me as long as I stayed at the farm?"

Fanny said it in passing but that was how Fanny said everything. Autumn often thought that Fanny would have made a horrible doctor. She could tell someone that they were going to die of a horribly painful terminal disease and make it sound like nothing.

"I just meant that no one would dare mess with you while you were on the McFarland property. That's all," she said as she put another croissant on their plates.

"No thanks Fanny, I'm saving room for pumpkin log and …" Autumn was cut short.

"You *are* going to eat that. I can tell by looking at you that you've been eating popcorn and soup for several days. Now, eat up and you'll still have room for pumpkin log."

Autumn knew there was no point in arguing. Fanny belonged to the school of thought that no man wanted a woman built like a twelve-year-old boy. In her book, bigger was better. Compared to the popcorn and soup, this tasted like heaven. "That doesn't tell me what you meant about me being safe. You just said the same thing a different way." Autumn asked while feeling better with every bite she took.

"Girl," Fanny said in a long, drawn-out way. "Sometimes I wonder what Jon saw in you."

Autumn looked hurt and confused.

"Now, don' go getting all upset. I just meant that you are so determined to see the world with your *eyes*. If you have learned nothing else, it should have been to look beyond the ordinary. The McFarland place is swimming in history and protected by powerful forces. You may not be a McFarland by birth, but the day you moved into that house, you became a McFarland. You ready for some dessert?"

Fanny squeezed herself out from the table to bustle into the kitchen. She returned with two very generous slices of pumpkin log. Autumn slid a bit of the moist pumpkin cake into her mouth. The cream cheese icing melted in her mouth. Autumn couldn't help but think of sitting at the nook at her mom and dad's house doing the same thing. With that, the emotion of the past couple weeks came pouring out of her.

Fanny, anticipating every move, ran over to wrap her arms around her. "You just get it all out. I knew this wasn't about lunch when you called. Go ahead. It's good to cry." After what seemed to be an eternity, Autumn pulled herself together. Fanny asked, "It's the pumpkin log, init?"

They both howled with laughter.

Autumn explained to Fanny what she had found at the house and what the people at Earthen Treasures told her. Finally, Autumn explained to Fanny that she may not be a McFarland by proxy.

"What do you mean," Fanny asked as she settled back into her chair, not at all surprised. Fanny leaned back in her chair with what appeared to be a grin on her face.

Autumn jumped right into the story of Florence McFarland and her grandmother's family. Fanny took all she was saying in stride, never flinching. At the end of the story, Autumn explained her theory of her great grandmother being a daughter of Florence McFarland. It was as if a great weight lifted once she shared her story. Fanny sat silent for a long time after Autumn concluded.

Fanny drew in a long slow breath and stared at her feet. "Jon thought that might be the case."

"What," Autumn asked incredulously. "Jon knew,"

"There were too many things about you that struck Jon as familiar. It could not have been a coincidence that you did more than remind him of Florence. You were a twenty-first century look-alike. This state always felt like a second home to you. There has always been something familiar in this place. There had to be a reason for that beyond your family vacationing here. I think that explains a lot. It explains why you saw all the things you did at the house-the girls at the lawn party, the slaves in the outbuildings, and Charles. These are all things that few or no one has seen before at the house. It must mean something. How interesting? Just when you thought the mystery was solved ..."

"Yeah, I end up back at the beginning again," Autumn finished Fanny's thought.

After too many slices of pumpkin roll, Autumn left Fanny. Even if she did not know anything more about the mysteries, Autumn's disposition changed immensely. That was the point of going to see Fanny. No matter the crisis or the situation, Fanny could always bring Autumn back from the depths of despair. "Fanny is what makes this bearable," Autumn thought as she turned into her driveway and underneath the security light that lit the way from the garage to the house. Autumn's spirits were a lot lighter now than when she left. The journey between the two emotions left her feeling very worn down. She couldn't wait to crawl into her big fluffy bed and cocoon herself in the linens until the morning. Before she headed upstairs, Autumn noticed the light on her answering machine blinking. Pressing the button, two new messages played for her.

"Hi, Autumn," her mom's familiar voice boomed from the machine. "I just wanted to see how you were doing. Your dad is heading out for football practice. I swear that man thinks he's a coach or something. I'm enjoying the peace and quiet here while he's gone. Well, I'll call you tomorrow if I don't hear back from you. I hope everything is well. I love you. Bye." Autumn knew that she should return her call tonight or face the "I was worried sick" guilt trip. However, she was too tired to get into what had been going on around the farm.

"Hey," Boyd's deep rich southern drawl sprang from the machine. "It's been awhile since I called you last." His voice sounded tired but happy. "Dad and I are finally narrowing down the field of contenders. Mr. Berlin would not sell the mare that won the Triple Crown. So dad is working on making another choice. I must have worked one hundred horses by now. Dad wants me to be absolutely sure of my choice which, of course, means no pressure on me." He laughed a little when he said that. Autumn could imagine the wily grin spreading across his face and the twinkle in his eyes as he said it. Boyd thrived on pressure. She often thought that the pressure of taking over the family business and exceeding people's expectations is what made him the beautiful person he was today. "Look, I'll call back tomorrow night when we get in. I'm hoping to have decided by this time tomorrow. I'm missing you and this cold weather is kicking my butt." Autumn couldn't help but laugh at his comment about the weather. Boyd froze in South Carolina from November until April. Autumn hardly wore more than a light jacket during the winter. Even though Boyd was in Virginia, it was north enough to be giving him the deep freeze. Autumn cleared the messages and headed off to bed.

CHAPTER 9

▼

BOOKS, BASEMENTS, AND MORE

"Hey," Autumn said as she slid up to Ian the next morning as he was working on the plaster in the downstairs hall.

"What did I do," he asked with a tone of disgust.

"Nothing," Autumn added innocently.

"Okay," he hesitated, "what did you do?"

"Nothing," she added again.

"I'm done guessing. What do you want?"

She smiled, "Your hammer."

"Sure." He handed it over reluctantly with a quizzical look on his face.

Before Ian had a chance to ask why she wanted it, she said "Thanks!" and was gone.

Ian's curiosity got the better of him and he decided to find out what she was doing. After listening to mysterious tapping noises, he found her on the floor in the den. "What are you doing?"

"Nothing," Autumn again replied offhandedly as if she were not doing anything out of the ordinary. She continued to tap the floor as she listened intently to the sound of the taps.

"Okay, okay. So, this 'nothing' involves a hammer, does it?"

"Yes," she replied as she slid over to a new section of the den to begin tapping.

"Well, if it involves a hammer then it involves me. So …," Ian hoped to draw an answer out of Autumn but she kept tapping. He walked over and grabbed her hand. "Please stop tapping for a minute and answer me."

Autumn and Ian were the only two people on the McFarland Farm who were not southern. Ian never adopted southern manners. Autumn wholeheartedly embraced the nuances of a southern disposition. With Ian, however, she kept her natural disposition which meant he stayed out of her way and she stayed out of his.

Autumn couldn't ignore him any longer. "I found another letter from Jon a couple of days ago."

"Let me guess. More mysteries." Ian shook his head with a grin. Ian had known Mr. McFarland for several years before his passing. He knew that Jon McFarland had been intelligent, shrewd, generous, and kind. Most of all, Jon had enjoyed a good mystery. "What is it that has you knocking on the floors?"

"He said to look for clues in the attic, the closets, and the basement. I have found clues in all of those places but one. Which one do you think I've missed?"

Ian looked a little confused. "I'm gonna guess the basement but …"

"But you told me there isn't a basement in this house," Autumn finished.

"Look, I don't know what Jon is playing at here. Sure, there are lots of places he and his relatives could have stored their 'skeletons' over the centuries. There is no way there is a basement. If there was one, I would know about it," Ian added firmly.

"What makes you so sure you would know about a basement," Autumn asked smugly. "You weren't born here or raised here."

"Please, I've worked on this big old house for more years than you have lived here," he shot back at her in a sort of good natured competition.

"Okay, you're the upper classman and I'm the green freshman. What does that prove," Autumn asked. "Couldn't the basement entrance have been built over or sealed over in the many additions to this house?"

"Is that what you are tapping around to find?" Ian paused for a minute and walked across the room to the window. He gazed out at the crisp fall day. "You remember the day you met me?"

"Yes, you were the mysterious voice coming from under the porch," Autumn laughed as she thought back to that day while continuing to tap.

"Then you remember what I told you I was doing," Ian asked still gazing out the window into the side yard.

"You were rebuilding a wall that had collapsed underneath the porch," Autumn said singsong voice like a child reciting a lesson in school.

"I told you then that the soil around here would not allow such a structure."

"Yeah, but it was a small wall with no supporting structure and," Autumn thought quickly, "we found that entire burial chamber for Alyson and Charles. It had not collapsed in over two hundred years of existence because it was built with a purpose in mind. You didn't know that it was there, did you?"

"No, but why would someone have built a basement in this house? Between the attics, the barns, and the outbuildings, why would anyone have dug out a basement?"

"I don't know," Autumn thought dejectedly. "All I know is that it *could* be done. The burial chamber had no deterioration."

"You went down there," Ian said in disgust and surprised.

"Yeah, why," Autumn turned to look at Ian.

"What was it like down there?"

"Well, surprisingly dry for the humidity of August," Autumn added non-plussed.

"Didn't it," Ian's face revealed a hint of morbid curiosity. "Didn't it smell?"

"No, it was surprisingly cool considering the beastly hot summer we had that year," Autumn's voice turned up at the end of that statement. Before Ian could respond, Autumn was out of the room again. Ian had no choice but to follow the banging sound he heard. He found her against the wall in the kitchen. Of the four walls that made up the kitchen, two walls faced the exterior of the house while two walls connected the kitchen to the rest of the house. Autumn was sitting and banging against the wall that connected the kitchen to the staircase and the hall.

"Thanks for letting me in on the secret," Ian chided her sarcastically.

"Oh, I'm sorry. Shh," Autumn replied quickly and returned to tapping.

"Aren't you going to tell me what your epiphany was?"

"Shh, listen," Autumn barked. As she continued to tap along the wall, she came to a place on the wall that made a hollow sound. Before Ian could say anything, she waved her hand frantically at him to keep quiet. The hollow tapping noise continued up the wall about five feet and across the wall around three or four feet. Autumn raised the hammer to give the wall a violent whack before Ian seized her hammer hand.

"WHAT ARE YOU DOING," Ian screamed.

"I'm looking for the basement. Now, let go," Autumn said as she yanked her hand away from his.

"That is not an answer when I see you about to make a big hole in the wall. I told you, there is no basement. There couldn't be a basement. So, what do you say to that?" Ian folded his arms in triumph. Before he could say stop, Autumn had sent the hammer through the sheet rock. "THERE IS NO BASEMENT!"

"No basement? What do you call that," Autumn pointed at the cavernous hole behind the sheet rock. The smell of undisturbed air hit them both.

"How did you know?" Ian asked as he pulled another hammer from his tool belt.

"You told me where it was," Autumn added coolly while banging away at dry wall. "Jon said there was a basement. I figured he knew more about this old house than you did. I didn't think about where the entrance to the basement might have been. I just thought I would start tapping around until I found a hollow spot. That's when you got to asking me about the mausoleum. I knew that the basement would have been part of the original house. Alyson and Charles would only have built an underground burial chamber if they knew that it could be done. After digging the basement for their house, they would have known that. The only part of the original house that remains is the kitchen and the dining room. The dining room has had electricity wired on both the dining room side and the kitchen side. That left only one wall in the original home untouched." By the time Autumn finished explaining her theory, they had a doorway in front of them to a small room.

Ian stood there with his hands on his hips as if utterly astonished at what he had helped uncover. "What is this?"

"My guess is that it is an old pantry of sorts. See," Autumn gestured to the shelves across from them. "The people who originally lived in the very small farmhouse probably used this to put up preserves for the winter months when fresh fruits and vegetables would have been rare."

Ian stepped cautiously through the hole in the wall. The stale air seized in his chest. He coughed to clear his lungs. Looking up, he could see the remains of an old ladder. "What do you suppose that was for? It looks like a ladder that goes nowhere?"

Autumn slid into the very narrow space. "These old farmsteads were not much for elaborate architecture. The kitchen of this house is the kitchen of the settler's house. The dining room was both living space and bedroom space, probably for the adults. This was once the ladder to the loft where the kids would have slept."

"You have got to be kidding me. It's probably only ten feet off the ground," Ian said as he easily reached the ledge where the ladder rested.

"I told you, simple design and even simpler building. Just think about where we are in the new house."

Ian took a minute to try to figure out where the rest of the house was in relation to this little room. He shrugged his shoulders.

"We are underneath the stairs to the second floor of the new house. They built the beautiful Georgian mansion right on top of the footprint of the old settler's cabin."

"How do you know this stuff?" Ian gapped at her.

"It is very common of the era and the region," Autumn replied as she began tapping again.

"Oh, well, then … *why* do you know this stuff?" Ian coughed again as Autumn tugged at a handle in the floor boards covered by years of soot, dirt, and dust.

"What do you think history majors study for four years in college?" Autumn grunted as she heaved the door in the floor open. The empty space below them was absolutely black. The smell of earth sealed off for a long time reminded Autumn of the excavation of the grave a year ago. People think of coastal South Carolina and think sand. In fact today if you walked through any parking lot in the area along the coast, sand was all that could be seen at the edges and borders. However, the soil in the Low Country was actually more complex. The sand exists on the surface throughout the area except near the inland waterways and rivers. The areas near fresh water have seen centuries of flooding and receding waters. Flooding had left fields of dark rich black soil. It was that soil that gave rise to the plantations. Once the sand and top soil are taken away, the dirt was far more stable than other areas in the country. This hole Ian and Autumn discovered had been in existence since the first McFarland came to America. It survived the family that dug it.

"Now what do we do, Sherlock?"

"If I've learned anything since moving to South Carolina it is not to jump into a hole without knowing what's down there first," Autumn laughed. "Let's get some light down there first."

Ian slid past her with a small flashlight. The small beam was swallowed by the darkness. Ian agreed to look into the hole to see if he could see anything with the flashlight.

"Well, what do you see?"

"Not a whole lot. There seems to be nothing down there. Wait. There are large crates over to the right. There are lots of them." Ian's voice was echoing through the cavernous space below them. "On the other side, there seems to be some furniture or something." There were a few moments of silence as Ian continued to look around in the faint light. He wriggled up to Autumn's excited face. "I'll be right back. I've got a couple of work lights in the back of my truck."

"Thank you," Autumn grabbed Ian and gave him a big kiss on the cheek. She then proceeded to jump up and down like a four year old on Christmas morning.

"Does Boyd know how lucky he is?"

"I don't know what you mean," Autumn asked slightly embarrassed after kissing him.

"Most girls would get excited if you sent flowers, surprised them at work, or presented them with an expensive piece of jewelry. Not you. Put a few lights in a damp dark hole in the ground and Autumn's wrapped around your finger." Ian left shaking his head.

While Ian went to retrieve the lights, Autumn thought about Boyd. The last time they talked, he thought his dad might be close to deciding on a horse. She wondered if that was Boyd's wishful thinking more than reality. Boyd might be in Virginia much longer than he thought. He may not want to even put that reality into words. Boyd sounded slightly homesick which would be a new emotion for him. The Masters family traveled all the time when he was growing up. Due to the nature of his business, Boyd frequently spent several days of each month out-of-town. Autumn smiled to herself as she thought, "Maybe he finally has someone at home to miss?" Before she could continue that train of thought, Ian had returned. "You look like a Christmas tree."

"Yeah, a safety orange Christmas tree. Can you plug this in?" Ian handed her the plug end of the string of work lights. Within moments, the lights were on.

"Now you really look like a Christmas tree." Autumn couldn't suppress her laughter this time.

"Okay, chuckles, do you want to do this or not?"

"Yes. I'll be good. What do you need me to do?"

"Grab a light and come down with me," Ian turned and handed her a light after dropping an adjustable ladder down into the hole.

"You are sure this will be okay?" Autumn looked suddenly unnerved.

"No, but I plan to figure that out before I put my foot down on the ground," Ian said as he descended the ladder.

The light now pierced the darkness. The rough walls of this room were visible. Autumn could only imagine the work that would have been involved to dig such a large hole. The cap of this room was probably only six feet from the floor of the room above it. However, if she was correct, the room they were now in was original to this farm. It would date back all the way to 1765. That would have meant that it had been dug by Charles with a small shovel. Autumn wasn't familiar enough with the dates on his family to know if any of his sons would have been old enough to help with the project. Alyson could have helped but might also have been pregnant when they came to America. Hopefully, it had been fall or early spring when they began work on the cabin. Fall could have given them time before winter would have set in. Though winter paled by comparison to New England, it was still wet and cold. Early spring would have given them time to get most of the heavy labor done before the oppressive heat set in. No matter when or who did the job, it would have been a tremendous amount of work.

Within half an hour, the space was fully illuminated and checked for vermin; small and large. The next step was to investigate the crates that were stacked all the way up from floor to ceiling on the right side of the basement. As Ian heaved down one of the boxes, he asked, "Tell me again how you knew this was here?"

"I didn't. I believed you when you told me there was no basement to this place. Then, I found Jon's letter urging me to thoroughly search the house. The letter mentioned a basement. I thought it odd that he would mention one if there wasn't one. Of course, he didn't give much more information than that. That's when I stopped and thought about it. I remembered how most plantation mansions came to be. They are nothing more than an elaboration on the original house. It required too much work and supplies to start a house all over from scratch. Plus, whether they did it on purpose or it was just a happy accident, most houses sit in the middle of all the land. Usually, it's on the prettiest piece of land. That's what led me here."

Autumn lifted the lid of the first crate once Ian pried it off.

Ian gasped in astonishment, "It is money!"

"Well, it *was* money," Autumn added nonplussed.

"You mean ..."

"Yep, it's Confederate money." Autumn reached down and grabbed two bundles of the colorful cash. It was in mint condition.

"It's still gotta be worth something because it's ... historical." Ian fumbled for words as he picked up some money to examine it more closely.

"Nope," Autumn shook her head. "There was so much of this stuff printed that you can still find it in any antique store and pawnshop from Maryland to Mississippi. People have insulated their houses with this stuff. Right after the Civil War, during the rebuilding, people burned it to cook with and keep warm. The only reason anyone would want this is because it is in mint condition."

"Why do you suppose it isn't all worn? Southerners replaced their money just before the war started and used Confederate money till the very last day of the war." Ian grunted as he brought another large crate down the ladder.

"I don't know if you know this, but the McFarlands have been financially shrewd for generations. Before the Civil War, the McFarlands were against secession. They felt that no issue was worth tearing apart the greatest democracy on earth. Remember, they were patriots all the way through the Revolutionary War. Alyson McFarland was Scottish and Charles was Irish. Somewhere in the Family Bible they wrote, 'British by rule—Celtic by birth.' It didn't matter why or for what reason the colonies were revolting, the McFarlands were happy to follow suit simply because they came from countries that had experienced the injustice of the English monarchy for centuries."

"You have way too much information in your head," Ian interjected.

"Sorry, where was I going with this? Oh, anyway, the McFarland family fortune was safely tucked away in a respected Boston bank owned by Alyson's brother. Just before the war broke out, she traveled to Boston to withdraw a portion of that money. She brought it back to Charleston where she quickly cashed it in for Confederate bonds."

"Okay, but that doesn't explain why it all looks brand new." Ian sighed as the second crate opened to reveal more Confederate money.

"The McFarlands knew that the South was not going to come out victorious for all the reasons they *didn't* come out victorious: no railroads to connect them, no armories, no natural resources, no factories, and no gold to back their money. They had Confederate bills merely to survive the war and pretend to be firm supporters of the Confederacy. Before you pry any more of these open, I would guess that several more crates are just like these."

"So, when the war was over," Ian started. "I mean, the McFarlands have always been wealthy, haven't they?"

"Yes, that's why this house was still owned by the family and in its original state. Once the war ended, the McFarlands had their amassed family fortune to live off of until they could turn the corner on the Old South image and find another venture to be successful in."

"I assume that was financing?"

"You'd assume right. Much of the money the McFarlands made under the practice of slavery went to build the dominant industries that propelled the Industrial Revolution up North. They were key investors in industries that developed after the war as well as generous philanthropists."

Ian climbed on top of the stack of boxes once again. "Why are we still looking? You said these are all probably full of Confederate money," he grunted as he slid another box down the side of the stack.

"I don't think all of these boxes have money in them," Autumn coughed as a new wave of dust was unleashed. "Besides, what pressing task do you have on the calendar for today?"

"Hey, I work hard for you and this big old farm. Don't you forget that," Ian scolded with a smile on his face.

"I know you do. Now, get down here and help me open this box." Autumn had been able to pry the previous boxes open easily. She didn't know if it was because she was getting tired or if this one was sealed better. Either way, she needed added brawn to open this crate.

Ian slid down off the boxes. He noticed that this box was different from the boxes containing money. After prying the lid off, they met the lid of another box. This box looked more like a luggage crate. There was a decorative design carved in the top and the large rotting leather belts had rusted buckles. Autumn and Ian both grabbed opposite ends of the crate and lifted the box out.

"What do you suppose this is," Ian asked as he ran his hand over the top of the box. "It looks like something you would unload off a boat."

"It probably was unloaded off a boat two centuries ago. Let's see what is inside," Autumn turned excitedly to undo the latches. Carefully, she undid the sturdy buckles. Autumn could feel the leather in her hands flaking off as she worked with it. Part of her thought about waiting and following proper procedure when handling a historical artifact while the other part just could not wait.

Inside the trunk there were many personal belongings that told volumes about the people who had once owned them. There were skirts, underskirts, blouses, sleeping gowns and such. Close to the bottom, Autumn discovered a baby's baptismal gown carefully pressed, folded, and wrapped in plain brown paper. The gown, unlike the other garments, was extremely elegant. It was made of fine linen with delicate embroidery along the hem of the dress and along the neck line. It was trimmed in beautiful Venetian lace. Autumn held it in her hands and, for a moment, could feel the life of this gown.

A precious gift from God had been given to Charles and Alyson in this wild and rugged place. That had been a miracle in and of itself. Charles' and Alyson's life had been hard. As she caressed the delicate folds and stroked the beautiful lace trim, Autumn's reality fell away into their time. Tears streamed down Autumn's cheeks as she felt all that the mother to these babies must have felt. There was the joy of the first born child, a boy. He would have been the one to carry his father's name to the future. This boy would have someday been the owner of this land. The future had been imminently bright for him. Then, there was the little girl. She had held her father's heart the moment she had entered this world. She would have been the lady of the manor until she married and had her own family to care for and love. The third baby was a boy full of his father's love of life and reckless nature. He would have been the one to give his mother grey hair before her time. The last baby, a boy, died in the gown. He had been a fighter. His parents had been overjoyed at his arrival. That joy had soon faded when it had become apparent that something was wrong. Autumn could feel this baby's intense struggle to stay where he had been so loved and wanted. At the same time, she could feel his life bubbling away from him.

"Bubbling away," she thought to herself. As she held the gown, it became clear to her what had happened. This baby who had struggled to stay had drowned. He had taken water into his lungs while being born. The grief Autumn now felt was all consuming. She suddenly switched from sensing the child to the mother. Autumn had no idea how any woman could handle the passing of a child, especially a helpless infant. Long ago, a woman would have had no help. Autumn could not help but imagine what an immense sense of helplessness the mother must have had. It almost felt as if her insides had completely left her. Like a jack-o-lantern on Halloween, everything that made her real and solid had been painfully scraped from deep within her.

Ian must have sensed something going on because she could hear him frantically calling her name and shaking her shoulders gently. "Autumn? Autumn, there's someone who wants to see you," Ian whispered frantically.

When Autumn looked at Ian, she could see that the color completely left his face. His pale blue eyes were as wide as any dinner plate. As she was about to ask him what was wrong, her attention fell to an old rocking chair in the corner where Ian was setting the boxes. In the chair was the figure of a woman dressed in late eighteenth century clothes gently rocking back and forth. She held a small tattered cloth in her hands lovingly caressing it. "There's my girl. You know what happened to my baby boy. Nothing any of us could do but give him a life time of love in a few short minutes. Be a good girl and find Thomas for me. He left so long ago and we haven't heard from him. I need to know where my baby is." The lady finished by looking down lovingly at what Autumn could now see was a baby's blanket.

"I will do my best. Do you have any idea where he is," Autumn asked coolly.

"He left to fight the British with that Marion fellow. Promised he'd look after my Thomas. Did a great good for the cause of freedom, they did, but Thomas never came home."

"Can you see where he is or what he sees?" Autumn felt Ian's hand on her shoulder. He was no longer clutching her but releasing his grasp. She heard a dull thud as he collapsed on the floor behind her.

"There are beautiful green rolling hills and white fences as far as the eye can see. He is in the shade of a large buckeye tree looking up on a hill where many cows as black as night are standing."

"Is there anyone there with him," Autumn continued.

"No one there with him now but the land has seen the blood of brothers wash over it. Find this spot and the fairy rings will lead you to my boy."

Autumn, tired from the emotional journey the baptismal gown led her on, nodded her acceptance of this task. With that, the lady vanished into the darkness of the cellar. Autumn slumped down to the ground alongside Ian.

After a few moments, she leaned over to him and asked, "Are you okay?"

No reply came from Ian. He was still pale and wide-eyed.

"Help me get this upstairs." With that, she closed and latched the lid of the heavy chest and dragged it toward the ladder. As she passed the rocking chair, she saw a tattered baby blanket lying on the rocking chair. Autumn reached down and tucked it under her arm. "Well, are you going to help me or should I just leave you here?"

Ian shook his head violently and muttered, "No. Let's get out of here."

When they hoisted themselves and the trunk out of the hole in the kitchen wall, Autumn had to make Ian sit. She turned and said, "How about a drink?"

"Yeah," Ian replied.

"Not here. Let's go into the living room."

Ian sank into the couch while Autumn settled into the roomy chair. Ian sipped his beer quietly while starring at Autumn. After a few minutes, he whispered, "What the hell just happened down there?"

"We were visited by a spirit." Autumn knew that was not the answer Ian wanted but in the end would be the answer he needed.

"A what?"

"You know, a spirit, a ghost, an apparition, a ..."

"Yeah I get it!" There was a long silence before he continued. "Why are you okay with this?"

"Hi, remember me. Stranger visited by spirits from the moment I stepped on this beautiful old farm. I'm not 'okay with this'. I have learned to be 'okay with it'. It was either deal with it or leave. I think you know which one I chose."

"Hello, its dark outside."

Autumn smiled. She knew this experience well. The first time she encountered it was when the group of children returned to the party after encountering what they believed were actors reenacting slave life at the plantation. The children said they had been gone for over an hour but that could not have been true. The adults had sent them off only twenty minutes earlier. What had seemed to be a little over an hour to the children had only been moments for the parents. During Autumn's encounters with Charles, she felt like she was crawling out of bed minutes after she just went to bed but an entire night had passed.

"I can't really explain why it happens, but when I encounter someone or something like we just did, time gets all screwed up. What felt like only a very brief time during our 'visit' actually must have been almost two or three hours?"

"You know the more you talk, the weirder this all gets." Ian finished his beer in one long gulp.

"You want another beer?"

"I think that would help," Ian said as he stared off into space.

Autumn got up to go into the kitchen. As she did, she apologetically added, "I wish I could give you a better explanation for all this but ..." Her train of thought was interrupted by the phone ringing. "Just a second, I'll be right back."

An exasperated voice spoke from the phone. It was Boyd. He decided that his father was not going to be happy until he spent a month living with the animals before he chose one. Autumn laughed to herself. Autumn had a strong impression that the apple didn't fall too far from the tree in the case of Boyd and his dad.

"What can I do to help?"

"Nothing unless you can divine some telltale signs to help him select *the* best horse."

"I don't know if it's divination but here's what I'd do."

"Yes," Boyd waited eagerly.

"Just pick the prettiest one!"

In his husky smooth voice, he laughed gently. "You are such a girl."

"You asked, I told." They both laughed at her simple suggestion. It wasn't until that moment that Autumn realized how long Boyd had been in Virginia and how much she missed him. "So, since I can't help your dad, can I do anything for you?"

"Well," he started hesitantly in the boyish tone he got whenever he felt insecure. Autumn could picture his coal black eyes burning a hole in the floor in front of him and the wily grin sliding from his face. "I wasn't going to ask but ..."

"But now that I brought it up. Yeah, what is it?"

"Would you fly up here for the rest of the stay? I'm losing my mind and I miss you. Heck, maybe you can convince dad of that whole 'just pick the pretty one' idea. Come."

"Sure. I'll get the first flight out tomorrow. Let me see Ian off and I'll call my flight crew." Autumn's heart began racing. She was missing Boyd and loved the idea of another adventure. "Plus", she thought silently, "he must be pretty serious about me or desperately lonely if wants me around his dad."

Her thoughts were interrupted by Boyd's question and tone, "Ian? What's Ian doing there so late?"

"What," Autumn blurted out in response to Boyd's tone. "Why Mr. Masters," she asked in her best cool and coy southern belle voice, "are you jealous?"

"No," he lied unconvincingly. "I just thought it was a little late to be working on home repairs."

"You *are* jealous!" Autumn didn't want to pick a fight tonight. She and Boyd could tear into things but it was always in fun. Tonight, however, Boyd seemed too tired and too lonely. "It is not too late for home repairs if the lady of the house has spent the day knocking out a wall in the kitchen. Plus, one of those strange things happened today that happen any time you uncover something here. You're tired, Ian's freaked, and I have got to pack. I'll give you the gory details when I see you tomorrow. Okay?"

"Yeah, sorry. Tell Ian I said 'Hey'." The fire and brimstone left his voice. The outburst seemed to have made Boyd even more tired. "I'm going to stay up till I hear back from you about tomorrow. I love you."

"I'll call back really soon so you can hit it. I love you. Bye."

"Bye."

Autumn grabbed a beer quickly and got back to Ian. It may have been a good thing that Boyd's call interrupted their discussion. Ian seemed to be less agitated than when she left him.

Autumn started things. "Sorry. That was Boyd. Here's your drink."

"How are things going in Virginia," Ian asked as he leaned over to get his drink.

"Not real good, I guess. His dad still hasn't decided on a horse."

"I've never met Boyd's dad but if he's anything like Boyd, he's not someone who would just jump head first into any big decision. Guess he's going to be gone a little longer than he thought." Ian seemed to have fully recovered from his first *ghostly* encounter.

"Yeah. I'm going to fly up to Virginia for a couple of days. Boyd's getting a little exasperated with his dad's thoroughness."

"So, how many ghosts have you encountered since you moved here?"

Autumn was not going to bring up the subject until Ian recovered. Now she was worried as to how much she should tell him. After all, she would be leaving the house in his care while she was away. Autumn didn't want him to avoid the house. "Oh, I don't know. Haven't you ever seen anything weird around here? You've worked here much longer than I have lived here."

"Do you really think I would have been so freaked out if I had seen ghosts here before?" Ian was looking at her with an ornery expression. Whenever he got that look, he would lead her to reveal more than she wanted to reveal.

"I don't know. They still freak me out and I've seen them a lot!" Just as the words escaped her mouth, she clasped both hands over her mouth. It was too late. She had done what she always did when Ian smiled at her that way.

"Hah! A lot, huh?"

"Not a lot. Well, maybe a lot but only on a few occasions." Autumn shook her head. She'd better quit talking before she made matters worse.

"I have never seen anything weird or out of the ordinary in all the years I've worked for Jon. This was definitely a first for me. I hope it is the last, too."

Autumn let out a sigh. "If it is any consolation, few people have ever seen anything weird or ghostly on the McFarland Farm. No one ever sees anything out of the ordinary except when I am around." She flopped down into the chair. "So, the best thing anyone can do around here is to stay away from me, I guess."

"Well, I don't know about that. Maybe it's just the fact that you are the first owner of this farm that isn't from the family." Ian took another sip and kicked up his feet.

"Didn't I tell you," Autumn reached for the little box sitting on the table in front of them. "I'm not sure yet, but I just might be a very distant relative of Jon McFarland. That's the latest twist in this crazy story." She cracked open the lid of the tiny box and thought she saw a glow coming from the large quartz.

"Why would that surprise you," Ian smiled as he finished his beer. "I'll tell you, I knew Jon McFarland pretty well but I had no idea he was hatching all this with you. Heck, he never even said anything about you."

Autumn looked up from the contents of the box. "I don't even know that Jon knew the full extent of his actions. I really think that I just reminded him of a friendly face from his past. The cold reality of his own mortality and the end of the McFarland bloodline caused him to act. He would have probably been having as much fun as we are with all these new discoveries."

"Fun," Ian said sarcastically. "Is that what you call this? Well, I've had enough *fun* for one day. Plus, you've gotta get ready for your trip. I'm going to get going. Will I see you in the morning?"

"I don't know. Are you coming back?"

"Me? Heck, yeah. There won't be any house to haunt without me. I'll be here like always." Ian got up and headed toward the front door. "You're not going to be here, so I should be safe."

Autumn got up and followed him to the front door. She laughed a little, "Yeah, you're right. Okay, then. If I don't see you tomorrow, it'll be because I've already left. Are you okay?"

"The beers," Ian screwed up his face. "Please, two beers in two hours? Yeah, I'm fine."

"Well, good but I was talking about all the stuff that happened in the basement today."

"Sure. Now I'm more upset that I have to figure out how to get all that stuff out of the basement, store it, and patch your hammer holes. I'll be sending you the bill."

"Fine. Good night."

"Night."

Autumn stood at the front door until she saw Ian's lights fade. While she watched, she arranged her flight to Reagan International Airport and quickly called Boyd so he could pick her up tomorrow morning. The conversation was brief. Once plans were made, Autumn ran upstairs and quickly threw things together. November was here and Virginia was not South Carolina. With enthusiasm, Autumn dug out her heavy winter coat and found her gloves. She looked forward to bundling up against the cold, seeing this Virginia horse ranch, and Boyd.

Autumn's plane landed at Reagan International Airport shortly after eight the following morning. It was another gray and wintry day. Autumn thought how much the day reminded her of winter back home. Even the gray days in South Carolina couldn't completely hide the sun. Winter in Ohio could seem endless. The airport was large and in a very urban place. It stood in stark contrast to her remote farm and the tiny Myrtle Beach Airport. The terminal was abuzz with business travelers to Washington D.C. Everyone seemed late for something. Cell phones rang. Hardly anyone made eye contact as they rushed from the gates to the luggage bays and out of the airport. Autumn couldn't help but laugh. She was the only one looking around at the sights and sounds that greeted her as she left the plane, gathered her bags, and went to wait for Boyd outside at passenger pick-up. Autumn had, indeed, become a southerner. Her pace changed. Two years ago, she lived life in a hurry to get from point A to point B but never really knew why. It was just the way life moved in her part of the world. Now, time was something to be savored rather than measured. Autumn stared at the faces that flew past. No one returned her friendly smile except the children moving through the airport trying to keep up with the adults. They would smile at her like they knew something these harried adults were missing.

Autumn thought, "Yeah. It's life. Everyone's so busy trying to *get* the most out of life that they've forgotten to *make* the most of life."

Within a minute or two of stepping out into the icy air from the Potomac, Boyd pulled to the curb. She knew it was him. Everyone else was driving fancy SUVs or elegant European sedans. Boyd rattled up to the curb in an old full-size pickup truck that he must have driven off the fields. It was coated from rims to rack in mud. "You need a ride, pretty lady?"

Boyd threw the truck into park and set the brake just before hopping out to greet her. He wrapped his lean muscular arms around her and lifted her into the air. "You can't imagine how happy I am to see you. Thanks for coming," he whispered just before placing a gentle kiss on her lips. He grabbed her suitcase and tossed it easily over the side. That was Boyd. His natural athleticism was easy to detect. Autumn did not realize how lonely she had been for him. She even missed the way he smelled. It was a mix of soap, cologne, and fresh air. Autumn could smell the wind on his soul. Even though he was complaining about his dad putting him through the rigors, there was no place Boyd would rather be than out chasing the wind on the back of a beautiful horse. "We'd better get back before dad once again decides I have no idea what I'm talking about when it comes to horses. Maybe once he sees you, he'll know I have good taste in something." Boyd hopped into the cab and quickly ran his fingers through his shoulder-length wavy sandy-blonde hair.

"So, do you love winter," Autumn ribbed Boyd. She knew he disliked winter in South Carolina which was barely winter.

"Right, let's just say that it's a toss-up between my dad and the cold."

Within minutes of hitting the beltway, the urban landscape faded away to gently rolling hills with miles and miles of white fences. "Where exactly *is* this farm," Autumn asked.

"It's technically in Manassas. That is the closest city or town. Sort of like your farm and mine aren't exactly in Georgetown but they are." Boyd cast a fox-like grin her direction. Autumn thought she saw a gleam in his eyes. Autumn loved his smile. It was a crooked smile set on a beautifully sculpted face. His perfectly proportioned and graceful features were like that of a statue. His eyes always revealed his duality. There was something playful and intense about his eyes. The way he looked at her always made her blush.

"What," Autumn asked hoping he hadn't noticed her blush.

"Nothing," he said still flashing the same look.

"What?"

"I'm trying to decide," he said in his rich southern drawl.

Autumn laughed, trying to hide the fact that he was making her blush even more. "Decide what?"

"Well, I've seen you in every season in South Carolina and couldn't decide which season made you look the most beautiful." He glanced once again in her direction. "Now, I think I've got a winner."

"Your dad's driven you crazy! What the heck are you talking about?"

"This is the first time that I have seen you in really cold weather. You know. All bundled up in your long suede and camel fur waist coat with ear muffs and gloves. I think you are the most beautiful thing I have ever seen." Boyd turned the truck off the main road and through the stone gates of the farm. There were white fences and fields. The fields were littered with large gray stones. Looking closely, there were masses of cows. "Well, we're here."

"What's this horse farm doing amid all these cattle farms," Autumn asked. She was flattered by his comments but wanted desperately to change the subject to something slightly less embarrassing.

"Beef," Boyd barked in a heavy tone.

"Beef what?"

"Beef. Beef cows to be exact. I don't know why these folk raise horses while everybody else raises beef cattle. Just is."

The road into the farm was not a straight shot like the dirt roads that lead to the Masters' ranch or the McFarland farm. After they had crested the large hill and were coming down the other side, Autumn could make out the large brick colonial style home that must belong to the family. "That's it. When I first got here, I thought I was in the wrong place."

"Why did you think that?" Autumn thought the house looked pretty typical for Virginia.

Boyd pointed in the direction of the house, "The directions ended with 'the large colonial house will be in view as you crest the hill of the main drive."

Autumn looked at Boyd, slightly puzzled. "Yeah, that's where I first saw it."

Boyd returned her bewildered look, "That's no colonial style house."

"Oh!" Autumn finally realized why he was confused. "You're right. It is not a colonial style house like in Charleston. It is much more of a Jamestown, Virginia style colonial. It's such a funny word for an architectural style because it is different depending on which part of the original thirteen colonies you are in. Believe it or not, New England and Pennsylvania have two more styles of colonial homes."

"See, I should never leave you at home. You know so much about that sort of thing. Oh look," Boyd's voice went flat. "There's dad. I hope you ate on the plane because it looks like he's raring to go."

Autumn squinted out the window to see the people in the distance. There was a short stocky man standing with a tall barrel-chested older gentleman. The shorter man was Harrison Masters. Autumn met him a year ago at Christmas when the Masters clan came to Boyd's for the holiday. Boyd and Autumn's romance was still new. She had the definite impression that Mr. Masters had been on his best behavior. Autumn wondered if that would be the case at this meeting. After all, she and Boyd had been together for more than a year now. Plus, Evelyn wouldn't be there to rein in her husband if he got out of line. The other gentleman had to be Mr. Berlin, completely gray but had the build of someone no older than forty. His face was red and cheery. The two men seemed to be locked in a debate.

"No. I ate before I left this morning. I sort of thought this would be the case." Autumn reached over the back seat to open her carry-on bag. "That's why I stuck these in my carry-on." She bent down to pull on her riding boots.

"I can't believe him. Sorry about this. I promise we'll have a nice dinner alone tonight, okay?"

"It's fine. The quicker we get your dad to decide, the quicker you and I can go home, right?"

"Right."

Autumn had sensed the frustration in Boyd's voice during their brief phone conversations. Now, she could see the rage brewing just below the surface in Boyd's eyes.

After polite introductions, the three of them were on horseback riding out to check the herd. Mr. Berlin would join them in a little while. The Masters both made horse riding look so natural. It was still very unnatural for Autumn. Never having ridden a horse before moving to South Carolina, Autumn was spoiled by her horse, Ebony. She always looked after Autumn. Ebony was patient when Autumn would be unnecessarily rough with her boots or the reins. Ebony understood that Autumn could not handle a full run on horseback. They always rode at a gentle trot. This morning, Autumn was not on Ebony and needed to keep up with the guys. By the time they reached the herd, Autumn's legs were numb from squeezing the saddle. Her backside felt every stride since they left the house.

Boyd reached over to Autumn. "We have to stay on horseback to keep up with them. They are used to people but can really take off if they want. Plus, the herd likes to spook horses with riders. Why don't you slide onto my horse just in case they decide to send you running?"

Autumn knew what Boyd meant. She was inexperienced on a horse. If the herd took off, she would not be able to keep her horse from following. She also couldn't control a horse well enough if it got spooked. He was protecting her from getting hurt, lost, or embarrassed. She gently dropped the reins of her horse and slid onto Boyd's. This was the closest she had been to Boyd in a long while. Autumn knew they were there to look at the horses in the field but it was hopeless for Autumn. All she could think about was how good Boyd smelled and how much she loved having his arms around her. As they rode along, she could feel his muscles flex as he steered the horse around the herd. At one point, Autumn thought Boyd must have been equally enthralled sharing the saddle with her because Mr. Masters glared over at Boyd with a disapproving frown.

When they had been out in the field for over an hour, Mr. Berlin and a couple ranch hands rode out to meet them. "So, Harry, which ones can we pull in today?"

"Same two I suppose," Mr. Masters added dryly. "You two lovebirds going to come in?" The droll expression on Mr. Masters' face made it perfectly clear that he did not approve of Autumn being there.

"You old bear. Leave 'em alone. There was a time in our lives when there were more interesting things than money and horses," Mr. Berlin added cheerily in his elegant Virginian accent.

Mr. Masters mumbled something under his breath and rode off.

"Come on you two. We'll let the boys wrangle the two up to the corral." Mr. Berlin saddled his horse alongside Boyd and Autumn. "Now, don't you go listening to that old bear. I for one am glad to see such a beautiful lady here on a gray winter's day. I know Boyd is too. Come on. I'll get your horse back, Autumn, dear. It'll take a little while to get the horses back to the corral. You two take your time." With that, Mr. Berlin spurred his horse and was out of sight in moments.

What had started out as a gray cold morning was becoming a sunny day with not a single cloud in the sky. Like most winter days, the sun was a fooler. It did very little to heat the air. The azure sky made the barren trees and yellow grasses of winter look especially stark by contrast. The air that had been cold became crisp. For several moments, Autumn and Boyd just rode in silence. One of the things that Boyd enjoyed the most about Autumn was that they didn't always have to be engaged in lively conversation. Autumn being a natural chatterbox found it very easy to be with Boyd and not say anything. Mostly, they just enjoyed the moment. Autumn was continually amazed at how hard a rider has to work to ride a horse. When looking at someone who rides well, it looks effortless. Boyd looked that way. However, riding in the saddle with him, she became aware of how many muscles he used to ride.

The scenery seemed almost as awesome as being alone with Boyd. The area of Virginia had gently rolling hills. It seemed funny to be just minutes from the nation's capitol without any sign of it. Just before the barn came in sight, Boyd broke the silence. "So, what happened yesterday?"

Autumn tore herself away from the sights to reply. "Oh, that was just yesterday? It seems like forever ago. Well, you know the strange things that happen at the house?"

"I know the strange things that happen when you are around at the house, yes."

Autumn was going to reprimand him but it was the truth. "I happened to have found a lot of things since you've been gone. They have sort of become a 'Pandora's box'. It started in the attic when I found this beautiful little box. That led me to one discovery after another that culminated in the basement."

Boyd pulled the reigns a little to slow down the gait of the horse. "There are no basements in houses like yours."

"That's what Ian told me. However, my house was built over and around the original settler's cabin. Anyway, long story short, when we were in the basement, someone appeared to deliver a message to me."

Boyd laughed uncontrollably, "You mean to tell me that big tough Ian was afraid of a ghost!"

"Now that's not fair! Haven't you ever seen something that scared you?"

"Not since I was nine or ten!"

"Well, then you have never seen a ghost. Mostly, I think he was surprised by the fact that it wasn't at all what he imagined seeing a ghost would be like."

"What does that mean?"

Autumn didn't want to get into a deep discussion with Boyd. "I just think he was surprised, that's all."

"So, is he going to stay away till you come home?"

"No. I told him that if he never saw one before he won't. I explained that those things usually only happen when I'm around. Ian seemed fine with that.

Plus, he can't stay away. I knocked a wall out in the kitchen. He's got a lot of dry wall and spackling to do before I get home!" Boyd was about to ask about the hole in the kitchen until Autumn added, "Don't ask."

By the time Autumn and Boyd reached the barns and the corral, the two horses Mr. Masters was debating over were there. Mr. Berlin waved to Boyd and Autumn whereas Mr. Masters looked slightly annoyed. When they dismounted and reached the fence, Mr. Berlin reached out an arm for Autumn.

Boyd climbed up the fence next to Mr. Masters. "So, what are you thinking *today?*"

Autumn could sense the deep sarcasm in Boyd's voice and flinched a little. "All this," Autumn thought to herself, "is not making his dad any happier that I am here."

Luckily, Mr. Masters just looked disdainfully at Boyd. Autumn could tell by the look on Mr. Masters' face that he was no closer to deciding on a horse. The two horses, a stallion and a mare, were beautiful animals. The stallion was penny-red with a black mane. There was something about him that still seemed wild and untamed. The mare was black from the tip of her nose to the end of her tail. She was the horse that won the Triple Crown. Apparently, Mr. Masters had negotiated that deal back on the table. She just stood in the corral eating carrots from one of the ranch hands. Each horse was wild and strong but with very different dispositions. After watching the two of them for a few minutes, Autumn blurted out, "Why don't you just buy their foal in the spring?"

It was apparent by the look Mr. Masters was giving her that her opinion was not welcomed or necessary. Boyd leaned back and gave her a grin that said, "I love it when someone else pisses my dad off."

Autumn sort of cowered behind Mr. Berlin. She was grateful he pulled her over and even more grateful that he was a tall fellow. Mr. Berlin grinned from ear to ear. "Well, that would be a wonderful idea, darling, if we could get these two to foal. There are qualities about each that he likes and doesn't like. What he doesn't like in one, he finds in the other. Like I said before, we can't get them to foal."

"But she's pregnant now. She should foal by late March or early April, right?" Autumn had no idea where the words were coming from but they wouldn't stop coming.

"What makes you so sure she's carrying," Mr. Berlin asked while waving one of the ranch hands over to him.

"I don't know. I guess it's just a feeling I have."

"A feeling, huh," Mr. Berlin added just before whispering something to the man he waved over. "Well, it's easy enough to check. He's going to take her in the stables and have the vet check your feeling out."

"You've got to be kidding me? You're going to haul that horse in because she has a *feeling*." All the disdain Mr. Masters felt since she arrived found a voice. He turned to Autumn. "I think Mr. Berlin would know if these two had foaled, dear."

Autumn wanted the earth to swallow her up. Mr. Masters was always curt but never as unkind as now. Mr. Berlin must have sensed her feelings. Before Mr. Masters even muttered a word, Mr. Berlin put his massive arm around her shoulder in a fatherly embrace.

"Dad! You've been nothing but mean to her since she got here and that was just a couple hours ago. She didn't do anything but share her thoughts on the subject." Boyd's eyes flashed with rage. His handsome angular jaw was set in an attempt to control his anger. Autumn felt terrible because Boyd was already frustrated with his father. She managed to make it worse.

Before anyone could say another word, Mr. Berlin calmly leaned around Mr. Masters. "Why don't you two go into town and get some lunch? Show this lady around Manassas. There are several shops in town she might like. It will take the doc an hour or so to get here." He reached his massive hand out to Boyd and put Autumn's hand in it. "Go on."

Without another word, Autumn and Boyd set off to his car parked in front of the barn. Autumn was happy to be leaving but still felt horrible for having opened her mouth.

"I'm sorry about dad," Boyd whispered. Autumn could still see the fury in his eyes.

"Don't worry about it," Autumn said meekly still cowering from Mr. Masters scathing comment.

"No, it's not right. He's had me up here almost all month yelling, lecturing, and just being shitty. I needed you to come and save me; not to be abused." Boyd stepped in front of Autumn. "I mean it. I needed you to save me. I am sorry."

"He is probably missing home too. It's been a tough decision for him and you said he never asked for your help before. Maybe it is bothering him that he had to ask for your help."

"Look at you," Boyd took her face in his hands. "My dad acts like the jerk of all jerks and you try to defend him. You keep amazing me." In the clear crisp air, Autumn could feel the warmth of Boyd's lips as they pressed against hers. It was a long warm kiss that eased the tension both of them were feeling. "Your chariot waits."

Leaving the farm, they passed more farms with cows and white fences. Just before entering the city of Manassas, Boyd and Autumn were passed the Manassas Battle Field. It was the sight of two of the largest and most pivotal battles during the Civil War. Battle fields were uneasy places for Autumn. Too many spirits were still tethered to this world. Each story and their eternal search could be sadder than the next. Battlefields made her want to cry and vomit all at the same time. Boyd asked if she wanted to stop. Autumn declined saying that places like that sort of short circuited her "feelings". There was too much input in places like that.

Just shy of the battlefield, Manassas's business district opened before them. They drove past the new businesses and restaurants to find a small café in the historic section of Manassas. After having a nice warm lunch, they decided to work their way down the road. Autumn wasn't a big fan of shopping but today was different. If shopping meant they didn't have to go back to the farm until the veterinarian finished, she'd shop till she dropped. Three shops into their journey, a small antiques store caught Autumn's eye. She asked to go inside. Boyd seemed more than happy to oblige because he was very uncomfortable in the winter air of Virginia. The antique shop was small but everything inside was carefully displayed. There was a huge glass counter in the back that held antique firearms. Boyd headed there. To the left of the entrance door was a display case in the window. Inside, Autumn could see several pieces of Confederate money and some war medals. To her surprise, the bills inside were being sold for face value or a few dollars more. The proprietor of the store approached her. He explained that the money was only worth what a collector was willing to pay. The money was also more valuable to a collector if it was worn and tattered. Not very much Confederate money had actually circulated but a lot had been minted. Circulated bills, being rare, increased their value. Autumn explained to the owner that she found several large crates of Confederate bills in her basement which had never seen the light of day. He explained that most people have had that experience with the bills. Suddenly, their conversation was interrupted by Boyd hollering for Autumn from the back of the shop. Autumn took off running and the shop owner followed suit.

"What is it?" Autumn was very confused because Boyd never found anything of interest in antique shops.

He grabbed her arm as soon as she came within reach. "Look at that pistol."

Autumn scanned the case but there were several pistols in the large case. "Which one?"

"Over here. It's the one with the dark gray body and the reddish brown handle."

The store owner reached them and asked, "May I show you anything in the case, sir." Boyd did not hear because he was so intent on making Autumn see the pistol.

Autumn still couldn't decipher which dark gray pistol with which reddish brown handle he was talking about. The shop owner finally got Boyd's attention, "Excellent choice, sir." He reached inside and withdrew the pistol Boyd was describing.

"Thank you," Autumn said as the shop owner handed Boyd the pistol. "Now, what are you talking about?"

"There is something inscribed on the handle of this pistol I think you should see."

Boyd thrust the pistol into her hands. On the wooden part of the handle, Autumn could make out the inscription. It read TJ McFarland SC. Boyd asked the shop proprietor if he knew anything about the pistol.

"Well, it is very old but in very good condition. The piece dates back before the Revolutionary War. It is one of the finest guns I have seen from that era. The handle is Old World cherry which implies that the piece had been fashioned in Europe."

Boyd and Autumn didn't care about the age or condition of the piece. They were more interested in the inscription on the handle. "Can you tell us anything about the inscription on the handle," Boyd asked as Autumn nodded in agreement. She was still in shock of finding something so old with the McFarland name in Virginia of all places.

"Well, no. All I can tell you is that people from that era usually carved in the butt of their guns." Autumn looked up. Boyd looked disappointed but Autumn learned a long time ago that something small and insignificant can be pivotal in uncovering a mystery. "People usually carved their names in the weapon. See, it would have been a very expensive purchase. A weapon like this would have been passed on from generation to generation. It would be a family heirloom."

"The family heirloom, huh," Boyd asked as he elbowed Autumn. "You wouldn't happen to know the history of this particular piece?"

"As I mentioned before, all I know is what era it dates to, who the manufacturer was, and that it is in excellent condition."

"You have to keep records just in case an antique comes back as stolen, right?" Autumn knew that was the case in most states. She hoped that was the case in Virginia.

"No, but I always issue receipts when I purchase an item. I guess it is to prove that I did not come across the item illegally. Why?"

"Can you tell us who sold this item to you," Autumn asked.

"Sure. I don't need to look it up. When a beautiful relic like this crosses my path, I always remember the seller. It was Mr. Berlin. When his wife passed on, he brought in several items. This was one of them."

Boyd looked shocked. "Why would he sell such a valuable piece that has such a legacy attached to it? He strikes me as the type who would proudly display this in his own home."

"Oh, I said the very same thing. I explained how valuable the piece is. He didn't seem to care. It's possible that no one ever told him the story behind this weapon. It sort of lost its history and therefore lost its value to the family.

"So," Autumn continued, "the original owner of this weapon could likely have been TJ McFarland?"

"Right."

"What does the 'SC' mean?" Autumn was still trying to pin down specifics.

The shop owner turned the piece over to take a better look at the handle. "The manufacturers mark is actually cast in the barrel of the weapon. So, that's not it. I really couldn't tell you what it is."

"It could be the state that this TJ McFarland was from, couldn't it." Autumn could hardly contain her excitement. It seemed almost unimaginable that she would come to Virginia and find a McFarland family heirloom. Yet, the name on the gun could very well be Thomas James McFarland of the South Carolina McFarland's.

"Again, I really couldn't say what that means. That is as probable an explanation as any."

Without hesitating, Autumn purchased the weapon. Fortunately, weapons of antiquity do not have to be licensed if they are purchased through an antique dealer. Plus, the weapon was a flintlock gun. One would have to pack and load it manually. In fact, the proprietor of the shop said that it would probably destroy the value of the weapon or destroy the weapon if anyone tried to fire it.

Two hours had passed since leaving the farm. Boyd hoped that had given the vet time to run his tests. With nothing but the gun on her mind, Autumn forgot all about the blistering comment from Mr. Masters. She couldn't wait to get back to the farm and ask Mr. Berlin what he knew about the pistol. When Autumn and Boyd pulled up to the corral, Mr. Masters and Mr. Berlin were grinning from ear to ear. The atmosphere appeared much more relaxed than it had been this morning. The two men saw the car pull in. They broke off their conversation to head toward the car.

"Great, here he comes. He's like a vulture. Can't even wait till I stop moving to pounce on me." Boyd's tone let her know that even though she forgot what happened this morning, Boyd had not.

"Well, boy, you ready to go home?" Mr. Masters was smiling. Autumn could see where Boyd got his crooked smile. "Did you hear me?"

"Yeah," Boyd grunted. "Why?" He could almost tell that he asked a loaded question.

"Cause," boomed Mr. Berlin in his deep bass voice. "That girl of yours is as smart as she is pretty."

"What do you mean?" The sour expression that had crept over Boyd's face as they got closer to the farm lifted like a mask.

"The mare," Mr. Masters interjected, "she's pregnant. Just within the last few days. She should foal by late March or early April. Isn't that right?" Mr. Masters reached out and grabbed Autumn in a big hug. He was not a man that would ever apologize for having wounded someone with his words or actions. However, the hug was his way of admitting what a jerk he had been. Autumn thought that Boyd got yet another trait from his father.

"Looks like you flew here just to ride home tomorrow. Look," Mr. Berlin gestured towards Boyd, "He looks like a prisoner who's just been told his sentence has been commuted. Your pa that bad?"

"No, he's worse." Boyd was grinning from ear to ear. He looked at the ground to hide it from everybody.

"Let's head in for some coffee. It's been a long day." Mr. Berlin said as he clapped his rugged hands on the shoulders of Boyd and Mr. Masters.

As the four of them made their way up to the house, Mr. Berlin asked Autumn where her packages were. "I told that boy to take you shopping. What did you two do for two hours, huh?" Mr. Berlin ribbed Boyd.

"It's not my fault. She hates to shop," Boyd replied slightly embarrassed by Mr. Berlin's insinuation.

"A woman who hates to shop? Boy you better hang on to this one!" Mr. Berlin's laugh was loud and boisterous.

"Well, that's not entirely true. I do love antiques." Autumn retrieved the pistol from her purse and laid it on the table in front of Mr. Berlin.

"Is that my pistol," Mr. Berlin's smile faded just a bit when he saw the piece.

"It is," Autumn added tentatively because she wasn't sure what it was, but she knew she had touched a nerve.

"Well, I'll be. You collect guns?" His voice became suddenly flat and lifeless.

"I'm sorry, Mr. Berlin. I didn't mean to upset you." Autumn's apology was sincere. At the same time, she was disappointed by his negative reaction. She hardly felt like she could press him for more information.

"Oh," Mr. Berlin shook his head like someone trying to wakeup from a bad dream. "You didn't upset me, dear. Just caught me by surprise. That's all." He drew in a deep slow breath as he leaned back in his chair. "You see, this gun is a family heirloom of my wife's. When she died, I got rid of anything and everything that reminded me of her. The shop owner probably told you how he tried to talk me out of it."

Autumn nodded.

"Foolish thing to do. My kids were furious but I wouldn't listen to them. They told me that later on I would regret doing it. I did. Then, I couldn't think of the future. It took all I could muster to deal with the moment. I'd loved her since we were ten years old. She wasn't supposed to leave me. So, if you don't collect guns, why buy one?"

Autumn felt the tears slowly running down her cheeks. She tried to keep her composure. No way could she do that if she tried to talk. That's when Boyd came to her rescue. "Well, you see the name on the handle: McFarland. Autumn's farm belonged to Jon McFarland. She thought maybe they were the same family. Do you know anything about the gun?"

Mr. Berlin went on to tell them what he knew about the gun. Apparently the Berlin name came recently to the ranch he now owned. The ranch existed for generations as had the Masters and McFarland farms. However, the ranch had been passed down from mother to daughter over the years. No one had a male heir. Some local folk said the farm was cursed. Plenty of male children had been born. None of them lived to be adults. The first daughter to inherit the ranch married a fellow by the name of McFarland. He was brought to Virginia during the Revolutionary War as a British prisoner of war. His internment had been interesting because the British took such care to make sure their prisoner didn't get away or have any contact with the other prisoners. From what Mr. Berlin remembered of the story, McFarland had suffered from post traumatic stress memory loss. He had been an honest man with a keen sense for business. He had worked for a few years until he had saved up enough to start his own farm. Shortly after the farm, he had met and married Mrs. Berlin's great-great grandmother. That was how Mr. Berlin came to own the farm. That was all he knew of the gun.

Autumn had finally pulled herself together enough to ask, "What was Mrs. Berlin's great-great grandfather's name?"

"Says right there on the gun, TJ McFarland. Thomas James McFarland."

"Then, I believe that this Thomas James is the long lost son of Alyson and Charles McFarland who were the original owners of my farm."

"This rightly belongs to you then." Mr. Berlin's smile and thunderous voice had returned.

"No, it belongs here with the descendants of TJ McFarland. I only own the farm. I'm not a McFarland by name. The gun would have been traditionally passed from father to son. But," Autumn paused, thinking about the request that Alyson made of her the other afternoon in the basement. "Would it be all right if I took it with me just for a little while?"

"Sure. Why don't you just bring it back when you come in the spring to collect the foal?"

"I don't …"

Autumn was interrupted by Mr. Masters, "Of course you and Boyd will come back when I collect the foal." Autumn knew she wasn't doing a very good job of hiding her surprise at this announcement. Boyd was worse than her. After all, this trip had been way more than he bargained.

"You two think about it. Worst comes to worse, I'll come to South Carolina to retrieve the pistol," Mr. Berlin added before either Boyd or Autumn could say anything.

Boyd and Autumn were headed upstairs when Boyd leaned over. He kissed Autumn passionately for the first time since her arrival. Pressing her against the wall, Autumn felt herself fall willingly into Boyd's love. He was not a man of words. Boyd was a man of action. Tonight, his body would tell her what she needed to know about his longing for her and the ache he felt at being away from her. Boyd gently lifted Autumn into his arms and carried her into his room. "Remember, no matter what happens, I will always love you," Boyd said as he gently laid her on his bed.

CHAPTER 10

▼

BLESSINGS AND CURSES

After returning from Virginia, Boyd became overwhelmed by all the work he missed at his farm. Boyd's farmhands maintained the horses and the work never stopped for them. However, the phone and computer logged more than a few messages from potential customers. Autumn did not hear or see from Boyd the first couple of days they were back. Saturday morning, there was a knock on Autumn's door. To her surprise, Boyd emerged from the solitude of the farm. "So, what are we doing for breakfast?"

"We are having whatever I decide to cook, I suppose," Autumn said groggily. She turned to walk into the kitchen. "Well, what are you waiting for, an engraved invitation?"

Boyd slid through the front door and caught up to Autumn. "I was going to take you out for breakfast but ..."

"Because I am the picture of loveliness first thing in the morning?"

Boyd ran up to her and grabbed her in a big hug. "You are such a morning person." With that, he planted a big wet sarcastic kiss on her.

"Quit clutching on me. You know I'm not a morning person." She playfully shoved him away and wiped the kiss off.

"Hey, what happened here," Boyd asked as he stopped in the doorway to the kitchen.

Autumn put her head in the refrigerator, "Remember, I told you. I took a hammer to the wall trying to find the basement."

"Yeah," Boyd hopped up on the kitchen counter, "I know but there's a door there. Why is there a door there?"

"So I wouldn't have to take a hammer to the wall the next time I wanted to go exploring in the basement. Ian really likes to patch dry wall."

In no time, Autumn cooked them a simple breakfast. There hadn't been a good time to fill Boyd in on all the details of the basement when she got to Virginia. The first chance they had to talk since coming back to South Carolina was today.

"What are you going to do with all the crates," Boyd asked as he smeared jelly on the last biscuit.

"I helped Ian move them out to the garage two days ago. I don't know if any one will want them. Remember what that guy told me in Virginia. I might as well burn them rather than haul them somewhere." Autumn stood to start cleaning up. "What do you think I should do with them?"

"It doesn't seem right to just burn them. Maybe you should ask Lillian. She might want them." Boyd leaned back on his chair content and stuffed. "If she doesn't want them, she might know someone who would."

Autumn placed the last of the dishes in the dishwasher. The kitchen was large enough for an entire cooking staff. When there are just the two of them, the room rang with every move. "I'll call her. She always gets me in on one of her research projects if I go there in person."

"Come on. I'll take you. That way you'll have an excuse to leave. She'd never ask you to stay if I am there." Autumn could see that Boyd was suffering from a serious case of cabin fever. He seemed in no hurry to get back home.

"Hi. Have you met Lillian? She gets so focused on a task that she'd ask a heart surgeon to postpone surgery if she thought he could help her."

"I can't go home yet. All I've done for three days is sit and talk to people who either want a horse or need help with a horse. I'm done." Boyd looked at her with his dark piecing eyes and a forlorn expression on his face.

"Give me a half hour to pull myself together," Autumn moaned. She had a feeling that she would regret this decision. When she came back downstairs, Autumn found Boyd and Ian in the kitchen. Ian told Boyd his version of the day he met his first McFarland ghost. Boyd looked stunned. Autumn secretly rejoiced that someone else Boyd knew and trusted had been there. Occasionally, she felt that Boyd thought she just had an overactive imagination when it came to stuff like that. He never said anything to suggest that and always would be the first to stand beside her when weird things happened at the farm. Ian could confirm everything she saw that day.

Ian planned on flushing all the pipes that fed the radiator system before Autumn turned the furnace on. Autumn became glad that she was leaving. The radiators in a big old house made so many weird noises when no one was working on them. When the pipes drained, it sounded like the house was being sucked into a great abyss. When the pipes refilled, the house creaked and groaned as the pipes and radiators resettled into the house. Autumn reminded Ian to bleed the pipes when she came back from Virginia. Otherwise, the radiators would pop and bang all winter.

"So, what are we doing for Thanksgiving this year," Boyd asked as they headed out the drive.

"What would you like to do this year?"

"Last year, your family came down for the holiday and weekend. Aren't they coming this year?" Boyd acted a little sad at the possibility that her family wasn't making the trip.

"Oh, didn't I tell you? Mom and dad are going to Massachusetts with friends for Thanksgiving. Apparently in Plymouth, they do this huge historically accurate recreation of the meal the Pilgrims had in 1621 at Plymouth Plantation."

"That sounds … um … interesting," Boyd wrinkled his brow and smiled inquisitively.

"Mom's best friend got the idea. Dad doesn't care."

"Your dad doesn't care about eating weird crap on Thanksgiving?" Boyd seemed incredulous at the idea. Autumn's dad rarely kept an opinion to himself and was very opinionated when it came to food, especially when her mom was the one doing the cooking. "You've got to be kidding?"

"Hey," Autumn slapped Boyd in the arm. "Okay, he did care. Then mom showed him the menu. Once he saw there was elk, oysters, lobsters, and corn pudding on the menu, he had a change of heart."

"No turkey?"

Autumn laughed. Her dad, without fail, always grumbled about the fact that the center of the Thanksgiving feast was turkey. He usually said he would have been thankful if the Pilgrims had T-Bone or filet that first Thanksgiving Day. "He was especially glad there would be no turkey."

Boyd let his smooth silky southern drawl fall into a back hill vernacular. "No turkey on Thanksgiving. Why, that's just plain unpatriotic."

"Hold on Billy Bob, don't get your overalls in a bind. The first Thanksgiving probably had everything I just mentioned but turkey. Tribes would hunt large game that could feed everyone in the tribe. They wouldn't have considered turkey worth their time. Plus, turkeys are especially hard to find from harvest till spring. Since the Indians brought the spread, there were probably no turkeys."

Boyd was laughing under his breath. "Did you just call me Billy Bob? So, what are your sister and brothers doing for Thanksgiving?"

"My sister is celebrating Thanksgiving with her boyfriend and his family in a cabin out in a forest in Pennsylvania." Autumn couldn't wait to hear what Boyd said about that.

"Your sister ... is camping. Did I just hear that?"

Autumn knew what he meant. Her sister was one of her best friends. Autumn couldn't imagine life without her. However, two more different sisters the world could not have invented. Autumn was a no fuss sort of girl. Boyd called her "low maintenance". She never did anything to her hair but wash and brush it. Her sister did everything to her hair. Everyday there was a huge ritual in grooming her hair for the day. Autumn hardly ever wore make-up unless it was a *very* special occasion. Autumn's sister would rather be dead than have someone see her without her make-up. Not the kind of girl one would find camping in the woods. "Yeah and I mean camping. No running water, no plumbing, and no electricity. Everything will be cooked in or on the wood burning stove. I can't wait to hear about her Thanksgiving. The boys are doing Thanksgiving at their in-laws'. What's your family doing this year?"

Boyd shrugged his shoulders nonchalantly and said, "Don't know. Don't care."

"Seriously," Autumn seemed a little concerned.

"Yeah. I saw enough of dad this month to last a lifetime. He's probably glad to be home. Mom's probably up to her eyes in work. My brothers probably will be going to France or Switzerland to ski."

"Well, since neither of us is going to go home for Thanksgiving, Fanny did invite us to her place."

"Let's do it," Boyd said enthusiastically. Autumn knew he meant it.

When they pulled up to the Rice Museum, they found Lillian knee deep in a quest. As Autumn predicted, Lil did ask Autumn for her help. Autumn said she could give her some hints to point her in the right direction but Boyd needed to get back home. "Oh, of course, I'm so sorry."

Coming back to the farm, Boyd and Autumn sat around and watched TV for awhile. Autumn could talk to anyone. Boyd was the first person she had ever met that she didn't *have* to talk to in order to feel connected. After much hesitation from both of them, the two said good night at the door back at the farm. He promised he would be right over anytime, day or night. She kissed him passionately and said, "I know. I love you."

"I love you too. Sleep well."

Just as Autumn latched the door, she heard the furnace click on. Ian had put a digital thermostat in when she moved in last year. She had the money to heat the enormous farm house. The thermostat would keep the noise of the rattling radiators to a minimum. The noise they could make in the middle of the night would scare even the nonbeliever into thinking someone or something was in the house. Autumn was glad to have the furnace come on. It hadn't really been cold until the last few days but the house had a damp chill about it.

Autumn headed up to bed. She retrieved her multicolor afghan from the cedar chest at the end of her bed. It made her feel warm and safe. Mornings in school, she would have rather rolled over and pulled the warm heavy blanket over her head than head down the chilly hall to shower in the drafty old dorm. Since coming to South Carolina, the old blanket did more than just keep her warm the few nights it got cold in the South. She could wrap herself in it to feel safe and secure in this big mansion. Autumn learned to live in her sprawling estate but it was nice to curl up under a heavy blanket. With happy thoughts of days gone by, Autumn slid under the covers. Maybe it was because of the heat from furnace and the weight of the old blanket, but Autumn fell deeply asleep in moments.

Things on the farm were just as normal as usual. Ian somehow found a safe place to put his experience in the basement. Autumn knew there were two ways people handled otherworldly experiences. Some, like her, sought answers to such encounters. The rest of the world let their rational mind tell them that it did not make sense. They tucked strange occurrences away and continued with life as usual. Most people could think of something in their life that seemed a little beyond the normal. Things people thought they heard or saw but could never explain dismissed them. That appeared to be what Ian had done. He came back to check each radiator in the house for leaks. He mentioned something about water pressure, boiler tanks, or something that Autumn didn't understand. Boyd managed to overcome the pile of work he found after returning from Virginia. Life simmered down to the usual slow pace of winter for him. Fanny called to see what Autumn was doing for Thanksgiving. Autumn avoided being so forward as to invite herself to Fanny's. However, the moment Fanny heard that Boyd's and Autumn's families were not going to be together for the holiday; Fanny insisted they come to her house for the holiday. Autumn insisted they be allowed to bring something to the feast. After several minutes of insisting, Fanny finally let Autumn bring the pies. Boyd could bring anything that didn't require cooking.

One morning, just after ten, Autumn heard a knock at the door. Ian and Boyd only knocked as a courtesy so it was not them. They would knock and then just come inside. There had been a time when Autumn kept all the doors locked during the day. Mrs. Hummel taught Autumn to lock everything all of the time. After all the things that happened on the farm, Autumn felt sorry for any intruder who would try to hurt the farm or the mistress of the house. In fact, there were several stories recanted by friends of the McFarlands when someone had broken in the house left without taking anything or harming the residents. People said it was as if the thieves had been scared out of the house by something. Speculation had been that the farm owners had a gun or owned a ferocious attack dog. Autumn knew what it really had been that kept intruders at bay. When no one opened the door, Autumn thought she had better see who was at the door. Autumn looked through the spy hole to see a nervous looking well-dressed couple. They weren't familiar to Autumn but she felt safe since Ian was upstairs checking the radiators in the bedrooms. She opened the door and the pair put on faint smiles.

"Ms. Hummel," the man asked in a shaky voice.

"Yes, may I help you?"

"I'm so sorry to bother you unexpectedly. It's just," his voice trembled as he looked to the woman to help him find the words he needed.

"We just don't know what else to do," the woman said through a barrage of tears.

"Please," Autumn reached out for the couple. "Please, come in." She didn't know these people from Adam and should not have invited two distraught strangers into her home. "Please, come and sit down. What's wrong?"

The gentleman began. "It's our daughter. We don't know what to do. I just don't think my wife and I can take much more of it."

Autumn thought it seemed obvious that there was something troubling this couple. Autumn didn't know what this could possibly have to do with her.

"Our housekeeper told her friend what was going on. That's how we found out about you. I think she said her name is Fanny."

Autumn finally had a connection with these people. Why Fanny would have sent them to her was unclear. "Why don't you tell me what this is all about?"

"Oh, I'm so sorry. Where are my manners?" His formal southern accent gave away the fact that he was a man of good rearing. The thought that he forgot his manners pulled him back together for a moment. "My name is Edward English.

This is my wife, Emily. I will try to make as much sense as I can. We live in Georgetown along Front Street in one of the beautiful old homes. My wife and I are originally from Columbia, South Carolina. I'm the editor of The Georgetown Times. We moved here a few months back with our daughter, Lauren." With the mention of his daughter, he broke down again.

"You see, Ms. Hummel," Emily continued.

"Please, call me Autumn."

"Well, Autumn, the house is everything we could have wanted. It is in a wonderful state of repair but needed to be restored." She looked around at Autumn's home. "Every era in home interiors left its mark on our modest Victorian home. It was just waiting for someone to roll up their sleeves and uncover its beauty. After a couple of weeks of settling in, we began to do that. That's when it all started." Emily dissolved into silent sobs.

"Our daughter, Lauren, is only three. We just thought she was adjusting to the move. We really didn't give it any more thought. Then, she just kept talking about her."

"Talking about whom?" Autumn forgot about everything else as they talked.

"That's just it. We don't know who. At first we thought it was an imaginary friend. Now we just don't know."

Autumn thought that she might know what they were talking about but did not want to speculate before the Englishs' could finish. "What makes you think that it is not her imagination? You know, children can have very vivid imaginations. It's something we loose a little of as we grow." Autumn tried to sound positive.

"We have seen her," Emily blurted. "I know that sounds crazy but its true."

"Wait. Why don't you tell me about your daughter?"

"She's a beautiful and inquisitive girl. We were both prepared for anything that might happen because of the move: sadness, anxiety, sleeplessness. Lauren didn't have any of that. It was almost as if the house had always been her home. Even still, we were going to set up what would have been the den as a playroom. It's on the main floor just off the living room. Edward and I thought it would be the perfect place. Lauren took to it immediately. As we unpacked boxes in the living room, we could see her playing. However, she seemed to be talking to someone. When we asked her who it was, she said it was her new friend Savannah. Lauren seemed happy to have a friend. We were prepared for her to do something like this to cope with the move. Like you mentioned, children have fabulous imaginations."

"So far, you haven't told me anything that sounds unusual or out of the ordinary."

Emily sighed heavily, "I will."

"Everything was fine. Shortly into September, Lauren came into our room one night. Lauren has slept through the night since she was an infant. So, I asked her what was wrong." Edward looked down at the floor. "She explained that I needed to help Savannah. Of course, I was slightly exasperated at this point. An imaginary friend at play time is one thing but not in the middle of the night. When I explained that she needed to go to bed, she balked and insisted that I help Savannah. At that point, I became very awake. I was about to scold her and carry her back to bed when I looked at Lauren. Standing beside her," Edward's voice became soft and low, "was a little girl dressed in a deep green coat with a white muff and hat. There was a strange look on her face. At that point, I gasped so loud that I woke my wife."

"Since that day, not a day goes by without us seeing Savannah somewhere," Emily added as she shuddered. "In the kitchen as I cook dinner, playing with Lauren, sitting in the garden ... everywhere." Their story came to its conclusion.

Autumn asked, "What does Lauren tell you about Savannah?"

"Mostly that she has fun playing with her but that Savannah cries a lot," Edward looked at Autumn with a glimmer of hope in his eyes.

Autumn reached out for their hands. "Does Lauren know why Savannah is so sad?"

With the beginnings of a smile, Emily said, "She says she can't find her mommy and daddy."

"That would make any little girl pretty sad, wouldn't it?" Autumn wasn't exactly sure of the situation at their house. She knew that they needed her help. "Does Savannah do anything that bothers you?"

Emily and Edward looked at each other and then back at Autumn. "She's there."

"Okay. Is there anything else that has happened at the house that concerns you?"

"No. Aside from Savannah, it is the perfect home," Emily added.

"Let me get my coat and let's go see Savannah." Autumn wasn't exactly sure what she could do for Emily and Edward but the place to start would be with Savannah. Before they left, Emily showed Autumn a picture they took to send to friends of their new home. In the far right corner was a little girl dressed in 19th century clothes, including the deep green coat, fur muff, and hat. Autumn's calm attitude seemed to have rubbed off on Edward and Emily. They both were very haggard but the hope of someone helping them seemed to have calmed the tempest in their lives.

"Did your housekeeper or her friend tell you anything about me," Autumn asked as she grabbed her keys and threw on her light coat.

Edward reached to help Autumn with her coat and said, "Don't you want to put a heavier coat on. It is very cold outside."

Autumn assured him that she would be just fine. "So, did your housekeeper tell you anything about me?" Autumn latched the door behind her and the trio made their way across the front lawn to the drive.

"Not much. Our housekeeper said she mentioned to her friend Fanny the strange happenings in our house. Our housekeeper is, well," Emily hesitated for a moment. "Well, she's black. *They* seem to have a different culture." Many people would have tried to put this idea in more subtle language. It could have been possible that in Emily's distress, she forgot common politeness.

"Yes, the Gullah culture is unique to this area of the coast." Autumn tried to avoid any racial language.

"Are they Christians," Emily asked, completely blind of her language. "I mean, it all seems so strange. Our housekeeper …"

"Has a name?" Autumn did not let the conversation go any further without trying to change Emily's language.

"Oh, yes, Rachel. There are so many things that she does that seem so primitive."

"The Gullah culture is a mix of African traditions, Christianity, and English customs. What did Rachel tell you about me?"

Edward seemed happy for the change in conversation. "Nothing. She just suggested that you might be able to help us."

With that, Autumn explained to them how she came to own the McFarland farm. As the story continued, Autumn told them about her strange encounters at the farm. Her story culminated with her trip to the hospital from all the stress of her "veiled" visitors. Emily and Edward couldn't help but ask how Autumn got through all of her encounters. Autumn was completely honest in the fact that strange happenings had not stopped at her house. Edward and Emily were pleased to find out that Autumn could not and did not handle what happened alone. Autumn thought that idea would be how she could help Mr. and Mrs. English. Like her mom and Fanny, Autumn could help simply by being an outside player in the situation. Most of the mysteries associated with her ghostly visitors, she had solved alone. What Mrs. Hummel and Fanny did was provide a perspective different from her own. That would be what Autumn planned to do when she got to the English's house.

Within fifteen minutes, the car pulled up to the curb on Front Street. The house sat back quite far from the road and on a slight grade. The home was a true Victorian lady. It was white with black shutters. There was a huge wrought iron chandelier hanging on the front porch. The ceiling of the porch was painted the palest shade of blue. Clearly, the ghosts did not know that they were supposed to avoid entering homes with a blue porch. As they made their way up the walkway, Autumn could sense the immense history of the home. Sights and sounds washed over her as they came up to the house. This house once saw the grand parades that sent soldiers to fight the British when the road ran away from the house towards the coast in the earliest days of Georgetown. Autumn saw mournful mothers gathered on the porch as fathers cheered South Carolina's vote for secession from the union. To the left of the house, Autumn could see crews of people diligently working to sort through bodies that had washed up from a hurricane tragedy.

As Emily and Edward invited her into their home, Autumn shook the images from the front yard out of her head. With so much outside the house, Autumn needed to prepare herself for much more inside the house. To her surprise, the home was very calm and warm. Any energy she could sense came off as completely benevolent. There had been happy times in the house: marriages, births, and gatherings. Like any place, not all the stories were happy but the sadness and tragedies experienced were muted by the love. "Your home is a loving place. It truly is a home."

With a blush, Emily thanked her and offered to take her coat. Rachel made her way from the kitchen to greet Mr. and Mrs. English. Autumn held out her hand to greet Rachel. Not surprisingly, Rachel gave Autumn a big hug. "I know all about you! Any person Fanny thinks so highly of is a friend of mine."

Autumn was embarrassed but not surprised. Autumn recovered with, "It's good to know that not everything she says about me is bad!"

Rachel laughed with her whole being. She turned to Mr. and Mrs. English, "I'm so glad you came. They don't deserve all this grief. Especially little Lauren, bless her heart. Luckily, like I told Mr. And Mrs. English here, I don't think little Lauren knows anything is wrong except that her friend is sad."

"Rachel, where is Lauren," Emily asked. Before Rachel could answer, they could hear a child talking to someone in the dining room. Without thinking, Autumn walked toward the dinning room. Edward and Emily were close behind her. Not unexpectedly, Lauren was hiding under the dining room table. The three adults squatted down to see Lauren.

"Hi, honey. Who you talking to?"

"Sabana. We hidin'," Lauren added through her giggles. A beautiful bright eyed little girl, Lauren's rosy cheeks told Autumn that this was a child who was more of a doer than a watcher. "Hi, Alum." Lauren turned her bright eyes toward Autumn and flashed an angelic smile. Emily gasped.

Autumn smiled right back at her. This small child clearly was not as upset by Savannah's presence as her parents were. Nobody taught Lauren that Savannah wasn't a normal everyday friend. Autumn bristled whenever she heard Emily gasp. If the English's weren't careful, they could make Lauren very afraid. Autumn did not want that to happen. Deep in her heart she thought, "Home should be the one place you feel safe, warm, and loved." Savannah did nothing to change what home should be for Lauren.

"Honey," Emily asked trying to regain her composure, "how did you know this lady's name."

"Sabana told me," Lauren replied nonplussed.

With that, Emily gasped again. Autumn sat down on the floor beside Lauren. Emily and Edward sat down, too.

"Can you tell me what else Savannah told you about me," Autumn asked in an upbeat and cheery voice.

"Yep, she said you gonna help her find her mommy and daddy. She lost them." With that, Lauren's smile faded a little. Autumn knew that it was because of Savannah's sadness that Lauren felt sad. Mirroring was how three-year-olds learn to empathize. Mostly, Lauren just aped the expression Savannah probably had when they talked about her mom and dad.

"Don't worry," Autumn added reassuringly, "I think we can help Savannah together. Would you like to help?"

In a flash, Lauren's face beamed with happiness at the thought that she might be able to help Savannah. She squealed, "Yeah!"

"Okay," Autumn continued. "Where is Savannah?"

"We hid'n."

"You and Savannah are hiding under the table," Autumn asked to make sure she understood Lauren's toddler talk.

"Uh-huh," Lauren nodded happily.

"Why doesn't Savannah come out," Autumn inquired.

"'Cause." Lauren's manner became slightly sheepish.

"'Cause why?"

"She scares mommy."

With that last statement, Emily gasped again and looked as if she were going to break into tears. Lauren looked as if she just did something terrible. "I sorry, mommy. I sorry," Lauren pleaded.

With that, Autumn turned to Emily and Edward. "I need you to either leave me alone with Lauren and Savannah or help me. Which will it be?"

"Help," they answered in unison.

"Then," Autumn's tone had become much more firm, "you are both going to have to reassure your baby that you are not afraid of Savannah and stop acting the way you have been these last five minutes. Can you do that?"

Edward was firm in his response.

Emily, however, agreed with a nod as she attempted to gather herself.

"Sweetie," Edward said with an insincere chuckle, "we're not afraid of Savannah. She just ..." His words trailed off as he thought of how to explain Emily's reaction to Savannah.

"She just surprises me sometimes," Emily added in a calm loving tone.

"You not mad a' me," Lauren asked longingly.

"No, honey, mommy could never be mad at you. Tell Savannah to come on out." The words had not quite passed Emily's mouth when a little girl in green appeared beside Lauren.

"See I told you, Sabana. Mommy not mad." To Lauren, there was nothing unusual about someone just appearing out of thin air. Savannah was as real to her as the other people in the room. Shockingly, Mrs. English managed to keep any surprise and horror from Lauren.

"Hello, Savannah. It's nice to meet you," Autumn said casually.

"Are you gonna help me find my mommy and daddy," Savannah asked in a soft thick southern accent.

"I am sure going to try. You look very pretty today. Where did you get that beautiful coat and hat?"

"Oh, it is lovely, isn't it? My mom and dad got it for me for Christmas." Savannah seemed to beam with pride at the elegant outfit she was wearing. "I wore it to Grandma's today. We went to her house for Christmas."

Autumn realized that Savannah had no idea that she had been dead almost a century and a half. Today, like every day since that Christmas, was Christmas day to her. "Really, what did your grandma think of it?"

"Oh, my, she said I looked like a little princess!"

"You sure do. It looks nice and warm. Where is your grandma's house?" Autumn hadn't gotten any sense of what this spirit might want. She thought that by talking to her, Savannah's manifestation would stay until Autumn figured out what it wanted.

"Grandma lives in Charleston along the bay. We were coming home from her house when," Savannah's gentile expression faded to deep sadness.

"When you lost your mom and dad?"

Savannah had tears rolling down her opaque cheeks. "We were riding home in the carriage when it happened. We were being thrown all about. Next thing, I was back here but my parents weren't. Can you tell me where they are?" Just as Savannah asked Autumn, a bright white light seemed to be glowing from behind Savannah. In a flash Autumn knew what happened to little Savannah and her family that Christmas night.

"Savannah, dear, do you see that white light," Autumn asked hopefully.

"I see it all the time. What is it?"

"Do you see it now?"

"Yes?"

"Okay. Now, you want to find your parents right?"

"More than anything."

"Then, I need you to be brave and listen very carefully. You and your parents died that night on your way home from your grandma's. Your mom and dad went into that bright light you always see. You didn't. You came here because you didn't know you died. I'm here to help you get to your mom and dad. See," Autumn looked at the light and could see several figures silhouetted by the light, "they are waiting for you."

"But," Savannah looked at Autumn, then to the light, and back to Autumn, "I'm scared."

"I know you're scared, honey, but there is nothing scarier than being here without your mom and dad, right?" Autumn could not help but feel badly. She knew that Savannah needed to cross over but didn't know how. It didn't make Savannah any less afraid or Autumn any less sad for her passing knowing that simply following the light would give Savannah what she has waited for all this time.

"You are right. I miss them so very much."

"Then, go ahead. Follow the light and you'll see your parents again. You don't belong here anymore."

Savannah got up to leave. Before she did, she turned to Lauren and said, "Thank you for being my friend, Lauren. Thank you for bringing Autumn here to help me." With that, Savannah turned and walked into the light until the image of her faded from sight. Autumn had not recovered from the blinding light when she felt a little body wrap itself around her. "Tank you, Alum. Sabana happy now. She home." As if nothing happened, Lauren ran into the kitchen to ask Rachel for a snack.

Autumn couldn't help but think to herself, "Kids are *so* cool."

"So," Edward asked as he got to his feet and offered a hand to both the ladies.

"Is she … gone," Emily stammered.

"She is. That is the last you will see of Miss Gribble."

"Who," Edward asked slightly confused.

"Savannah. Savannah's last name was Gribble. You can look her family up in the deed records or tax records for this house. Savannah's dad had been a wealthy textile merchant and they had lived here just before or just after 1900. They had traveled down old King's Highway to Charleston. On the way home, something had spooked the horses. The carriage had been dragged several miles into the wooded area just off the road. I'm sure there is probably an old police account or newspaper article about them since he had been so prominent a figure in Georgetown."

"Why didn't we hear any of that," Edward asked in amazement.

Emily took hold of Autumn's arm, "All we heard her say was that she couldn't find her parents and the whole bit about the light."

"I'm sorry. Savannah didn't tell me any of those things. It's just what happened. Your life can go back to normal now."

"How do you know those things," Edward pressed on. He seemed determined to understand what had just happened.

"I really can't explain how I know. I just do. Like I said, I'm sure you can verify that the Gribble's lived here around the turn of the century. Census records may even be able to tell you Savannah was their daughter. She really wasn't trying to bother you. She just wanted to find her parents. You may be the only people to live here that have ever seen her."

"Us," Emily seemed nervous at the thought. "Why would she have come to us?"

"She probably wanted to play with Lauren. Savannah may have even found you resembled her own mother."

"These other things about Savannah," Edward continued. "Did you see them in a vision?"

"Okay, I don't even know if I can explain this. I don't always see things. Sometimes I see apparitions like Savannah. Other times, I just get this picture in my head about what happened or whatever. It sounds crazy but it's what happens." Autumn tried to explain her experiences before and without much success. "Now, do you think you could give me a ride home?"

"Oh, my goodness," Emily sighed. It was as if the concept of returning to their normal life just hit her. Autumn could see the delicate beauty of a young thirty-something woman return to her. Even Edward seemed less guarded. "How much do we owe you?"

"Owe me," Autumn asked astounded at the thought. "You don't *owe* me anything except a ride home."

"No, no. You have given us our home and our daughter back. I cannot even begin to tell you what that means to us." Edward let a single tear roll down his face. "I thought for sure I was going to have to find a new job and move far away from here. Can't we give you something?"

With that, Autumn's stomach let out an audible gurgle. She skipped lunch and it was nearly dinner time. "How about dinner *and* a ride home?"

"I think we can manage that," Rachel boomed as she set the table for one more person.

Shortly after arriving home, Autumn called Boyd over for the night. Even though she was becoming more accustomed to the weird things she encountered in her life, Autumn had not completely learned to have nerves of steel. Boyd was on her doorstep within five minutes. "So, I hear Georgetown has an official ghost buster on call now."

"Very funny, now, get in here and kiss me!"

Autumn rolled over to slap the snooze alarm that was ringing just before dawn Thanksgiving Day. Autumn and Boyd were going to Fanny's for the holiday. Fanny said that they didn't need to bring anything other than their appetites. Boyd felt like he should bring something. So, he was in charge of bringing the adult beverages. Autumn was baking her family's traditional Thanksgiving bread called Monkey Bread. Autumn didn't know where it got the name because it was a traditional German dessert. The name could have come from the fact that it can be eaten with the fingers like a monkey. Autumn preferred to think it came from the fact that it was so easy to make even a monkey could do it. Autumn was going to make that over at Fanny's house. Autumn wanted to be over at Fanny's when Fanny started cooking. Autumn had never been to a Thanksgiving feast in South Carolina. Fanny's feast would be a traditional Gullah extravaganza of food. The recipes were not written down. Autumn knew the only way to learn how to cook Hopping' Johns or sweet potato pilaf would be to stand there and watch Fanny do it. So, Autumn drug herself out of bed, took a quick shower, and dressed for the day. The sun was just coming up and Autumn snickered as she looked at herself in the mirror. She was all dressed for Thanksgiving dinner at 6:30 a.m. Before she swung out the front door, Autumn stopped by the kitchen to grab an apron to preserve her holiday outfit.

Traveling down the dark road from her house onto the state route, Autumn could see the sun rising beautifully over her shoulder. The sunrise was vividly red with just a few streaks of purple in it. The sun was still rising and still terribly red as she neared Fanny's. Without cause, a violent chill came over Autumn that made her shudder and the hairs on the back of her neck stand up. Autumn recited the sailor's adage she learned long ago. "Red sky at night, sailors delight. Red sky at morning, sailors take warning." Autumn had never seen the sky red in the morning. She always thought that it would be like the red at sunset. At sunset, the sky usually dipped a deep shade of orange more than red before dark. The sky on the horizon this morning looked as red as blood. After parking behind Fanny's house, Autumn stepped out of the car and turned once more to look at the sky. A familiar voice rang out from the porch, "I's just sittin' heah drinkin' my coffee wonderin' the same ting. Guess time'll tell." Fanny's Gullah drawl was more pronounced when she was tired or when she was deep in thought. She seemed to be both this morning.

"I've come to help," Autumn turned and announced proudly.

"You will in time. You will. Now come have a biscuit and some fruit with me then we'll get started." Fanny sat in her cotton robe and terrycloth slippers. "Oh, I don't know if my kitchen can handle such a fancy cooker in it."

"Very funny. I just didn't want to bring a change of clothes." Autumn helped herself to the homemade biscuits and fruit. It wasn't often that Autumn was up so early. Her mom raised her that breakfast was the most important meal of the day. More than that, Autumn couldn't really function without a glass of juice or something in the morning. This morning, she had left before she could even think about breakfast.

In the kitchen, Autumn found a veritable feast for the eyes. Some of the ingredients Autumn never saw before except in the grocery store. The first thing Autumn noticed was all the seafood. There were big blue-gray shrimp in a bucket. There were oysters chilling in a vat of ice. On the stove, a big pot boiled. From the smell of it, Fanny already put the crabs in to boil. In a bowl so big it could have been a sink there were things that looked like little black and white stones. Autumn knew they were beans soaking for the Hopping' Johns. On the center island sat a grater and a pile of sweet potatoes. To the left of the sweet potatoes, a pile of long green vegetables sat that Autumn could only assume were okra.

"Where can I start?"

"Well, the crabs' gonna be dunn soon. We'll take 'em out and cool dem in the fridge while we throw in the oysters. Dem won't take long. We should be able to shell the crab by den and mix up da stuffin'."

"Okay, why are we boiling the oysters in the same water as the crabs," Autumn wondered out loud.

Fanny giggled, "Girl, ain't you ever made seafood bullion?"

"No. I've never made anything. If I did, it would have to come from a can in the grocery store."

"Then you woulda gone an ruined what ever you's makin'. That stuff tastes like the water on the fishing docks smells." Fanny shook her head in disgust. "De only way to make seafood broth is with de food of de sea. Come on, let's get the crab out."

As they fished the crab out of the huge pot of water, the aroma of fresh crab filled the air. Autumn couldn't help but think about her dad. This was the kind of Thanksgiving feast for which he could be thankful. Before they tossed in the fresh oysters, Fanny put another handful of sea salt into the water. She told Autumn that the stock would get watered down with the water from the oysters. Plus, the sea salt helped keep the meats tender. Within minutes, the two were fishing the oysters out of the pot. While the oysters sat on the table cooling, the two quickly shelled the crab. Once they diced the crab, Fanny threw it in a bowl with some spices and bread cubes. Next, they threw the oysters in the crab and bread mixture.

"What is this, Fanny?"

"It's stuffing, child. Don't you stuff turkeys for Thanksgiving in Ohio?" Fanny reached in both hands and started to mix all the ingredients together.

Autumn laughed and nudged Fanny playfully. "Yes, we stuff turkeys in Ohio. We just don't have crab and oysters in our stuffing."

"Well, tell me, what's in your stuffing?"

"There's bread, onions, celery, salt, and pepper."

"Dat don't sound like much of a stuffin?"

"Yeah, compared to this, it sounds pathetic."

"Can't cook a feast of the harvest without the harvest of the sea in Low Country. Now, you can start stuffin' this inside the bird. We don't get that on soon, we won't be eatin' till tomorrow!"

As Autumn dressed the turkey, she watched as Fanny threw other ingredients into the large boiling pot. There were tomatoes, diced onions, green peppers, shrimp, and sausage. They put the turkey in the oven to roast for the next four hours. Once it was in, Autumn started shredding sweet potatoes as Fanny started another pot to boil alongside the seafood stockpot. When it came to a boil, Fanny added a ham hock to the pot, turned down the heat a little, and covered it. "It's for Hopping Johns," Fanny answered without even being asked.

With the pile of potatoes nearly as tall as Autumn, Fanny placed a big frying pan on another burner after adding the beans to the pot with the ham hock in it. In the frying pan, Fanny put a large blob of butter. Once the butter had melted, she added a little bit of maple syrup to the pan. As the butter and the syrup caramelized, Fanny directed Autumn to start throwing the potatoes into the hot pan. Fanny stirred and stirred as the potatoes softened and became a beautiful rich orange color. Fanny turned the potatoes out into a greased casserole dish. She sprinkled a little brown sugar over the top of them while Autumn ground up some pecans to finish the dish. All this had taken them up to around eleven thirty. They chopped up the green vegetables Autumn assumed were okra. Before Fanny added the okra, she asked, "What is this?"

"Okra," Autumn said confidently.

"Now, what's in the pot?"

Autumn thought for a minute, "I don't know?"

"Well," Fanny paused for a moment, "What do you call a pot on the stove that has broth, meat, and vegetables?"

"I'd call it stew, probably." Autumn couldn't tell what Fanny was getting at with all this.

"Right, it would be a seafood and sausage stew. Now," she dropped the big bowl of chopped okra into the pot. "Now, I have something different. What do I have?"

Autumn felt tired and a little hungry. Not knowing what to say, she knew Fanny was trying to teach her something. "Okra stew?"

Fanny laughed. Autumn loved when Fanny laughed. She did it with her whole body. From her mouth and eyes to her fleshy figure, Fanny laughed. "You right. Okra stew sept we call it gumbo. Gumbo is the Angolan word for this vegetable, okra."

"All that for gumbo," sighed Autumn. "Now can I go sit down?"

"Last thing, Hopping Johns and gumbo ain't done till you add this." Fanny dumped huge containers of rice into each pot. Fanny explained that all the food people call Gullah has a little bit from all over the world. The food house slaves prepared for the families they served. So, a little came from what the white people knew. Some came from food familiar to the African continent. Most of it came from the local harvests: venison, meats from the sea, and rice. No meal would be complete at anytime or in any place along the coastal islands of South Carolina and Georgia without rice. Long gone as a money crop, it was still a staple food in the area.

Fanny's guests started showing up a little after twelve. Autumn met distant relatives of Fanny's who lived just doors away. Then, there were Fanny's own children and grandchildren who live several states away. Fanny's son had four beautiful and lively children all under the age of six. His wife was affectionate and eternally patient. Boyd showed up at quarter till one with the spirits. They set the table at promptly one o'clock. The small house was filled to the brim. No one felt crowded. They served the food buffet style. They all made their plate, found a place to sit, and ate where they could. The conversations ranged from Autumn and Boyd's trip to Virginia to someone who had relatives in Virginia and on and on. The house stayed full until around four o'clock when people started to make their way home.

As people were coming to thank Fanny for an outstanding feast, Fanny excused herself to talk to Autumn. Fanny put her hand firmly on Autumn's shoulder. Autumn looked up, a little concerned when Fanny said, "You need to take a nap."

Autumn was both confused and surprised at Fanny's serious tone. "No, I'm okay, Fanny."

"No. You *need* to take a nap. Go on in my room," she gestured to the room just across from where Autumn sat.

"But Fanny …" Autumn was cut off before finishing.

"No, you need to take a nap. I'll tell Boyd. You can call him later. It'll be okay. Just go to sleep."

Autumn furrowed her brow in confusion. Fanny's tone changed from insistent to adamant. Life was always a chuckle and grin to Fanny so it took Autumn by surprise to hear her tone. Autumn thought about asking what could be wrong but could tell by looking at Fanny that there would be no discussion.

Boyd made his way to the screened porch where Fanny's son and some of the other men congregated while digesting.

Autumn went into the small bedroom. She closed the door behind her and pulled the shades. There were very few things in the room other than the bed. Beside the bed was a nightstand with a lamp and an alarm clock. At the end of the bed facing the head board was a small set of drawers. Autumn lay down on the bed spread because she didn't want to disturb the bed. At the foot of the bed was one of Fanny's beautiful rag quilts. To hear them described as "ripped" or "rag" quilts would imply that they are less than the amazing pieces they are. Rag quilts were made from left over pieces of material. The material could be left over from another sewing project or they could be from an old garment or blanket. The central piece of Fanny's quilt was made from Fanny's childhood winter coat. Autumn smiled to herself as she wrapped up in the warm quilt. These quilts were as important for warmth as communication. Folklore says that these quilts were made during the days of slavery when they had to mask communication. The slaves were encouraged not to sit and share stories. They forbade writing anything down. Lack of community was the fastest and easiest way to subjugate a person and that had certainly been what the institution of slavery did. However, everybody needed blankets and quilts to keep warm. Slaves were allowed to get together and make quilts. The quilt patterns, stitches, and knots were all part of keeping their verbal history alive in a nonverbal way. Later, as abolitionists became more active, slaves hung these quilts out to air or dry. Under the guise of bed linens, people found a map to freedom. Autumn happily wrapped herself in the history of this beautiful linen and let the turkey dinner she ate lull her to sleep.

Autumn shot straight out of bed. Fanny stood by the bedside with Autumn's purse and coat. Unfortunately, Fanny's expression had not lightened. If anything, Fanny looked even more concerned. Before Autumn felt really ready, Fanny pulled back the quilt. In a quivering yet motherly voice, Fanny spoke to Autumn quietly. "I would go with you but I can't. Sometimes, in situations like this having someone there only gives them more ammunition. I be prayin' for you." Fanny attempted a smile but it quickly faded.

"What about Boyd?" Autumn asked trying to pull herself out of a deep sleep.

Fanny turned to the porch as she ushered Autumn out the back door. "Those fellas out there gonna keep him jawin' well into the night. I'll just tell him you got a bad piece a shrimp and were gonna call your mamma and go to bed. You listen now, hear."

"Yes, ma'am," Autumn said as she hugged Fanny.

Autumn pulled her coat around a little closer. The wind picked up and was coming in from the north. Had she not been in South Carolina, Autumn would have sworn there was a big winter storm about to blow in. The sun seemed to be strangely absent. The sun appeared faint on the horizon. Autumn drove home in what could only be described as a daze. When she turned into her drive from the main road, Autumn thought she saw a glow coming from the cross that sat on top of the chapel steeple. Autumn felt an icy chill that she couldn't blame on the weather. The feeling made her think of Jim. The last time she and Jim met, it ended strangely. Autumn felt too tired and too weak to even think of what she would do if it was Jim. Autumn stepped out of the car and raced to the front door. The wind blew so hard that light debris floated around in the air. The moss hung to the trees for dear life. The few leaves that were still on any of the deciduous trees were being ripped off. Autumn closed the door and locked it in one motion. To her delight, the phone rang just as she was coming back up the hall from hanging her coat in the closet.

"Well, look at you! Here we are in Massachusetts for Thanksgiving and you're the one getting the snowstorm!" Her mom's vivacious voice boomed from the other end of the phone.

"Really, I wondered what was going on. I'm surprised to hear from you," Autumn started as she curled up onto the puffy couch in the living room.

"Now, I'm your mother. How could I not talk to you on Thanksgiving?"

"I don't know. Well, how was it?"

Autumn's mom laughed. "Oh, it was wonderful. If we decide to do it again, you kids are going to have to come. It was at Plymouth Plantation. Everything was just so amazing. There were costumed Pilgrims and descendants of the Narragansett tribe there. It really was wonderful."

Autumn could just imagine all the beauty and brotherhood without the plague.

"What did dad think?"

"Well," her mom's tone dropped a little bit, "you could ask him yourself, but he's already in bed. He swears it's from the food we ate."

"Really?"

"There wasn't anything wrong with the food. There's something wrong with your father. He ate more at this Thanksgiving meal than he has in all the Thanksgiving dinners before put together."

"Oh, so he enjoyed it?"

"He enjoyed it … over and over and over again. How was your Thanksgiving?"

"It was great. Fanny had a real house full. You guys will have to do Thanksgiving down here sometime. There's the turkey and all but the other dishes are truly Southern. Dad would love them. They all have seafood in them."

"So, what are you doing tonight?"

Autumn could hear her dad in the background mumbling about his stomach.

"Not much. I think I'll just watch a little TV and then call it a night. Did you say it is supposed to storm here?" Autumn planned on hanging out and watching TV but who knew what the evening would bring.

"Yep. They said that even the coastal areas of South Carolina could see a few snowflakes before the evening was out. Unlike up north, though, the storm could be quit forceful with thunder, lightning, and damaging winds. You'll have to call me tomorrow and let me know what happens."

"I will. This is on your dime …"

"And I need to call your brothers and sister before I call it a night. Well, Happy Thanksgiving. I love you."

"I love you too. Tell dad too."

"I will. Goodnight."

"Goodnight."

Autumn still didn't know what the evening would hold but felt a little more prepared for whatever it would be after talking to her mom. She flipped on the TV and pulled the afghan over her. **It's A Wonderful Life** was coming on. Autumn thought that would be a wonderful way to pass the time. The movie was a holiday classic. No matter how many times she watched it, the ending always gave her a wonderful holiday glow. Who couldn't rejoice as George's world turns right around before his very eyes or when he gives a wink to Clarence when he hears the bell ring? If she could not be at home, she could come close by watching this old favorite. Just as George was about to jump from the bridge, before Clarence comes on the scene, the network went to commercial. With that, Autumn decided to get a glass of water from the kitchen before the movie came back. The Thanksgiving feast had been amazing and filling. A little water would go a long way in helping wash down all that food made with such love. Just as Autumn entered the kitchen, the whole room went dark. Autumn could not see anything around her. As if that weren't bad enough, she could feel herself falling. Autumn couldn't tell if her body was falling or if her mind was. It almost felt like the falling sensation in dreams. Autumn could not wake herself to stop the feeling. Then, there was nothing.

After what seemed like an eternity to Autumn, she slowly opened her eyes and found herself lying in her bed with Boyd in a chair next to her. Autumn's first reaction was embarrassment. Boyd clearly found her unconscious on the floor of the kitchen and carried her all the way up to her room. She did not even want to think of the fact that she essentially ditched him at Fanny's on a major holiday. As her head became clearer, she looked around more carefully. On her chest sat a huge quartz crystal. On her head rested a very cold rock. In her hands, she found the purple amethyst stones.

Boyd noticed that she was coming out of it. "Here, have a sip of water." The wonderful smell of Jessamine washed over her. An intense sense of security wrapped around her tenuous spirit. He propped her up on the many pillows she had on her bed. Autumn was too weak to ask any questions but she did sit up a little more. The look on Autumn's face prompted Boyd to say, "No, I am not upset that you came home alone. There are things you and Fanny understand that I don't. Sometimes, it's just better that I stay on the edge of things. Okay?"

Autumn sank a little into the pillows with relief. As she gathered the stones, Autumn looked to Boyd again for answers.

"I don't know where they came from or how they got there. This is how I found you. I thought they must be for something so I put them all back where I found them once I got you upstairs." He laughed and smiled that boyish smile he sometimes has.

Autumn smiled and patted the spot beside her on the bed.

Without hesitation, Boyd was holding her in his arms. "Fanny said you were in trouble. She wasn't sure what kind of trouble but she thought it was that guy from the Halloween party again. Jim, I think was his name."

Autumn thought about what happened for a minute. The only experience that she ever had in her life that came close to this was the night Jim appeared intentionally in her dream. Jim must be doing it again tonight. The difference? She was still awake. Asleep, the conscious mind surrendered control to the subconscious mind. That was where scientist believed people did their most creative thinking because the subconscious didn't have all the rules and obstacles the conscious mind did. Her brain was forced to let her subconscious mind be in control and her conscious mind would not give up control without a fight. All of this happened at the discretion of someone other than herself. Jim attacked her psyche. Looking at the stones in her hand, she thought they must do something to protect or empower her against such an attack. What little she remembered about the stones was that the quartz was a power crystal that people often wore around their neck to center and focus their energy. The cool black stone was a grounding stone that was believed to take negative energy and send it into the ground. The purple meant something as well but she was too tired to think of what it was. Lying in a comfy bed on a full stomach with protective arms wrapped around her, Autumn could not resist the call to sleep.

When Autumn woke the next morning, she could put her thoughts together. The first and most important thought, Autumn knew Jim was behind the attack.

Autumn and Jim's last encounter did not go as he hoped. This time she stopped him with a bit of white magic. She wondered how that would raise Jim's level of desperation. Jim clearly underestimated Autumn. He may have been under the impression that Autumn would have no idea how to fight off a psychic attack let alone block it completely. Blocking the attack let her survive it. When Autumn detected a threat, her brain simply shut itself down to protect itself.

Boyd smiled at her when she woke up. He spent most of the night watching her and thinking of what he would say. "I couldn't be more white bread if I tried."

Autumn laughed. Not for a moment would she have ever described Boyd as being white bread. "Because you don't understand any of this. Ple-e-ease, join the club!"

"Seriously, I grew up here. I know about voo-doo. People seem to think New Orleans has the corner on that market." Boyd got up to get Autumn a glass of water. "Fanny said you need lots of this."

"Ugh," Autumn groaned feeling slightly water logged at this point. "I just can't drink any more. And, this isn't voo-doo." She paused for a minute, "Well, maybe it is voo-doo but I don't know what voo-doo is. I guess all that I have experienced is sort of 'spiritual' but I don't know if it is a faith."

"Well, I'm Methodist but I'm pretty sure there are no tenets in the religion that involve … psychic abilities. I pray to God who is the God of Abraham. That God sent His only begotten Son, Jesus, to save us from death. It is the details after death that we are not real specific about!" Boyd joined her back in the bed. "Apparently, that side of death is perfectly clear to you."

"What do you mean," Autumn asked hesitantly as she got a strange sinking feeling in her stomach.

Boyd explained that while his grandmother had been battling cancer, he had struggled with his faith as he understood it. During that time, he had found himself asking God several very tough questions. In fact, he had struggled with the very concept of God. Boyd thought, looking back on it, that his struggle had probably been very similar to that of other people. He had wondered why God would have let something like this happen to someone as caring, loving, and wonderful as his grandmother. Then, it had escalated to more serious doubts. Soon he had found himself questioning if God existed or not. Boyd had begun to think that maybe when you die, you just die. Heaven might be a creation of our own fear of mortality. We simply cannot stand the thought that maybe when our life leaves us that was all. This period of doubt had lasted a very long time. It had ended when a butterfly landed on his shoulder one day. From that day on, he had seen a butterfly everyday. Eventually, he had begun to wonder what the significance of the butterfly was. As he had watched the beautiful Monarch sit gently folding and unfolding its wings while it had sat on the bumper of his car, he had asked out of utter frustration, "What's with all the butterflies?" Just as he said it, a brilliant white light filled the space around him. It didn't blind Boyd but it made everything he saw clearer.

He had heard a voice in his head reply, "Finally!" Boyd had recognized the voice. It belonged to his grandmother. It continued, "I've been waiting for you to see me!" His grandmother explained that she asked to appear to him so that she could put his doubts to rest. From that day forward, Boyd had believed but did not understand.

"That's how it is with you. I believe you when you tell me that you saw a ghost in the basement or a little girl who's been dead a hundred years. I believe. I just don't understand."

Autumn felt badly for Boyd. He believed. She just wished she could make him understand something that she didn't even really comprehend. "Let's imagine that God created us out of His thoughts, not *in* His image but *of* His imaginings. Had he created us in His image, wouldn't He have done away with that troublesome free-will aspect? That must mean that the world is here for our experiencing. I mean, why give us free-will and then not give us any choices as to how our life would go. How boring would that be? We know God is infinite so He cannot take up residence on the earth. His entirety would overwhelm it. So, He made us His extension into the world. The whole world revolves around Him but we have to show it to Him; live it for Him. Each of us has a unique way of bringing the world to Him. No one is better than the other. Just different."

"So, that means we are all divine?"

"Yeah. The writer, painter, musician, scientist, criminal, actor, lawyer, politician. We all experience the same world but in vastly different ways."

"Wait. You're telling me that someone who has committed, oh, let's say murder is divine," Boyd asked. He thought for sure he knew the clear cut answer to this question.

"Well, I guess according to my theory, yes. They were imagined by God. That person has a completely different viewpoint of the world. Okay. Have you ever met someone for the very first time and you don't know why but something about the person is completely off putting? They might be handsome or beautiful, intelligent, respectable by worldly standards, well kept, all those things but you still just have a terrible feeling in your gut?"

Boyd nodded.

"Well, maybe that is the divine within you recognizing the divine within them and telling you to keep clear of this person. Unfortunately, most of us ignore that part of our being and let our upbringing and social skills overcompensate. How else do you think Hitler rose to power?"

"So," Boyd said breathless from the marathon Autumn asked his mind to run, "what did your gut tell you about Jim?"

"Run away!"

Boyd began to sense a long day ahead of him. "So far, none of this sounds too weird."

"No, I guess it really isn't." Autumn smiled "Have you ever seen a spirit?"

"Nope."

"What would you call the butterfly who sounded like your grandmother?"

"Oh-"

"Exactly. I don't know if any of that made sense to you but talking about it is helping it make sense to me."

"And last night," Boyd asked.

Autumn shook her head and scrunched up her face in thought, "I'm still working on that one. But, thank God Fanny sent me home. Whatever it was would have been ten times worse if I hadn't been here on the farm!"

Boyd pulled away from her to look her in the eyes, "How do you know that?"

"Fanny told me that a long time ago."

CHAPTER 11

▼

BELIEVING IN MIRACLES

Life slowly reawakened from its winter slumber. Spring was in the air. By February, the last of the cold weather passed. By the first of March, the flowering trees were covered in buds anxious to burst open. Autumn knew that Mr. Master's foal would be arriving soon. That meant another trip to Virginia. At Boyd's request and Mr. Berlin's insistence, Autumn packed for the trip to Virginia. Boyd and Autumn arrived at the Berlin farm two days before Mr. Masters. Mr. Berlin swore he just got the days mixed up when planning the visit. Autumn felt that he did it on purpose. Mr. Berlin genuinely enjoyed having people at the house. Mr. Masters was a little bit of a wet noodle during their last trip. Mr. Berlin probably wanted Boyd and Autumn to have a positive experience at his house on this visit. Autumn brought her copy of the McFarland Family Bible. Doing some research on Thomas McFarland, he had been listed as a son of Alyson and Charles but where the other children go on to have wedding dates, spouses, and children; Thomas did not. Mr. Berlin didn't have any information to help clarify the mystery since Thomas McFarland had been his late wife's relative. He was very interested in the McFarland Bible as its own unique history of names, dates, and stories.

Several days after Mr. Masters arrived, the mare foaled. Autumn never saw anything as beautiful as the little horse. The horsemen all made fabulous assessments regarding the inherited traits of the foal. Mr. Berlin, Mr. Masters, and Boyd agreed that it possessed the best qualities of each parent. Autumn could not get over the fragile nature of the foal. Legs the men predicted would win races were so long and weak they trembled beneath her as she struggled to stand. Her eyes were like black jewels. New eyes looking at an old world and giving it hope. After several hours, the foal was leaping wildly on those spindly legs. The foal seemed to be celebrating this life she was given. Autumn thought, "What a wonderful day to be born!" The temperature fell somewhere between sixty-five and seventy. There were big fluffy white clouds sparingly placed on a bright blue sky. In the wind, she could smell the wet earth coming to life with the warmth of a spring day. A few of the flowering trees could not contain themselves any longer. Their buds burst to reveal the first blossoms of spring. It seemed as if new life could not be contained this day.

The mare had a fiery spirit and was a ferocious protector of her new baby. After several people tried to approach mother and baby with no success, Boyd took Autumn's hand. "You try. We just want to get the foal use to people. I don't want to take her from her mom but she and her mom don't know that!"

Autumn hesitated, "I don't know anything about being around horses. You know that Ebony is the first and closest contact I've ever had. Why would I do better than all you experienced hands?"

In his velvety voice Boyd urged, "Just try."

The mare held herself up as tall as she could when Autumn entered the pen. Autumn moved slowly and gingerly as Boyd closed the gate behind her. The shaky foal wobbled slowly over to Autumn. The foal brushed Autumn's hand. Autumn could feel the soft warmth of her breathe on her hand and the dampness of just being born. She reached out to stroke the foal. As she did, the mare turned and walked to the water trough.

After watching the foal for a couple of hours, Autumn asked Boyd to go for a walk. Boyd and Autumn were readily excused for now Mr. Berlin and Mr. Masters had the business of buying and selling a champion foal. Boyd wanted to hop on a pair of horses. Autumn asked that they use their own feet to take a walk. She would have been concentrating so hard on riding that she would have missed the scenery around her. Today, on this day of new life, she did not want to miss one detail. Boyd reticently agreed and they set off. They had been walking for an hour or so when they came to the edge of the Berlin farm. The landscape seemed refreshingly different from Georgetown, South Carolina. The hills were small and gently rolling. The grass was coming back from its long slumber. It appeared especially green; the color of an emerald. In the valley of two rolling hills, Boyd and Autumn found a creek that ran along the property. Beside the creek grew a large deciduous tree. On the opposite side of the creek, a white fence surrounded the entire farm. Across the fence, there were fields full of cows. Each and every one of them was black.

Autumn turned and asked, "What kind of cow is all black?"

Boyd chuckled as he always did when Autumn proved she was a city girl. "Haven't you ever heard of Black Angus?"

"Well, yeah. I guess. I just never really thought that they were black. You know like they just referred to all beef cows as Black Angus. I had no idea they were actually a breed of cow. Come on. Let's go down to the creek."

As they came closer to the tree, they could hear the creek. It was small but fast from all the snow Virginia had received over the winter. The tree was more enormous up close. The little girl in Autumn could imagine playing with her friends in the numerous branches of the tree. Around the base of the tree were the remains of buckeyes that had fallen the previous fall. Autumn smiled and wondered how many springs the large tree had seen on this farm. Then like a bolt of lightening, she remembered something. "There are beautiful green rolling hills and white fences as far as the eye can see. He is in the shade of a large buckeye tree looking up on this hill where hundreds of cows as black as night are standing … find this spot and the fairy rings will lead you to my boy. Bring him home for me, won't you?"

Boyd grabbed Autumn's arm, "Are you okay?"

"Yeah," Autumn replied but wasn't really sure.

"Another one of those *things* that happen to you?"

"Sort of. Remember when Ian and I first found the basement?"

"Sure. It was back in the fall when I was here. What about it?"

"I told you that we were visited," Autumn sank to the ground. The wind had sort of left her at the moment. "She said to find her son. He would be where there were green rolling hills, white fences, black cows, and a buckeye tree."

Boyd sat down beside her. "How were you to find his grave?"

Autumn thought for a moment and then looked around. "She said to look for the fairy rings. They would lead me to his grave." Autumn's voice sounded far away and her expression was absent and glassy.

Boyd didn't know where she went or what to do to get her back.

Without thinking, Autumn got up and began wandering around.

"What are you doing," Boyd asked softly. He had never been with Autumn when she had one of these moments. Boyd wasn't quit sure what to do. Something in his brain kept telling him that startling her would be as bad as waking someone who was sleepwalking. To him, Autumn seemed to be in some weird trance.

Again, without expression or emotion, she said, "Help me find the fairy rings."

"Okay," Boyd jumped up and ran to her side, "but, you're going to have to tell me what the hell a 'fairy ring' is."

"Sounds weirder than it is. Just look for a circle of toadstools or mushrooms on the ground. Don't know why they are called fairy rings. Just the spore pattern of a capped fungus. The parent has died with the new ones growing in what is a circle. There should be more than one."

It didn't take them long to find the fairy rings. There were about five of them standing in a row and were a bright beautiful color. The caps were a glowing shade of orange while the stems were a pristine white. "The angel-of-death," Autumn muttered.

Boyd went as far as he could with patience. He grabbed her arm and pulled her around to face him. "Fine, enough with this. You need to stop right now."

Shaking the cobwebs from her head, Autumn's expression returned. "If you are going to be around me, you need to be okay with what happens. Supposedly, someday I will have control over this. Right now, it just happens and I can't stop it. Are you okay with that?"

"Look," Boyd's frustration became apparent, "I don't like feeling you've gone away."

"Tell me why? I'm okay. Nothing happened to me!"

"I know but what if," his voice faltered as if saying what he thought might make it happen, "you can't come back. I can't come get you. I can't save you."

Autumn gave him a big kiss, "Thank you for caring that much! I know it's scary but I always come back."

"Okay, but can you work on controlling it?" He wrapped his arms around her and pulled her close.

"For you." Autumn lied. She didn't know when or how she would ever have control over something that she did not even understand.

"Okay, well, let's go get Mr. Berlin and ask him what the story is?"

Back at the farm, Mr. Berlin became keenly intrigued by Autumn's experience. The gun was an obvious tie between her farm and his farm. He couldn't enlighten Boyd or Autumn on what might be out there in the fields. He suggested that they visit the Recorder of Deeds. Boyd and Autumn could find the original deeds to the land. If there were graves on the property, the office might also have record of that. Mr. Berlin sent them off as quickly as possible since it was nearing three o'clock on a Friday. The office would be closed in just two hours. He was as anxious as Boyd and Autumn to find new threads in this mystery.

Once in town, Autumn and Boyd literally ran to the office. Since the farm has always been one large tract of land belonging to the same family, the deeds were very simple. The records showed the transference from generation to generation. There was nothing remarkable or revealing in the records. The gentleman in the office did look into recent surveys of the land. The property sat near the creek which was a feeder for the city of Manassas' water supply. The Environmental Protection Agency had ordered a soil sample from all the land along the creek. The EPA had taken a sample every five yards of length and three yards out from the banks. The report filed by the EPA found human remains at the Berlin farm just east of the creek. The visual landmark the report gave was the lone buckeye tree. Autumn asked the Recorder if he would know who to contact to find out who might be buried there. Autumn knew none of the state or local government agencies would have any record of a burial older than the early eighteen hundreds. If it were Thomas McFarland, the grave could date back to the late seventeen hundreds. The Recorder sent them to the oldest church in the town. The church had records of funerals going all the way back to colonial times. If Autumn and Boyd could find anything, it would be at First Episcopal Church of Manassas.

Driving over to the church, Autumn felt this would be a hopeless venture. Very few churches before the independence of America bothered keeping records. Autumn knew that the McFarland's were religious. Even though they had built a chapel on her property, she couldn't tell what denomination the McFarland's were. Simply because First Episcopal Church of Manassas had been the first and only church in the area for generations did not necessarily mean that the people who died out on the Berlin farm were God-fearing people. Her doubts were many and her hopes were very few. However, the odds of finding the place Alyson described could have been the same.

Boyd could sense her disappointment when they left the city offices. "Look. You are always up for an adventure. Think of this as just another adventure. Whatever happens?" Autumn could not help but smile. Boyd was right. All she could do was ask. There was no way she could leave Virginia without following the trail of clues *wherever* it led. The worst that could happen would be nothing. With that, they made their way across the town circle to the small brick building with the white wooden bell tower.

The church was elegantly simple. It reflected the architecture of colonial Virginia. Just as Virginia colonial homes were small and brick, so was the church. A white fence encircled the churchyard. To the left and rear of the yard, a small old cemetery sat. A bronze plaque next to the gate contained the name and age of the building. The name stuck in her mind: St. Thomas Episcopal Church. At some point in the life of this church, St. Thomas changed its name to First Episcopal Church of Manassas. Autumn marveled at the age of the building. First must be not only the oldest church in Manassas but the entire county. The church was built in 1746. The lawn appeared small but well kept like the rest of the old church. The pair made their way up the six steps that led to the beautiful wooden doors. Autumn pushed gently on the doors. Boyd seemed very uncomfortable at entering the church. As the door swung open, Autumn reached back and pulled Boyd through the entryway. The interior of the church was narrow and entirely white accept for the wooden pews. Autumn was a little surprised that the walls inside were not brick. On either side of the center aisle were several rows with short pews. Although small, they seemed to be of thick heavy wood with ornate carvings at the end. Up at the front of the church, a young man was busy preparing the altar. He seemed completely unaware of their entrance. Autumn thought she would make her way down the aisle rather than yell the length of the church. There are certain manners to be kept within God's house. Again, she found herself pulling Boyd who was dragging his feet. As she hoped, the sound of their feet caught the attention of the young man.

"Oh," he said in what could only be described as a Virginian accent, "I didn't hear anyone come in. Welcome to First, how can I help you?" His accent seemed similar to Boyd's in that it was southern. The difference being it was an aristocratic southern accent. Boyd's vowels were very round and all the syllables got fair time on his tongue. Virginian accents rounded vowels but syllables didn't linger as long.

"Hi. We hate to bother you," Autumn said cringing at how loud her voice came out and rolled around the sanctuary.

"No. Please. I was getting things ready for Sunday because I've run out of things to do. Please," he waved them forward. "What can I help you with?"

"Hi. My name is Autumn Hummel and this is Boyd Masters." When Autumn looked over at Boyd, he held out his hand very timidly. Boyd's body language usually exuded confidence. He normally filled the space he was in. This was a side of Boyd she had not seen. "The gentleman over at the Recorder of Deeds Office sent us over. We have been looking for information about a grave out on a farm we are visiting. The records at the town hall hadn't given us any answers. Due to the age of your church, he thought that maybe the church records would yield more information." Autumn paused. "I don't know if you have the time to help us."

The young minister leaned in with intrigue. "Well, I sure would love to try. You tell me what you're looking for while we head back to the office. Now," he smiled a little, "it might be a little tight in there."

Boyd cleared his throat. "You know," he said sheepishly, "I can meet you outside."

"I didn't mean to offend you, sir," the minister leaned around to catch Boyd's eyes.

"No, it's not you. I'd just feel more comfortable outside. No, really. I'll be over at the hardware store. Just come get me when you're done." With that, he slid out of the pew and walked quickly to the back of the church. Autumn didn't know what caused it but she could sense that Boyd couldn't breathe inside the church. He literally suffocated in there.

The minister was indeed correct about it being a little tight in the office. The office was little more than a hallway with a desk at one end. The records the church had were in big leather bound books. "With all the technology, you'd think I'd happily trade the books for CD's or disks but, to be honest, I would miss them. You get a real sense of history from these old books."

"I know what you mean," Autumn smiled. She knew exactly what he meant. It was nice to meet another book aficionado. As long as there were people like Autumn and the minister, there would always be a reason for publishing books.

"So, what are we looking for in these?"

Autumn began to tell him how her journey began and the pieces she found along the way to First. Halfway through the telling, the minister stopped pulling down books and started shelving them again. Autumn silently wondered why he stopped looking through the books. Her heart sank to a new low. She thought it must be that the church documents could not help her. "You don't think anything you have will help me, do you?" Autumn needed the answer but hated to hear it.

With a broad smile on his face, he answered, "No. Nothing in these books is going to help you." Just as Autumn was about to thank him for his time, he interrupted her. "But I can." Autumn couldn't hide her confusion. "You see my mother's family owned that farm. It is where she was born and raised. The gun you found belongs to the man in the grave you are trying to identify. It is Thomas' grave. You have given me a piece of the puzzle that my family has been searching for generations to find."

"You've got to be kidding me," Autumn was dumbfounded at this piece of news. "What piece have I given you?"

"Let's go get your friend. I'll tell you both over dinner if you'll join me? The old Westman Inn has fabulous food. That's an unbiased opinion even though my sister is the chef there." The young minister, Jeff, led her out the front doors. He turned to lock the doors of the church when Boyd made his way across the street. "I hope he's all right *eating* with a minister?"

Autumn met Boyd at the gate. She told him about what Jeff said about the family and the grave. Before going into detail, she leaned close, "He said he would tell us the story over dinner at the Inn. Are you okay with that?"

"Sure." Boyd looked at her as if he had no idea why it wouldn't be okay with him. "I just got off the phone with dad to let them know we wouldn't be back till later. Mr. Berlin recommended the Westman Inn. He said you'd love the history and I'd love the food."

"So, you're okay?"

"Yes, quit asking me. I wouldn't say it if I wasn't."

The three made their way out from the town circle and down two blocks to another beautiful brick building. The wood trim of the porch and windows had been painted a deep green. The windows were nine paned candy-glass. They were either very old or they were made to look very old. Candles illuminated each window of the Inn. Jeff told Boyd and Autumn that the Westman had been a carriage stop. The restaurant was as old as the Inn itself. Weary travelers would need a place to eat and sleep. The Westman mostly had a reputation as a restaurant now but the six rooms were still available for rent each night. His sister had bought it in a terrible state of disrepair. The old restaurant once had been a bar. The Inn's various rooms had served as an apartment for the bar owner once. Fortunately for his sister, the bar owner had not done much to the building. All the original architectural nuances were still intact when she came to own it. As they entered the building, Autumn noticed the rough hewn floor. The floor was heavy wide hardwood planks. No one would have put a beautiful finished wood floor in a place that would see as much wear and tear as a tavern. Unlike the church, the walls inside The Westman Inn were brick. The tables and chairs were dark wood. Each small table and booth held a small candle. There were lanterns scattered here and there. The lighting gave a real sense of nostalgia. The atmosphere sent visitors back in time.

The bar was full of regulars. Jeff seemed to know everybody there. Jeff spotted an open booth in the corner and waved Boyd and Autumn to follow. A bright eyed youthful looking waiter greeted them and took their drink orders. Since Jeff was intimately familiar with the specialties of the house, Autumn and Boyd let him order. During dinner, Jeff began to tell his side of the Thomas McFarland story. "He married my … oh, let's see … great-great-great grandmother, Rebecca. That is not the interesting part of the story. Nor is the fact that he is buried out on the farm. Apparently, owning a large farm was paramount if he wanted to marry Rebecca. Not from her family's point of view but from his."

"See, she came from a wealthy and prominent family. In those days, people rarely married outside of their social classes. Thomas would not tarnish Rebecca or her family's social status by having people think she was marrying beneath her. So, he had acquired the large tract of land that is now the Berlin farm and had worked tirelessly to make it a thriving success."

"I can understand that," Boyd added between bites of Shoofly Pie.

"I know you can. As a southern man, we both can. Thomas didn't have to prove that to anyone. You see, he had fought bravely alongside Manassas' men during the battle of Manassas when the British were desperately trying to re-establish themselves in the area. In fact, he is credited with winning the battle because of his battle tactics. The British lined their big guns up on the hill over-looking the field where the battlefield park is today. The people below were suffering terrible casualties. He had found a group of men who had known the woods surrounding the open field like the back of their hand. The woods had been where the men had hunted before the conflict. The men made their way into the woods and around to where the British were. They had ambushed several British soldiers, taken their uniforms, and had made their way to the big guns to blow them up. In the chaos that ensued, the band of Revolutionists had slipped back into the forest while the local militia overtook the British. No one knew where he got the idea but everyone knew Thomas was a hero. There couldn't have been a more honorable person in town to marry."

Autumn dropped her fork. "I know where he got the idea. He served in the South Carolina militia under Frances Marion."

"Who," Jeff asked.

"Frances Marion. The Swamp Fox," Autumn said.

Boyd furrowed his brow and squared up his chin in indignation that someone would not know who Frances Marion was. Jeff inadvertently insulted Boyd's southern pride. "Frances Marion. He defeated Cornwallis. Sent him back to New York in disgrace and probably cost him his commission." Boyd leaned back in his chair. He glanced over toward Autumn, "No. I get to tell him this." Boyd smiled his cool smile. "Frances Marion used the swamps and old Indian trails to move around the British. Because of his tactics, the British were unable to secure the towns around Charleston. Eventually, they had to give up Charleston because they couldn't get supplies or reinforcements to Charleston. Frances Marion was a Revolutionary War hero."

Jeff seemed fascinated by how much the stories wrapped around each other. "Well, that explains a lot. See, Thomas was brought to Virginia as a prisoner of war." Jeff pointed to the logo of the Westman Inn. It bore the British flag. "Virginia was not so fortunate during the War for Independence. In fact, many captured patriots found their way here. Remember," Jeff said to Autumn, "the butt of the pistol has S.C. on it. People in town didn't know his name but because of the weapon they suspected that the S.C. stood for South Carolina."

Autumn and Boyd gave Jeff a confused stare. Then, they looked at each other. "Didn't Thomas know his name," they asked in unison.

"No," Jeff chuckled. It seemed that everyone in the trio was enjoying the twists and turns of this story. "When Thomas came to Manassas, he had suffered a severe head trauma. He had no memory of who he was, where he was, or from where he came. After being treated for his injuries, the British released him. They no longer considered him a threat. That is how Thomas came to Manassas, Virginia. The Berlin farm is *his* legacy because he couldn't remember his real legacy."

After several cups of coffee, Boyd and Autumn thanked Jeff for a wonderful evening. Jeff answered all of Autumn's questions. Autumn gave Jeff a link to the founder of his family and a heritage that seemed long lost. Boyd and Autumn made their way back to the Berlin farm. Mr. Masters and Mr. Berlin were sitting in the parlor finishing up the deal for the foal. The foal would be kept in Virginia until she was weaned. Mr. Berlin felt that a certain date could not be established. Boyd concurred with Mr. Berlin. That date would be set by the mare and her foal. Mr. Masters wanted a champion and would do what would be best for the foal. Mr. Masters arranged to fly home the following morning. Autumn and Boyd decided they would leave before breakfast as well.

Autumn arrived back at the farm bringing the whole story full circle. Her first night back, Autumn went down to the basement and sat there for almost forty-five minutes talking to the spirit that initially petitioned her. Autumn finally walked over to the old rocking chair and placed her hand on the back of the chair. With that, the woman reappeared in the chair. The spirit seemed consoled to know what happened to her son. Once Autumn finished retelling the tale, she explained that Thomas did not come home or contacted her because he simply did not know his own identity. It seemed that in his lifetime, Thomas never remembered who he really was. In her heart, Autumn knew that Thomas had crossed over. She assured the ghost of Alyson McFarland that her son was at peace on the land he came to know as home.

Spring began with a flurry on the farm. Everyone came back: the field planters, Tom, Fanny, and Albert with his crew. Autumn enjoyed having people back on the farm. The days did not seem so long when everywhere she went there was someone to visit. To Autumn, the farm came alive with all the activity. Over the winter, the local school district approached Autumn. They wanted to know if she would be willing to open the farm to groups of students. The teachers thought it would be a wonderful way for the students to experience the history of the area. Autumn, being a history major, thought that it was a wonderful idea. The first groups were scheduled to arrive once the rice field work started again. Each grade would have the material presented to them at their own comprehension level. The younger students would have many hands-on experiences. The high school students would discuss the sociology of the antebellum era with all its inherent inequities. The state would fund the field trips including a fee for the use of the McFarland farm. Autumn originally declined the fee because she knew that the money could be used somewhere more in need. After thinking how a bureaucracy worked, she knew the money would not get to other educational projects. So, she decided to take the money and donate it for the restoration other historical sites in Georgetown County.

The day after the second grade classes from Sampit Elementary School came to the farm, Autumn received a letter in the mail. The writer expressed deep concern and much hostility at the fact that Autumn was promoting slavery and the forced oppression of an entire race; not the first time Autumn encountered accusations of glorifying slavery or the Confederacy. Even though the letter personally hurt Autumn, she felt the best response would be to not respond at all. Unfortunately, Autumn would come to regret that decision. The following week, a small group of concerned people showed up at the farm. To their dismay, they found Autumn out by the river watching the first flooding of the rice fields. Albert and all but one or two of his workers were African-American. Two years ago when Autumn contacted Albert about starting rice cultivation on the farm, she gave no thought to what color Albert or his crew were. Albert knew how to grow river rice the way they did in the 1800s. Autumn provided the land so he could do it. In fact, Albert's financial status improved tremendously in a year's time. Fine restaurants from New Orleans to New York fell in love with the red river rice Albert grew exclusively along the Santee River. She was standing and talking to Albert about how the very dry fall required them to move the fields almost six feet from last year. The image was something very much out of the past. Unfortunately for the visitors, it seemed much too out of the past.

When the group reached Autumn, the horror in their faces was apparent. It didn't take Autumn long to see the scene the way they did. Despite her great sense of dread, Autumn held out her hand with a smile on her face. "Hello. May I help you?"

"I doubt seriously that you can," said the leader of the group in a quiet voice that seemed to be suppressing rage. The woman did not receive Autumn's hand. Autumn retracted her hand awkwardly to straighten her shirt in an attempt to hide the slight. The woman dressed in a royal blue pant suit with her hair pulled back in a very tight bun had many freckles dancing across her cheeks and the bridge of her nose. Her pursed lips were a very vibrant shade of red. "We came to talk to you about the letter I sent last week. I am *speechless*. I had no idea it was this flagrant!"

Albert, who was always so friendly, seemed stunned that an uninvited stranger would lash out at Autumn so ferociously. "Ma'am, what is it that has your bees all in a buzz?"

The woman's ire turned sharply to Albert. "You, sir, do not *see* what is going on at this farm?"

Albert looked at the fields, then at Autumn, and back to the woman whose anger was bubbling over at this point. "I see two business people discussing their business arrangement while watching a crop being cultivated." A broad smile lit up Albert's face. He, too, saw the scene from a different perspective but found it humorous that this woman would interpret it as a white master overseeing her slaves.

The woman scoffed at his statement. "This woman has African-American workers working rice fields while her privileged white face lives in this stately mansion. You see nothing *wrong* with that?"

"Correction, ma'am. I have black workers working rice fields while *Autumn* lives in the stately money-pit of a house." Albert's glee escaped him in the form of a gentle chuckle. Albert did not mean to insult the lady. He was trying to calm her down. It did not work. The woman seemed to be offended by Albert's casualness about the situation.

"The stately mansion built with money earned from the forced labor of African-Americans." The group that came with the woman physically rallied behind her at this moment.

Albert shifted his weight and looked down at the ground. "Are you calling me an African-American?"

"Yes, sir. I am."

"Well, that would be where you are wrong. See me and the rest of the men out there in the field have never been to Africa. Born and raised right here in the United States of America. And," he continued without the usual lilt in his voice, "we *choose* to be here. You see, our forefathers were brought here because we were the best rice growers the world had ever known. No one grew rice like the farmers of Angola. We choose to honor our heritage by continuing the ancient tradition of our people. As for Autumn," Albert stopped and drew a long breath then he looked up, with a smile on his face but defiance in his eyes and added, "Autumn gets nothing from us being here. I farm her land. My company does the work and makes the money. She pays the taxes on the land and asks for nothing in return. My workers and I make a living doing what we know and love."

A young man from the group stepped forward. The woman in the blue suit retreated a bit with Albert's last comments. "Then, sir, you are okay with this woman glorifying slavery?"

From behind the crowd, Autumn heard a familiar voice emerge. The voice sounded winded but Autumn could still tell it was Fanny's. "When are you people going to get a life? You got questions about what's going on with the black folk on this farm? Come to the black folk on this farm! This girl has given Georgetown and the country a wonderful treasure. She has given all of us Americans a piece of our past." Fanny was winded and sweaty. Autumn could only figure that Ian or Joe must have given her the scoop since Fanny had been working in the slave cemetery clearing away the overgrowth for the new fence Ian was building around it.

With the grace of a born and bred belle, Autumn collected herself and invited the group up to the house for some lemonade and discussion. Fanny wanted to keep working but Autumn insisted that she wait. Fanny and Autumn came to a compromise. Fanny would come up to the house but only if the hostile group agreed to stop by the cemetery on the way to the house. As Fanny led the group away from the river, Autumn turned to Albert. "Thank you for that. You didn't have to say anything. I guess being a white girl who owns a former plantation is bound to get me in trouble from time to time, huh?"

"White girl," Albert chuckled. "Are you sure about that?"

"They don't come much whiter than me, now do they?" Autumn looked down at her hands. She didn't know why, but any time the subject of race came up, Autumn felt very self conscious. The reason being that she never really thought of Ian as her male friend or Fanny as her black friend. She always just thought of them as friends until someone pointed out their differences. She gave

Albert a big hug and a kiss on the cheek before heading off to the house to make lemonade.

The rest of the day was spent in discussion. Autumn explained that the farm was a working farm. Albert just happened. The business agreement was exactly as he told them. When the discussion turned to her glorifying the antebellum period, Autumn assured them it was not her intent to glorify slavery. The only reason she opened the farm was because it was a part of history. Autumn did not think it was a proud moment in time but it was an important period. Fanny told them slave heritage should not pull their children down but lift them up. In a very short period of time, the status of African-Americans in society had changed tremendously. That was an accomplishment that should cheer on future generations not shame them.

Fanny told them, "You can't really know where you are going in this life until you know where you came from."

Fanny's last words hit home to Autumn. Since coming to South Carolina, she had been trying to solve all the riddles the ghosts of the McFarland family laid before her. She solved all their mysteries while adding to her own. It became very clear that the events in her life recently were not random or accidental. These events were leading her deeper into her own mystery. As Fanny said, Autumn would never really know where she was going until she found out where she came from. Maybe all the weird phenomena that had been happening since the day she came to the McFarland farm was leading her to find her own heritage. Autumn thought it was time to focus her energies on her mystery.

Autumn took stock of the phantoms she met since inheriting the farm. Without fail, each party had guests who were welcome yet uninvited. They caused no harm. Autumn took pictures in the third floor of the house where phantom figures had appeared. Not only had there been phantom figures but phantom writings in the closet wall. Recently, Autumn found a connection between herself and the McFarlands. The line between the Hummels and the McFarlands found, Autumn felt certain that Jon McFarland had been completely unaware of the connection. Last, there was the little box that belonged to Alyson. Autumn sat for a very long time thinking how all these pieces went together. Before long, her head was swimming in all directions. Life always had a mysterious way of working itself out. Autumn thought that time might be the only way to solve this puzzle.

Spring was not a season unto itself in South Carolina. Spring was the gradual introduction of summer. Some days could be mild with pleasantly cool breezes.

Autumn enjoyed those days the most. She would meet the field crews down at the barns. It felt good to work planting the fields. Autumn loved the way the wet black earth smelled. After sitting undisturbed all winter, the soil seemed to breathe when the tillers came through. There were large crops which were planted mechanically while others, like cotton, preferred being planted by hand. Planting took only a week if there were no rainy days. This year, there were two rainy days during the planting week. For two straight days, an intense thunderstorm put everything on hold. During those two days, Autumn opened all of the windows of the house. As anxious as Autumn had been in November to turn the furnace on, she couldn't wait to air out the house. Most people wouldn't have picked a stormy day to do it, but the storm had been caused from a tropical front. The warm air came off the ocean. Autumn loved the way it smelled. To her, the way the air smelled triggered a sentimental memory. The air felt like summer in South Carolina. That brought back happy memories. Not to mention, the lightening seemed to purge the air around the coast. It did wonders for the air in the two hundred year old house. On the second straight day of rain, Autumn took a shopping trip down to Charleston. The most amazing place to shop in Charleston was the Market. The Market was smack dab in the middle of the historic district and just off the wharf. It was a long thin brick structure that dated back to the earliest days of Charleston. It had once been a place where farmers could come and sell their produce. The structure itself looked like a long brick garage or pavilion. When inside the Market, one was outside since there were no solid walls. The Market had every kind of merchandise imaginable. Autumn usually came home with a treasure trove of goodies. Despite the storm outside, everything was business as usual for the Market. Autumn made her way from the Gullah rag dolls with their colorful dresses and corn row yarn hair to the tacky velvet paintings.

Shortly before calling it a day and heading out for lunch, Autumn passed a booth selling jewelry and pewter pieces. Autumn made her way over to the tables that were covered in deep green cloths. The green set off the silver of the jewelry and the pewter pieces. The flames inside the candle holders flickered tenuously each time the storm winds raged. After gazing at the different items, Autumn noticed a familiar symbol. There was a beautiful silver necklace with the same knot that her mysterious box had on the top. Autumn ran her fingers over the necklace. As she moved from the jewelry to the pewter works, she noticed the knot was on many of the cups and bowls. A tall thin blonde woman appeared from behind one of the pillars in the Market. "Can I help you with something," she asked in a pleasant southern drawl.

Autumn pulled her thoughts away from her mysterious box to smile. She was amazed at the stunning beauty of the woman. Her skin appeared opaque. The features of her face were very thin and elegant. Autumn couldn't help but think she looked surreal. "I was just noticing the designs on some of these items. They are really beautiful."

"Oh, the knots. Yes. They are very popular."

"What are they called," Autumn asked.

"They are knots. Celtic knots to be exact."

"Celtic? Like from Ireland," Autumn asked again. She saw a few more of her puzzle pieces coming into place.

The woman seemed to sense her pensiveness. "Yes," she laughed quietly, "Ireland and Scotland commonly."

With her last word, Autumn thanked her quickly and made her way back to her car. The rain started coming down in sheets. Autumn's stomach pained her for a moment but she didn't give lunch another thought. Since finding the box, Autumn had pondered the meaning of both its contents and its design. Autumn got some information about the stones that seemed vague and rooted in superstition. This knot, this Celtic knot was the first tangible information Autumn had on the box. The art design of the box came from the British Isles. The culture of the Celts went back well beyond the Roman Empire. History concerning the Celts was incomplete and biased. The only record of the Celts was from outsiders such as the Romans. The Celts had no written language. After centuries of assimilation by the Roman Empire and later the Gaels, their culture had been lost to domination from central and southern Europeans. The last bastion of the Celts had been on the British Isles. It had not taken long for the Celtic ways to be lost with the rise of Christianity.

The link was made. The box held mystical rocks frequently associated with nature or "earth" religions. Pam brought up the word "witch". Celtic sages or shamans had been called Druids. The Druids had been scorned and persecuted by early Christians for their pagan ways. Throughout history, Druids had been the owners of an ancient knowledge. A knowledge people feared. The Druids had been the builders and users of the great stone formations that were scattered from Ireland to central Germany. The stones and their positions mystify modern scientist who ponder how such primitive people could have set the heavy stones in place. Some even wonder how the stones got to the formations after being quarried over ten miles from the circles. Autumn arrived home with all those thoughts still spinning in her head.

Autumn unlocked the front door. She stormed passed the answering machine which was blinking frantically. Upon entering the kitchen, she tossed her purse and keys to the counter and practically pulled the door from its hinges as she made her way into the basement. Autumn flopped down on the cool dirt floor and placed the box in front of her. She didn't know what she was doing but she came to one consistent thought from all the information she had received. The box had a Celtic Knot on it. Celtic culture was most commonly thought of as being from the British Isles. Alyson McFarland emigrated from Scotland. The box had been engraved to Alyson McFarland. She was the matriarch of the family that had owned this land for almost two centuries.

"ALL OF THIS. WHAT DOES IT MEAN?" Autumn felt like a small child and her frustration boiled up inside. "What am I," Autumn asked the air.

Sitting still, one word kept coming back to her over and over again: witch. That must be who she was or what she was. No mention had been made of this growing up in a Catholic family. Autumn thought, "I think I would remember hearing something about a relative being a witch or having psychic abilities." At least Autumn had the peace of mind that she had also never heard of any of her relatives being institutionalized for being insane. Both would have stood out in a person's memories of their family. Then a thought came to her. What if the box was not the important thing? What if it was the items *in* the box that was important? Pam said the cards were older than the box. Maybe the items inside the box had been handed down generation after generation like some eclectic heirloom. For an instant, Autumn thought about returning them to the attic. A wave of fear overcame her when she thought about going about her life without the small bag of gems. There was no immediate relative to claim the items. If Jon felt her worthy enough to inherit the farm, he would want her to have the strange contents of the beautiful box.

Dirty, tired, and cold; Autumn made her way back upstairs into the kitchen and the real world. She went upstairs to change her clothes. The chill of sitting on the basement floor had gone right through her. Autumn slipped into a hot bath to chase the chill away. After almost a half hour, Autumn left the tub more tired than she entered it. Rather than getting dressed again, Autumn pulled on her pajamas and headed to bed.

The sun greeted Autumn the next morning bright and early since she had not closed the blinds or the curtains the night before. The rain had finally stopped after two solid days. The workers would be back to finish planting the fields. Autumn leapt out of bed happy to have something to do with the day besides think. She put on an old t-shirt and a cut-off pair of jeans. As she rounded the bottom of the steps on her way to grab a quick breakfast in the kitchen, Autumn noticed the answering machine. The light was blinking frantically which meant she had several messages. Not wanting to be late to the fields, Autumn pressed play as she went to grab some food. All but two messages were from Kendra. Hers was the same, "I just felt you were in need of something last night. Hope every-thing's okay. Call if you need anything." Autumn was touched by her concern. Autumn would call Kendra later today to put her at ease. The other messages were from Boyd and from her parents. Boyd was asked to deliver his dad's new foal to South Dakota. He apologized for not seeing her before he left but, as he put it, "You know what a pain my dad is. When he says jump, we ask how high!" Her parents were concerned because her mom went to bed last night and "just couldn't find her." Autumn shook her head and thought, "Great, now my Mom's getting in on the creepy stuff!" Of course Mrs. Hummel couldn't find Autumn. It was the middle of the night and they were separated by over fifteen hundred miles.

With a thermos of ice water in her hands, Autumn set out to the fields. She was rather impressed at what a well oiled machine the planting crews were. They had been off for two days but were right in step as if they were planting yesterday. When everyone received their assignments for the day, the crews headed off to do their jobs. The day was clear and pleasant. Autumn was planting cotton plants. Last year's small field was taken out by bole weevils. This crop was not designed to be a cash crop. Cotton fit into the historic scheme of the farm. The students would love taking home raw cotton from the field. Fanny made the most beauti-ful cotton angels from boles at Christmas.

An hour before breaking for lunch, Autumn heard what sounded like voices coming from the west cornfield. Before she knew it, Tom grabbed her by the arm and was pulling her along in a panic. From what she could gather through his panting and her running, one of the workers was hurt badly while plowing the fields. Tom said something about a blade snapped off and flew through the cab of the tiller. The sight that waited Autumn was nothing short of horrifying. The other workers had pulled the wounded operator out of the cab. He was lying on the black newly turned earth. The ground pooled with blood. The clothing of the operator was soaked in blood. He appeared unconscious, barely breathing, and as white as a sheet. Autumn saw that Tom had given his cell phone to someone who was calling for help.

All Autumn kept thinking was, "This man is going to die if I don't do some-thing." Despite her severe aversion to blood, Autumn told two workers near her to pin his shoulders to the ground. There was a man standing by his feet who Autumn barked to sit on the injured man's legs. Once the three people were in place, Autumn reached down to the large metal blade that had pierced the driver through the upper abdomen. She carefully grasped the blade and with one swift strong motion pulled the blade from the man. Though unconscious, his body wrenched up in pain. Onlookers questioned Autumn's decision to remove the blade. She heard some say he would bleed more because the blade was removed. Others insisted she did more damage by not removing the blade carefully. Still others were convinced the pain of having the blade removed would send him into shock. Autumn didn't care. She knew she had to do something or the man was going to die. Shutting out all the noise from the scene, Autumn placed both her hands on the large gapping wound. Images began swirling in Autumn's head. She saw the man as he had been before the accident. The smell of the earth after it had been turned over. The blood she saw pooled around him. The fact that the black earth and blood were life struck her. The blood gave the man life. The dark black soil of coastal Carolina gave the earth life. Autumn then felt a warm rushing sensation from all the way up her arms out through her finger tips.

The next thing she knew, she was being loaded into an ambulance. Autumn blacked out again. "You really shouldn't have done that," Autumn thought as she started to gain consciousness. "Okay, you shouldn't have done that YET. Ask them for water." The voice was hers. "I know you feel like closing your eyes and not waking up. There is nothing wrong with you. Nothing they can fix. Sit up and ask for some water."

"Could I please have some water," Autumn forced herself to say. Lifting her head felt like lifting the world. Her body seemed to have fused with the stretcher she was lying on. She felt as if someone had tied lead weights around her wrists. Autumn sat up on her elbows.

"We need to check you out. Just lie back," said the round faced female paramedic.

"No, you have to get that man to the hospital. He's hurt very badly. I think he might die," Autumn croaked again as she struggled to sit up.

"The man." The older female paramedic asked, "What man?"

"Did he die already?" Autumn felt as if she might collapse at any moment.

Both ladies looked completely perplexed. "Everyone is fine. You are the only one in the ambulance."

Autumn looked outside the ambulance at all the worried faces. Suddenly, she remembered what had happened. Not knowing what else to say, Autumn asked for water again as she slid down to the bumper of the ambulance. The faces in the crowd changed in a heartbeat from worry to awe. The man who had been lying in a pool of his own blood made his way through the small group gathered around the back of the ambulance. Other than his shirt being soaked through in his own blood, he looked perfectly fine. When he was at her knees, he lifted his shirt up for her to see. Autumn automatically reached out and touched where the wound had been. Nothing remained of the wound; not even a scab or a scar. In almost a whisper, the man said, "It is a miracle. I should be dead. You saved my life."

Autumn pulled back her hands as if they were touching something hot. "What just happened here," she thought to herself. Autumn looked up with tears in her eyes. All the people shared the same emotion as the man. They all thought they had seen a miracle. Autumn climbed down from the ambulance and walked over to the broken truck. Beside it, a deep black wet mark remained on the ground where the man had laid dying moments ago.

She turned to the group and said, "If someone hadn't done something, he was going to die. So, I did something."

"A miracle is what you did," one of the onlookers said. Autumn remembered him as the one scolding her for pulling the blade out of the wound so carelessly.

"Never," said a gray haired worker while shaking his head in disbelief, "in my life have I ever seen anything like that. The hand of God worked through this lady."

A chorus of people agreed with him.

Autumn suddenly felt the invisible weights that had been tied around her wrists. She wanted to collapse onto the ground and just go to sleep. Before that happened, she felt arms supporting her. Then, a familiar voice echoed in her ear as a bottle of cold water was pressed to her lips. "Drink this. I'm gonna take her home now, ya hear. Don't none of y'all go talkin' about what happened here. Autumn needs the quiet. Go on. Y'all have two days of missed worked to get done. Go on!" Autumn had no idea how Fanny always happened to be at the right place at the right time but Autumn was thankful. "Go on, you heard me, drink this." Fanny led Autumn back to her old beat-up station wagon. The car must have been at least from 1972. It was big and brown with fake wood paneling on the side. Fanny claimed it was her pride and joy. Autumn slid in the passenger side and focused hard on staying awake. It only took five minutes by car to get back to the house. Fanny helped Autumn into the house. "Come on to the kitchen. I'll fix us some lunch," Fanny said as she patted Autumn on the back.

"I just ..."

Autumn couldn't finish her statement before Fanny interrupted. "Want to go to bed? You can't go to sleep right now. You have to stay awake. Drink some more of that water and come with me."

"How do you know what I need?!"

"Child, are you really that slow," Fanny chuckled as she shook her head. "Lord, I'll tell you if you promise to sit here and drink that water. Well?"

Autumn hopped up on one of the stools that sat along the counter in the kitchen. "Yes, ma'am."

"I don't see the things you do. I can't hear the things you do. Lord knows I can't do the things you do. But, when I need to, I get the information. I came to you because you got in over your head today." Fanny turned, "Don't you eat when nobody's here. Not a scrap in the fridge. Oh, there's something."

Autumn laughed. Fanny's refrigerator was full of comfort foods. Autumn's refrigerator had food, not good food, but food. Fanny hardly considered it food. As Fanny quickly threw together a feast, Autumn realized that she may have used a lot more than water out there on the field. Once every scrap of food was gone, Autumn turned to Fanny with a feeling of impending disaster.

"What," asked Fanny.

Autumn took her bottle of water and walked out the kitchen door. There was someone or something pulling her to the river. All the weakness and nausea that had come like a crushing wave after the accident vanished as if it happened a lifetime ago. In fact, she felt stronger for having experienced it. Two steps away from the house she knew who was waiting for her at the river. It was Jim. The last she heard from him had been at Thanksgiving. That unpleasant experience disturbed her but paled in comparison to their encounter in October. Today, the thought of taking him on made her anxious but not nervous. All she could think was, "A man almost died today. Somehow that man was saved. Whatever saved him will surely protect me through this encounter."

The land gently sloped down toward the water. Autumn stood on the rise when she saw Jim with his back facing the river. He seemed as cool and soulless as ever. This time Autumn did not shutter when she felt his absence of all that makes people human. Jim was somehow less than human. Just as she reached out with her "gift", she could not breathe. It was almost as if there was a hand around her throat. Autumn knew why she had brought the bottle of water with her. She had learned a lot about herself over the past five months. She dumped most of the contents of the bottle of spring water over herself. As she did so, her breath returned and she continued to walk towards Jim.

A swashbuckler's grin crawled over Jim's face.

The ground beneath Autumn began to crunch with every step she took. Looking down, the ground had become covered with all manner of creeping insect. Her natural reaction to this would be to get as far from the bugs as possible. Autumn got goose bumps a mile high but did not run. She stopped for a moment, reached down with her hands then straight up to the sky and made a motion like a bird flapping its wings. Within seconds, the thunderous sound of hundreds of birds could be heard. Autumn looked around to see the ground now spotted with red and white. Cardinals and doves were feasting on the insects that had covered the ground. Autumn could not help but laugh at the irony of the two birds with such strong symbolism in her life showing up to help her. Silently, she thanked them for coming. When they had lighted, she began to walk to Jim again.

"What is all this about," Autumn demanded.

Jim's smile faded. His eyes became dark and sullen. "Do you still not realize what power you have?"

"Trust me," Autumn said. "I am well aware of my gift but it is just that: a gift."

Jim growled, "What do you mean?"

Autumn laughed. For a moment, she almost felt sorry for Jim. He desperately wanted something from her. "Don't you know what a gift is?"

"What?"

"First, this land that I am on is a gift. I didn't do anything to get it. It just came to me. The 'power' that you refer to is a gift. It is not mine. Someone or something gave it to me. So anything that you think I can do, *I* cannot."

"See!" Jim strode purposefully over to Autumn with his nose nearly pressed to hers. "That is where you are wrong! The power belongs to you and that is why I am here." Jim kneeled beside the river and touched his finger to the water. Seconds later, the river as far as Autumn could see had fish floating to the surface. They were all dead, thousands of them.

"Look," Autumn stated calmly. The water rippled slightly. Soon, the fish were swimming back into the depths of the river. "Death is never the end. It is just another beginning."

"You are the beginning I intend to end," Jim roared. "You know what you are?"

"Why don't you tell me?"

"You are something my people thought they had exterminated ages ago."

Autumn became angry and confused. "WHAT?!"

"Autumn Hummel, you are a witch," Jim declared. "A powerful one as well."

"And who or what are you?"

"I belong to an order nearly as ancient as yours. We have vowed to rid the world of your kind."

Autumn sunk to her knees. "You are here ..."

"To kill you. Yes. That is what my people have done since time in memoriam."

"I don't understand."

Jim explained that history does not reveal the true story. The oracles had been what the Spartans protected in Greece. They were witches. The Persian Emperors had belonged to an ancient order that had exterminated women with Autumn's ability. They had done so centuries before in Egypt and Babylon. The oracles of Greece had been thought to be the last of their kind. The true oracles had escaped to many different lands as did the people sworn to rid the world of witches. Time and society had turned against witches and had subjugated women as being less than men in the order of creation. With the rise of Rome and Christianity, women like Autumn had been pushed to the furthest regions of the known world. It was in the British Isles that they had made their last stand as a cultural influence. Wisely, they had gone underground or were shipped off to the New World.

"You specialize in American history," Jim finished. "We found and slaughtered anyone who may have been a witch."

"Innocent people as well?"

"If need be."

"Even men?!"

"We weren't sure that the witches weren't teaching their sons their ways to pass them on to future generations."

"And they call witches wicked!" Autumn stood toe-to-toe with Jim again. "Why kill me?"

"Men own the power in the world. Men dominate the culture and shape it to our liking. If I let you live, people will wonder. People wonder and things change and ..."

"Men might not be the ones in power!"

"See. Beautiful and smart!"

"Men loosing power would be bad because ..."

"No more poverty. No more poverty means no more wars. What would the world do with itself? Oh, I don't know: feed the hungry, shelter the homeless, and clothe the naked. Well, actually, that is quite a lot. Never heard that before, have you? It would be so much easier than living a life of take, take, and take!"

Jim's eyes flashed with malice. He attempted to physically grab Autumn. Rather than being terrified, all she thought was how wonderful the earth smelled. The ground under her feet felt warm on the surface but a hint of winter's chill could be felt underneath. All around her she could hear life. Trees were waking. Grass was growing. Birds were nesting. All animals who called the river home were bustling with life. A bright light blinded her for a moment and she remembered what Fanny had told her long ago. "As long as you are here, nothing can happen to you."

Jim was lying on the ground in front of her. He did not move. His eyes were closed but she could see his chest gently rising and falling. Jim was unconscious because of Autumn. Autumn did not intend to hurt Jim. All she wanted to do was protect herself. The wonderful and beautiful sights around her had pulled her into a meditative state that unleashed something so good that it rendered Jim unconscious. Autumn cautiously approached Jim. As she did, she saw tears streaming down his cheeks. Jim slowly opened his eyes. Autumn could not believe what she saw. Until that moment, Jim's eyes had always been an ice blue color. Now, when he opened his eyes, they were a deep aqua blue. He seemed to be seeing something Autumn could not see. Autumn worried that he was about to die. Autumn sat with Jim until the distant sirens had reached them. Fanny came down to let Autumn know that the authorities had been notified.

She walked up with Fanny once the police had Jim in custody to find Boyd waiting for her. He raced over and gently wrapped himself around her.

"I don't want to hurt you," he said softly.

Autumn laughed, "You never could." She hugged him back as hard as she could to show him that she was alright. When she stood back to look at him, Autumn saw that Boyd must have torn up his hands in his haste to get to her. She took his hands in hers and lifted them up to her mouth. Tears streaming down her face, she gently kissed each mark. When she let go of his hands, each and every mark was gone.

"What the hell?"

"Yeah, I can do that sometimes. You okay with that."

"You are one strange lady, Autumn Nicole. No, I'm not okay with it because I don't understand one damn bit of it."

Autumn looked saddened and was scared for the first time all day.

"But," Boyd began, "I love you and it is part of you."

Fanny said. "Girl, you are going to be the death of me. I swear."

"Sorry Fanny," Autumn mumbled. Autumn never liked being a burden to anyone. She certainly did not want to burden Fanny.

"I was just foolin' with you. Lord, you moving here is the closest thing to having my own children here. Don't you worry none about me. Now, Mr. Masters," she turned to Boyd, "you and I are gonna be busy this evening."

Boyd looked confused. "Busy? Doing what?"

"What happened with the field worker today? People, even though Fanny told them not to, are going to talk. They are going to want answers. Everybody will be asking *me* for answers."

Fanny looked up at Autumn with a smile on her face, "And?"

"And," Autumn looked confused. "Didn't Fanny know what had happened out there? Maybe she thought healing a dying man from being impaled with a large farming tool wasn't that out of the ordinary.

"I know two things. Your soul needs mending as well as your body. Boyd and I are gonna take care of your body."

"We are," Boyd asked.

At the same time, Autumn said, "You are?"

"We all need a good solid dinner after the day we've had. Lord knows there's nothing in this house to cook. So," Fanny looked at Boyd, "you are going to the grocery store and get the fixin's for a proper meal while I turn away all those fools who are gonna be beatin' down her door thinking she's the second coming or something."

Autumn swallowed hard, "And how are you gonna do that?"

"Well, I haven't quite figured that out yet. You leave that up to me. As for your list, you can't go to one of them fancy grocery stores for what I need. You know where you need to go?"

Boyd rolled his eyes. Some places in the South were clearly still segregated because that was how some people wanted them to be. The grocery store Fanny spoke of was three miles west of Georgetown. People would stare at him as he wandered up and down the aisles because white people just didn't shop at that store. Boyd had been there many times before on just such errands as a teenager. "Yes ma'am, what do you need?"

"I'm gonna write it down for you. Have you looked around here? There ain't nothing I need. Oh, and stop by Bubba's. I heard he just brought in a boat load. Get some clams if they got 'em too."

"What should I do," Autumn asked wearily.

"You need to get outta here for awhile. Too much happened here today. This is your home but you need to go be where your soul can find some peace."

"Where is that?"

"Child, don't ask me. Search your heart. Where is the one place that you can loose yourself?"

Autumn paused for a moment and thought, "Where do I always go when I get in South Carolina and where do have to go before I leave?" Without hesitation, Autumn knew where to go.

She could see people coming down the drive when she looked out the living room windows. It had started. Those stunned people in the field apparently did not understand Fanny. Without hesitation, Autumn asked Fanny if she could borrow her car. Fanny took her hand and led her over to one of the two hollow panels on either side of the fire place in the dining room. Autumn screwed up her face in question. Fanny pushed open the left panel. Then, she pushed up on a small bit of molding around the interior door frame. The lower half of the back wall turned sideways just enough for a person to slip through.

"You stand here till I get the door. I'll invite them in and you can slip out to my car."

"But, Fanny," Autumn whispered to her, "you need to take my keys. I don't know when I will be back."

Fanny patted her on the back, "You take all the time you need, sweetie."

"Thank you." Just then, Autumn heard the doorbell ring.

"Go!" With that Fanny closed the panel beside the fireplace and yelled loudly "I'm on my way!" to cover-up the sound of the panel being reinserted.

Autumn waited until Fanny asked them in. The hidden compartment had a small door that opened beside the chimney. The average person would miss it. Ian still didn't know about it and he had painted every inch of the exterior five times in all the years he worked on the farm. Autumn hurried to the car and pulled out without anyone even giving a second thought to the old station wagon driving away. Within five minutes, Autumn made it out to the main road heading towards the beach. The state park seemed the best chance Autumn could have to be at the beach. No one would go looking for her there. Autumn replayed the events that led to this moment over and over again. In the forty-five minutes that it took to drive down Route 17 to Huntington State Park, Autumn was able to disassociate her emotions from everything so that she could be open to whatever would happen.

Route 17 had a small stretch from Pawley's Island to Murrell's Inlet where there was truly nothing to be seen on either side of the road except for the small sign to mark the entrance of the park. The road to the park wound for several miles through marshes, inlets, and small little bridges that were scattered across the land that eventually led to the ocean. The beach at Huntington could very well be the purest landscape on the Atlantic Coast. The dunes stood nearly three to five feet high, over eight feet wide, and covered in the most amazing diversity of flora and fauna. Autumn parked her car several yards from the beach and hiked to the ocean. The only sound Autumn could hear were the roar of the surf, the wind coming hard from the southwest, and the cry of a few sea birds. There could be no more perfect sound track for a meditation tape than the ones that rang out true and clear for Autumn.

When she finally reached the beach, Autumn pulled a hair tie out of her pocket to gather her long thick dark hair back into a knot so it would not whip in her face as she searched for whatever her soul needed at this moment. Taking a seat on the beautiful white sand, Autumn could not help but notice how different this beach was from the other beaches around. Very few people made their way down to Huntington. That left the beach just as the surf made it. People came to Huntington to avoid sun bathers and observe nature or to surf. There were shells of every shape and size. Some of the shells Autumn had never seen before on her travels to South Carolina. Shells were not what Autumn came for this day. Combined with the gentle breeze, rhythm of the surf, and the stressful events of the day, Autumn soon found herself relaxing and being in the moment.

Before long, Autumn could hear the familiar voice of Jon coming from somewhere in the distance. Autumn could hear him saying, "You just could not wait for this, could you? True to the McFarland nature. You are impatient, reckless, and head strong. They will be here in a few moments if they think you are ready."

Autumn did not even bother to reply to Jon for fear of interrupting. Not long after Jon finished speaking, Autumn could see a host of beautiful people making their way to her. They were not walking to her. They were more like things you imagine when you are half asleep. Rather than becoming less distinct as in a dream, the people became clearer and clearer. Before long, Jon and the group of people joined her in the sand and made a circle. A beautiful woman with long silver hair, a light blue flowing robe, and the most amazing body art on her arms, hands, and face spoke to Jon, "She is your charge. Please introduce us."

"Autumn, these are the ancient ones. They come to you from across time, across nations, and across the veil. For centuries, they have kept the knowledge that time and mankind have sought to destroy. The ancient ones speak to those of us who are willing and capable of listening. I wasn't capable of listening."

"What do you mean?" Autumn could not be sure that this was not a creation of her mind due to the stress of the day.

"If I could have heard them the day I saw you on the street in Georgetown when you were just a teenager, there would have been no reason for all the detective work you have had to do when you came to the house." Jon shook his head and slipped his hands into the front pockets of his pants. Autumn thought it must have been a habit of his from life that had lingered. "I could have shown you everything about the house. The little box with gems. I knew its story. It had been told to me years before by my nanna. You see me clearly today because you accepted your gift. It wasn't until I was so close to the veil that I understood. I had to make you fall in love with the farm. I appealed to curiosity. I could never walk away from a good mystery." Jon turned to face Autumn. He seemed somehow younger to her than when she had seen him in her dream two years ago. "Listen to them now as they share with you what they know."

The beautiful painted woman began, "What do you know of your kind?"

Autumn paused for a moment uncertain of whether to speak for fear that the council before her would disappear. The woman seemed to sense this. "We are the ones that have brought you here. Speak openly for only we can separate the bond that links us together now."

Autumn still did not say anything for she was unsure as to what "kind" the woman meant. Without thinking, Autumn said the first thing that came into her mind, "I know that women in my family were witches."

"That is a harsh and ugly word invented by men who feared us but you are correct. Many women in your family possessed the gift. Do you understand what that gift is?"

"I don't. That is why I am here. It seems that I can use my gift but am very uncertain as to how to consciously use that gift or why I suddenly have this gift."

"First, you have not suddenly developed this gift. It is your birth right. The land is what has forged your gift and pulled it out of you. The land you dwell on is full of energy."

Autumn knew in her heart what the woman said was true. Autumn felt it every time she returned to South Carolina. "So, it is the land that gives me my gift."

"It is not. The gift you possess was given long ago by that which created the world and all that dwell there in. Because everything came from that which created the world, it all resonates with the power."

The people proceeded to explain the world as it had been meant to be. Starting from the beginning of time, men and women had both been created as equal images of that which created the universe. Man and woman had been true partners in a very real sense of the word. Neither superior to the other since each served a purpose in the continuation of creation. Without the seed, there can be no fruit. Without the fertile soil, there can be no fruit. However, creation was different for a man and a woman. Men are observers in creation. Women live it. It grew within them. It moved within them. It transformed them as new life came into the world. No woman was the same after that experience. Because women can bring new life into the world, they have a connection to the divine that was unique and powerful. That did not make women superior to men. Ancient people understood this.

Women had held a unique status in the ancient past because even ancient people understood that women were the ones that bore life. Women could not do it alone but only they could do it. Naturally, people looked to them for help when life seemed to be in jeopardy. Ancient people lived as one with the rest of creation and learned to preserve this precious gift known as life through using what they had. Ancient people had lived the words from Genesis that everything man and woman had needed was placed in the garden for them. In desperate and unique moments, some women could even channel the power that created the world in order to heal someone. The decision did not ultimately belong to the woman. No one could decide when life should end. We all leave when we are supposed to leave. These women had been there to make sure that no one left before their time. They acted as a channel for the power in this world. It had been the role of healers in the ancient world.

Humans, however, fear what they do not understand. As the population of the world grew, people began to forget. They warred with each other. Men took up arms to kill each other rather than to kill food for themselves and their families. As people forgot who they were, they became frightened of those who remembered. The people who possessed the knowledge had been placed as corner stones of society but eventually were seen as a threat. Since that pivotal moment in time, things had changed forever and the course of human history had been off-course ever since.

One of the spirits added, "In my day, African's were thought of as subhuman in order to oppress them into slavery. Before them, the native people of this country were subjugated the same way."

"You are telling me," Autumn said, "that people with a gift have been subjugated since that point in history when violence came to be the dominant cultural influence."

"You are a bright and educated woman, can you not think of several different cultural practices that have caused innate nature to be suppressed?"

Without much thought, Autumn recalled how the world had changed. History had been written by the victors because they had annihilated those they had conquered. The world had been full of cultures that had been amazingly advanced and complex but had been decimated by the mind set of "might vs. right". All the strides humanity had made toward the arts and sciences had actually been to regain that which had been lost generations ago.

"Think of what this idea has done. You used the word 'witch' to describe women of your line. Where did that concept first appear," the beautiful woman continued.

"I'm not sure," Autumn replied.

Jon spoke next. "Well, I am. When the Christian church first came to the British Isles, they encountered spiritual leaders. Not only were the majority women but they held powerful influence within the community. In order to convert the peoples of Brittan, they began witch hunts. Any woman with influence or power within a community was seen as a witch. The Romans conquered England and the like by eliminating the cultural centers of the conquered. It was all too easy to graft Roman culture into these communities after the cultural pillars had been removed."

Autumn began to see the path emerge before her. She still felt a long way from understanding. "The witch trials in this country? Were they for the same purpose?"

The council laughed. "In New England, a different nature of women developed than in the South. New England women were outspoken and formally educated. This gave them the foolish notion that they were free to follow their intuition and do as they saw fit. Women were no freer of men in the 1700 and 1800s than slaves were of their masters. Women lost their lives for forgetting their place in a man's world. To make sure the message got out; witch trials ran rampant to make sure women stayed in their place."

"You said that there was a different nature that developed in the South. What do you mean," Autumn asked.

"In the South," Jon replied, "the women knew their place but so did the men. Women were submissive and demure *in public*. The men were the ones who were in charge. They owned the land and ran the government. Women stayed at home to raise the children and did not concern themselves with the workings of government. In reality, women had equal say in the home and on the farm. Women were the ones to decide when and if the men could share their beds. Girls were educated with the boys so they could educate their own children. Women of the South cared for the slaves that worked the land. In the South, women knew their place but so did men."

Autumn was proud to be related in anyway to the people gathered around her. She began to understand. All she had experienced over the past two years had been her birth right and not a curse. The painted woman held out her hand to Autumn. She rose and they walked to the waters edge. "That which moves the sea and gives it life runs through you. Understand that and that is all you need to know."

"And Jim?"

"Man fears what he does not understand. Man must either possess power to control it or destroy power if he cannot possess it. Be clear, Jim is that sort of man. Let me leave you with these words,

'Over oceans vast and deep,
In you the blood of continents meet.
Wisdom and knowledge will you align
When along forgotten paths you wind.'

Autumn stood alone with the sea washing over her toes. Though she could not say what would happen next, Autumn knew that the wisdom of the ancient ones would be with her as she made her way along those forgotten paths.

978-0-595-68575-2
0-595-68575-7

Printed in the United States
96363LV00004B/106-123/A